Fighting for Fiona

Fighting for Fiona

A single dad billionaire boss,
teacher, age gap, sports romance.

Galactic Wrestling Association
Book 1

Leah Mae Wright

Copyright

Contents

Dedication

To my cousin and childhood best friend, David Wayne Daniels, also known as Blue Thunder Tornado. Without you, I would have never gotten the chance to live our dreams in the ring. Though you moved up to Heaven's Wrestling Federation way too young, you're still my favorite wrestler of all time. I hope you have a Kindle in Heaven, so you can read all about the GWA. I'm writing the promotion to be run the way we dreamed of running our own when we were kids. Feel free to visit me in my dreams to correct me if you see something I'm missing.
Love ya lots, Cuz!
Lightning

Introduction

Rick Robertson lived his dream life as the second-generation owner and promoter of the world's most successful sports entertainment company—the Galactic Wrestling Association. As a single dad and billionaire boss, his life was spent traveling the world with his twelve-year-old daughter and the crew he considered a second family. But seeing his staff and talent falling in love made him realize there was still one thing missing in his life—his soulmate.

Not that Rick ever believed he'd meet a woman and fall in love like the crew surrounding him. He'd thought he found the one in the mother of his daughter, but she had only been interested in him for his fame and fortune. Seven years after his disastrous divorce, Rick refused to be suckered into another relationship, no matter how jealous he felt of all the lovebirds on his company jet.

He certainly wasn't going to fall prey to the overly flirtatious English teacher he currently had working for him to teach all the children that traveled with their parents who worked for the GWA. So, Rick was looking for her replacement, along with a history teacher, since several of the kids would be going into high school in the next couple of years and would need more education on the history of the world than they currently received by touring historical sites in each city they visited on tour.

Fiona Harrison was tired of living the sheltered life of a preacher's daughter in a small Texas town. She craved adventure and excitement, like she read about both with her middle school English students and alone at home. She wanted to get out of Heart's Destiny and see the world. And maybe meet a man who could make her feel more than the friendly affection she felt with the guys she grew up with.

Fiona jumped at the chance to travel with the GWA when her coworker and friend, Charlotte Burleson, told her about the traveling English teacher position. She interviewed for the job when the GWA was in Heart's Destiny for Charlotte's youngest brother's wedding over Thanksgiving break. She was scheduled to start her new job at the beginning of the new year, and hoped the instant attraction she felt when she interviewed with the owner of the company wouldn't make the working conditions too uncomfortable.

Rick didn't think his attraction to the new English teacher, who was ten years his junior, would be a problem. She was too young to be interested in a single father with too much responsibility on his shoulders to ever have time to take her out and treat her the way a beautiful young woman like her deserved. He considered himself more than man enough to appreciate her beauty from afar and keep all their interactions professional.

Then he went home to New York over Christmas break and hired a male history teacher closer to Fiona's age. When the two new teachers both started work in the new year and seemed to be spending an awful lot of time together, Rick struggled to fight his natural alpha tendency to claim Fiona as his own.

Which battle would Rick win? The battle with himself not to pursue Fiona? Or the fight for Fiona's heart?

DISCLAIMER: This single dad billionaire boss, teacher, age gap, sports romance book contains references to fertility issues, profanity, and graphic sex scenes. It is intended for adult readers (18+) who are not easily offended.

Glossary of Professional Wrestling Terms

As you read this book, you may find some terms that don't make sense to people outside the professional wrestling industry. Hopefully, this glossary will help you understand the vernacular of the industry to improve your reading experience.

An updated version of this glossary is available to download for free on Book Funnel at
https://dl.bookfunnel.com/eg7nfw06hb

Agent: The individuals employed by a wrestling promotion to assist the wrestlers in planning out their matches to fit the angles written by the bookers. Often former wrestlers who no longer perform due to injury or age.

Angle: Storyline or feud between wrestlers.

Armbar: When a wrestler grabs their opponent's arm at the wrist and twists. Multiple variations exist depending on the position of the two wrestlers' bodies.

Babyface (or Faces): Wrestlers in the good guy role.

Bear Hug: When a wrestler in a standing position wraps their arms around their opponent's chest, midsection, or thighs and locks their hands to hold their opponent tightly to their chest. Sometimes lifting their opponent completely off the ground. Their opponent's arms can be trapped in the bear hug, or they can be free to fight the tight grip around them.

Beatdown: When a wrestler or other performer is the recipient of a beating, usually by a group of wrestlers.

Booker: The individuals employed by a wrestling promotion to write the angles and plan the shows.

Breather: When a wrestler takes a rest break, usually outside the ring, in the middle of a match. Can be due to needing to catch their breath after a cardiovascularly intense sequence of moves or having the breath knocked out of them by a hard impact. Can also be a work to sell the intensity of their opponent's attack.

Card: The order or series of matches on a given show.

Collar-and-Elbow Tie-Up (Lock-Up): When two wrestlers are standing facing one another and grab each other with their left hand at the collar, back of the neck, or on the trapezius muscle while gripping their opponent's left elbow with their right hand.

Dark Match: A match on the live card that's not televised when the rest of the show is broadcast. Often used as a tryout for local talent on TV days.

Dirty Finish: When a match ends because of cheating, outside interference, or disqualification.

Double Leg Takedown: When two wrestlers are standing facing one another and one of them ducks down and grabs both of their opponent's calves to pull their legs out from under them.

Double Turn: The rare occurrence when both the heel and face switch roles during an angle or match.

Faction (Stable): A group of wrestlers within a promotion who have a common element that puts them together as a unit of three or more.

Figure 4 Leglock: When the wrestler performing the move is standing over their opponent, who is laying on their back on the mat, grips both feet of their opponent, performs a spinning toe hold to bend their opponent's left leg at the knee, and drops down to sit on the mat with their legs straddling their opponents straight right leg and looped over their opponents bent left leg at the ankle and calf. Invented by Buddy Rogers and made famous by Ric Flair.

Finish: The planned end of a match or card.

Finisher: The primary wrestling move a wrestler uses to finish a match. Usually, their favorite or best move, thought to be most effective for incapacitating an opponent to win a match.

Professional wrestlers often try to add drama to their matches by naming the move and over exaggerating its usage.

Future Endeavoring: When a promotion fires someone, they often send a letter or issue a public statement wishing them well on their "future endeavors," thus leading to the term future endeavoring meaning firing.

Gimmick: Anything made up about a wrestler or the props used in a wrestler's performance from their ring name to their costuming to the origin story of the character they portray. *Example: The Dangerous Twins have a biker gimmick.* Can also be used as a verb to describe a prop that has been prepared to be used in a match without causing actual harm to an opponent. *Example: The table was gimmicked before the Dangerous Twins slammed their opponents through it.*

Go-Home Show: The final televised show before a pay-per-view.

Go Over: To win a wrestling match.

Gorilla Position: The staging area just behind the curtain where wrestlers come out to the ring. Named after Gorilla Monsoon.

Heel (or Heels): Wrestlers in the bad guy role.

Hook (Left or Right): A boxing punch where the person throwing the punch bends their elbow at a 90-degree angle to strike their opponent in the side of their head or body with the punch arcing through the air from off to the side of the body toward the midline of the body. Punches of any kind are not legal moves in the sport of wrestling, but they are often used by heels in professional wrestling as a way to cheat when the referee isn't watching.

House Shows: Shows performed live but not televised.

Jab (Left or Right): A boxing punch where the person throwing the punch extends their arm straight out in front of them to strike their opponent's head or body. Punches of any kind are not legal moves in the sport of wrestling, but they are often used by heels in professional wrestling as a way to cheat when the referee isn't watching.

Jerking the Curtain: Wrestling in the first match on the card.

Job: To lose a wrestling match.

Jobber: Wrestlers who primarily lose their matches.

Local Competitor (Local Talent): An unsigned wrestler who works a show either as a tryout or as a jobber to keep the main talent roster from having to job.

Main Eventer: A wrestler who is seen as the highest talent level in a promotion. Typically headlines shows. Usually, the current or former champion, or other performers who often wrestle for the title of a promotion.

Mid-Carder: Most of the wrestlers who work for a promotion are classified as mid-carders because they perform in the middle of the card, not the first match or the main event, a majority of the time.

Plancha: An aerial wrestling maneuver where one wrestler flies out of the ring or off the top turnbuckle into an opponent on the floor outside the ring in which they land chest-to-chest in a crossbody position.

Ring Psychology: Using wrestling skill to draw an emotional reaction from the fans watching.

Ring Rats: Groupies. Fans who follow the wrestlers with the hope of having sex with them.

Ring Rust: When a wrestler's in-ring skill declines after not working in the ring for a while. Can be from just a few months off after an injury, or after several years off after retirement.

Roundhouse (Roundhouse Kick): When a wrestler, who is standing with one foot in front of the other, spins their body to strike their opponent with the shin or top of the foot on their back leg, not stopping the spin of their body until their leg has completely passed their opponent's body.

Selling: Acting as if something is real when it is choreographed or faked for the show. Pretending a move or hold is more painful or effective than it really is.

Side Headlock: When a wrestler wraps their arm around the head of their opponent, squeezing their opponent's face into the side of their chest.

Spinning Toe Hold: When the wrestler performing the move is standing over an opponent laying on their back on the mat with their legs in the air, the wrestler performing the move grasps their opponent's foot and spins around 360 degrees to make it

Leah Mae Wright

look like they've twisted the toe, foot, leg, or ankle of their opponent.

Splash: When a wrestler jumps from a position raised above their opponent, who is laying on the mat, and lands stomach first perpendicularly across their opponent's body. Usually performed from the top turnbuckle, but can be launched from any of the ropes around the ring.

Suplex: When a wrestler in a standing position lifts their opponent off their feet and uses their own body weight to propel them both toward the mat with both wrestlers landing on their backs. There are different variations of the move depending on the body position of the wrestlers before the lift and how the offensive wrestler grabs their opponent for the lift portion of the move.

Swerve: Confusing the fans by doing the opposite of what they expect or doing something off the wall that nobody would ever expect.

Tapping (Tapping Out): When a wrestler slaps their hand on the mat, their opponent's body, or on anything they can reach to signal they are forfeiting the match or to get an opponent to release a hold. Usually three slaps of the hand, but can be more or less depending on the rules of the promotion.

Turnbuckle: The metal component of the wrestling ring that connects the ropes to the corner posts. Usually covered with padding. One of the top turnbuckles is usually used as the platform wrestlers jump off of for aerial moves.

Tweener: A morally ambiguous wrestler, who is neither a face nor a heel.

Uppercut (Left or Right): A boxing punch where the person throwing the punch bends their elbow at a 90-degree angle to strike their opponent under the chin or in the torso with the punch coming from their waist upward. Punches of any kind are not legal moves in the sport of wrestling, but they are often used by heels in professional wrestling as a way to cheat when the referee isn't watching.

Work: Fake but presented as real to the audience. Can refer to a wrestler's overall performance, specifically appearing to target a body part to cause an injury, or an injury if it is scripted as part of the angle and the wrestler isn't really hurt. Can be used as a noun or a verb. *Examples: (Noun) His broken arm is a work. (Verb) They worked the crowd. James really worked Dion's left knee in their last match.*

Worker: Another term for a professional wrestler. Often used in the context of describing in-ring skill level.

Workrate: The in-ring performance level a wrestler puts into their matches. Judged by a combination of skill and effort. A wrestler considered talented in the ring has a high workrate.

Author's Note

In the course of writing this book, I've had to do a lot of research about places I've never been to come up with settings for the sightseeing the families of the GWA do on their midday breaks in their work schedule. I also had to come up with a schedule for the cities where they travel each day with no idea if there is an airport in the cities I've chosen that's big enough for the GWA plane to land. Therefore, I ask that you please forgive me for any inaccuracies in my descriptions that have no basis in reality.

As is always the case with my books, reality is irrelevant. My characters live in my fantasy world, which just happens to share some city names and sightseeing attractions with the real world. Only in my imaginary world, even some smaller cities have private airports with runways long enough for a 747 to land. Of course, the 747 the GWA uses in my head only has one level of seating with the upper level waiting to be used for the oversized suitcases of the crew when all 120 of the seats on the main level are filled. The seats on the GWA plane are also only available for use in my head. As of the end of this book, there is a maximum of 83 people on the GWA plane, including both flight crews, all of their families, and the new members of the roster hired in this book.

*With all that being said, every museum and historical site mentioned in **Fighting for Fiona** is actually a real place. So, if any of my readers live in the areas mentioned in this book, check them out and let me know if I've been extremely way off in my descriptions, since I pieced them together from online research only. And if you're like me, curious but unable to travel for whatever reason, do an online search for anyplace I mention that interests you. Some have fabulous websites, including virtual tours, like Mullme in Tijuana.*

Chapter One

Monday, October 22, 2018, Heart's Destiny, Texas

Fiona Harrison went about her day just like she did every other day of the school year. She was up at five in the morning to have time to go for a jog, even though she hated jogging, because it was the only thing that worked to keep her only about twenty pounds heavier than all her friends. After that, she came home and had a sensible breakfast before showering and getting dressed. She tended to stick to a style that camouflaged her curves by wearing one of a rainbow of colors of t-shirt dresses and sandals. She opted for a bright Halloween orange dress that morning, hoping the bright color would lift her melancholy mood. She finished her morning routine at home by applying minimal makeup, pulling her long light-red hair up in a messy bun once it was mostly dried, and gathering her things to go teach sixth- and seventh-grade English at Heart's Destiny Middle School. Seven weeks into the school year and she was already bored with her routine.

Is it possible to have a seven-year itch when I've just started my fifth year of teaching? Fiona wondered as she gave her current class of sixth graders the same writing assignment she'd given her earlier classes. *Like being burnt out and wanting to go do something more adventurous can pertain to a job just as much as it can to a relationship, right?*

Not that Fiona had ever been in a relationship long enough to experience the seven-year itch like in that classic movie. The longest she'd ever been in a relationship was her senior year of high school, when she'd dated Justin Burleson all year before breaking up when they got to college and didn't have any of the same classes.

Growing up in a small town didn't give her many opportunities to date. Especially since her father was the preacher at the only church in town, so none of the boys she grew up with wanted to face him on Sunday morning after kissing her goodnight on his front porch at the end of a Saturday night date.

The only reason Justin hadn't had an issue with dating her was because most of their dates were group dates, where they hung out with his cousins and a few of their other classmates after school or at football games, and there weren't any kisses when other people were around. Even when they lost their virginity together on Prom night, Justin had kissed her goodnight in the car before taking her home and giving her a one-armed hug goodnight on the porch when her father could have seen them. That one-armed hug was all the affection he ever showed her with their parents around, even though they fooled around on the Walker's trails all summer long before going off to college.

After breaking up with him during their first semester at the University of Texas, Fiona had dated a few more guys while she was in Austin at school. But none of them lasted more than a couple of months, or ever made the journey home to Heart's Destiny to meet her parents. Not even the two she'd thought she knew well enough to have sex with after dating them during her junior and senior years of college.

Since graduating from college in 2014 and moving back home to start teaching, Fiona had been in a dating dry spell. She still hung out with her high school friends, but none of them were a love match for her. Not even Justin, who had also moved back home after college to work in his family business.

Hooking up with him, even for old times' sake, was no longer an option for her, after she started working so closely with his cousin, Charlotte, the other English teacher at Heart's Destiny Middle School. Between working together in the English department at school, coaching the middle school softball team together, and starting a book club together, Fiona and Charlotte quickly became best friends. Once they started regularly hanging out, it was just too weird to ask Charlotte about her cousin, or to think about confiding in her about anything Fiona might do sexually with anyone Charlotte was related to, even though she'd dated Justin before getting to know his cousin.

Charlotte had actually convinced Fiona to go out for girls' night in San Antonio a few times over the last four years. Both of them had hoped to meet a man when they'd gone out, but neither had been lucky enough to find someone who wanted more than a one-night stand. And that was not something Fiona was comfortable with doing. She might not be as strict in her religious beliefs as her parents to insist on saving sex for only after marriage, but she at least wanted to have a few dates before she went to bed with a guy.

Maybe not having sex in over four years is why I'm so restless? Maybe I should just give in and have a one-nighter the next time Char and I go out? I wonder if she already has plans for Friday. I'll have to ask her at lunch.

Fiona slogged through the rest of the class she was teaching, anxiously awaiting the bell dismissing them for lunch as much as the kids in her class. She didn't have to wait long before she was headed to the teacher's lounge while her students beelined to the cafeteria.

She nuked her leftover lasagna from dinner the night before at her parents' house while waiting for Charlotte to arrive.

"Hey girl, what's up?" Charlotte asked as soon as she walked into the room.

"My boredom level," Fiona replied, shaking her head.

"Burnout hitting early this year?" Charlotte sat her stuff down beside Fiona's at the table where they usually ate lunch. "I thought we didn't complain about being bored and ready for the school year to be over until Spring Break."

The microwave beeped for Fiona to get her food out, so she waited until she sat down at the table where Char was pulling out a salad before answering. "Yeah, well, I'm already feeling it. I'm never going to make it through another seven months of the school year if I don't do something to shake things up."

"Please tell me you're not thinking of changing the syllabus in the middle of the school year to shake things up." Charlotte's eyes were wide as she looked at Fiona.

Fiona thought her friend might have some OCD tendencies with the way she liked to have the whole year meticulously planned out and couldn't veer from the schedule. Luckily for Charlotte, Fiona had no plans to mess with her routine.

"No, absolutely not." Fiona held her hands up in surrender to calm her friend. "I was thinking more along the lines of going to San Antonio this weekend and trying one more time to have a one-nighter. Like maybe I just think I'm bored teaching the same thing every year, when I really just need to get laid."

"I suppose that's possible." Charlotte tilted her head to give Fiona an inquisitive look. "And I'll be glad to go out with you this weekend to be your wing woman." There was an awkward pause, where Fiona felt like Charlotte was examining her under a microscope before continuing. "But I may have another option for you to shake things up, if it really is you being bored teaching the same lessons year after year."

"Yeah? What's that?" Fiona took a bite of her lasagna to allow Charlotte time to gather her thoughts and explain her idea.

"You know my brother, Anthony, works for the Galactic Wrestling Association, right?" Fiona only nodded with her mouth full of food. "Well, I talked to him over the weekend while he was sitting in the backstage classroom they have set up for all the employees' kids. Apparently, they need a new English teacher to travel with them. I don't know any of the specifics, but I doubt you'd be bored traveling the world and teaching kindergarten through high school."

Fiona almost choked, trying to swallow her lasagna before it was fully chewed to ask, "Seriously?"

"Yeah, Tia tried to recommend me for the position, but you know I have no desire to leave Heart's Destiny." Char shuddered at the thought of a job traveling so much. "Apparently, the English teacher they have now has a problem with being overly flirtatious with the hot wrestlers, regardless of whether they're single or married. So, they're looking to replace her pretty quickly. If it's something you'd be interested in, I'll get the info from Anthony for you to apply."

"Yeah, I'm interested." Fiona nodded her head excitedly. "Would it be his crazy five on, five off schedule, or like the Hunters who only come home on holidays?"

"I think Anthony's schedule is an FAA thing, so probably only coming home on holidays." Charlotte stabbed a few pieces of her salad with her fork. "But I'll ask him."

Charlotte reached into her bag and pulled out her cell phone as she took her bite, swiping it alive to send a text.

Fiona's heart fluttered as she sat there eating, while waiting for Charlotte to finish her text conversation with her brother to give her more information on what could be a really cool job.

"Okay, so apparently, they have a listing up on the GWA's website for the two teacher positions they're looking to hire for." Char put her phone down on the table and picked up her fork once more. "But Anthony said to have you email your résumé straight to his boss and mention him as a reference. I forwarded the email address to you, along with the web address, so you can look up all the particulars of the job before you apply."

Fiona quickly pulled her phone from her purse and powered it on, too excited about the job prospect to wait until the end of the school day to check it out. As soon as it came to life, she went to her messages with Charlotte and clicked on the link to the GWA's website. It took a little surfing to find the job listings and scroll through to find the English teacher position.

"Holy moly!" Fiona exclaimed when she saw the salary for the position. "Is this right?" Fiona turned her phone, so Charlotte could read the salary. "It can't be right. Can it? Teachers don't make six-figure salaries. This is, like, more than double what we make."

"Yeah, that's right." Charlotte bobbed her head between bites of her salad. "Anthony said his boss has a tendency to pay at least one-and-a-half times the average pay rate he's found for other people doing the same or similar jobs to compensate for all the travel required."

"But this also says all the travel expenses are covered by the company," Fiona pointed out. "So, what is this extra pay?"

"A bonus for not being able to be home with your family except on holidays?" Char shrugged. "Not enough of an incentive for me, but with you wanting to change things up and go on an adventure, the extra pay seems like icing on the cake for you."

"Yeah. I mean, I don't need to make that much extra money," Fiona replied. "But it could go a long way with helping the shelter we work with in San Antonio and with the youth center here in town."

"Exactly." Charlotte smiled at Fiona. "So, should we plan on getting a couple of rooms for Friday night, so we can go straight to the shelter to volunteer on Saturday?"

"Definitely," Fiona agreed, looking through the rest of the GWA website while Charlotte put in their usual reservations for nights when they didn't want to risk driving home from San Antonio after drinking. Spending the next day volunteering at the homeless shelter helped ease Fiona's guilt for going out drinking, even though she volunteered every Saturday whether she went out on Friday night or not.

Wow, I can see why the previous English teacher got fired for flirting with the hot guys who work with the company, Fiona thought as she looked at the pictures of the talent roster for the GWA. *Guess it's a good thing I'm not the flirty type. Though it might be hard not to flirt just a little with some of these guys, at least my morals will keep me from flirting with the ones already in committed relationships.*

Fiona floated through the rest of her day, mentally updating her résumé before going home to her apartment over her parents' garage, where she actually updated it and sent it off to the email address Charlotte had given her earlier in the day.

$\sim\sim\sim$

Wednesday, November 21, 2018, Heart's Destiny, Texas

Rick Robertson appreciated the support system he had on staff to help him take care of his daughter, Britney, while he was working, even though technically they were all on vacation for Thanksgiving. Since one of his pilots was getting married and had invited the whole company to the wedding and all the festivities the week before the wedding, Rick and most of the GWA talent and their families were in the small Texas town of Heart's Destiny for the week.

Rick was glad the Traversons, the couple he'd originally hired as tutors for his daughter and the other kids who traveled with the company, were included in the group in town for the wedding. Otherwise, he wouldn't have been able to schedule the interviews he had for that morning without his daughter sitting in on them, since his driver, who was also his head of security, was off for the week.

Normally, Rick scheduled interviews while they were touring during the time Britney would be occupied with the tutors in the backstage classroom. If he interviewed during a holiday break, they'd be in New York, so Britney could stay with his parents. But since his parents weren't joining them in Texas for Thanksgiving, Rick had to rely on the Traversons to keep his daughter occupied while he did the two interviews he'd set up that morning.

Thankfully, it's just the two interviews, he thought as he took a seat behind a desk in the library of the bed and breakfast where they were staying. *And they're mostly formalities to get the human resources paperwork filled out, since I've gotten excellent recommendations for both of the women I'm interviewing.*

The first interview was with Fiona Harrison for the English tutor position. After Anthony Burleson and both of the Hunters had told him about their preacher's daughter, Rick was pretty sure she would be a good addition to the team. *At the very least, I know she won't be a sexual harassment lawsuit waiting to happen, the way Stacy has been by hitting on me and every other man who works with the company.*

Since he'd only spoken to Fiona once on the phone to schedule the interview, Rick couldn't be positive her coming to work for the company was a done deal. But he certainly hoped he'd be able to convince the woman, whom his other employees highly recommended, to come to work for the GWA as soon as possible, so he could terminate Stacy Jones' employment contract on their first day back from their Thanksgiving break.

The second interview was really more of a farce than the first one. It was with Randi Lee for a job as a production assistant. Randi was James Hunter's girlfriend, and would be Anthony Burleson's sister-in-law after the wedding at the end of the week. Rick didn't actually need another production assistant, but he couldn't say no when one of the main eventers on his roster came to him asking about job options for his girlfriend to be able to travel with him.

Of course, I'm going to hire a woman who wants to work to support herself instead of letting her boyfriend take care of her, like Colleen expected me to take care of her before we were married. Rick shook off the negative thoughts about his ex-wife. *No point in thinking about that gold-digging bitch.*

Colleen had traveled with him when they first got together, acting like she'd loved him and not the rockstar-like lifestyle of professional wrestling. Thinking they were both in love, Rick didn't mind taking care of her expenses to have her with him on the road when they first started seeing one another. Once their daughter was on the way, Colleen decided she preferred to stay at home in New York while Rick traveled with the company, where he worked as a wrestler on the shows at the time. Rick hated being away from his family all the time, but he knew it couldn't be helped if he wanted to one day step into his father's shoes as the owner and promoter.

Truth be told, while Rick missed his daughter like crazy, he hadn't really missed Colleen while he was wrestling. He wasn't as in love with her as he'd originally thought. Looking back, he now realized they hadn't really loved each other at any point in time. He was only twenty-four when he met her and followed his dick to her bed. She seemed to like his rougher tendencies in the bedroom, so he paid for her to travel with him because he wanted easy access to pussy and his younger self confused sexual chemistry with love.

Looking back at the punk kid he'd been in his early twenties made him cringe, so he tried not to think of those days often. He certainly had to grow up fast when she told him she was pregnant and would only keep the baby if he married her.

Needless to say, their marriage wasn't a good one. He could count on one hand the number of times they'd had sex in the five-and-a-half years they were married. At first, she'd used the excuse that he was too rough and would hurt the baby. Then after Britney was born, Colleen had complained about him not being gentle enough, even though she only came when he pounded her hard. It got to the point that sex wasn't satisfying for either of them, so Rick spent the next few years in a celibate marriage.

He settled into life on the road, taking care of his sexual needs with his own hand in the shower because his ethics wouldn't allow him to be with anyone else while they were married, even though they were no longer sleeping together. He thought they were both happier as friends and co-parents than lovers, so he played the part of the happy husband to make sure his daughter was raised in a loving home.

Their lives all changed dramatically the day Rick got the call that his father had collapsed in their corporate office in New York. He took the first flight home from the tour to be by his father's side as he recovered from a heart attack. His father insisted he go take care of the business at the corporate office, instead of sitting at his bedside, so Rick headed home to change out of his gimmick wear to go do his father's bidding. When he got to his house, he found his wife, Colleen, naked and riding the guy he paid to mow the lawn on their living room sofa, while their five-year-old daughter was on an outing with the nanny he didn't even know Colleen had hired.

It had been seven years since he'd walked in on her screwing the gardener and promptly kicked them both out of his house. He'd retained the services of the nanny at first, while they went through their messy divorce. But once he was awarded full custody of Britney, and Colleen signed away all her maternal rights for a big, fat paycheck with more zeros than she deserved, Rick let the nanny go, too. He hired the Traversons to provide his daughter with an education while she traveled with him full-time.

When his father decided to retire and put Rick in charge of everything with the business, he changed things around, no longer having the CEO position tied to a desk in New York. He bought the corporate jet and offered the tutoring services he used for his daughter to the children of his employees, so families could travel together and be less likely to have issues leading them to split up or divorce.

With the exception of Stacy and her overly flirtatious ways, the system had worked wonderfully for the last few years. But with almost two dozen kids now touring with the GWA, and the older kids needing more in-depth history education than just the sightseeing trips they took with their parents in different cities each week, he had to find a history teacher within the next few months, as well.

Though I'm still going to enjoy taking Britney to places such as the Alamo whenever I can, he thought, looking forward to the afternoon outing he had planned with his daughter. With being limited to only a day in each city while they were touring, and only a couple hours of that day being free for sightseeing, Rick was really enjoying having the time off in a city other than New York to explore more of the sights with his daughter.

He couldn't dwell on his plans for the afternoon as Fiona Harrison stepped into the room. *Holy shit! Maybe hiring her isn't the best idea,* Rick thought as his dick twitched in his pants from his first look at the beautiful young teacher. He stood and buttoned his suit coat, hoping to hide the evidence of his body's reaction to her. It was the first time in his thirty-seven years of life that he'd been instantly aroused by a woman, and he wasn't sure he wanted to fight the attraction he was currently feeling every time he had to interact with the woman who would be teaching his daughter.

Fiona Harrison was a gorgeous goddess walking across the library. Rick estimated her to be about five-foot-four, not quite a foot shorter than his six-foot-two stature, and at least a hundred pounds lighter than his two-hundred-and-forty-pound body weight. But it wasn't just her perfectly proportioned body with curves that, while covered, couldn't be concealed by the emerald-green dress she wore that caught his attention. Her eyes perfectly matched the emerald green of her dress, and her strawberry blonde hair that flowed around her shoulders was almost the exact same shade as the rose-gold sandals she wore on her petite feet.

"Mr. Robertson?" His name came out as a question when she reached the desk and extended her hand to him.

"Please, call me Rick." He took her hand for a polite shake. He noticed the way her fair complexion contrasted with his tan skin tone, but the instant jolt of electricity he felt when their hands touched shocked him so much that it kept him from imagining how they would look lying naked in bed together, just as his thoughts started to veer there. It wasn't a feeling he'd ever experienced before and he didn't know what it meant, much less how to deal with it. "And you must be Fiona."

"Yes, sir, um, Rick." Fiona blushed lightly as they shook hands, and Rick couldn't help but wonder if she'd turn such a pretty shade of pink anywhere else on her body.

Like those perky tits that are way too covered up right now.

"Please have a seat." Rick released her hand and took his own seat once she'd sat in the chair across the desk from him. He didn't dare unbutton his jacket, no matter how unusual it was to sit with it buttoned, knowing his erection was tenting his trousers and would be obvious to her and anyone else who saw him sitting there staring at her beauty. "After looking over your résumé and talking with your references, I can see that you are very qualified and would be an asset to our children, if you're hired for the English tutor position. So, please, tell me why you're interested in leaving the school where you currently work to travel with us."

"Honestly, the idea of getting to travel the world is what's most appealing about the job." Fiona's emerald eyes lit up with excitement as she spoke. "I was born and raised in Heart's Destiny. The farthest I've been away from here was a family trip to Dallas. And the only time I've lived anywhere else was in my dorm room in Austin during the four years I was in college. I love my family and my hometown, but I want to see more of the world than the few places in Texas I've lived and visited."

Damn, she's even more sheltered than I thought after talking to the guys about her. I wonder if she's still a virgin? Fuck! I can't think about a potential employee that way.

"I see you've only taught middle school for the last four years." Rick scrolled through her curriculum vitae on his tablet to refresh his memory of the dates of her education and employment. *Fuck! How fucking old is she? If she was nineteen when she graduated high school like the Hunters, then going to college for four years would make her twenty-three when she graduated. Four more years of teaching would only make her twenty-seven now. Ten fucking years younger than me, and way too young for me to be lusting after.* "Is that age group what you focused on in college? Or do you have other experience that would prepare you for teaching kindergarten through high school, as will be required for a tutor working with us?"

"My internship in my final year of college was at a Christian school where I spent time working with children in each grade, preschool through twelfth grade."

Fiona's skirt shifted slightly when she crossed her legs while answering, allowing Rick to see about an inch of cream-colored skin above her knee on her top leg. That small slip of his attention distracted him from hearing her full answer about her experiences during her internship, but he knew she was more than qualified for the job.

Fucking hell! I have to give her the job if she wants it. I'll just have to take a whole lot of cold showers to keep from acting on this attraction to her. Surely, after a couple of months of seeing her have no reaction to me, I'll come to accept that I'm obviously too old for her and won't keep getting hard as a rock from just talking to her.

Besides, someone that young and innocent would never be able to handle the rough way I like to fuck, so we'd never work out, even if she was interested.

"Very well." Rick nodded when she finished telling him about all the things she'd done in her internship. "How soon can you start work?"

"I'll need to give the school enough time to find my replacement." Fiona fidgeted in her seat. Rick fought to keep his eyes on her face and not on her luscious legs again. "If I call my principal today, she should have time to hire someone by the time we go on winter break. So, possibly as early as right after winter break, the beginning of January."

"Excellent." Rick closed her documents on his tablet to open up the HR portal for her to fill out the paperwork. He slid the tablet across the desk to her before continuing. "Our winter break starts when we land in New York on December twenty-first. We fly out of New York on January second, so I'll need to schedule you a flight to New York on the first to meet up with the crew and start work the next day. If you'll just fill out our human resources forms on here, taking a picture of your driver's license and social security card when prompted, we can get everything scheduled for you to be our new English tutor."

"Seriously? I got the job?" Fiona's voice went up at least two octaves, showing her excitement as she asked the questions.

"Yes, Fiona." Rick was unable to stop himself from returning her beaming smile. "You got the job."

She was practically bouncing in her seat as she filled out the online forms on his tablet. Her excitement was contagious, causing Rick to struggle to maintain his normal stoic composure with her making cute little squeaking noises that he could only interpret as glee.

Fuck, I wonder if she'd make those same noises with me balls deep inside her? I'd love to hear what she'd sound like, moaning my name as she comes on my cock. Too bad she's way too young and innocent for someone like me.

When she handed him back the tablet, Rick stood to shake her hand once more to dismiss her from their meeting. Fiona surprised him, though, by bounding around the desk as soon as she was standing.

"Thank you so much!" Fiona wrapped her arms around his waist and pressed her cheek to his chest. "I'll be the best tutor you've ever hired. I promise."

Fuck, she even smells like strawberries! Rick bent slightly, pulling his hips back, so she couldn't feel his erection. He patted her on the back to return her unexpected embrace, without hugging her to him the way he really wanted, which would be very inappropriate with a new employee.

"I'm sure you will." Rick chuckled lightly, unable to hide his smile while witnessing her happiness about the job. *And you'll also be the only tutor I'll hire that I'd rather have in my bed than in our backstage classroom, teaching my daughter and the rest of the kids. Not that I'll ever let that happen.*

"Um, just a fair warning…" Fiona's words trailed off as she pulled back, a pensive expression crossing her lovely, heart-shaped face. "Tomorrow at Thanksgiving, my dad is probably going to want to meet you and ask you a million questions about the job. I hope that won't make you change your mind about hiring me. Because I really want this job, no matter what Daddy thinks about traveling outside of Texas being too dangerous for his daughter."

"I'll make sure to tell him all the safety protocols I have in place with my daughter traveling with me to put his mind at ease." Rick smiled slightly as she started to walk away.

"Oh, good. A Daddy-to-Daddy talk is probably the only thing that will keep him from freaking out too much." Fiona's smile grew wider as she lightly giggled. "See you tomorrow, Boss."

A Daddy-to-Daddy talk? Why the hell does her referring to me as Daddy sound so appealing? I must be more of a pervert than I thought if I want her to call me the same thing she calls her father.

"See you tomorrow, Fiona." Rick couldn't stop himself from chuckling again at her childlike excitement as she skipped out of the room. *Too bad I can't think of you like another daughter, Fiona. Hopefully, when I talk to Fiona's dad tomorrow, I can fake it enough that he won't recognize how I'm fantasizing about spanking his daughter before fucking her in every way I can possibly imagine.*

Chapter Two

Friday, December 14, 2018, San Antonio, Texas

Fiona was on cloud nine after the way the last few weeks had gone. Her new boss had put all her parents' concerns at ease when they grilled him at Thanksgiving. Her almost former boss had posted her job on all the national job boards the following Monday and had scheduled interviews for the last week to find the perfect candidate. If all went as well as Lisa Walker seemed to think it would in the final round of interviews she had scheduled that afternoon, Fiona could receive the call she was waiting for to hear her replacement had been hired, so she could start her new job at the beginning of January.

If Lisa would just hurry up and call, Fiona thought as she drove into San Antonio for what could possibly be her last night out drinking with her friend, Charlotte. *Maybe we can turn girls' night into a celebration before my last week of work in Heart's Destiny. Though, no matter whether this interview goes well to set me up to start my new job when we originally planned, or if it takes them a little longer to find someone to replace me and I have to wait another month or two to start my new job, tonight is still probably going to be mostly conversation about how I can stop myself from lusting after my silver fox, new boss when I eventually get to work with him every day.*

Fiona had been lusting after Rick Robertson, since the day she met him for the interview. He epitomized the words *Tall, Dark, and Handsome* in a way that no other man had for her. While he was obviously way older than her twenty-seven years with the touch of silver in his dark hair, the way he filled out his dark gray suit made it evident that he was still in excellent shape, no matter what his age.

I wonder what he looks like under the suit? Is he still as muscularly defined as he was back when he wrestled? Fiona thought as she parked her car in the parking garage attached to the hotel. *Not that I'll ever find out, since there's no way a man as debonair and sophisticated as Rick would ever be interested in a country bumpkin like me. And even if he wanted to come over to my place for a one-night stand if he's ever in town again, he'd run as soon as he stepped into my pink princess bedroom that I probably should have outgrown over a decade ago.*

She put her negative thoughts out of her head as she made her way into the hotel lobby. Since Charlotte had to meet up with her brother to drop off his recently adopted daughter that had been staying with her all week to take the state acceleration tests for school, Fiona was the first to arrive at the hotel where they normally met up. She got checked in, took her things to her room, freshened up, and made her way to the hotel bar, knowing that's where Char would meet her.

Just as she was taking a seat at the bar, her phone buzzed in her bag. When she pulled it out, she had to stifle her squeal of excitement at seeing the text from her school principal.

Lisa Walker: You can alert your new boss that you can start immediately after winter break. We hired your replacement today.

Fiona: Thanks so much for letting me know!

She ordered a glass of wine to celebrate and sat watching people come and go. One of her favorite things was people-watching. She and Charlotte often sat there making up stories about the various people around them. The couple who looked like they were there on their honeymoon. The older couple who looked like they were in town to visit their grandkids. And since they mostly drank in the hotel bar, more often than not, they picked out the couples that were there for an illicit tryst or the business people looking for a one-night stand while in town.

I wonder if the people watching will be the same when I'm in a different hotel every night for my new job? Fiona wondered what the protocol was for going out after the wrestling shows. *Will there even be anyone traveling with the GWA who will be friendly enough to want to have a drink after work? I'd ask Anthony's new bride, but I doubt Kay will want to socialize with me when she could be with her husband and kids. But maybe she'll know if there are other single women I can make friends with within the company.*

Fiona was pondering how best to go about making friends in the company without seeming like she was flirting with any of the guys when Charlotte walked in and took the seat beside her at the bar.

"You look deep in thought." Charlotte flagged down the bartender and ordered a Chardonnay and some appetizers for them to share in place of dinner.

"Yeah, just trying to picture how I'm going to fit in on this new job, now that I've gotten confirmation from Lisa that she's filled my position, so I can start right after winter break." Fiona took a sip from her own glass.

"You'll fit in wonderfully." Char smiled as she shook her head, as if to indicate Fiona was worried about nothing. "Just like you instantly fit in at the middle school."

"Yeah, but I already knew everyone at the middle school." Fiona gave Charlotte a skeptical smile, shaking her head. "The only people with the GWA that I've had more than a brief interaction with are your brother and the Hunters. And with them being a couple of years younger than me, I'm not exactly close friends with any of them."

"I'm sure you'll make friends quickly." Charlotte waved off Fiona's concern. "You met Kay and her sister the week of the wedding. They're both super sweet and will introduce you to the ladies they've made friends with so far and will point out the ones to avoid. Although, I think the only one I've heard anything negative about from Kay is the woman you're replacing, so I'm sure you'll get along fine with everyone else. Though you might have your hands full with some of the wrestlers I met that week."

"What do you mean?" Fiona didn't remember any issues with the GWA crew at Thanksgiving. Well, other than the conflict with Kay's family and James Hunter, but that was all cleared up with Kay announcing the pregnancy test was hers and not her sister's.

"Some of the single guys can be over-the-top flirts." Charlotte rolled her eyes. "Much to my mother's delight in the way she was trying to fix Becky, Jen, Julie, and I up with them."

"Yeah, I did notice you seemed to be seated with them at every event I attended that week," Fiona giggled. "I was half surprised my mom wasn't teaming up with her to throw me in there with you. Well, until she and Dad gave my new boss the third degree about my safety while traveling with them."

"Girl, if we weren't a year apart in age, I'd wonder if we were switched at birth." Char chuckled at the confused look Fiona gave her. "My mom would gladly send me flying off with the GWA in the hopes I'd fall in love with one of the guys, when I'd rather stay in Heart's Destiny. And your folks would rather keep you safe at home, when you're the one wanting to fly off on an adventure."

"I guess it does seem like we each got the wrong set of parents when you put it like that." Fiona grinned at her friend.

"So, having met a few of the guys already, were there any that you might be interested in breaking your dry spell with?"

"There were certainly a few who were attractive," Fiona admitted. "But you know me. It'll take a lot more than good looks to get me to break the dry spell."

"Yeah, I know, but you're going to be traveling the world with them, so surely you'll get to know at least one or two of the guys well enough to go on a date or two, maybe more. I'm just wondering if any of them caught your eye to possibly be candidate number one."

Fiona took a large gulp of her wine, finishing off her first glass, not sure if she was stalling because she was embarrassed about how hot she thought her new boss was, or if she just needed the extra liquid courage to divulge her interest in him to her best friend.

"Oh, shit, girl!" Charlotte shouted. "Someone did pique your interest!"

Fiona swallowed her wine quickly and motioned with her hand for Charlotte to take the volume down a notch or twenty. "Not so loud. I don't want to announce it to all of San Antonio."

"Sorry." Char lowered her voice, speaking in a more conversational tone. "But I need the details."

"Fine, if you must know," Fiona whisper-shouted, shaking her head at her BFF. "My new boss, Rick."

"Seriously?" Charlotte shouted once again. "The DILF my mom kept trying to get me to talk to?"

"Don't call him that!" Fiona could feel herself blush at the crude acronym and was glad they were at the River Walk and not the airport, knowing her face was so red it probably glowed enough to outshine the runway lights and would cause a plane or two to crash.

"Why not? If ever there was a man that description was made for, it's Rick Robertson. Just because I don't want to marry him and fly around the world with him, like my mom wants, doesn't mean I'd kick him out of bed for a night or two." Charlotte raised an eyebrow, as if to challenge Fiona to disagree with her statement. "You can't tell me he's the one guy you're attracted to and then not agree that he's a DILF."

"Fine!" Fiona threw up her hands in defeat. "I agree it's an apt description, but it's still too crass for me to say."

"Whatever." Charlotte laughed. "Hanging around all that testosterone daily, I bet you'll be saying that and a whole lot worse by the time you come home for your first holiday break."

"I'll mostly be hanging around with children daily, so I'm sure I'll keep my language clean." Fiona disagreed, but she still laughed with her friend. *But I might start thinking a few dirty words, or rather all the dirty things I'd like to do with my hot boss.*

"So, what are the chances you'll say yes if Daddy Rick asks you out?" Charlotte flagged down the bartender for another round of Chardonnay, just as the nachos and quesadillas they'd ordered to counteract the effects of the alcohol arrived.

"Oh, geez, Char." Fiona almost had a spit take from the mental picture of her boss that Charlotte's newest moniker for him caused. "Don't call him that either. That sounds like something out of one of those books Kay recommended when you first brought her to book club."

"Of course it does." Char grinned as she lifted a cheese-covered chip from the plate of nachos. "Where do you think I got it from?" She wagged her eyebrows at Fiona as she popped the chip into her mouth.

Fiona just shook her head, but she still giggled with her friend as she lifted a section of quesadilla from the plate to take a bite. *I guess he did kinda give off a Daddy vibe during my interview, and especially when he was talking to Mom and Dad about keeping me safe while traveling.*

"But seriously, quit deflecting and answer the question." Charlotte pointed to Fiona with her newly filled wine glass. "Would you go out with him and give him a shot at breaking your dry spell?"

Fiona took another large drink to gather her thoughts while Charlotte let the silence linger by stuffing her face with nachos. On the one hand, she'd love to go out with Rick and see if he had half the attraction to her that she had to him. On the other hand, she knew it was probably a bad idea to date her boss. The more she thought about him, the more she thought about how she'd had to go home and change her panties from how wet they got during her interview, and wondered if the term *dry spell* was really an accurate description of her current situation.

"Maybe," she drawled out, shrugging as she went back to eating. "But I don't think I can really call it a dry spell when just thinking about him makes my panties wet."

Charlotte choked on her wine, having the spit-take that Fiona barely avoided earlier. "Well, I guess that's my answer," Char giggled once she'd regained her composure from the shock of Fiona talking about her wet panties. She held up her glass, as if to give a toast. "Here's to my beautiful friend, Fiona, taking Daddy Rick the DILF off the market in the new year!"

Fiona burst out laughing at her outrageous friend, but she still clinked her glass with Charlotte's before they each finished off their second glass of wine and their dinners. They ordered a third round before Fiona finally turned the conversation off her new job and potential romance with her boss.

"So, what are the chances you'll finally find Mr. Right in the new year?" Fiona asked Charlotte, looking around the bar to see if there were any guys her friend might be interested in, if only for the night. She noticed the guy sitting on the barstool on Charlotte's other side and wondered if he was really as focused on the drink in front of him as he appeared, or if he was listening to their conversation.

"Oh, I'm probably just going to stick with book boyfriends for another year." Charlotte shook her head. "Maybe I'll get Cassidy, Lexi, or Kayla to come out for a girls' night when I want to look for a one-off, but I'm not about to give Mom the satisfaction of marrying me off anytime soon."

"You seriously weren't interested in any of the GWA guys?" Fiona knew Char was tired of her mother trying to hook her up with one of the Walkers, as she had for years, but she thought at least one of the hot wrestlers would have attracted Charlotte's interest.

"Don't get me wrong, they were nice eye candy when they were in town." Char wagged her eyebrows suggestively. "But I didn't really feel a connection with any of them. Not that I need that connection for a one-time hookup, but I won't go there with anyone who works with my brother."

"I get it." Fiona bobbed her head in agreement. "For anything long term, you want that connection like our parents have, and the couples have in all the romance novels we read."

"Gross! Don't mention our parents and romance novels in the same sentence." Charlotte made a gagging face. "For long term, I'd need the connection. But I wouldn't mind the passion of a romance novel for a night or two, even without the connection."

Fiona thought the passion portrayed in romance novels was because the couples had the connection Charlotte was talking about, but she wasn't about to argue semantics with her friend. The only thing that would do was kill their buzz.

"Okay, if you could have a hot hookup with a real-life version of a passionate book hero, who would it be?" Fiona asked the question that she knew she couldn't answer herself. Not only because she could only think of her new boss, Rick Robertson, as her romantic lead in her imaginary world, but also because there were too many book heroes who were described as too good to be true.

"Ian Taggart," Charlotte stated matter-of-factly.

"That is definitely not whom I expected you to pick." Fiona giggled as she thought about the Lexi Blake books they'd recently read on Charlotte's new sister-in-law, Kay's recommendation.

"No? Whom would you have thought I'd pick?"

"Someone more studious, like that librarian in the Pippa Grant series we read last year," Fiona replied, remembering how much she enjoyed the hot hockey players in that same literary universe. *Huh? Guess I have a thing for athletes, since my new boss was a wrestler before he took over the company.*

Fiona wasn't going to mention to Charlotte how she'd looked up pictures on the internet of Rick and saw a few of him in his younger days dressed in wrestling tights. She'd even saved a couple to her laptop, since they were as close as she thought she'd ever get to seeing him naked.

"Yeah, I could see that." Charlotte tilted her head thoughtfully before nodding. "And if we were talking about forever together, I'd probably agree. But since you said it was only for a hot hookup, I figured I could handle the excitement of Ian for a night. I mean, the opportunity to spend the night in a dungeon being dominated by a Nordic God, former spy, is too rare to pass up. So, if I ever met a real-life Ian, I wouldn't be able to say no."

"I guess I can see your point," Fiona admitted, giggling. "And your name is Charlotte, so Ian certainly fits with you."

"Yeah, but I'm no Russian assassin, so I wouldn't have to worry about either of us falling in love." Charlotte giggled.

They ended up ordering one more round of drinks before turning on their stools and scoping out the place.

"One o'clock, blue dress, and bad toupee." Charlotte indicated to a couple across the bar. "Go."

"Midlife crisis, hired a hooker for the night." Fiona slapped a hand over her mouth after saying it because she felt so guilty for judging them so harshly.

"You are so, one-hundred percent, right on that one," Charlotte laughed.

"Ten o'clock, red dress between the two suits. Go." Fiona pointed out the next group of people for Charlotte to figure out their story.

"In town on business, and the two bosses are planning to share their secretary for the night." Charlotte shocked Fiona at the mention of a possible ménage between the threesome at the table she'd indicated. "Far-right corner, black dress, sitting alone."

"Oh, she looks sad," Fiona observed, wishing she could go cheer up the stranger in the corner without coming across as a weirdo. "I bet she's here for work and missing her family back in Tupelo."

"Tupelo?" Charlotte chuckled. "You could pick any city in the world for the narrative, and you pick Tupelo, Mississippi?"

"It was the only place that popped into my head." Fiona shrugged, not sure why she didn't think of a more exciting city.

"And I don't think she looks sad." Charlotte tilted her head to examine the woman more closely. "Though I could understand being sad if she actually lived in Tupelo."

"Quit picking on me about Tupelo and give me a better narrative." Fiona rolled her eyes and shook her head at her friend.

"She's bored, stuck here for work when she'd rather be somewhere like New York or Los Angeles, where she'd be the life of the party."

"I can see that," the guy on Charlotte's other side said. "She's definitely bored, not sad."

Is that the same guy that was staring into his drink earlier? No, this guy is actually smiling and being friendly. The broody guy must have left when I wasn't looking in that direction.

"And not from Tupelo." Charlotte turned and grinned at the stranger.

"Definitely not from Tupelo." The guy chuckled and extended his hand to Charlotte. "Name's Ian. Mind if I join in your game?"

Charlotte had just put her hand in his to shake when her eyes went wide, and she turned to look at Fiona at the mention of his name. Fiona burst out laughing at the strange coincidence of Charlotte meeting a guy named Ian less than an hour after talking about her fantasy book boyfriend with the same name.

"You are definitely welcome to join the game," Fiona said when she got her laughter under control. "In fact, I think I'm going to let you take my turn. I have an early morning tomorrow and think it's time for me to head up to my room."

"Fiona!" Charlotte growled her name with her hand still clutched in Ian's.

"Yeah, I'm not going to stick around and be a third wheel on your once-in-a-lifetime opportunity." Fiona downed the last of her drink and tossed two twenties on the bar to cover her tab. "I'll call before I leave in the morning to see if you're up for going with me. Night."

Fiona waved at Charlotte and Charlotte's new friend, Ian, as she left the bar to go up to her room. She knew Charlotte was more than capable of handling herself with the stranger, even if she was somehow able to say no to the man, who looked an awful lot like what Fiona imagined the book character with the same name looked like.

If Charlotte just got her Christmas wish to have a hot night with her own Ian, maybe my Christmas wish of breaking my dry spell with my hot boss in the new year will come true, too?

~~~

Thursday, December 27, 2018, New York City, New York

Rick knew he was cutting it close to the new year deadline he'd given himself to hire a history teacher by doing interviews while everyone else who worked for the company was technically on their year-end holiday break. But since none of the history teachers he'd interviewed while traveling seemed like a good fit, he didn't have a choice but to keep interviewing until he finally found a history teacher that would be the correct addition to the GWA roster.

Hopefully, one of these interviewees today will be a good fit. And will be available to start next week. And already has a passport, so I don't have to fast-track another one before we start our international events in a couple of weeks.

Rick's dick twitched at the reminder of the phone conversation he'd had with Fiona a week and a half before, when she called to confirm her start date. He had been in the middle of confirming all his employees and their families had their passports, as he was finalizing tour dates in Mexico, the Caribbean, Canada, and Europe for the first quarter of the new year, when she called to tell him that her old position had been filled, so she could start work with the company on January second as he'd requested. Since it was fresh on his mind, he told Fiona to be sure she brought her passport when she flew to New York to start working for the GWA.

Rick leaned back in his desk chair and adjusted himself in his slacks at the memory of the sexy little noise she made before admitting she didn't have a passport. As much of a pain in the ass as it was for him to pull the strings to expedite getting her passport, the way she profusely thanked him on their next call made him feel better than anything else had in a long time.

He didn't really feel like the hero she claimed he was for her. But he certainly enjoyed feeling like he was taking care of her, even
~~~

though it was only in a small way. He didn't have much time to bask in the fleeting feelings, as the phone on his desk rang.

He pushed the button to place the phone on speaker, answering with a curt, "Rick Robertson."

"Mr. Robertson, there's a Jaxon Nolen here to meet with you," Jamal, the security guard on the ground floor of the building, said through the phone.

"Yes, I've been expecting him," Rick replied, shuffling through the résumés on his desk to find the correct one. "Please send him up."

"Will do, Sir."

"Jamal," Rick barked the man's name, hoping to catch him before he hung up the phone.

"Yes, Sir?"

"There hasn't been anyone else that's come in for an interview this morning?" Rick wondered why the two people scheduled to interview before Jaxon Nolen hadn't already arrived.

"Um, there were a couple of women that stopped in." Jamal sounded like he was uncertain about what he was saying. "But they were dressed like they were going to the club, so I thought they were ring rats and didn't believe they actually had an appointment with you, Sir. I gave them some autographed pictures of the talent and sent them on their way."

"You didn't happen to catch either of their names, did you?" Rick wasn't sure if they were the two women he'd also scheduled to interview for the history tutor position, or if they were groupies, as Jamal suspected. But if their names matched the ones on the résumés on his desk, then he would at least know he only had to stick around for the one interview before going to pick up his daughter from his parents' house.

"Um, no, sorry, Sir." Jamal at least sounded apologetic as he answered.

"Thanks, Jamal. Just so you know, I am expecting Tammy Thomas and Debra Stevens to interview for a tutor position." *Though I probably won't hire Tammy just because she's forty-five minutes late for her scheduled interview time.* Rick looked at his watch and noted that Debra wasn't scheduled to be there for another fifteen minutes, and Jaxon was over an hour early for his scheduled time.

"I'll let you know if they arrive. And I'm sorry again if they were the two I sent away this morning. But if they were, I don't think you'd have hired them." Jamal chuckled. "Unless you're looking to hire someone to teach pole dancing to keep the single guys entertained on the road."

"No, I'm not hiring a pole dancing teacher." Rick chuckled, glad his employees were comfortable enough to joke around with him.

They said a quick goodbye just as Jaxon Nolen knocked on Rick's open, office door.

"Come on in." Rick hung up the phone and stood as the blond-haired, blue-eyed man, who looked like he could be a model instead of a history teacher, stepped into his office. While Jaxon was a couple of inches shorter and probably forty pounds lighter than Rick, the twenty-something young man almost looked like he belonged on the talent roster as a manager or announcer instead of in the classroom.

"Mr. Robertson?" Jaxon extended his hand to Rick as he stepped up to the desk.

"Yes, but please call me Rick." Rick shook the younger man's hand, impressed with his confident grip. "And you must be Jaxon Nolen."

"Everyone just calls me Jax." They took their seats across the desk to begin the interview.

Rick glanced over Jaxon's curriculum vitae to see his teaching experience, noting that he hadn't worked in a school setting for the last six months. Though prior to that, he'd worked at a private school for five years, starting there right after graduating from college.

"Please tell me about your teaching experience." Rick placed the paper on his desk to focus on the man's answers, hoping to read in his body language what he couldn't find between the lines on the page.

"For the last six months, I've been working as a private tutor," Jax began, seeming to relax in his seat. "In that time, I've worked with kids as young as second grade all the way up to college students. In that capacity, I've taught a little bit of everything from spelling to world history and even a little math and science, though math and science are definitely not my strong suit. Prior to that, I taught history exclusively at a private school upstate."

"Yes, I saw you were there for five years, right out of college. Why did you decide to leave that job?" Rick noticed Jax tense momentarily at the question.

Once he had schooled his features to hide his discomfort, he finally answered. "It was a combination of things. The school is located in a small town, which was a nice change of pace at first. But over time, the lack of leisure-time activities in the area, and peers in my age range to socialize with outside of school activities, started to make me feel like I wasn't really the right fit for that position. So, as much as I loved teaching young minds what should and what shouldn't be repeated in history, I moved back to the city to look for a position where I am the right fit."

Rick wasn't sure how he felt about the possibility of Jaxon socializing with his peers as a tutor with the GWA, but he couldn't exactly pass on hiring a qualified candidate to keep him away from a woman that Rick himself had no claim on either.

"And what makes you think you're the right fit for our history tutor position?"

"First and foremost, because it's a history tutor position." Jaxon smiled brightly. "While I won't mind helping out with another subject if one of the other tutors is unavailable, I like the idea of being able to focus on my primary subject of interest for the most part. Second, I've come to enjoy working with a wide range of age groups through the last six months of tutoring, so the fact that your students range from kindergarten through high school will keep my skills sharp in all areas of history and not just in the one area of history I taught tenth graders for five years."

"And you understand our schedule is literally a different city every day, all year round?"

"That's the third thing I find perfect about this job." Jaxon grinned. "I love to travel, but haven't been able to budget in much the last few years on a teacher's salary. In fact, I'm leaving tomorrow for a week-long ski trip that I'm only able to take because my parents gave it to me as a Christmas present. So, getting to teach history while traveling to all the places where it occurred is my dream job."

I definitely can't fault the man's enthusiasm for the job, Rick thought as he watched Jaxon practically bouncing out of his seat with excitement. *But I have to make sure his socializing doesn't border on sexual harassment like Stacy's before I can hire him.*

"What exactly did you mean when you mentioned wanting to socialize with your peers earlier?" Rick tried to school his features as he asked the question, but he wasn't sure how successful he was when Jaxon raised an eyebrow at him quizzically. "We recently had to terminate a tutor's employment for overly flirtatious behavior with some of our married staff members. I need to make sure that won't be a problem in the future with anyone else we hire."

"Oh, no, that definitely won't be a problem." Jaxon raised both hands, palms out, while shaking his head to indicate he wouldn't behave that way. "I was just talking about making friends. Talking over dinner or hanging out after work. Not anything inappropriate like that. And I abhor cheating, so I would never even think about flirting with a married coworker. In fact, I find it best not to date anyone I work with, just to keep everything professional."

"While I appreciate that, we don't have a company policy against dating coworkers. Hell, half the people who work here are married to coworkers, so I'd lose most of my talent roster and half my staff if I tried to instigate such a policy." Rick chuckled at the irony of his inability to prevent anyone who worked for him from dating the woman he shouldn't want to keep for himself. "I just ask that we all keep our private lives private and don't even flirt without consent."

"You won't have to worry about that from me, Sir."

While Rick appreciated the younger man using the moniker as a sign of respect, he hoped Jax would eventually address him by his first name, just as he asked everyone else to do. *Unless he defers to me that way in front of Fiona, so maybe she'll pick up on it and do the same. Fuck, I wouldn't mind hearing Sir from her lips.*

Knowing it was inappropriate to keep thinking about the pretty, young, English teacher in a sexual manner while he was interviewing Jaxon, Rick pushed her from his thoughts and focused on the task at hand. *He does seem like a good fit for the history tutor position. Hopefully, my gut instinct isn't too thrown off by thinking about Fiona, so I won't regret following it to hire this guy.*

"When will you be back from your ski trip to be able to start work?" As much as Rick wanted to hire someone to start on January second, when they went back to work after the holiday break, he figured he'd be okay with a later start date, if the kid was willing to start as soon as his ski trip was over.

"I'll be flying back from Breckenridge on the sixth of January, so I can start on the seventh."

"We'll be flying out of New York on the second." Rick pulled up the schedule on his tablet to check where the GWA would be on the sixth and seventh. "Can you change your flight home to meet us in Minneapolis on the sixth? Or do I need to book you a flight out of New York on the seventh to meet us in Sioux Falls?"

"I can switch my flight to meet you in Minneapolis, if that's when you want me to start work." Rick just thought Jaxon's smile was beaming earlier. *Damn, he definitely doesn't have a poker face.*

Rick closed the schedule on his tablet to open up the human resources forms and passed the tablet across the desk to Jax. "Fill out these forms, so I can have you added to our hotel bookings. And let me know your flight information, so I can have someone pick you up at the airport and bring you over to meet us at the Target Center when you land in Minneapolis. You won't actually start work until Monday the seventh, but we'll go over the daily schedule and introduce you to everyone that night over dinner in catering. We all eat together at six o'clock local time every day, so I'm sure you'll make plenty of friends then."

"Thank you, Sir." Rick raised an eyebrow at Jaxon's continual usage of the honorific. "Um, Rick. Thank you, Rick, for this opportunity. I'm really looking forward to working with you and the rest of the GWA staff."

"Thank you, Jax, for coming on board and helping me get the rest of my staff off my back about needing a history tutor."

Both men chuckled as Jax filled out the online forms to begin working with the GWA. Once the new hire left his office, Rick called down to the security desk.

"GWA Security." Jamal's voice was sharp when he picked up the line.

"Hey, Jamal, I just wanted to let you know that I filled the tutor position. I doubt either of the other applicants will show up since it's well past both of their appointment times. But if they do, you can send them home and let them know the position is no longer available."

"No problem, Boss. Guess it didn't really matter if those girls I sent home this morning were them after all."

Rick huffed out a small chuckle. "From the way you described them, it sounds like you saved me from having to suffer through interviewing them."

"More like I cock-blocked you from one or both of them trying to get the job by demonstrating their oral skills in your office." Jamal laughed at his own joke.

Rick cringed, afraid there was too much truth behind Jamal's joke. "Well, thanks for the save, Jamal. I'm heading out now, so you can lock the place up. Nobody should be back in the building until the second."

"Will do, Boss. Enjoy the rest of your holidays."

"You, too." With that, Rick hung up the phone, gathered his things, and left the office to go spend some quality time with his family. And hoped he could keep his New Year's Resolution to not lust over the new English tutor to the point of making things awkward at work.

It's not like someone as innocent as she could handle the rough and dirty way I want to fuck her, so I need to quit thinking about her so fucking often.

He knew better than to try to shut down all thoughts about her. That would be an impossible task. But he thought everything would work out just fine if he limited his lustful thoughts about her to when he was jacking off in the shower.

Fuck, if I keep getting this hard just thinking about her, I might have to start showering more than once a day to keep from popping a boner like a teenager every time I see her when she starts working with us. At the very least, I should probably pack my compression shorts from when I was wrestling to keep my hard-on from being obvious to everyone when we all start back to work next week.

Chapter Three

Tuesday, January 1, 2019, Traveling between Heart's Destiny, Texas, and New York City, New York

Fiona was glad she had thought to ask Kay and Randi for advice on what all to pack before her first flight to head off and start her new job. They had not only given her an excellent checklist to make sure she brought everything she needed, but they'd also offered to let her ride to the airport with them, since they were all on the same flight out and planned on caravanning to the airport.

She ended up riding in the backseat of Dean Hunter's truck with Randi, while the Hunter twins were in the front seat and all their luggage was under the tonneau cover in the bed of the truck.

"Thanks again for letting me tag along with ya'll." Fiona was nervous as they grabbed their luggage before making their way to the airline counter to get checked in for their flights. "I'd be so lost if I were going alone this first time."

"No thanks necessary, Fiona." Dean grinned at her as he handed her rolling suitcase down from the back of his truck. "We all had to be shown where to go our first few days traveling with the company."

"And you're welcome to ride with us anytime," Randi added, smiling as she grabbed the handle of her own rolling suitcase with one hand, while hooking her free arm with Fiona's to lead her out of the long-term parking area. "Though I'm sure you'll end up making lots of friends to carpool with between airports, hotels, and arenas as you get to know the rest of the crew. So, don't feel like you have to ride with us if you'd rather ride with a new friend."

Randi gave Fiona a look she couldn't quite interpret. Her smile was friendly, but she seemed to have a gleam in her eye that indicated

Randi thought Fiona would pair off with a coworker as more than friends.

Goodness, did Charlotte tell Kay or Randi about my crush on our boss? Surely, she doesn't think I'm going to act on that attraction and start riding with Mr. Robertson to and from the various airports, hotels, and arenas. Does she?

Fiona didn't have the chance to work up the courage to ask Randi what she knew, or whom she thought Fiona might become more than friends with, because they were joined by the Burlesons and a few other wrestlers that had been vacationing in Heart's Destiny when they got in the line at the airline counter. Reintroductions were made as they all got in line, but Fiona knew she would probably get some names mixed up over the next few days, as she was getting to know everyone.

Fiona tried to keep up with the small talk going on around her, but she was too fascinated with all the new experiences of checking her larger bags for the flight, going through airport security, and people-watching as they made their way to their gate.

When they boarded the plane, she was surprised that the GWA crew took up more than half of the first-class seats, filling three of the five rows. When she took her seat, she was glad her friends had talked her into upgrading from the business class seat she'd originally been booked in because they looked cramped when she looked farther back in the plane.

I probably shouldn't get used to this comfort level on the plane, she thought as she put her backpack and purse under the seat. *I'm sure with as many people as the GWA employs, I'll be stuck back in the cramped seats on that plane each day.*

"You nervous about flying?" Dean asked as he took the seat beside her after putting his carry-on in the overhead bin.

"No, not really." Fiona shook her head and smiled.

"Then what was that look for a minute ago?"

"Oh, just thinking I should probably enjoy the space of first class while it lasts, since I'll probably be sitting back in the cramped seats on the GWA plane." Fiona waved away the momentary melancholy she felt at being crammed in like sardines for their daily flights.

"Oh, no, the pods on the GWA plane are all bigger than these seats. And we have thirty rows of them, so nobody has to suffer in a cramped seat on the company plane." Dean grinned as he buckled his seatbelt.

"Nobody but the pilots and flight attendant," Anthony corrected from his seat in front of Dean. "But those pods won't fit in the cockpit or galley."

"Yeah, I think it's funny that Kay gets to sit in the pods with the rest of us, while you have to cram into the cockpit." Dean laughed as he poked fun at Anthony being so tall and cramped into the pilot's seat, while his petite wife sat in the luxury seats with the rest of the crew.

"Yeah, she might not need the leg room, but I'm glad she's able to ride in comfort on the company plane." Anthony smiled across the aisle at his wife. "And I imagine she'll need the extra space when we get closer to our son's due date."

They talked a little more about the baby before settling into a comfortable silence for the rest of the flight. During their layover in Dallas, Fiona talked more with Kay and Randi about the way their travel schedules usually worked. So, once they landed in New York, Fiona knew to ride with them or someone else with the GWA between the airport, hotel, and arena daily to avoid having to drive herself each day in unfamiliar cities where she wasn't comfortable driving.

When they got to the hotel, her friends walked her through the procedure to check in under the GWA's group reservation. Then she tagged along with Anthony, Kay, and their daughters to go ice skating at Rockefeller Center, stopping on the way to buy a heavier coat than the lightweight one she'd brought from home.

She felt a little foolish, at first, for thinking her lightweight coat she wore on the rare days South Texas temperatures dipped below fifty degrees would be enough for her to wear in the colder cities where they traveled. But then Anthony pointed out how impossible it would be to find a coat heavy enough for below-freezing temperatures in their hometown, where lows were only in the forties in the middle of the night, maybe half a dozen days a year.

While she didn't have time to explore everything she wanted to see in New York on her first trip to the city, Fiona had a wonderful time seeing the iconic Christmas tree and trying to ice skate for the first time in her life. And she knew she'd be back to the city multiple times in the course of her employment with the GWA to see the other sights in due time.

Along with the sights in several hundred other cities around the world, Fiona thought as she drifted off to sleep that night in the hotel bed.

~~~

Wednesday, January 2, 2019, 8 a.m., New York City, New York

Rick took one last look out of the floor-to-ceiling windows in his bedroom, appreciating the view of Central Park from his penthouse at 15 Central Park West that he wouldn't get to see for a couple of months. He had bought the penthouse after his divorce, thinking he was better off no longer owning property that required lawn maintenance services. He thought having Central Park right across the street would give him plenty of space to take his daughter out to play when they were home. But with only spending maybe fifty days a year in New York, he was beginning to wonder if the four-bedroom condo was mostly wasted space.

Shaking off the melancholy thoughts, Rick turned away from the spectacular view to grab his bags and place them on the luggage cart waiting beside the elevator that opened up straight into the gallery in his penthouse.

"Is this everything?" Rick yelled down the hall to his daughter's room when he noticed Britney's bags were already on the luggage cart ready to go. When she didn't respond immediately, he called her name, "Britney Bear, you ready to go?"

"Almost, Daddy!" Britney's voice rang out from the other side of the condo, instead of from the hallway out of his room leading to her bedroom and the two guest bedrooms.

Probably in the kitchen, Rick thought, mentally chuckling at his daughter's recent fascination with baking, since spending time in the kitchen with her friends and their mothers when they were all in Heart's Destiny for Anthony and Kay's wedding. *Most likely packing up the rest of the cookies to take to her friends now that our holiday*
~~~

break at home is over. I still can't believe she got Mom to bake them with her this week.

Britney proved him correct in his assessment when she came around the corner carrying two gallon-sized plastic bags of cookies in each of her hands.

"How many cookies did you and Nonna bake this week, Pumpkin?" Rick pushed the button to call the elevator, while Britney piled the bags of cookies on top of their luggage.

"A hundred and forty-four," Britney replied absent-mindedly, while trying to make sure none of her precious cargo would tumble off the top of the luggage on the cart. "But we ate a bunch of them, so there's only about a hundred left to take with us."

Rick rubbed his belly and chuckled. "Yeah, I'm already planning the extra workouts I'm going to have to do to work off all of the ones you fed me. Thank goodness you saved most of them to share with your friends, or you'd have to roll me on the plane."

"Naw, I'd just get some of the wrestlers to carry you," Britney joked, giggling as the elevator opened.

"You keep trying to fatten me up like you have this last week, and it'll take at least four of them to lift me." Rick grinned at his daughter, as he pushed their luggage cart onto the elevator.

"Then you might want to push them to lift more weights because Tia and I are planning to bake every time we stay in a hotel that has a real kitchen in our suites." Britney grinned back, as she followed him onto the elevator and pushed the button for the lobby. "She said our new English teacher was talking to her mom and offered to supervise our baking whenever Mrs. Kay needs a break."

"That sounds awfully nice of her, but she's probably going to need some time to get used to our travel schedule before she's ready to supervise one of your slumber parties." Rick hated being the one to burst his daughter's bubble, but he knew there wouldn't be any baking in the standard hotel rooms he had reserved for Fiona Harrison. Even if the girls convinced her to supervise their slumber parties, which was when they'd done a little baking in the last few weeks, while staying in the family suites he reserved for the families that traveled with the GWA, her room wouldn't have a kitchen for them to bake in since single staff members didn't stay in family suites.

There's no way I can invite her to our suite to bake with the girls. Rick discreetly adjusted his stance, as his cock started to swell from imagining Fiona in his hotel suite. He was glad the cart stacked with luggage was between him and his daughter while they rode down in the elevator, so she didn't notice his discomfort. *If just the thought of Fiona doing something so domestic with my daughter is arousing, I'd never be able to keep my hands off her if she was still there after the girls crashed for the night.*

"I know, Daddy." Britney rolled her eyes at him. "Just like when Mrs. Kay started working with us, we have to wait at least two weeks before we can start planning slumber parties with new people babysitting us."

The eye rolling was already getting old in Rick's opinion, even though it had only started recently and would be a staple of Britney's attitude throughout her teenage years, at least according to the other parents he'd spoken to about raising teenagers. He knew it was useless to reprimand her for it, as none of his previous corrections had stopped the behavior, so he let it go as they exited the elevator and made their way through the lobby of their building. They made small talk with the doorman, who assisted them in loading their luggage into the car that was waiting for them at the curb.

It was probably overkill to have a full-time bodyguard on staff to drive him and Britney around, but Rick liked knowing his daughter was safe, even if he didn't always need the extra driving time to work on keeping everything about the company running smoothly. Having security on staff had eased Fiona's father's worries about his daughter traveling with the GWA back on Thanksgiving, too.

"Hey, Munchkin, you ready to blow this popsicle stand?" Cage Dalton, their driver and security expert, asked Britney as he opened the back door for her.

"You know it!" Britney squealed as Cage reached out as if he was going to tickle her as she sped past him into the vehicle.

Though Cage had been an employee of the company for just over five years, he felt more like family with as much time as he spent with Rick and Britney. She often referred to him as Uncle Cage, and Rick had to admit he considered him as close a friend as he'd ever had. He was only a couple of years younger than Rick and would have made a good addition to the talent roster when he was originally hired in the fall of 2013, if it wasn't for the fact that he wanted to keep his war wounds covered. Cage was a former Navy SEAL who went into private security after he was medically discharged.

Rick had tried diligently to talk him into training to wrestle when he first started working with the GWA, just a few months after his discharge from the Navy. But Cage had adamantly refused, saying he'd scare away the fans if he went shirtless in the ring and exposed his scars to the viewers. Rick quit pressuring his friend, trying to be understanding of his feelings, even though he didn't think anyone would really be offended by Cage's appearance, especially if they knew how he got the scars.

They carried on their usual banter as Cage drove them to the airport. At least until Britney started talking about being excited to meet the two new teachers Rick had hired to start working with them in the next week.

Cage gave Rick a knowing look as Britney rambled on about what Tia had told her about Fiona in their online chats over Christmas break. Cage was the only person Rick had told about his attraction to the young English teacher. Rick knew his friend was eager to meet Fiona, so he could formulate a plan to help keep Rick out of trouble with the younger woman.

Seeing as how Cage was the only man in the company who was as celibate as Rick, he figured he'd have the best chance of coming up with the best suggestions to resist temptation than anyone else he might talk to about his need to control his desire for Fiona. Cage hadn't mentioned why he wasn't interested in dating or even picking up a one-night stand, but Rick assumed it had to do with the scars he mentioned when he was first hired.

Rick's reasons for avoiding women were more about the scars nobody could see than having his daughter travel with him, as everyone around him assumed. If he wanted, he could still pick up a ring rat on the nights Britney spent with one of her friends. That was what he had done in the first year or so after his divorce. But after everything that happened with Colleen, he found he needed more control in the bedroom than he could expect a one-night stand to give him.

After studying a little about BDSM online, he thought about trying to find a club to find a partner to meet his needs. But with his travel schedule, it wasn't feasible to buy a membership in a club he couldn't use ninety percent of the year because of not being in New York. So, he resigned himself to a life of celibacy and fantasizing, while jacking off in the shower when he needed a release.

Once they were parked at the private airport where the GWA plane was kept for maintenance on holiday breaks, Rick let Britney run ahead to her friends, who were gathered a hundred yards away, so he could have a private word with Cage.

"Hey, about the stuff I told you…" Rick trailed off, not wanting to mention specifics when his other employees could possibly overhear them.

"Rick, man, come on," Cage said, shaking his head. "You know I'm a vault when it comes to that stuff. Nobody will hear a word from me."

"Thanks," was all Rick could say before they were close enough to the crowd that others might overhear. They fell in line with the rest of the crew, who were all lining up to board the plane.

He didn't see Fiona in the group until he boarded the plane and found her seated with Randi Lee and the Hunter twins. *What's she doing there instead of sitting with Kay and the kids? Fuck, I hope she doesn't have a thing for Dean Hunter!*

Rick stowed his and Britney's luggage and looked around the plane to make note of where his daughter was sitting with her friends. He waited until most everyone had their things stowed away and had taken their seats before walking down the aisle of the plane to stand beside the grouping of seats where Fiona was sitting in the rear-facing, window seat beside Dean.

"Fiona." Rick extended his hand to her as an invitation to have her stand up, so he could introduce her to the rest of the crew. He stifled his smile when she misunderstood his gesture and shook his hand instead of taking it to stand. He schooled his features to cover the jolt of electricity that ran from where he held her hand in his straight to his cock.

Damn, I really should have looked for those compression shorts while I was home this week. Thank fuck, I always wear a suit to help hide these inappropriate erections. I can't let anyone see how my body reacts to how alluring her naïveté is, or everyone on this plane will know I'm attracted to her.

"Rick, it's nice to see you again." Fiona smiled up at him as she continued to shake his hand for far longer than truly appropriate.

"Yes, you, too. But I was actually offering to assist you to stand, so I can introduce you to everyone."

"Oh." Fiona's lips stayed in that perfect circular position to say the word as she released his hand to unbuckle her seatbelt. Her pink cheeks perfectly matched her dress as she pushed herself up out of the seat without his assistance.

Damn, I wish we were alone, so I could see if she blushes like that everywhere, or if it's just on her cheeks, Rick thought, while trying to maintain a straight face.

Rick stepped back and motioned for her to step out into the middle of the aisle as he cleared his throat to get everyone's attention. "As I'm sure most of you have already noticed, our former English tutor is no longer with the company. With the new year comes a new semester for our students, and Fiona Harrison will now be the English tutor working with our children. Dan and Ivy, please raise your hands."

When the couple, whom he considered to be the lead teachers in the company, raised their hands, Rick turned to look at Fiona. "Dan and Ivy Traverson teach science and math. Dan is actually our principal, for lack of a better title. He keeps track of all our students' academic records and will be who you report to each day for classroom time. Please get with him once we land in Nashville to get started with your teaching duties and anything else you might need to know to stay on schedule with the rest of us."

"Yes, Sir." Fiona smiled up at him before turning to wave at the Traversons. "Um, should I go sit back with them now?"

Yes, go sit with the married couple now, and not my single talent. "Entirely up to you. You're not technically on the clock until three this afternoon for classroom time, but we will be in the air for a couple of hours, when they could fill you in on everything without taking away from the time with the kids later."

"Good point. Just let me grab my bags and I'll go ahead and talk to them now." Fiona turned and grabbed her purse from beneath the seat she'd previously occupied.

When she went to open the overhead storage compartment, Rick stopped her with a hand over hers on the latch. The jolt of lust that hit him when his hand made contact with hers felt as if he'd been shocked, causing him to lift his hand quickly while hoping nobody else noticed the reaction. "Unless you need a laptop bag to learn how to log into our system, the rest of your luggage is fine where it is."

"Oh, okay, thanks." Fiona continued to open the overhead bin and retrieved a backpack before closing it and turning to walk toward the middle of the plane, where the Traversons were seated.

Rick returned to his seat and buckled up, knowing he couldn't pull out his own electronics to work until after take-off. As he peered down the aisle, Rick regretted sitting in the first row, rear-facing, aisle seat for the first time since he'd bought the company plane. He usually liked being able to see almost everyone on board to be able to call over whomever he needed to discuss the next show with, but he found he couldn't take his eyes off Fiona now that she was on the company plane.

When he forced himself to look away from the woman he knew he could never have the way he wanted, he caught Cage looking at him with an expression that clearly said, *"You're fucked."*

No. Rick tried to project his thoughts to his friend without anyone else catching on to what he was thinking. *I'm not going to fuck her, and that's the problem. I'm just going to be stuck in the hell of seeing her daily when I want her more than I've ever wanted another woman, and I'm not able to act on that desire for her.*

~~~

Wednesday, January 2, 2019, 11 p.m., Nashville, Tennessee

Fiona reflected back on her first official day at her new job as she crawled into the hotel bed in Nashville. While she wished she had more time to explore New York City, she looked forward to exploring a different city every day, too.

She had certainly enjoyed touring the Country Music Hall of Fame in Nashville with the Traversons before going to the arena for the afternoon and evening. They were a nice couple and very welcoming from the first moment she'd sat down with them on the plane. They'd not only prepared her well to start teaching as soon as they got to the
~~~

arena, but they'd also given her tips about traveling with the GWA that Kay and Randi hadn't mentioned.

Who knew our arrival time matters when it comes to using the hotel laundry services? Randi had just said to drop my laundry off whenever I arrive at the hotel. She didn't say anything about the possibility of it not being returned the same day if it isn't turned in before noon. I wonder if she knows that? I should probably pass that info on to her tomorrow, just in case she hasn't learned that in the short time she's been with the GWA.

She was certainly right about it being easy to make friends with others in the company, though. The kids are all great. Fiona took a moment to run through the roster in her head, needing to make sure she had all the children's names memorized before seeing them again the next day.

Shawn Evans, Archer Everett, and Kendrix Grady are all five years old and in kindergarten. Carter and Courtney Westbrook are both in first grade, along with Laci Kirby. Laci and Courtney are both six, and Carter is seven. Jason Moore and Baylee Grady are both seven years old and in second grade. Baylee is Kendrix's older sister.

Maria Burleson is in third grade with Sarah Evans, and they're both eight. Sarah is Shawn's older sister. Katie Moore is our only fourth grader, but at nine years old, she usually sits with her best friends, Sarah and Maria. Katie is also Jason's older sister.

Our ten-year-old fifth graders are Addison Everett, Archer's older sister, and Skye Fields. Skye's brother, River, is a year older and in the sixth grade, along with Dillon Kirby, Laci's older brother.

Our seventh graders are Britney Robertson and Noelle York, who are both twelve years old. Noelle's schedule is the opposite of the Burleson girls' because her parents are on the other flight crew, so when I see her and the Burlesons on the same day, our flight crew is changing the next day.

That just leaves the teenagers. Connor and Cody Stafford are both in eighth grade, with Connor being fourteen, a year older than Cody at thirteen. And, of course, thirteen-year-old Tia Burleson, who tested out of high school last month and is starting online college courses next week.

That girl absolutely amazes me with how she uses her brilliant mind while maintaining the innocence of childhood. It's a testament to how wonderful a job her parents are doing with raising her. Kay is a wonderful woman and so perfect for Anthony.

Speaking of wonderful women, all the moms I met today were super friendly, though it's going to take me more than the one day of meeting them to remember all their names. Some of the dads were a bit standoffish, but with what I heard about their last English tutor, I can understand why.

Thinking about the other dads she'd met in the company brought Fiona's thoughts back to her hunky boss, Rick. She wouldn't say he was as standoffish as the rest of the men in the company, but he wasn't as welcoming as the women in the company, either.

He actually comes off a bit untouchable in the tailor-made suits he wears. Though he does wear them well. Guess ZZ Top had it right when they sang about a **Sharp Dressed Man**.

The tingles she got while shaking his hand and when he covered her hand with his briefly, as she was getting her backpack with her laptop out of the overhead bin in the plane, came back with a vengeance at just the thought of him. She shuddered in her bed as she realized that those innocent touches led to jolts of lust straight to her core.

I really need to figure out how to control the lustful thoughts I have for my boss. He's obviously not interested in me as anything more than an employee. So, I need to shut down any thoughts I might've had about flirting a little to see if I could gain his interest.

But that's so hard to do when my ovaries explode every time I see him interacting with his daughter. She's clearly the most important person in the world to him, which is exactly as it should be for all parents and children. But seeing this man, who is in charge of everything in the GWA, delegate his tasks to others, so he can go sightseeing and have lunch with his daughter is truly heartwarming.

Fiona appreciated that same kind of unconditional love from her own parents. That was probably why seeing it between Rick and Britney made him so attractive to her. It was a trait she wanted to see in her hypothetical future life partner, so she found it highly attractive when she noticed it in eligible males.

And she saw it several times that first day on the job between Rick and Britney. Not only as they were all exiting the plane when Britney convinced Rick to go ziplining with some of the other kids and their families, but also when they were at the arena, when Rick put his tablet away to focus on having dinner with his daughter, instead of continuing to plan the show for the evening.

Though she didn't really have much interaction with him other than that morning on the plane, Fiona couldn't keep her eyes off her hunky boss whenever they were in the same space. *I hope nobody noticed me drooling over him all day,* she thought as she laid there in bed.

While I don't think he's married, since he doesn't wear a wedding ring or have his wife traveling with him, I don't know for sure that he's single. I mean, he could be dating someone and just keeping it private until he's ready to introduce his girlfriend to his daughter.

Although, if he was in a relationship, he would have mentioned that to someone back at Thanksgiving to avoid all the matchmaking going on in Heart's Destiny. So, he's probably single. Not that it really matters, since he hasn't shown even the slightest bit of interest in me, or any other woman working with us today.

I need to drop all thoughts of ever flirting with him or possibly dating him. But gosh, it's so hard when all I can think of is how his beard would feel if he kissed me, or what his big hands could do if he touched me.

Without conscious thought, Fiona's hands slipped under her pajamas. She cupped her breast under her pink tank top with one, while the other delved under the waistband of her pajama pants and panties to cover her mound at the apex of her thighs. With her palm resting on her pubic bone, her fingers were free to explore her delicate folds from her clit to her slit.

Fiona let her mind wander, imagining it was Rick touching her most intimate places. As she slipped her fingers through her folds, she knew her own touch would never compare to his. But that didn't matter, since she knew she'd only ever have him touching her in her fantasies.

He probably prefers thinner women than me, anyway. I hope he's not secretly dating one of the beautiful female wrestlers I saw backstage tonight. I really like this job and don't want to have to leave it because of being jealous of the skinny Minnie he'll eventually end up with.

Pushing all potential negative thoughts out of her head, she went back to imagining Rick was touching her. She spread her wetness around, using her own arousal to lubricate her fingers, so she could insert two inside her while rubbing her thumb over her clit. She moved back and forth between her breasts with her other hand, kneading her mounds, as she imagined how Rick would squeeze them.

I bet his beard would tickle if he sucked my nipples. Or maybe it would feel rough and scratchy against the most sensitive parts of my skin.

She pumped her fingers in and out of her channel, as she spread her arousal over her bundle of nerves with the pad of her thumb. She imagined running her hands through Rick's dark hair, as he used his mouth on her breasts and filled her with his fingers.

Knowing he was older and more experienced than she was, she tried to envision what he would do differently than her former lovers, who hadn't mastered the art of lovemaking when she was with them in her teens and early twenties.

With at least fifteen years of experience more than me, I bet Rick would know exactly how to play my body like an instrument. He'd make sure I came every time, instead of fumbling like those guys in college who couldn't get the job done.

And with the way he has such a strong, take-charge personality, but also shows his sweet, compassionate side with his daughter and the rest of the kids, I'm sure he'd exert a loving dominance in the bedroom like some of my favorite book boyfriends.

Oh, yes, Rick, tie me up and tease me for both our pleasure, Fiona imagined herself saying to him as she sped up the movement of her fingers inside her sex and the pressure of her thumb circling over her clitoris. *Make me come before you claim me with your cock.*

The thought of him bringing her to the brink and replacing his fingers with his dick as she climaxed brought her over the edge to achieve her release. As the waves of pleasure flowed through her, Fiona finally felt relaxed enough to drift off to sleep.

I'll clean up in the shower tomorrow morning, after dreaming some more about my studly boss.

Chapter Four

Rick felt like he was doing a pretty good job of hiding his attraction to Fiona the past few days, even though his morning jack-off sessions in the shower did very little to prevent him from getting hard every time he saw her. It helped that he'd spent so many years traveling with the GWA that he had a gym he could sneak off to most mornings for his workouts, no matter what city they were in on the tour. So, he didn't have to take the chance of running into her in the hotel gym when he wasn't dressed in the proper attire to cover his body's response to her.

"Damn, Boss, aren't you hot?" Brent Crockett, the wrestler with the lumberjack gimmick, asked as Rick walked by him while taking his daughter to the classroom area for the afternoon.

"No, why?" Rick maintained his normal stoic expression, knowing the wrestler, who was dressed in gym shorts and a t-shirt to head to the ring for some sparring before rehearsing for his match that night, was referencing the fact that Rick was still wearing his suit coat inside the building, when he normally took it off to keep from sweating while running all over the arena making sure everything was ready for the show.

"No reason, just thought you normally took your jacket off as soon as you got to the arena." Crockett held his hands up in surrender, as he backed away toward the exit from the backstage area to head out to the ring.

"And I will when I get back to my office," Rick replied as nonchalantly as he could muster. "Got to take Brit to the classroom first."

"Oh, um, okay." With that, Crockett turned and jogged away.

"Why's Crockett being weird, Daddy?" Britney scrunched her nose as she asked the question.

"I have no idea, Britney Bear," Rick lied, knowing his crew was starting to notice that he kept his jacket on any time he was around the new English tutor to cover his inappropriate erection. *Guess I'll have to come up with a better idea to keep my dick under control than just hiding my hard-on under my jacket. Maybe I can find some time to sneak off to an Under Armor store to buy some new compression shorts.*

Thankfully, she didn't ask any more questions before they got to the classroom, where the tutors and a few of the other kids were already gathered.

"Bye, Dad, see ya at dinner." Britney didn't even give him a hug as she ran over to the table where the tutors were standing.

"What happened to the little girl who always gave me a hug and kiss before going off with her friends?" Rick mumbled under his breath. Thankfully, his words deflected from the fact that he was staring at Fiona instead of Britney.

He couldn't take his eyes off her ass the way it was hugged in her bright green dress. If it wasn't for the fact they were surrounded by several of his employees and their children, he'd be tempted to slip up behind her, lift the dress, slide her black leggings down, and take her from behind.

Fuck! It would be so easy, even with the leggings she's added to keep warm while still wearing her dresses. Rick took a moment to picture a similar scene. Fiona bent over his desk in his locked office with the skirt of her dress pushed up around her waist and him pushing into her from behind. *Maybe in a warmer climate, so she could ditch the leggings.*

"She became a preteen," Matt Moore, the mid-carder who used the ring name of Madman, chuckled. He brought Rick out of his fantasy about Fiona by slapping a hand on Rick's shoulder, as he and his family walked into the classroom. "At least you got public hugs and kisses a couple years longer than Katie gave us."

"Miss Fiona, you should have come to the Mall of America with us," Britney shouted, as she hugged the English tutor after dropping her backpack on the table. "There's a whole amusement park inside the mall and we had so much fun, even though Daddy wouldn't let me ride the log ride because of it being too cold outside to get our clothes wet."

"Rick might be more confused about why the new tutor is getting his daughter's affection when he isn't," Emily, Matt's wife, pointed out, as she noticed the exchange at the front of the classroom. "Don't let it bother you, Boss. Your daughter isn't the only one who's smitten with the new tutor. But once the newness wears off, Britney will return to hugging you instead of Fiona."

"Yeah, that's probably it." Rick chuckled to cover his jealousy at hearing others in the company were smitten with Fiona. *Hopefully, it's just the kids hugging her like that, and not anyone whose ass I'll have to kick to keep them away from her.*

Trying to shake off his jealous thoughts, Rick excused himself from further conversation with his employees and retreated to the backstage area that was made up as his office for the duration of the show prep that day. He struggled through his normal daily tasks, barely comprehending the updates the bookers were giving him on the plans for the show that night to be able to approve them.

It was hard to focus on how the matches that night would progress the overall angles for the local fans without giving away the plans for their weekly televised show coming up on Tuesday, with Fiona being at the forefront of his mind. All Rick wanted to do was go back to the classroom and watch Fiona as she worked with Britney and the rest of the kids.

Fuck, she was back in that emerald-green dress that matches her eyes today. And even though she was wearing black tights and boots under it to be warm enough for her to wear in the cold weather here in Minneapolis, it's still my favorite of all the dresses she wears regularly. Too bad I'll never get to see how it looks in a puddle on my bedroom floor, while she's naked in my bed.

Somehow, he made it through the afternoon without giving in to the temptation of Fiona Harrison. He even managed to spend some time ringside, observing the rehearsals. That's where he was when Cage tracked him down, escorting Jaxon Nolen down the ramp to meet with Rick, now that he'd finally arrived at the arena.

"Jax, good to see you again." Rick extended his hand to the younger man as he walked up. "How was the skiing in Breckenridge?"

"Excellent," Jax replied, shaking Rick's hand. "Though I don't think it was as cold there all week, as it is here today."

"Really?" Rick hadn't ever thought about the differences in temperature in the various parts of the country, other than to have an idea of how many layers to wear when they left the hotel to go sightseeing before going to the arena. But with that comment about the temperature, Jax reminded him of his thoughts about Fiona earlier, and how he wished their schedule included more stops in warm enough climates that she didn't need to wear those leggings under her dresses to stay warm.

"Yeah, it was barely below freezing in Colorado all week, but they said it was only twenty degrees out when the plane landed here earlier." Jax shrugged. "So, it's ten degrees colder here today than in the mountains in Colorado."

"Well, don't pack away that warm coat just yet," Rick chuckled, trying to keep focused on his surroundings and the conversation he was having with Jax instead of fantasizing about Fiona once again. "We have another week or so of northern, cold weather before we hit California, Tijuana, and the southwest for a week of warmer weather. Then we'll have you back in Colorado in mid-January to kick off a few days of cooler Midwest stops before we hit the deep south, Florida, and the Caribbean, where we can lose the heavy coats for a couple of weeks at the end of the month."

"Wow, you weren't joking about being in a different city every day, were you?" Jax's eyes lit with excitement at the thought of the schedule he was about to embark on with the rest of the GWA.

"Nope. Since we left New York on the second, we've been to Nashville, Indianapolis, Chicago, Milwaukee, and now Minneapolis. It'll be a different city every day until mid-February, when we'll spend three days in San Antonio for the *Saint Valentine's Day Massacre* pay-per-view."

"And we have time each day to do a little sightseeing?" Rick nodded in response to Jax's question. "Wow, this is going to be awesome."

Rick couldn't stop himself from smiling at the enthusiasm of the young tutor. "Come on, let me show you how we normally set up the backstage area, so you can find where you need to be tomorrow. Then I'll introduce you to everyone over dinner and have Cage show you to the hotel, so you can get checked in before the front desk closes for the night."

Rick gave Jax a brief overview of their daily schedule, as they walked back up the ramp to head backstage. He then explained that the backstage layout might change some depending on the backstage space available in each arena, but they would always have locker rooms, catering, and a classroom area, even if there wasn't room for Rick to have a separate office space.

By the time they were through with the tour, everyone was heading to catering for dinner, so Rick whistled to get everyone's attention. He stepped up on a chair, so everyone could see him, whether they were already seated to eat or still standing in line to fix their plates, before introducing Jax in a similar manner to the way he had introduced Fiona a few days before.

"Hey, everyone, this is Jaxon Nolen. He's our new history tutor starting tomorrow. Please try to introduce yourselves to him over the next few days. Dan and Ivy, where are you?"

Dan waved from the line to get food. "I'm going to have Jax sit with you for dinner tonight, so you can go over what he needs to know for tomorrow. But don't keep him too long because he still needs to go get checked in at the hotel for tonight."

"Will do," Dan shouted from his place in line.

Rick hopped down from the chair he was standing on to get in line for his own dinner. Jax followed him and they chatted more about the schedule until they got their plates.

Once they were each ready to sit and eat, Jax went to sit at the table with Dan, Ivy, and the Yorks. Derek York was one of the pilots that rotated shifts with the GWA. His wife Mia was the flight attendant on the same flight rotation. Their daughter, Noelle, was the same age as Britney and apparently needed to spend a little extra time with the Traversons for her tutoring before the family left for their time off on Tuesday.

Rick caught up with Britney and Cage over dinner before they split up for the rest of the evening. Britney went back to the classroom with the rest of the kids and tutors. Cage took Jaxon to the hotel to get him checked in before coming back to the arena to pick up Rick and Britney at the end of the night. And Rick went back to his temporary office to ensure the show went off without a hitch for the rest of the night.

If only I could do my job while observing in the classroom area, so I could get more than a passing glance at Fiona. Just because I can't act on the attraction, doesn't mean I can't enjoy the view.

~ ~ ~

Monday, January 7, 2019, Flying from Minneapolis, Minnesota, to Sioux Falls, South Dakota

Over the past few days, Fiona had moved around quite a bit on the company plane, sitting with different people each day to get to know her students and their families better when they weren't focused on an actual tutoring session. But after meeting the new history tutor the night before in the Minneapolis arena, Ivy Traverson had pulled her aside and asked her to sit with Jaxon Nolen on their short flight to Sioux Falls to make him feel welcomed to the team without anyone in a supervisory position seeming to micromanage them.

Fiona wasn't sure how much she could help him with settling into the job since it was only her fifth day, but she decided to look at it as the newbies sticking together to make sure they were both successful in their new jobs.

"Hey, Jaxon," Fiona flagged down the six-foot-tall man, who looked like he should be on the cover of GQ instead of working as a teacher, as she made it to the gate to board the plane. With his blond hair, blue eyes, and boyish good looks, Fiona suspected the other women on board the plane were going to enjoy the new eye candy, even though she didn't feel the same spark of attraction for Jaxon as she did for their boss.

"Hey, um, sorry, I didn't catch your name yesterday." Jaxon shook his head and lightly blushed at the admission.

"Oh, no worries, I still haven't learned everyone's names yet either." Fiona smiled as she pointed to the line of people who were making their way onto the plane. "I'm Fiona. And this is my fifth day on the job as the English tutor. So, I thought we might sit together on the plane and…" Fiona's voice trailed off as she tried to figure out how to end her sentence.

And what? And get to know each other before we start working together in a few hours. And answer any questions you might have on your first day, even though I probably don't know all the answers.

"And commiserate on how overwhelming all this is for us newbies?" Jaxon finished her sentence for her.

"Yeah, something like that." Fiona laughed at how much more accurate his statement was than the ones she'd thought in her head.

"I'd like that, Doll. And please, call me Jax. Hearing Jaxon makes me feel like I'm in trouble with my mother."

"Sure thing." Fiona wasn't sure about him calling her Doll, but she'd let it slide until she got a better feel of why he used the moniker, instead of calling him out on it being inappropriate during their first interaction.

"So, do we have assigned seats on the plane or something?" Jax asked as they made their way down the walkway in the crowd of families boarding.

"No, not really." Fiona shook her head. "The first few rows seem to be for the wrestlers and production people to plan the shows during the flight. Everyone else seems to congregate in the middle of the plane, but not in any specific seating arrangement."

"So, if we want to gossip we should sit at the back of the plane for the most privacy?" Jax grinned with a playful glint in his bright blue eyes.

"Oh, no, I'm not gonna let you get me in trouble like that." Fiona laughed, lightly slapping her hand on Jax's bicep, as they stepped into the plane. She didn't notice Rick's glare as they walked by him, where he was already in his seat.

"No trouble." Jax raised both hands in surrender and shook his head. "Just getting to know all about our new coworkers."

"Uh-huh, sure." Fiona found herself relaxing with Jax and his jovial personality. Though she'd planned to sit across the aisle from the Traversons in case he had any questions she couldn't answer about their jobs, they ended up sitting further back in the plane than she'd sat previously, with a couple of rows of oversized luggage between them and the rest of the crew.

Once their luggage was put away and they were buckled into their seats for take-off, Jax finally asked a more serious question. "So, what's the normal procedure for us once we land? Do we shuttle to the hotel? Or go straight to the arena?"

"I've been riding to the hotel with whomever I sit with on the plane each day," Fiona admitted. "We're technically off the clock until three o'clock local time, so most everyone carpools in different rental cars to the hotel and either gets lunch or goes sightseeing or whatever until then."

"So, when we get to Sioux Falls, who are you riding with, and do you think I can tag along?"

"I'm not sure since we're not sitting with anyone else on the flight." Fiona giggled as she realized she hadn't asked anyone about the procedures for getting a rental car, even though she knew the company would cover the expense. "I guess we should probably ask the boss what we need to do to get a company card for rental cars like everyone else."

"Yeah, you can ask him, Doll." Jax grinned and fanned himself with his hand. "I get too flustered just looking at our Greek God of a boss to be able to remember what I'm supposed to ask him."

Realization dawned then, that Jax calling her Doll was in no way flirtatious because he wasn't attracted to her in that way. His statement about their "Greek God of a boss" seemed to indicate he was gay, but Fiona wouldn't be rude and ask him outright to be sure.

"Why do you think I haven't remembered to ask him before now?" Fiona raised an eyebrow at Jax. "My first day on the job, I got so tingly from shaking his hand that I missed most of what he said to introduce me to everyone."

"Oh, boy, aren't we a pair?" Jax laughed loudly, drawing the attention of a few people in the rows ahead of them. He covered his mouth before ducking down in his seat to get everyone to turn back around before looking at Fiona. "How about we just split a cab until one of us gets over our crush enough to talk to him?"

"I have a feeling we're going to be splitting a lot of cabs." They both broke out in giggles at Fiona's words. When they finally calmed down, she said, "Seriously, though, I'm sure we can ask the Traversons what we need to do to get our expense account cards this afternoon. But with my limited experience driving in large cities, I'll probably still ride with someone else in the company, regardless of whether it's in a cab or a rental car."

"Yeah, it's probably safer to stick with a group in strange cities," Jax agreed. "I might feel comfortable renting a car when we're in the US, but I'm not sure I really want to risk getting pulled over for violating a traffic law I don't know about when we go international."

"I hadn't even thought about the logistics of getting around outside the United States." Fiona shook her head at the thought of what her dad would say if he knew she would be traveling around the world and not just inside American borders.

"What's that face for?" Jax waved his hand around in her general direction. "You're not freaking out about international travel, are you?"

"No," Fiona huffed. "Just thinking about how much worse Rick would have been grilled by my dad back when I first interviewed for the job if Daddy knew we wouldn't be staying in the United States."

"So, you're not just a small-town girl, you're a small-town girl with an overprotective daddy?" Jax raised an eyebrow at Fiona.

"Overprotective is only half the story when it comes to Daddy." Fiona laughed while shaking her head once more. "He's also the only preacher in Heart's Destiny."

"Heart's Destiny?" Jax looked confused by the name of her hometown.

"Heart's Destiny, Texas, is the small town where I grew up," Fiona elaborated. "The Dangerous Twins are also from there." Fiona pointed out the twins, where they were seated close to the front of the plane. "And my best friend's brother is the pilot on the other flight crew. You'll meet his family tonight or tomorrow when they start their flight rotation."

Fiona went on to explain how the Hunters had helped Anthony Burleson get his job with the GWA, before leading into how Anthony had passed the information about the teaching positions to Charlotte for Fiona to be able to apply. Then she explained how she'd interviewed for the job back at Thanksgiving, when the GWA was in Heart's Destiny for Anthony and Kay's wedding.

"So, that's how you're able to talk to the hottie wrestlers without drooling on them," Jax joked. "You knew them when they were gangly kids and don't see the sex-on-a-stick the rest of us do."

"That may be partially true for the Hunters, especially since they're a couple of years younger than me." Fiona bobbed her head from side to side as she contemplated Jax's theory. "But I'm not completely blind. I can appreciate the fact that everyone on this plane is clearly a ten without personally being attracted to them."

"Uh-huh, sure you can." Jax rolled his eyes at Fiona. "You know it's okay to admit we're attracted to the hotties, right? We just can't act on that attraction in any way that might make our work environment uncomfortable."

"Well, I guess it's a good thing I'm a firm believer in all my hometown stories about only having eyes for our one true love." Fiona shrugged, not sure she was comfortable enough with Jax to admit to her crush on Rick just yet. "So, I'm not tempted by the attractiveness of my coworkers while I'm looking for my Mr. Right."

"Fair enough." Jax tipped an imaginary hat at Fiona before changing the subject. "So, what are we doing when we get to Sioux Falls?"

"I'm not sure." Fiona pulled out her laptop, since they were at altitude and could log into the plane's Wi-Fi to make plans for the rest of the day.

"What sightseeing have you done since you started with the company?"

"The day before I officially started, I flew into New York and went ice skating at Rockefeller Center with the Burlesons. Then the next day, after flying to Nashville, I went to the Country Music Hall of Fame with the Traversons." Fiona started an internet search for attractions in Sioux Falls as soon as her computer connected to the plane's Wi-Fi.

"Yeah, as much as I'm looking forward to seeing places I'd never travel to otherwise, I'm not sorry I missed the Country Music Hall of Fame." Jax chuckled. "Now if it was the Rock-N-Roll Hall of Fame, I'd be first in line. But having grown up in New York City, I'm not into country music."

"You'd have probably enjoyed the Benjamin Harrison Presidential Site in Indianapolis, where I went with the Moores last Thursday." At least Fiona assumed the history teacher would be interested in a historical site.

Leah Mae Wright

"Yeah, probably." Jax nodded his agreement. "Who are the Moores?"

"Katie and Jason Moore are two of our students. Their parents are Emily and Matt." Fiona pointed out where the family was sitting on the plane. "They're originally from Indiana, so they were able to show me around a little while we were there."

"We'll have to find out where everyone else is from, so we can stick with the locals to show us all the places we wouldn't normally think of to check out." Jax smiled at the thought of finding the hidden gems in their sightseeing trips.

"That's a good idea. Maybe we can even convince the kids to show us the most historical places in their hometowns." Fiona's idea was rewarded with an excited head nod and a huge smile from Jax. "Although, I really had a blast on the Chicago Crime and Mob bus tour with the Staffords, even with the interruption of some fans wanting their autographs. And I don't think they are originally from there."

"And who are the Staffords?" Jax sat up in his seat for Fiona to point them out to him.

"Connor and Cody are our oldest students, both working in the eighth-grade modules, though they're a year apart age-wise." Fiona pointed out the boys, who were sitting with their mom. "Their mom's name is Tiffany. Though I'm not sure if you can see her sitting across from them with her back to us, you'll recognize her as the backstage announcer if you watch the GWA's weekly TV show." She then looked around the plane to find their dad before explaining his location to Jax. "Their dad, Cooper, is the guy sitting across from Rick, probably planning his match for tonight, since he's currently the GWA champion."

"Wait," Jax whisper-shouted, holding up his hand in a stop motion. "'Crusher' Cooper is married to Tiffany and they're both old enough to have kids in the eighth grade? No way! Neither one of them looks a day over twenty-five on TV."

Fiona could only shrug in response, since she wasn't sure how old either of the Staffords were to know how far off Jax was in his estimate of their ages. While she could somewhat estimate a person's age as late thirties or early forties if they started to show signs of aging, like the silver hair sparsely spattered in Rick's otherwise dark hair and beard, she couldn't differentiate someone in their thirties from someone in their twenties if they didn't have obvious signs of being older.

"I'm seriously going to have to talk to them about their skin care regimen, so maybe I can reverse some of the lines on my face before my thirtieth next year."

Fiona giggled at the serious look on Jax's face.

"What?" Jax looked at her incredulously before waving a hand over his face. "I have almost fourteen months to get control of these crow's feet before thirty hits me in the face and makes them worse. Surely, that's enough time to fix the cracks with the right spackle."

Fiona cracked up laughing at Jax's over-the-top dramatics. "I don't think spackle is the right product for someone's face."

"Yeah, I knew that didn't sound right the moment I said it," Jax laughed along with Fiona. "But you know what I mean. The right cream to keep the skin glowing and wrinkle-free, like yours and the rest of the beautiful people of the GWA."

"Oh, no, I'm not defying the hands of time by using a miracle cream." Fiona waved off his compliment, not feeling it was deserved, since she wasn't old enough to have to fight wrinkles yet. "My secret to preventing wrinkles is not being old enough to have them yet."

"Well, obviously." Jax waved his hand around her. "You're what? Twenty-two, fresh out of college with skin so young and flawless, you don't even have to wear a drop of makeup to look gorgeous. But there are creams out there that will allow those of us, with a few years on you, to look closer to your age."

"Twenty-two?" Fiona choked out, shocked at how old Jax thought she looked. "Thank you for the compliment, but I'm actually twenty-seven."

"Seriously?" Jax bugged out his eyes to show his surprise at her age.

"Yep, actually closer to twenty-seven-and-a-half. My birthday is August twenty-third, nineteen-ninety-one."

"Well, you're obviously doing something right to take five years off your appearance." Jax shook his head as if he still struggled to believe Fiona's age.

"It's twenty-seven years of country living," Fiona joked, though she believed the fresh air of living in the country versus living in the smog of a big city might have had an impact.

"And what does country living have that city living doesn't?" Jax raised an eyebrow at her.

Instead of discussing her theory of fresh air versus smog, Fiona decided to tell her new friend, Jax, about the one thing he might actually enjoy seeing in her small hometown. "Cowboys in tight Levi's."

Jax's smile spread as he thought about her answer. "Oh, yeah, that might be worth some country living."

Chapter Five

Fiona was having a great time seeing things she'd only dreamed of seeing before starting her job with the GWA. Not only was she enjoying the variety the job brought to her teaching with such a wide range of ages of the children she worked with daily, but she was also making friends with the parents and her peers while visiting historical sites and attractions in a different city each day.

The other tutors had gotten excited about her idea to have the students pick places they were most interested in visiting, even in cities where none of them had been before. They had started convincing a few of the parents to go places such as hands-on science centers, art museums, libraries, and historical sites in small groups based on the age and grade level of the kids, instead of each family doing their own thing. It seemed to be more conducive to educational sightseeing than having the older children being bored while doing an activity with their younger siblings, or the younger children not comprehending the significance of the places the older children chose to visit.

For their day in Las Vegas, however, she felt they'd picked an activity that all the children would enjoy—Cirque du Soleil at the Bellagio. Well, at least all the school-aged children. Tank and Tina Olson's twin infants, Travis and Trent, slept through the whole thing.

It was also the first outing she'd gone on with Rick joining the group. While Britney and their driver, Cage, had accompanied them to The Science Zone in Casper, Wyoming, on Tuesday, Rick had stayed at the arena to supervise all the extra tasks of producing a live television show.

Fiona couldn't stop herself from watching Rick as they all walked outside to see the fountain show. He was as impeccably dressed as always, in a dark, navy-blue suit. *I wonder if he sleeps in a suit and tie, too?* Fiona tried not to openly giggle at her silly thought as she realized she'd never seen him wear anything more casual.

"What's that look for?" Jana Evans asked Fiona, trying to follow Fiona's line of sight to see whom she was looking at.

"What look?" Fiona turned her head toward Sarah and Shawn's mom to make sure the other woman couldn't catch her ogling the boss.

"The goo-goo eyes look," Jana explained while circling her finger at Fiona's face.

"Who's Fiona making goo-goo eyes at?" Kay Burleson asked, turning around from where she was walking in front of them to see what Jana was talking about.

"I'm not making goo-goo eyes at anyone," Fiona protested, shaking her head and raising her hands, as if the actions would get the ladies to stop pointing out her lustful look toward Rick. Unfortunately, it didn't work.

Soon, Holland Everett, Addison and Archer's mom, joined the other ladies in asking her who she'd seen that caught her eye. "Was it someone with us? Or someone in the crowd that we need to track down for you to go out with after the show tonight?"

"Nobody's caught my eye," Fiona lied, not wanting to tell her new friends about her crush on Rick, when he could possibly overhear them talking. "I was just watching the fountains."

"Yeah, I'm not buying that," Emily Moore, Katie and Jason's mom, said, shaking her head before turning to look directly at Kay. "Kay, do you know who her bestie is back in Heart's Destiny?"

"Yep!" Kay exclaimed, popping the p. "My sister-in-law, Charlotte." Kay's grin widened as mischievousness glistened in her eyes. "And we're flying home tomorrow just in time for her birthday party. So, if Fiona doesn't tell us who in the company she's interested in, I'm sure I can get the deets from Charlotte tomorrow."

And Char will probably try to get Kay to play matchmaker for me, like her momma is for her and her siblings back home, if she's the one to tell Kay about my crush on Rick. Fiona hoped throwing herself on the mercy of the women around her would prevent them from bringing Charlotte into it and save her the humiliation of any matchmaking stunts she might suggest. *I guess I shouldn't have pushed her toward Ian last month.*

"Please don't talk to Charlotte about this," Fiona whispered, shaking her head. "I can't ever act on my attraction, so I don't want to be set up for any of the Burleson matchmaking schemes."

"It's not one of our husbands, is it?" Shauna Grady, Kendrix and Baylee's mom, asked, looking around uncomfortably. "'Cause you know Holland and I already had to threaten to drag the last language arts tutor in the ring to get her to back off our husbands. Right?"

"No," Fiona whisper-shouted, wanting to emphatically make that clear while not alerting everyone in the vicinity to their conversation. "He's not married. He's our boss."

"Rick?" Cheyenne Fields, River and Skye's mom, asked a little too loudly, causing the boss to turn toward the huddle of women from where he was standing a good ten feet away from them. Cheyenne looked apologetically at Fiona as their boss raised an eyebrow at them to question why his name had been called. "Um, is there an overnight childcare facility at the hotel? We'd like to have a casino night with all the adults, instead of some of us having to stay in the rooms to watch the kids."

"Oh, yes, I believe so," Rick nodded as he spoke, his lips in a flat line that was neither a smile nor a frown. "You'll have to check at the front desk before heading to the arena to see if there's any availability for tonight."

"Thanks!" Cheyenne smiled at Rick, but still only got a nod in return before he turned back toward the men and children surrounding him watching the fountain show that was still going on. Once his attention was elsewhere, Cheyenne turned back to Fiona and the rest of the women and lowered her voice before speaking. "Sorry. I didn't mean to say his name so loud. I was just surprised at who I thought you were referring to."

"At least you were able to come up with a good cover story." Jana grinned at Cheyenne. "Though now at least a few of us are going to have to see about childcare and going to the casino after the show tonight."

"She says that as if we weren't already planning to go to the casino tonight," Emily chuckled.

"Yeah, but now Kay & Anthony and Holland & Tanner have to join us if there are enough spots for all our kids in the hotel's childcare center," Jana smirked.

"If I have to go, then so do you." Kay pointed at Fiona to emphasize her point. "And if Rick doesn't come with us, then you have to dish all the deets about your crush on him."

"Fine," Fiona whisper-shouted, hoping Rick went to the casino after the show, so she wouldn't have to talk to her new friends about her attraction to him. "But I'm not saying a word when he's around to overhear us."

Fiona wasn't sure what the looks the other women were giving her meant. *I don't know which would be worse,* she thought as they made their way back to their hotel after the fountain show ended. *Them trying to play matchmaker by setting it up so Rick comes with us tonight, or them pushing him not to come tonight, so I have to admit to crushing on him since my interview back in November.*

~~~

Saturday, January 12, 2019, 6 p.m., Las Vegas, Nevada

Rick wasn't sure what was going on with his employees and their wives. Since they'd all left the Cirque du Soleil show that afternoon, they were all whispering and giving him strange looks. If he didn't know better, he'd think they were all plotting a huge prank against him.

No, that can't be it, Rick thought as he went back to double-check that everything was in place for the show before heading to catering for dinner. *They know better than to prank me in the middle of a show. Right? Maybe I should ask Cage to look into whatever they're up to?*

Rick found his security expert and friend talking to the head of security for the arena on his way backstage. "Everything set up for tonight?"

"Yes, sir, Mr. Robertson." The arena security officer nodded his head a little too enthusiastically, in Rick's opinion.

"Good." Rick gave the man one solemn nod of acknowledgment before speaking to Cage and starting to walk back toward the
~~~

backstage area. "I need to talk to you about some other matters when you get a chance."

"Yeah, I'm good now." Cage turned away from the arena security officer to catch up with Rick. "Can we talk on the way to catering, or do we need to head to your office first?"

Rick shook his head to indicate it wasn't that private a matter. "I just wanted your opinion on what the crew is up to tonight. They're either whispering or shut up completely when I walk by, and they're giving me some strange looks since the Cirque show this afternoon."

"Geez, Boss, paranoid much?" Cage chuckled. Rick raised an eyebrow at his friend. Cage held his hands out, palms up. "Sorry, anyone, in particular, I need to question about this, or should I just observe everyone in general?"

"If it were just one or two people, I wouldn't be concerned." Though Rick wasn't exactly sure what he was concerned about, he couldn't shake the feeling that something was being planned that he wouldn't like for later that night. "It might have something to do with the casino trip the ladies were talking about while we were at the Bellagio fountains."

"Oh, that." Cage shook his head and half rolled his eyes. "They're probably just wondering if I got childcare set up for Brit, so you can go, too."

"Wait." Rick stopped walking as they reached the gorilla position just inside the backstage area. "They asked you to set up childcare for Britney, so I can go to the casino with them?"

"Yeah." Cage nodded and grinned as he stopped walking just a couple of steps past where Rick had stopped. "And I've got it all taken care of for all the kids, not just Britney."

"Why would they ask you and not me?"

"Because your employees like you, Boss. And they want to surprise you with a night out, so you can't say *no* like you did back in November for your birthday." Cage slapped a hand on Rick's shoulder. "So, quit being paranoid, and don't ruin the surprise."

"The cake in catering was all I needed for my birthday." Rick tried to defend his position on not going out after the show in Saint Louis a little over two months ago. "Besides, you know I'm not one to want to party after the shows when I could spend that time with Brit."

"Yeah, I know." Cage gave him a wry smile. "And so does everyone else. But they also know you need to have a life outside the GWA and your daughter. So, relax and have a good time tonight."

"Fine, but make it known that I'm only going to let my crew strongarm me into accepting their poor excuse for therapy once a year," Rick huffed, maintaining his normal stoic expression on the outside, while smiling at his friends' antics on the inside.

They walked the rest of the way to catering, where Rick and Cage got in line to fix their plates behind the two new tutors.

"You have to come with me tonight." Fiona looked at Jax imploringly. "I've never been to a casino, and I need you there, so I'm not a third wheel with all the couples going."

No, you don't need him as your date. You need me.

"Of course, I'll go with you, Doll." Jax gave Fiona a one-armed hug while holding his plate in the other hand.

Get your fucking hands off her! Rick growled in his head. *And quit calling her Doll. She's not yours!*

"Hey, Boss, let's step over here and talk for a second." Cage grabbed Rick's arm and pulled him away when he heard Rick's low growl at the sight of Jax touching Fiona. Once they were a good twenty feet away from the line and the rest of the crew, Cage released his grip on Rick. "Unless you want to claim her as yours, you've gotta chill out and let her live her life with whoever she wants to date."

"Fuck," Rick cursed under his breath. His fists balled up involuntarily as he stood there trying to figure out what he could hit without getting into trouble for assault or property damage. *If only I could book a match between Jax and I on tonight's card.*

"You okay, Boss?" Anthony walked up behind Cage and looked at Rick skeptically.

"Yeah, fine," Rick barked, his voice coming out way harsher than his pilot deserved to be spoken to, since Rick's anger wasn't really directed at him.

"Ya know, I've learned the real meaning of that word since getting married and becoming a dad." Anthony's lips turned up in a half smile. "And based on the fact that your fists and jaw are all clenched, I suppose I'd have to agree that you're fine, since the real meaning of *fine* is *pissed off*."

"Well, it is better to be pissed off than pissed on," Cage joked, obviously trying to lighten the mood around them.

"Yeah, but none of us want Rick to be either," Anthony replied, grinning at Cage.

Rick couldn't hold on to his own anger when the guys were joking around with him. He released his fists and the clench of his jaw, but he still didn't smile with his friends.

"So, what's up, Boss? You pissed that the girls are trying to fix you up with Fiona tonight? Or pissed that Jax is moving in on your woman before they get the chance?"

"What are you talking about?" Rick was confused about how the women of the GWA were planning to fix him up with Fiona. "They can't fix me up with Fiona."

"Oh, yeah, they can," Anthony laughed. "And I'm afraid my wife might be their ringleader when it comes to making plans to ensure you're practically glued together all night, in the hopes you'll start dating her after. Well, if they don't get ya'll drunk enough to get married while we're here in Vegas, anyway."

"I can't marry Fiona," Rick growled low enough that only Anthony and Cage could hear him. "Hell, I can't even date her."

"Why not?" Anthony shrugged as he looked back and forth between Rick and Cage. "It's obvious that you want to, based on how you look at her."

"Because she's ten years younger than me," Rick argued.

"So? Kay's almost eight years older than me." Anthony shrugged once more. "And our age difference doesn't mean shit in the grand scheme of things."

"I can't date anyone because I don't want to confuse Britney."

"Yeah, Kay tried that excuse with me, too." Anthony shook his head. "The right person will love your daughter as much as you do, and Fiona has already shown how much she adores Britney and the rest of the kids. So, you have to nix that excuse, too."

"She's my employee." Rick knew he was grasping at straws to come up with more excuses for why he couldn't pursue Fiona, but he couldn't allow himself to give in to his baser desires. And he didn't want to admit to them to his employees, so he couldn't tell Anthony and Cage about his primal proclivities in the bedroom to convince them he was all wrong for Fiona.

"And there's not a policy in the company preventing you from dating her."

"You do realize that I fired the last English teacher to prevent a sexual harassment lawsuit," Rick pointed out. "Hitting on the new English teacher would just set me up for another one."

"So, ask her out politely, instead of hitting on her like a sleazeball." Anthony smirked at him. "Ya might as well give it up, Boss. Ya'll fell for each other Heart's Destiny style the week before my wedding, and I'm not the only one who saw it. If ya don't give in and let Kay fix ya'll up tonight, the Matchmaking Mommas of Heart's Destiny will do it when we're all in town whenever James and Randi decide to get married. You're just delaying the inevitable."

"We're not inevitable," Rick grumbled, feeling his blood pressure rise from the whole situation.

"I agree, Boss," Cage interjected. "You're definitely not inevitable if you keep giving her the time and space to pick somebody else for her forever."

"Fuck!" Rick's shouted expletive drew the attention of everyone in catering. Not having a ready explanation for his outburst, Rick lowered his voice, so only Cage and Anthony could hear him. "I'm done talking about this. I'm going for a run around the arena while the two of you come up with an excuse for why I'm pissed off that doesn't include Fiona in any way, shape, or form."

With that, Rick speed walked out of catering, taking off in a slow jog as soon as he could no longer be seen by his employees. *Damn, maybe I should bring my workout gear to the arena, so I could actually run instead of half-assing it in these dress shoes.*

Or maybe I should start sparring with the wrestlers in the afternoon, instead of going to the gym at five in the morning when I'm more likely to have to punch a heavy bag than I am to find a random sparring partner. I wonder if Jax would get in the ring to spar with us?

Rick made laps around the arena until it was time to let the fans in for the night. Luckily, he was able to expend enough energy for his anger to fade some and for him to realize what a bad idea it would be to invite the history tutor into the ring with him.

~~~

Fiona wasn't sure what was going on with almost everyone who worked for the GWA meeting up in the casino at their hotel. She had just expected to meet up with the half a dozen women she'd started getting to know in the last couple of weeks, their significant others, and Jax. Somehow, they ended up with half the single performers, writers, and production crew joining them. Oh, and of course, Rick, and his security specialist and driver, Cage.

Fiona wasn't sure if it was better or worse that Rick was part of the group going to the casino. Obviously, it was better because she didn't have to come clean to her friends about how smitten she was with their boss. But it was also worse because she couldn't act on her attraction to him, like she wanted to do every time she was close enough to smell his citrus and sandalwood scent.

And somehow, with all those people around, Fiona kept finding herself right beside Rick. *It's like the whole company is trying to play matchmaker, and they keep maneuvering us to have to sit together no matter what game we go to play.*

It had started at the slot machines when they first arrived. Fiona hadn't thought anything of it when she ended up at a machine with Jax at the machine on her right and Rick at the machine on her left. When she lost her ten-dollar limit in the first few minutes at the machine, she stepped back to let someone else play on her machine, and watched as some of her coworkers won and others lost.

Rick apparently had the golden touch, since he won a whole lot more than he lost. In fact, Rick was the only one who was still winning when they got up from the slot machines to spread out to the other sections of the casino.

They ventured through the casino to see sections set up for craps and roulette and a few other games that Fiona had never heard of before. Granted, her gambling knowledge was limited to what she'd seen in movies, but she was still surprised to not recognize a few of the specialty game tables set up before they made it to the area set up for various card games.
~~~

Somehow in the shuffle, everyone seemed to pair off into couples and separate into small groups around the various card tables. Fiona found herself in a group with Kay & Anthony Burleson, Emily & Matt Moore, Jana & Jeff Evans, Holland & Tanner Everett, and Rick Robertson. That's when Fiona started to feel like her friends were pairing her up with Rick.

Kay has obviously been spending too much time with her mother-in-law and has started to follow in Hazel's matchmaking footsteps.

"Ladies first." Rick motioned for Fiona to take the seat he'd just pulled out at the blackjack table.

"Oh, no, I don't know how to play this game," Fiona protested, knowing she hadn't planned on betting more than her ten-dollar limit for the night.

"It's not hard." Kay grabbed Fiona's hand and pulled her down into the chair beside her. "You just try to get the value of the cards to add up to as close to twenty-one as you can without going over."

"And I'll be right here to help you strategize, just like these guys are doing for their wives." Rick stood behind her chair and patted her shoulder with his hand reassuringly.

Fiona tingled from his innocent touch and couldn't say no to playing with Rick encouraging her. Her friends explained the rules as the dealer started setting up and issuing betting chips to each player.

"How many chips can I get for you?" The dealer smiled at Fiona as he asked the question.

"Oh, um, sorry." Fiona felt herself blush as she looked up at the man on the other side of the table. While he was attractive and about her age, that wasn't why she was blushing. "My friends were explaining how to play the game and I didn't hear what you said about the cost of the chips."

"The chips are a dollar each, bundled in increments of twenty-five. The minimum bet is five dollars, so one bundle only gets you five bets. Most people start with a hundred, so they don't have to interrupt the game to buy more."

"Oh." Fiona did a little mental math to determine how much was left in her checking account after paying for her various outings since starting her new job. She thought she could spare the hundred dollars and still be fine until her first paycheck from the GWA was direct deposited on the fifteenth, but she wasn't certain how close she was cutting it.

Before she could ask the dealer if he could swipe her debit card, or if she needed to go back to the machine at the casino entrance to add money to her casino card, like she had the ten dollars she'd already lost at the slot machines, Rick handed the man his casino card. "We'll take two hundred."

"Oh, no, I can cover my own." Fiona objected while opening her purse to get out her wallet.

"Consider it an advance, since you haven't gotten your first paycheck from the company yet. If you win tonight, you can just return the initial buy-in. If not, we can settle up on payday." Rick gave her one of the few genuine smiles she'd seen from him in the whole time she'd known him, as he put his casino card back in his pocket. "Besides, only half of those are for you. The other hundred are for me when we swap out players."

"Oh, okay." Fiona turned back to the table to find the eight stacks of chips in front of her and made a mental note to only pull from four of them when she was placing her bets.

A waitress came by and took their drink orders once again, just as the game started. As she had all night, Fiona ordered the same thing as Kay, knowing the pregnant woman wouldn't be consuming anything alcoholic. She wanted the Vegas experience, but she didn't want to risk getting too drunk to remember it.

With Rick's help, Fiona ended up winning most of the hands she played. Though she couldn't remember any of the strategies he tried to teach her because she was mostly focused on enjoying the date-like feeling of the night.

When they swapped seats for the guys to take their turn playing, Fiona looked around the room, thinking she might venture over to see what some of her other new friends were doing.

"Oh, no, you stay right here." Rick clasped her hand in his, directing her back into the seat he'd been in while she played. "I need my good luck charm to keep our winning streak going."

"I'm not a good luck charm." Fiona shook her head as she took the seat slightly behind and to the right of where Rick was at the table in her former seat. "I think you're the one with all the good luck, since you won everything you've played tonight, including helping me win here."

"Aw, but you're wrong, Fifi," Rick slurred, making Fiona wonder just how many alcoholic drinks he'd had, while she sipped her juice mocktails and played the game. "I've only won when you were beside me. I lost every time you walked away. So, you're my good luck charm and need to stay right beside me. All. Night. Long."

Rick punctuated each of his last three words with a kiss on the back of her hand that he was still holding. The innuendo laced in his statement went straight to Fiona's core, sending a jolt throughout her body that caused her panties to flood, her heart to skip a beat, and her brain to short circuit. She was so caught up in the excitement of her crush giving her a cutesy nickname, as if he was crushing on her, too, that she had no idea what to say in response, so she just sat there dumbfounded as the guys' game started.

"I think this is the first time I've seen you drunk, Boss." Anthony's words brought Fiona out of her lust-filled haze.

Of course, he's drunk, and not really attracted to me. Fiona sat back in her seat, pulling her hand out of Rick's. *I'm just conveniently here right now. He's not really attracted to the only chubby girl employed by the GWA.*

"I'm not drunk," Rick argued with Anthony as he reclaimed Fiona's hand. "I'm just having a good time, like you told me to earlier. And I'm switching to water for the rest of the night, so I don't get drunk enough to fall victim to your plot to marry me off like the rest of you."

"I'm not plotting to marry you off." Anthony chuckled and shook his head at Rick while placing his next bet on the game.

"That's not what you said earlier." Rick glared at Anthony before turning to point toward Kay. "You said I could either give in to Kay's matchmaking tonight and let her get me drunk enough to get married here in Vegas, or your mom will do it next time we're in Heart's Destiny. And since Britney has already said she wants to stay in Heart's Destiny when we go to San Antonio for the pay-per-view in February, I figured you were setting me up for a wedding live on pay-per-view. If it's inevitable, then I'd rather it not be broadcast around the world."

Fiona was confused by Rick's rambling and her arm was starting to get sore from the way he was waving it around as he talked with his hands while he was still holding hers.

So, Anthony told Rick to have a good time tonight? And how does that translate to a plot to get him drunk enough to marry a stranger in Vegas? Fiona tried to decipher Rick's drunken outburst and missed hearing Anthony say that Rick had twisted up their earlier conversation. *But wait, if Kay's matchmaking tonight, that means I was right earlier when I felt like I was being pushed to pair up with Rick all night. Does that mean they were trying to get us both drunk, so we'd wake up married to each other in the morning?*

No! Surely not! Kay might write about stuff like that in her books, but she wouldn't try to make it happen in real life. Would she?

Fiona wasn't sure what to think about the events of the night, and especially about the things Rick revealed in his drunken rambling. All she knew at that moment was that she wanted no part of a potential drunk, Vegas wedding. She pulled her hand from Rick's and fled the casino, grateful her hotel room was just a few floors away.

I'll deal with figuring all that out in the morning when I know we're all sober!

Chapter Six

Rick couldn't believe what he was seeing as he walked into his bedroom in the hotel suite he was sharing with his daughter. Fiona Harrison was laid out on his bed, naked and waiting for him. He quickly shut and locked the bedroom door, so Britney couldn't accidentally walk in and see them first thing the next morning.

"If I'd have known this is where you ran off to, Fifi, I'd have left the casino a lot sooner." Rick confidently sauntered up to the bed and ran his palms from her ankles to her knees and back down again. "I hope you being here means you're prepared to take everything I want to give you tonight."

"Yes, Sir." Fiona's throaty purr made Rick's cock twitch in his pants. He was already harder than he'd ever been in his life, and knew the things he had planned for her would be just as torturous for him as for her.

He gripped her by the ankles to pull her down to the end of the bed before he dropped to his knees between her spread thighs. He propped her feet on his shoulders and lowered his head to taste the smooth folds of her pussy.

Rick flattened his tongue to lap up as much of her cream as he could with the first lick over her slit. Her sweet cream tasted like the strawberries he always smelled whenever she was near.

"Oh, Rick," Fiona moaned. Her fingers weaved through his hair and her hips bucked when he closed his lips over her clit and lightly sucked. "Yes, just like that."

Rick didn't have to be told twice what to do to please his woman. He continued to suckle her clit while inserting a finger to start opening *her up for his dick. She was so tight he really had to massage her inner walls to allow him to insert a second digit.*

He felt his cock leaking precum in his boxers at the thought of how her cunt would grip him like a vise. It took every ounce of willpower he had to take the time to prepare her, instead of ripping off his pants and rutting in her like a wild animal the way he really wanted.

Thankfully, it didn't take long before his responsive woman was squirting her cream into his mouth, with her pussy clamping down on his fingers. She chanted his name repeatedly as she came. Rick didn't let up on his ministrations until all the waves of her orgasm subsided, and she relaxed back into the bed, releasing the death grip she'd had on his hair as she came.

Rick licked his lips, enjoying every last drop of her sweetness as he stood and started to remove his suit. The meticulous man, who normally hung each piece as he removed his clothing to take it to be dry cleaned, was replaced by the man too desperate to get inside Fiona to care what happened to his clothing. He wasn't entirely sure his shirt would still have the buttons on it when he picked it up off the floor later.

Once he finished stripping with his clothes strewn around the room haphazardly, he instructed Fiona to scoot back up on the bed. She crab-walked back up the mattress until her head hit the pillow, her strawberry-blonde hair fanned out over the white sheets. Rick crawled on the bed, trailing open-mouthed kisses up her body as he went.

He pressed his torso against her pubic bone as he took his time worshiping her bountiful breasts. Her pretty, pink nipples were as hard as diamonds under his tongue and fingers. Fiona writhed beneath him as he brought her to the brink once more without even really touching her pussy.

Rick wanted to be inside her the next time she climaxed. He needed to feel her come on his cock. So, he kissed his way up over her collarbone and long, graceful neck as he lined his dick up with her pussy.

He kissed her lips softly first, planning to impale her with his cock at the same time he deepened the kiss.

BUZZ! BUZZ! BUZZ!

"Why are you buzzing, Fifi?" Rick asked his empty room, still caught in the moment between dreamland and waking.

As the buzzing continued, Rick finally woke up enough to open his eyes and realize it was his alarm on his phone. "Fuck," he groaned, wishing he could go back to sleep and especially back to dreaming about Fiona.

He reached over to the nightstand and grabbed his phone to shut off the alarm. The events of the night before flooded back to him, as he noticed it was just a couple of minutes after seven in the morning. He only vaguely remembered changing the time on his alarm when he made it back to the room, but after the amount of Macallan he'd consumed the night before, he was glad he'd opted to skip his normal five a.m. workout.

"What the hell was I thinking, drinking that much?" Rick stumbled out of bed and into the ensuite bathroom to search through his toiletry bag for some over-the-counter pain relievers. He popped two pills, swallowing them dry, since he hadn't grabbed a bottle of water from the mini-bar in the room before stripping out of his boxers to get a shower. "Oh, yeah. I was thinking that if I couldn't taste Fiona, I'd at least enjoy the best scotch they had available."

Rick wanted to kick his own ass for getting so drunk. He couldn't believe he'd ruined the wonderful night he was having with Fiona by arguing with Anthony for trying to fix them up. "If I'd have stayed sober, and appreciated my meddling employees' efforts, maybe I could have actually had her in my bed last night, instead of just dreaming about it."

As he thought about the dream, Rick couldn't stop himself from palming his cock to relieve his morning wood. He imagined the parts of the dream he didn't get to finish, as he stroked his length in the shower.

Fuck, I bet she's so tight that I'd still have to work my way in slowly, even after stretching her with my fingers first. Rick squeezed his dick as hard as he could stand while fantasizing about fucking Fiona. Just a few strokes with a vise-like grip had him leaking precum.

Imagining her arms and legs wrapped around him as he pounded into her pussy had his balls drawing up in record time. Rick almost felt as if he was seventeen again, instead of thirty-seven, with how quickly he painted the shower wall with his cum like an eager teenager.

Too bad I'll only ever come in my hand like that, since she's way too sweet and innocent to handle how rough I need to be when I fuck.

Rick shook off the errant thought as he rinsed the evidence of his indiscretion down the drain and got cleaned up to start the day. He toweled off and brushed his hair and teeth before trimming his beard and applying a little beard balm to keep any unruly hairs in place.

He got dressed and went to wake Britney before gathering the rest of their things from around the suite to head back to the airport. Thankfully, she was already up and getting ready, since he was running later than usual, after being out until the early hours of the morning at the casino downstairs.

Rick was once again grateful that he could call most of his employees his friends, as he put the envelope from where he'd cashed out at the end of the night in the inside pocket of his suit jacket. They had not only made sure he remembered to take care of that, so he could give Fiona her winnings from the night before. But they'd also helped his drunk ass carry a sleeping Britney up to their suite from the childcare center.

I should probably give Anthony and Cage a raise, Rick thought as he finished packing up and carried his bags to the main living area of the suite. He helped Britney finish packing her things, noticing she was slower and quieter than usual.

"Did you stay up too late last night having fun with your friends, Britney Bear?" Rick raised an eyebrow at his grumpy girl.

"No," Britney grumbled. "Last night was not the problem. It was fun hanging out with everyone without our usual adults. But we had to get up way too early this morning."

"Well, at least you can take a nap on the plane, so maybe you won't be too tired to check out the Hollywood Walk of Fame when we get to L.A."

Britney only nodded in response before plopping down on the couch and closing her eyes. She didn't get to rest there long before Cage knocked on their door promptly at eight o'clock.

Once everything was loaded on the luggage cart Cage brought with him, they stopped for the continental breakfast as they checked out of the hotel. With a full belly, Britney fell asleep in the car on the way to the airport. Rick was glad they were flying out of a private airfield, so he could carry his sleeping daughter straight on the plane without having to go through a security checkpoint before flying to Los Angeles.

As everyone was slowly filtering onto the plane, Rick noticed Fiona looking around, as if she was looking for someone in particular before boarding. He got Britney buckled in the pod beside him, so he'd be able to lay it out into a bed once they were at altitude. Then he went back down the stairs to help Cage with their luggage.

Instead of going straight to the SUV to get the luggage, he walked over to where Fiona was standing off to the side. *I should probably do this now, while everyone else is preoccupied and not close enough to overhear our conversation.*

"Fiona, I want to apologize for last night," Rick started, pulling the envelope from his pocket, and extending it out to her. "I don't remember what all I said in my drunken state, but I hate that I offended you to the point that you left without collecting your winnings."

"Oh!" Fiona's mouth formed a perfect O as she took the envelope from his hand without actually touching him.

"I assure you, my irritation and rambling last night were not directed at you in any way. And I hope you can forgive me for my outburst, so our working relationship can go back to normal."

"Of course." Fiona blushed as she smiled up at him. "You have nothing to apologize for. It's Anthony and Kay who need to explain what they were trying to pull last night." She looked around once more. "But I guess I'll have to catch them later to ask…"

"Yeah, in a few days." Rick ran a hand through his hair as he interrupted her sentence. "They're at the commercial airport this morning to fly home for their time off."

"That's right!" Fiona slapped her hand to her forehead. "The Yorks came to the arena last night, so the Burlesons are off. I should have remembered the flight crew changed when I saw Tia, Maria, and Noelle all on the same day."

"Don't worry about it." Rick smiled at the beauty before him. "The only reason I remember when the flight crews change is because they check in with me to make sure the other crew has arrived before they head home."

They both chuckled at his self-deprecating statement. Rick would gladly be the butt of any joke just to see her smile again.

"So, we're good?" Rick needed to make sure she had no reservations about continuing her employment with the company.

"Yeah, we're good," Fiona confirmed before looking at the envelope in her hand, as if she was just realizing she was holding it. "But what's this?"

"Your winnings from last night. And I already took out the initial hundred I bankrolled you to play blackjack," Rick lied, realizing at that moment that the envelope contained not only both their winnings from the night before, but also the initial five hundred dollars he'd put on a casino card at the beginning of the night.

"Oh, I didn't expect to keep any of that since I didn't pay to play." Fiona tried futilely to give the envelope back to Rick.

"But you won it fair and square, so it's yours." Rick put his hands in his pockets, so she couldn't push the envelope back in his hand. He wasn't sure why he was so adamantly trying to give her more than she'd actually won, but he didn't want to question his caveman tendency to take care of her right at that moment.

"Oh, um, okay." Fiona gave up and put the envelope in her purse when Rick backed away from her. "Thanks."

"You're welcome," *Fifi.* Rick barely stopped himself from using the cutesy nickname once again, as he turned to go get his and Britney's luggage to load it on the plane. *Where the fuck did I even come up with that? I don't use pet names like that with anyone but Brit. And I definitely don't have fatherly feelings for Fiona.*

Rick pushed the nickname and everything else to do with Fiona out of his head, so he could go about the rest of his day without popping an inappropriate boner while sightseeing with his daughter and working the rest of the night. Well, at least, he tried.

~~~

Monday, January 14, 2019, 9 a.m., Flying between Los Angeles, California, and Tijuana, Mexico

Life had basically gone back to normal for Fiona after her brief talk with Rick the previous morning. They hadn't really addressed the inappropriateness of Kay and Anthony trying to fix them up Saturday
~~~

night, but Fiona took Rick's avoidance of the subject to mean he wasn't interested in her, and would probably be addressing the setup with his employees when they returned from their time off work in a few days.

Fiona had gone back to sitting with Jax on the plane and ended up going with him and a couple of the families who toured a Hollywood studio when they landed in Los Angeles. She and Jax had briefly discussed the events of Saturday night on the plane, including how she thought the amount of money in the envelope Rick gave her was three times what she thought she'd won at blackjack. Jax laughed it off as the boss being too drunk to remember who won what, but Fiona still felt guilty for taking more than she'd actually won. Knowing Rick had already refused to take it back when he gave her the envelope, she didn't think he'd take back a portion of it if she confronted him about the discrepancy. So, Fiona had found an ATM to deposit it into her checking account, and would be calling her bank later in the day to transfer the full amount into the mission fund her father used to keep the shelter in San Antonio up and running.

Maybe I should wait to make that call until payday tomorrow, so I can put half my first check with it on the transfer, Fiona thought as she boarded the plane in L.A. to take her first trip outside the border of the United States.

She was excited to be going to Tijuana, Mexico, to get her first stamp in her new passport that Rick had arranged to be fast-tracked for her less than a month before. *I just won't mention it to Dad when we talk next, so he doesn't worry about me being in Mexico, where he hears about all the horrible cartel stories happening from the people we help in the shelter.*

Thinking about the shelter made her anxious to check in with Charlotte to find out how four-year-old Antonio Reyes was doing with her helping him with his speech every week. Fiona had met Antonio and his father, Roberto, about six weeks before, when they first arrived at the shelter where she used to volunteer every Saturday. Two weeks later, when Charlotte came to volunteer with her after their girls' night in San Antonio, Fiona had introduced her friend to the little boy, so she could continue working with the child, whose speech was practically nonexistent after spending his first four years of life in a home where it wasn't safe to go outside because of the cartel war going on in his hometown. He had already lost his mother to the crossfire and his father was struggling to know how to help his son, until he finally had the chance to flee across the border for help and safety.

It was people like Antonio and Roberto Reyes that made Fiona wish she could figure out a way to volunteer while traveling with her new job. She almost felt guilty for not being there to help at the shelter every week, the way she had for as long as she could remember. But then she remembered that if she was there, then she wouldn't have the extra income to donate to help keep the shelter going with other volunteers.

And I can still go volunteer whenever I'm home for holiday breaks.

"Miss Fiona, sit with us," Britney shouted as Fiona walked down the aisle of the plane. Britney was sitting across from Noelle York with two open seats in the quad seating area across the aisle from the Fields. Well, Cheyenne, River, and Skye Fields anyway. Stone Fields was seated at the front of the plane with Rick and the other writers to plan the GWA show for that night during the flight.

While she knew the girls weren't truly unsupervised during the flight while their parents were working because of being surrounded by the other families, Fiona thought it was still probably best if at least one adult was sitting with them. So, she put her luggage in the overhead bin before taking the seat beside Britney. She wasn't too surprised a few minutes later when Jax took the seat across from her beside Noelle.

"So, what are you ladies planning to do when we land in Tijuana?" Jax asked, smiling at the girls.

"Mom, Dad, and I are going to the History Museum Tijuana to learn about the local history of the city." Noelle shrugged, as if she couldn't care less where they were going sightseeing.

"Oh, that's where I was hoping to convince a few of you to go today," Jax replied, sounding more excited than the twelve-year-old beside him about the museum visit that afternoon.

"Yeah, good luck with that," Britney giggled.

"What? You don't think the rest of the kids will enjoy a local history lesson?"

"Oh, no, I'm sure they'll enjoy the history museum just fine." Britney shook her head. "But this is a wrestling company, so their parents are probably going to want to take them to Mullme with Dad and me."

"What's Mullme?" Fiona asked, wondering why Rick would skip a history museum to take his daughter there instead.

"It's a lucha libre museum," Britney said, as if that made it clear to those around her. When both Fiona and Jax looked at her with blank expressions from not understanding, Britney continued. "Lucha libre is Mexican wrestling. And it's so popular in Mexico that they have a museum full of wrestling stuff."

"Ah, so that's why you think the wrestlers will want to take their kids there, instead of the history museum." Fiona nodded in understanding.

"Yeah, Dad said I have to go to learn as much about the industry as I can for when I eventually take over the GWA when he retires." Britney didn't look very excited about that prospect for her future.

Fiona wanted to ask Britney if she had other ideas for what she wanted to do when she grew up, but she didn't want to step on her boss's toes when it came to parenting his daughter.

"Is that what you want to do when you grow up?" Apparently, Jax didn't have the same qualms about overstepping those boundaries as Fiona.

"I want to be an author when I grow up." Britney's eyes lit up at the thought of living her dream. "But unless Dad gets remarried and has more kids, who want to grow up and run the GWA, I'm gonna have to write in my spare time like Mrs. Kay. But if she can publish her books while traveling with us and taking care of her kids, then so can I. Besides, writing storylines for the shows isn't that much different than writing books, so I should be pretty good at it."

When Britney mentioned Rick getting remarried and having more children, Fiona felt as if her ovaries were clamoring to volunteer for the position of wife and mother. Though she could easily picture herself as Rick's wife and raising a passel of kids with his black hair and steel-gray eyes, she didn't like the idea of her children feeling as if they were forced to take over the company, if it wasn't what they wanted to do for a living.

What am I thinking? It's not like I'll be able to give him a passel of kids, even if we miraculously got together. Fiona pushed her worries about her fertility issues from her mind and focused on the preteen sitting beside her instead.

I wonder if he realizes running the GWA isn't what Britney wants to do with her life? And if he doesn't know, is it really my place to inform him?

No. I'm just his daughter's English tutor. Not her mom, or stepmom, or even someone he's interested in dating. So, it's not my place to question his parenting decisions.

Fiona was so lost in thought that she missed what Jax and the girls were saying about Jax going with the group to the history museum and Fiona going with the group to the wrestling museum. Having a teacher at each location would give them the knowledge to grade both of the seventh-grade girls, when they wrote reports about both of the locations and presented them to the rest of the kids later in the week.

It wasn't until Britney said, "We're gonna have so much fun at Mullme, Miss Fiona," that she realized their talk about combining the oral book reports from their language arts module with the sightseeing they did as part of their history module would require Fiona to spend the day with Rick and his daughter. *Yeah, that's not going to be awkward at all!*

Fiona hoped Britney was right about all the wrestlers wanting to bring their kids to the wrestling museum, so she wouldn't be alone with the Robertsons for the afternoon. *It's hard enough not drooling over the man when we're surrounded by the rest of the people who work for the GWA. If I only have Britney as a buffer between us, I'm not sure I'll be able to keep my attraction to him hidden.*

~~~

Monday, January 14, 2019, Noon, Tijuana, Mexico

Rick wasn't sure what had transpired on the plane to have Fiona riding with him, Britney, and Cage to the hotel and then sightseeing in Tijuana, but he feared it had something to do with Cage continuing the matchmaking from the weekend, while Anthony and Kay were off work and couldn't do it themselves. Luckily, Cage had only rented a
~~~

standard SUV instead of a limo of any kind, so Rick could sit up front with him, while Fiona rode in the back with Britney.

While Rick was glad the security measure to conceal their wealth, as a means of preventing them from being targeted by criminals, also allowed him a little more separation from Fiona on the drive, he was seriously regretting listening to Cage with the relaxed dress code while they were in Tijuana. Rick understood his normal suit and tie would stand out like a sore thumb and make him a target for pickpockets, but he wasn't comfortable wearing the jeans they were all informed they should wear while sightseeing in the city.

It wasn't just because he hardly ever wore the pair he owned specifically for situations like this. They were actually pretty comfortable every other time he'd worn them. But the other times he'd worn them, he wasn't sporting a hard-on from seeing Fiona in figure-hugging denim walking hand in hand with his daughter.

I have got to quit looking at her ass, Rick thought as he followed Fiona and Britney through the door into Mullme. As soon as they were in the lobby, Rick stepped up to the desk to pay for their admission, while the girls looked at the items in the display cases in the lobby. Cage stepped into his security role and scoped out the place while keeping his distance, which made Rick feel even more like he was alone with Britney and Fiona.

Normally, Rick liked the way Cage stepped back when he had father-daughter time with Britney. Family time was important to maintain, even with their busy schedule. But he wasn't sure what to make of feeling like he was having family time with both Britney and Fiona, as they posed for a picture with the life-size luchador figures just inside the museum.

"Dad, did you ever wear a lucha mask when you wrestled?" Britney asked as they perused the display of various wrestling figurines.

"Yeah, back when I first started wrestling." Rick chuckled at the memories his daughter's question brought up. "Your nonno insisted on it when I was a teenager because he didn't want to get in trouble for letting me start wrestling at fifteen, even though he didn't let me on TV until I was eighteen. Then later, I brought several masks on the road in case we were short on talent, and I had to wrestle multiple times on the card without anyone figuring out I wasn't two or three different wrestlers. But that was back before we all traveled together."

"You started wrestling at fifteen?" Fiona looked shocked as she asked the question.

"Technically, I started wrestling with my dad as soon as I was able to walk as a toddler, but I only traveled the circuit and worked house shows in the summer after bulking up for football my sophomore year of high school." Rick explained as they walked on to the next area of the museum. "It wasn't until I graduated high school that I was able to start wrestling full-time."

"Dad, why do they have Spiderman and Superman posters? I thought everything here had to do with wrestling?" Britney pointed out the display dedicated to the wrestlers of the past, who paid homage to their favorite superheroes through their gimmicks.

"Well, back in the early days of the sport, trademarks weren't really enforced." Rick shrugged at the incredulous looks both Fiona and his daughter gave him. "We'd be sued if we ever tried to use those characters now, but back before the internet, smaller organizations weren't likely to get caught using characters they didn't have the right to use."

Rick went on to explain the difference in theatrics between wrestling in the United States and lucha libre in Mexico, as they went upstairs to walk through the hall of masks. The more he talked about the history of professional wrestling, the more he felt like he was having family time with more than just his daughter.

Fiona asked insightful questions about the memorabilia they were seeing, as well as questions about his own career in the squared circle. If it were just the two of them, it might have felt like a first date with the way they were getting to know each other. But with Britney along, and Fiona's questions seeming to focus more on his life before his daughter was born, Rick felt more like he was giving his wife and child more information about his early life.

They fell into such easy conversation that Rick found himself walking side by side with Fiona while following Britney through the museum. He often unconsciously placed his hand on the small of her back to guide her to the next level of the building or through a narrow passage into a different section of the museum, as if she was his significant other.

Leah Mae Wright

It wasn't until they were coming back downstairs from the third floor, where the various posters from famous lucha libre cards were displayed, that Rick even realized he'd been touching her for most of their tour of the museum.

Damn, man, get it together! Rick told himself as they made their way toward the exit. *Just because I'm attracted to her, doesn't mean I can start treating her like she's my girlfriend, for fuck's sake.*

She's Britney's teacher, my employee. Act, fucking, professional!

As they met up with Cage to head back to the car and off to the arena, it took all of Rick's self-control to keep from reaching for Fiona's hand, the same way he had Britney's, to keep them both safe on the walk.

Fucking hell! I can't let them wrangle me into any more of these intimate family outings, or I'll never be able to keep my hands off her.

Chapter Seven

Rick thought his day would be easier when he went to the arena, while his daughter went with Cage and the rest of his employees going to the Children's Museum in Phoenix for their midday break. Not being on the outing with Fiona should have kept her off his mind, but he found he kept wondering more and more about what she was doing every moment.

Fuck! I need to focus on making sure the backstage set is ready for promos tonight, not on how that plum-colored dress she's wearing today accents both her emerald eyes and strawberry-blonde hair.

Rick tried to force his thoughts back to the work at hand, as he walked through the backstage area to where the interview set was being put together. He found Caleb Quinn, his head of production, talking to a member of the ground crew that traveled by truck to the various arenas to start setting up before the talent arrived each day.

Most days, the ground crews had the ring and backstage areas set up as early as possible, so they could head to the hotel and rest while the card was performed each evening. But on days they had extra work for the GWA's weekly live television program, they had to stay longer for the extra backstage set and camera setups.

Rick knew the ground crew schedule was brutal with days that started before midnight, when they started by tearing down and loading up the ring and all the other furniture the GWA utilized daily. Then they drove to the next city to set it all up again, as soon as they got into town, before trying to sleep in the afternoon and evening. That was why he had three ground crews alternating working for him, so none of them would get burned out by working too many days in a row.

Seeing the ground crew still working reminded him that he only had six weeks to get everything set up for them to temporarily switch to traveling on a second plane for the two-week-long European tour. Rick pulled out his tablet and sent a message to his executive assistant, Patrice, in New York to find out where she was with scheduling the extra plane and flight crew, as well as making flight arrangements for the volunteers from each of the three ground crews who wanted to work the European tour.

He also sent a group email to both of his current flight crews to see if they wanted to travel with the company on their days off during that same two weeks, so none of their kids would miss seeing the sights of Europe. Since it was the first European tour in company history, Rick wanted to give as many of his employees and their families as possible the opportunity to be there with them, especially the kids.

I can't wait to see how excited Fiona is for the European tour. I bet she'll be as excited as she was to visit Tijuana. The more he thought about it, the more he realized she seemed excited about every city they went to, no matter how big or small, just as long as it was outside of Texas. *But Tijuana seemed to be her favorite so far. I wonder if that was because it was her first time outside the States? Or could she possibly have enjoyed it more because of our time together there?*

"Hey, Boss," Caleb waved Rick down as he walked toward him. "Have you seen Ron since you got here?"

"No. Why?" Rick hit the button to put his tablet to sleep and put it back in his messenger bag, wondering why Ron Langston, one of the bookers, would be looking for him so early in the day.

"He was looking for you earlier." Caleb motioned toward the gorilla position for them to walk that way, presumably because that was the direction Ron had gone the last time Caleb saw him. "Said something about the tryout tonight and cutting one of the women's matches to accommodate it."

"No, we're not cutting one of the women's matches tonight." Rick shook his head, as they started walking to the curtain separating the backstage area from the ramp down to the ring. "It's bad enough we only have enough women on the roster to have two women's matches on TV nights. I'm not cutting one of them unless one of the women is injured and needs the night off!"

"I agree." Caleb held his hands up defensively, making Rick realize he was yelling at the wrong person. "We need as many women on TV as possible. I'm just telling you what he said, so you can go talk some sense into your booker."

"Yeah, sorry, didn't mean to bite the messenger," Rick apologized, as they walked through the curtain to see Randi Lee training with the Hunters in the middle of the ring. There were four female performers outside the ring, only three of which he recognized as the women's division heels under contract with the GWA. They were all four talking to Ron, presumably about the tryout Rick had scheduled for the fourth woman at ringside for that night.

"Hey, Ron, heard you were looking for me." Rick waved at the booker to get his attention, as he and Caleb approached the group.

"Yeah, we need to change the card for tonight." Ron motioned for Rick to step away from the group at ringside.

Rick had no intention of changing the card, but he masked his expression, appearing as his normal stoic self to let Ron say his piece. Rick wasn't sure why Ron didn't want the ladies to hear what he had to say, but he hoped it wasn't something that would end up with him firing the booker for inappropriate comments about the female talent.

"You have all four of our best female performers booked for the show." Ron's words came out in an accusatory tone that rubbed Rick the wrong way. "That only leaves Allissa to work the dark match for Amber's tryout."

Rick didn't agree with Ron's opinion on the four best female workers he had on the roster. Nor did he see what the problem was with Allissa working the try-out match. So he stood there silently, waiting for Ron to elaborate. *Unless she was injured last night and didn't inform me.*

"Allissa!" Rick hollered across the ring at the wrestler, who used the ring name of Victoria Vicious, to get her attention. When she turned to look at him, he asked the only question he had that was pertinent before she had a chance to speak to acknowledge him. "You weren't hurt last night while adding a little luchador flair to your ring repertoire, were you?"

Allissa shook her head in the negative, as she answered with a wide smile on her face. "No. In fact, I'm planning to add that Plancha to my matches whenever I can because of how good it felt."

"Good." Rick smiled back at the excited performer before schooling his features to turn back to Ron. "So, why do you have a problem with Allissa working the tryout?"

"She's only been on the roster for three months." Ron huffed indignantly, rubbing his wrist as if it was hurting him. "I don't think that's enough time to know we can trust her judgment to assess a potential new hire."

Based on the look on Ron's face, Rick didn't think her short time with the company was the only issue Ron had with Allissa. *Fuck, he objected about starting to push her toward the women's title with her promo tonight, too. I wonder what happened to piss him off enough to start trying to undermine her career?*

Back on October fifth, when Allissa had her try-out match in Las Vegas, Ron had agreed with Rick and the other bookers that she was one of the best performers, male or female, they'd ever seen. So, Ron's about-face on Allissa's ability had Rick confused.

Is it really just that she hasn't worked with us as long as our other female performers? Does the amount of time we've known her really matter when it comes to trusting her judgment to assess another wrestler?

If so, does that mean I shouldn't trust our new tutors to teach my daughter and the other kids because I haven't known them very long? How long does it really take to build that trust?

Just the brief flicker of the new tutors in his mind shifted Rick's mental gears to think about Fiona exclusively, causing him to, once again, get sidetracked from what he was supposed to be dealing with at the moment.

If trust can't be built in several months of working with someone, does that mean I shouldn't believe the way I instantly felt I could trust Fiona when I first met her?

Was that instant connection really love at first sight like everyone in Heart's Destiny believes? Or am I just thinking with my dick and trying to label my attraction to Fiona as more than lust, so I don't feel like a dirty old man for lusting after a woman ten years younger than me?

I certainly can't argue that there isn't a lust component to what I feel for Fiona. But I don't really think that's all there is to it. If I was only feeling lust, then I'd only think about sex when I think about her. But I want to know everything about her, not just her favorite sexual positions, so there's definitely a friendship component to what I feel for her, as well.

I keep having these crazy thoughts about taking care of her, too. More than just providing for her financially as her boss. I want to make all her wishes and dreams come true, just to see her smile as my reward for helping her with them. That's an affection component to my feelings that I've only felt with my daughter before. Is that love?

Fuck! I've fallen in love with Fiona. That's why I want to call her Fifi and take care of everything for her. I love her. Now, what the hell am I going to do about it?

"So, if you don't want to cut one of the women's matches tonight, we can have Allissa take Emerald's place in her match with Shauna." Ron's continued rambling finally broke through to Rick's Fiona-fogged brain. "And Emerald can work the dark match for Amber's tryout. Although, maybe we should have Shauna work it and have Allissa wrestle Emerald, so we can add Amber as our next Precious Stone."

"No, the card is staying as we planned it on the plane this morning." Rick held his hand up to stop Ron from objecting again. "I don't know why you suddenly have a problem with Allissa, but you need to get over it. I trust her judgment to assess the local talent and know she's already a main eventer. So, you need to get with the program." He left the *"or find a new job with another company"* unsaid.

Rick turned and walked away, unsure which woman he'd just decided to trust more. Allissa with helping to build up the women's division of the GWA? Or Fiona with his heart?

~~~

Friday, January 18, 2019, 11 a.m., Tulsa, Oklahoma

"Girl, you need to relax," Jax told Fiona as they followed the Burlesons in the car Jax had rented that morning. They were part of
~~~

the caravan of GWA employees and families that were going to visit two of Tia and Maria's favorite places in their hometown. Jax had originally tried to get the older kids and their families tickets to Greenwood Rising to learn the history of Black Wall Street while they were in Tulsa. But since it was sold out for the one day they would be in town, Tia and Maria had convinced everyone to check out the Center of the Universe and the Tulsa Zoo instead.

"Yeah, but it's hard to relax when I know Rick is going to be sightseeing with us." Fiona felt a flutter in her belly as she mentioned his name.

She'd felt those same flutters every time Rick had placed his hand on her low back to guide her through Mullme in Tijuana on Monday. But when he was actually touching her, the butterflies were accompanied by a flood in her panties. That outing on Monday had felt almost like a date, and it would have been a dream come true if Rick had kissed her to end it. Unfortunately, her dream kiss never happened. And on top of that, Rick had actually pulled back from having any interaction with her since then.

"Just because he's going to be there, doesn't mean you have to talk to him like you did on Monday." Jax reached over and patted her hand reassuringly. "You've got half the GWA acting as a buffer today, so quit stressing."

"Having everyone in the GWA at the casino didn't help me keep my distance from him," Fiona reminded Jax, shaking her head at her friend. "In fact, I think they were actively trying to push us together, which I don't want a repeat of today."

"You know it's offensive to those of us, who wish we were being fixed up with our silver fox boss, when you complain about that, right?" Jax raised an eyebrow at her without taking his eyes off the road.

"You wouldn't say that if you were the one he'd vehemently rejected last Saturday night. Or if you'd lived through the whiplash of him acting like the perfect boyfriend one minute and rushing to get away from you the next on Monday." Fiona had already told Jax all about the events he hadn't witnessed earlier in the week, so she didn't understand why he still thought she should try to get Rick's attention yet again.

"Pul-ease!" Jax groaned the word, drawing it out dramatically. "That hot and cold act is just him fighting his attraction to you as much as you're fighting your desire for him. If you'd just let your walls down and flirt a little to let him know the feeling is mutual, he'd be all over you."

"You do remember the last English tutor was fired for flirting with Rick and the other dads, right? I have no intention of following in her footsteps."

"I'm not saying to throw yourself at him like the stories I've heard about that ring rat wannabe." Jax shook his head in exasperation, as he pulled into the parking space at their first stop for the day. "Just smile at the man, instead of scowling every time you're in the same place, and quit avoiding him like the plague. He'll eventually give-in to temptation and make a move on you."

Fiona didn't have a chance to argue with Jax, as the rest of the cars parked around them, and it was time to get out to walk over to the Center of the Universe. Regardless of whether or not she agreed with Jax's opinion on the subject, she did follow his advice to smile, instead of scowling when her eyes met Rick's, as the group walked through downtown Tulsa.

I'm not flirting. I'm just trying to be a pleasant, professional person.

"What is that?" Addison Everett asked, as they approached a strange-looking steel structure on their walk.

"That's the Artificial Cloud," Tia explained to her ten-year-old friend. "It was designed by a Native American artist as a statement about pollution, and how we should work with nature instead of against it. That's why the metal isn't treated to prevent the sculpture from rusting."

Dan Traverson went into a short scientific lecture about why the metal rusted, but Fiona let it go in one ear and out the other. She was too busy enjoying the eye candy that was her boss, while she thought nobody else would notice. Just because she didn't think she could ever act on the attraction she felt toward Rick, didn't mean she couldn't enjoy the view when they were in close-proximity.

Keeping her eyes off her hot boss was even harder when she ended up walking behind him from the Artificial Cloud statue to the Center of the Universe. Since he had ditched the jacket of his suit somewhere between the castle-like hotel where they were staying that night and their first sightseeing stop, she had an exceptional view of how his tailored black slacks fit so nicely over his backside. He wasn't dressed as casually as he had been when they were in Tijuana at Mullme, but having also removed his tie and rolled up the sleeves of his white button-down shirt, he appeared much more relaxed than his normal buttoned-up businessman persona.

When they arrived at the rather nondescript circle of bricks in the otherwise concrete walkway, Tia and Maria explained where they needed to stand, with only one or two people at a time going to talk while standing in the middle of the circle.

"When we came here last year on a field trip, my teacher said we're supposed to whisper our secret wishes in the middle. And if the universe yells them back at us while nobody outside the circle can hear them, then they'll come true." Maria explained, looking excited about getting to make a wish.

Tia rolled her eyes at her sister. "It's really a vortex phenomenon that makes whatever you say in the circle echo back way louder than the words were originally spoken. And because the soundwaves are bouncing back at the person in the middle of the circle, they're too distorted for anyone outside the circle to understand what's being said."

"So, if two people stand in the circle, can they hear each other?" Katie Moore asked.

"Yes, it's a great place to tell our best friends our secrets when nobody else can hear us." Maria smiled at Katie conspiratorially.

"But if we tell each other our secret wishes, they won't come true," Sarah Evans whined, shaking her head.

"So, don't tell us your wishes when we're in the circle together," Maria shrugged. "We can all go tell secrets first and then take turns going back alone to make wishes."

Ivy Traverson took charge of corralling the kids to get them to take turns going to the center of the circle and talking, while her husband, Dan, looked around the area, mumbling about not seeing a cause for the vortex effect.

"Looks like Tia has stumped Dan once again," Emily Moore chuckled, as she pointed to where Tia had joined Dan in trying to find the cause of the phenomenon.

"Not just Dan." Anthony ran a hand through his hair before stepping away from the group of parents to join the kids who were huddled around Dan.

Fiona noticed then that Britney, Cody, and Connor were huddled close together with Tia.

"Um, Rick, you and Cooper might want to keep an eye on that situation." Kay giggled, as she pointed to where Anthony was standing between his and Rick's daughters and Cooper's two sons. Even though Connor and Cody were tall for their ages, Anthony's six-foot-six stature towered over them.

"Damn it, Anthony. My boys are just trying to learn. They aren't going to do anything inappropriate with your daughter." Cooper Stafford stomped over to where the older kids were all gathered with Anthony and Dan.

"Come on, guys, knock it off," Rick groaned, as he followed Cooper. "Even if they went to the center of the circle to say they like each other, we're all clearly able to see them to know there's no inappropriate behavior going on."

"I don't think it's a secret that they like each other," Jana Evans laughed.

"No, they *like*, like each other," Tiffany Stafford, Connor and Cody's mom, corrected, putting extra emphasis on the first "like" as she also laughed.

"Oh, Lord, don't let Anthony hear you say it that way," Kay chuckled. "I'll never be able to convince him that he's overreacting to Connor's interest in Tia if he hears that. And I can't deal with his overprotectiveness if it gets worse because he thinks he's right about the boy's interest in more than studying with Tia."

The ladies all laughed as Ivy approached them to see if any of them wanted to check out the phenomenon of the Center of the Universe.

"Yes!" Kay grabbed Fiona's hand and pulled her toward the circle. "We need to share some secrets."

Fiona was surprised at how strong Kay was since she was a good four inches shorter than Fiona's five-foot-four. But she wasn't about to fight against the pull of the petite, pregnant woman and make a scene with all of their coworkers around.

Kay positioned Fiona slightly off center of the circle and stood inches away on the other side of the line dividing the centermost circle in half. "Now that we know he can't hear, you have to tell me how you feel about Rick," Kay whispered, and her echo repeated much louder.

"No, not until you tell me what was up with trying to get us drunk in Vegas to get married by Elvis," Fiona whispered back and was also echoed much louder.

"I had nothing to do with anyone getting drunk." Kay raised her hands, palms out, as her echo repeated the statement. "We were drinking virgin sunrises all night, and there's no way we could get drunk on orange juice and grenadine."

"Then what was Rick ranting about?" Fiona and her echo both asked.

"That was Rick getting drunk and misremembering a joke Anthony made earlier in the day, when he was trying to calm Rick down from being jealous of the time you spend with Jax." Kay paused to let her echo catch up. "While I'll probably write a drunk-wedding-in-Vegas-themed book eventually, I wouldn't push my friends to actually get married while drunk in Vegas."

"But you were trying to fix me up with Rick that night?" Fiona's words came out sounding like a question, even though she thought she could say them as a true statement.

"Look," Kay whispered defensively. "We can all see you like each other. So, yes, we set it up so that you two would be paired up for the night. But that's all we did. There were no plans to make either of you act on your attraction or marry you off."

Fiona didn't know how to respond, so she stood silently contemplating everything Kay had just said as their echoes died down. That's when she finally comprehended what Kay had said about Rick being jealous of Fiona's friendship with Jax.

"What was the joke and why did Anthony say he thought Rick was jealous of Jax?"

"I wasn't there to hear the conversation firsthand, so I can't say for sure. But Rick was losing his shit when you invited Jax to be your date for casino night, so Anthony said something about getting you drunk and marrying you that night to keep you from dating anyone else."

"But Jax is gay, so we're just friends. There's no reason for Rick to be jealous over our friendship."

"Yeah, you know that, and I know that." Kay shook her head. "But Rick apparently has no gaydar and hasn't figured that out yet. Although, if I can get my friend Brayden to come to the show tonight to meet Jax, maybe Rick will figure it out."

"You seriously have a problem with trying to fix people up," Fiona laughed, hugging her friend.

"Yeah, Hazel and Susan have had more of an influence on me than I'd like to admit," Kay giggled, returning the hug before the ladies stepped back out of the circle to let the next people have a turn sharing their secrets in the strange sound vortex.

Once everyone else had a chance to step into the circle and talk to observe the phenomenon and started to walk back to their cars to head to the zoo, Fiona stayed back a moment to make a wish in the Center of the Universe.

"If this is really a portal to God to ask for our most secret wishes to come true, then I'd better take advantage of my time here to let you know my fondest dream. I wish that my friends are right about Rick being as interested in me as I am in him, and that we'll eventually find our happily ever after together."

Fiona waited for her echo to shout her whispered words back to her before running to catch up with everyone else to go to the zoo.

~~~

Friday, January 18, 2019, 1 p.m., Tulsa, Oklahoma

Rick felt a little like a stalker as he snuck a few pictures of Fiona while taking pictures of his daughter with his phone on their group outing. When he first snuck a couple at the Center of the Universe, he justified it to himself as no big deal, since she could clearly see him taking pictures of Britney and could easily step out of the background if she didn't want to be in the pictures. But then Fiona and Kay had stepped into the center of the circle to talk, and he had no excuse for taking their picture, other than to try and figure out what they were saying.

He felt guilty about overstepping the boundaries of decency by photographing her without permission the whole drive between downtown and the zoo. But that didn't stop him from continuing to
~~~

take her photo every other time he took a picture of Britney, as they walked through the zoo.

She looked so stunning, in her royal blue and black abstract printed dress, black tights, cardigan, and boots, that he couldn't resist the temptation to capture her beauty on his phone, especially after his realization a few days before that he was starting to fall in love with her. *Starting? Ha! I fell for her the instant I first saw her back in November.*

When they first got there, they went to the right from the entrance to see the Gem Dig exhibit, where he really had to be sneaky to get a picture of Fiona since she was helping the younger kids, instead of being close enough to Britney for him to get them both in the same shots. As they walked through the Life in the Cold exhibit and then the Life in the Desert exhibit, Rick observed the way Fiona interacted with the kids.

She had turned the zoo trip into a learning experience for the younger kids. She had the kindergartners looking at the signs to find the names of animals that started with each letter of the alphabet. She paired up each of the first through fourth graders, with a fifth through eighth grader, to help them read any of the signs they had trouble with reading.

She may have the most experience working with middle grades students, but by the time they got through the Life in the Forest and Life in the Water exhibits, Rick could tell the kindergarten-aged boys were the students who were most attached to her in her short time with the GWA.

"Look, there's Honker!" Maria shouted, pointing to one of the ducks as they were passing between the duck pond and the children's petting zoo.

There was a lively discussion about the strange-looking duck that didn't really look like the rest of the ducks in the pond. Rick didn't pay much attention to what was being said about the Burleson girls' former pet, which was actually a mix of a mallard duck and a blue goose. He was too focused on watching Fiona with the little boys who were more interested in the animals at the petting zoo.

It took some real creativity not to get caught taking her picture when he was going back and forth between Fiona in the petting zoo and Britney with her friends over by the ducks. Though he thought he'd pulled it off, he was really glad when they moved on from that area of the zoo.

Fuck! I have got to stop staring at her like a perv, Rick thought, as they walked toward the Rainforest exhibit. *I need to focus on what my daughter is doing, not my employee I want to fuck.*

Even if I want more than sex with her, I have to play it cool, so I don't freak her out by acting like a perv. I can't be the one to initiate anything, so I have to maintain my professional appearance and let her make the first move, so I don't scare her off. If she's even interested in me.

Hell, even if she is interested now, I'm not sure she'll still be interested in me if I can't learn to control the beast inside me, so I don't hurt her if I ever get the chance to fuck her.

Rick tried to pay attention to what Britney was saying about the animals in the Rainforest, but he failed miserably when Fiona caught his eye once again.

"Being jealous of five-year-old boys isn't really a good look on you, Boss," Anthony pointed out as they exited the Rainforest exhibit to head to the Macaw Landing Grille for lunch.

Rick tried to play it off with a shrug, as if he didn't know what Anthony was talking about, as they followed everyone else in their group. But he slowed his steps to allow the rest of the people with them to go into the restaurant, so he could talk to Anthony one-on-one without witnesses.

"It's not just the five-year-old boys monopolizing her attention today that I'm jealous of," Rick admitted when they were finally alone. "It's anyone she talks to or smiles at when it can't be me."

"You really need to give up your hang-ups about your age difference or whatever and ask her out, so it can be you she's talking to and smiling at." Anthony took a couple of steps away from the door to the restaurant, so they could talk without being in anyone's way who might need by.

"Even if the age difference isn't as big a deal to everyone else as it feels in my head, I still can't ask her out because I'm her boss." Rick shook his head at his young friend, wondering if he could somehow still be naïve about workplace relationships because of only being twenty-five years old.

"So? Do you pay her more than the other tutors?"

Rick shook his head at Anthony's ridiculous question. *The extra money in that envelope from Vegas was a mix-up, not me paying her more than the other tutors.*

"Does she get special benefits that none of your other employees get?"

"No, but it's still inappropriate…" Rick's voice trailed off as Anthony held up a hand to stop him from talking.

"As long as she's not getting special privileges, or being punished through her job, if she turns you down when you ask her out, there's nothing inappropriate about seeing what could develop between the two of you." Anthony smirked at him before continuing. "Unless you have some kind of fetish that crosses over her boundaries, then that might be inappropriate."

"Even if I wanted to do something she wasn't into, I would never force her to go along with it," Rick objected. *Though it might be hot to have her pretend to not want it once in a while, so I can get rough the way I like, I still wouldn't do it if she really wasn't into it.*

"I'm joking, Boss." Anthony held his hands up in surrender. "Just like I was joking last week about Kay wanting to get ya'll drunk in Vegas, so you'd wake up married the next day. You really need to quit taking everything so seriously all the time. You're going gray before your time because of stressing too much over things the rest of us laugh about."

"You might be right about that," Rick huffed out a chuckle. "Fine, I'll try to be a little less serious all the time, if you will make sure your wife doesn't pull any more matchmaking shenanigans on me or the rest of the crew."

"Deal," Anthony agreed as they turned to walk into the restaurant before anyone noticed they'd been gone from the group too long. "Though she'll be disappointed when I tell her you won't give her friend a backstage pass to meet Jax tonight."

Damn, maybe I was a bit hasty in stopping the matchmaking, Rick thought, as Anthony walked over to the group of tables where the rest of the GWA employees and families were sitting to order lunch. *I'd be fine with one more ploy, if it gets Jax's attention off my Fifi.*

Chapter Eight

Fiona took advantage of Saint Louis being in the same time zone as her hometown to know it was a good time to call her best friend while everyone was taking a break in catering for dinner. They had kept in touch via text for the last couple of weeks, but Fiona needed to hear Char's voice to know how she was really feeling about Ian being Fiona's replacement at Heart's Destiny Middle School. In order to have a little privacy for the conversation, she stayed in the classroom area to make her call to Charlotte.

"Hey, world traveler! Finally have time between seeing the sights to actually talk?"

Fiona couldn't contain her smile at Charlotte's upbeat greeting. "Yeah, something like that. I'm actually taking time from my dinner break tonight to call you, since you're always busy in the middle of the day when I have time for sightseeing."

"What did you see today? And what's your favorite place you've visited so far?"

"Today I saw the Gateway Arch in Saint Louis." Fiona was unsure how to pick a favorite place she'd been since starting her job with the GWA. She thought back to the various things she'd done on the daily outings, from ice skating at Rockefeller Center to the various museums and educational outings with the kids, and felt she'd enjoyed them all pretty equally, even the ones that got interrupted by wrestling fanatics asking the wrestlers for autographs.

Don't lie to yourself, Fiona! Your favorite was Tijuana. Not because of the city or the wrestling museum you visited, but because you felt almost like it was a date with Rick.

"And?" Charlotte prompted when Fiona let the silence stretch too long. "Your favorite place so far?"

"I can't pick a favorite," Fiona fibbed. "I've enjoyed everywhere I've gone so far. Though Tijuana might be the most memorable, since it was my first time out of the country."

"From what Kay said last week, I'd have thought Vegas would be your most memorable."

"Yeah, it probably would have been if not for how the night ended," Fiona admitted, knowing Kay had probably already filled her sister-in-law in on all the details of that day.

"So, did the drunken rambling kill the attraction, or are you still pining for your DILF boss?"

"I'm still attracted to him, but I wouldn't say I'm pining for him. I know it's a one-sided attraction, so I'm not going to let my feelings go any deeper than thinking he's hot."

"Sorry to hear that." Charlotte's tone of voice sounded melancholy. "I was hoping you'd found *The One*."

"Speaking of *The One*, what's going on with you and Ian?" Fiona was anxious to get the conversation on any topic other than her and Rick's lack of a relationship.

"Don't even go there with suggesting he's *The One*." Charlotte sounded exasperated. "He's a total *PITA,* but definitely not *The One*. I've spent the last two weeks fighting with him daily about the seventh-grade syllabus. And he still won't admit it was him at the hotel last month. He claims he never met me before our late Christmas celebration. And that I'm not his type, so he wouldn't have gone to my room that night, even if it was him."

"Darn, guess neither one of us has found *The One*," Fiona sighed. "So, what else is going on with you? Is Antonio becoming any more vocal, since you've been working with him?"

Char took an audible deep breath before answering. "Antonio is a little more vocal, but not as much as I'd like to see. Roberto has been really hands-on trying to help me with the sessions on Saturdays, but I think he's too busy with immigration paperwork and trying to find a job during the week to work with him as much as Antonio needs."

"I hate to hear that he's not progressing as quickly as we'd hoped." Fiona's heart ached for the four-year-old, who had suffered too much loss in his young life and was struggling to learn to speak because of it. "Maybe once Roberto finds a job, you can get Paige to work with Antonio while he's in the childcare center. I'd suggest having her work with him now, but Roberto only leaves him there sporadically, so she couldn't do anything consistently to be much help."

"Yeah, I've already talked to her about that." Charlotte sounded a little more hopeful.

"So, anything else exciting going on back home?"

"The only really exciting thing that happened this week was seeing Anthony and Kay's ultrasound pictures Monday night."

"Yeah, I got to see them yesterday when the girls insisted on showing their friends the pictures of their baby brother." Fiona smiled at the memory of how excited Tia and Maria were to show off the grainy black-and-white images. "I still don't see how they can tell the baby is a boy from those pictures."

"Oh, that's not why they think they're having a boy," Charlotte chuckled. "Anthony dreamed about his family for over a year before he met Kay, and in those dreams, they had two daughters and two sons. So, now they're convinced that the baby is a boy because his dreams were so accurate when he saw Kay and the girls before meeting them. Truth be told, I'm kinda hoping they have another girl, so the whole family will drop their belief in prophetic dreams."

"You don't believe in prophetic dreams?" Fiona inquired, curious about her friend's thought process.

"No," Char replied adamantly. "If God really allowed us to see our future in our sleep at night, then we'd have some forewarning about the bad events in life as well as the good. How can I believe Anthony saw his future wife and children in his dreams, when he didn't get any warning before losing Nancy and AJ? If he'd have dreamt about losing them, maybe he could have done something to prevent it."

"So, you'd believe prophetic nightmares, but not good dreams?" Fiona couldn't imagine how horrible it would be for the person to live with the guilt of not preventing a tragedy, if they had a nightmare about it beforehand. So, she hoped, if she ever experienced the phenomenon, it was only good dreams. "I don't think I could sleep at night if I had nightmares that came true."

"No, I don't believe in either being signs of what's to come." Fiona couldn't see her friend, but she knew by the vehemence in her voice that Charlotte was shaking her head as she spoke. "But if they were real, they wouldn't always be good dreams with positive outcomes. Life doesn't work that way. We have to take the good with the bad. Just like we all have bad days, we all have bad dreams. So, I don't think we can pick and choose which ones to believe will come true."

"But it would be really nice if we could pick the erotic ones to come true." Fiona sighed at the thought of her dreams about Rick making love to her coming true.

"If you'd have said that a month ago, I might have agreed with you," Charlotte laughed through the phone. "But since all my erotic dreams lately have included a certain PITA English teacher, who lied to me about who he was before the best sex of my life, I really don't want them to play out in real life now."

"Really? If it was the best of your life, I'd think you'd want to have a repeat." *Lord knows, one night with Rick wouldn't be enough for me.*

"Well, he did have a glorious dick, so maybe. If I could gag him and put a bag over his head." Charlotte barked out another laugh. "But only if there was no way for me to know it was him, since his asshole attitude has killed any attraction I had to him as a person."

Fiona chuckled along with her friend, even though she hated that her friend hadn't found true love with Ian.

They talked for a few more minutes before Fiona had to go, so she had time to eat before the kids would be ready to head back to the classroom. For the rest of the night, Fiona contemplated what Charlotte had said about Anthony's dreams and whether or not she thought they could really be prophetic. *If only I knew for sure that I could pick my sexy dreams about Rick to come true…*

Later that night, just as Fiona finished getting ready for bed in her favorite flannel pajamas, there was a knock on the door between her room and the adjoining room. She knew it was probably one of her coworkers, but she hadn't paid attention when they were going to their rooms earlier to know who had the room right beside hers. So, she threw her robe on over her pajamas before answering it.

"Who is it?" Fiona asked with her hand on the door handle.

"It's Jax, Doll. I just wanted to see if you were possibly as wired as I am and want to watch a movie."

Fiona opened the door for her fellow tutor, who was also decked out in flannel pajamas. Jax bounced into the room and grabbed her television remote before flopping on her bed.

"I don't know if I can stay awake for a whole movie." Fiona shook her head as she walked around the bed to sit on the other side from where Jax was making himself comfortable.

"Oh, well, gossip it is then." Jax grinned at her before dropping the remote back on the bedside table. "What were you up to tonight that made you late for dinner? And don't tell me you called your girlfriend again. Girlfriends don't cause those dreamy smiles you had the rest of the evening, like hot guys do."

"I really was talking to my friend, Charlotte, from back home," Fiona protested, raising her hands in surrender. "But the smiles weren't from thinking about her."

"Oh, and what were they from then?" Jax rolled on his side and pushed up on his elbow to look her in the eyes.

"I was thinking about something she said about prophetic dreams," Fiona admitted before explaining what Charlotte had said about Anthony's dreams before he met Kay and their daughters, and how that was why they thought they were having a baby boy. She glossed over Char's belief that there were no such thing as prophetic dreams. "Anyway, after all the talk about the possibility of dreams becoming reality, I couldn't stop thinking about my own recent dreams."

"So, was it remembering the dreams that made you smile languorously, or imagining them coming true?" Jax dramatically imitated her lost in dreamland look before they both started laughing.

"Maybe a bit of both," Fiona admitted through her giggles.

"Oh, now I need all the juicy details of your dreams." Jax's eyes and grin widened as he rested his head on his hand, waiting for her to tell all.

"I'm not telling you the details of my dreams." Fiona lightly slapped a hand on his shoulder.

"Not even if I tell you all about the dreams I've been having that I hope come true?" Jax raised an eyebrow inquisitively.

"I don't think I'm mature enough to hear your dreams," Fiona joked. She was both curious about what Jax would reveal, and afraid she wasn't prepared for the jealous feelings she'd have if he was also dreaming about Rick.

"Oh, pul-ease!" Jax flopped back on the bed dramatically, as he drew the word out to emphasize his indignation. "You're not that much younger than me. Besides, I've seen the way Rick looks at your ass, so someone should probably give you a heads up for what to expect when he wants anal."

"I doubt he wants to do butt stuff with me," Fiona exclaimed, covering her bright red face with her hands in embarrassment at talking about this with Jax. "And I don't need you to tell me how it works."

"Oh, Doll, you really don't think *'butt stuff'* is limited to us gay guys, do you?" Jax shook his head as he used air quotes around her term for anal sex.

"No, I know it's not." Fiona grabbed for a pillow to cover the mortified expression on her face when Jax pulled her hands down, but she wasn't successful in hiding completely. "I mean I've read about butt plugs and the preparation and training needed in enough romance novels to know what to expect, so I don't need you to tutor me on butt stuff on the off chance Rick will want to do *that* with me. I mean, I don't even know that he wants to kiss me, much less have kinky sex with me."

"Oh, yeah, he wants it. You're just still in denial." Jax shook his head. "Remind me after we finish talking about our dreams to check out your Kindle library. Miss Prim and Proper, preacher's daughter, has a hidden kinky side. I definitely need to know more about your reading habits. But first, tell me what you think about the reality of prophetic dreams."

"I don't know if they're real or not." Fiona sat up and put the pillow she'd been trying to cover her face with on her lap now that they were changing the subject off of things she found embarrassing to talk about. "I mean, Charlotte did make a good point about not being able to pick and choose which dreams we believe are prophetic and which are nightmares we don't want to come true."

"Yeah, I definitely wouldn't want my nightmares to come true." Jax's expression turned serious for a moment before he went back to his normal, jovial self. "But wouldn't it be great if we could pick the super sexy ones to come true? I'd definitely pick my erotic dreams with Cage to live out in real life."

"Cage?" Fiona was shocked to hear her friend had a crush on Rick's brooding bodyguard. "He's so quiet and reserved. I thought you'd pick someone a little more outgoing, like you."

"You know what they say about opposites attracting?" Jax shrugged one shoulder. "Besides, there's nothing hotter than a dominant, alpha, brooding, bad boy. And Cage is all that and a bag of chips."

Fiona had to agree with Jax's assessment of Cage Dalton. She just hoped her friend wasn't setting himself up for heartbreak if Cage didn't play for his team.

She and Jax stayed up half the night talking about their crushes and their favorite romance novels. Jax finally went back to his own room when Fiona couldn't stop yawning long enough to complete a sentence.

When she finally went to bed that night, she said a prayer that her dreams about Rick would one day come true.

~~~

Sunday, January 20, 2019, Flying from Saint Louis, Missouri, to Memphis, Tennessee

After checking in with Anthony in the cockpit for their flight time to Memphis from Saint Louis, Rick stopped in the galley behind Fiona and Jax, who had just boarded the plane. He wasn't close enough to get a whiff of her strawberries and cream scent, but he appreciated what he could see of her red dress peeking out of the bottom of her coat.

Fuck, she must have one in every color of the rainbow, Rick thought, as he stepped up just close enough to hear their conversation.

"You alright, Doll?" Jax asked Fiona as they stopped beside the first row of seats to wait for the aisle to clear, so they could walk the rest of the way to their seats in the middle of the plane.

"Yeah, just tired," Fiona replied with a yawn. "*Someone* kept me up too late last night." She put special emphasis on the word "someone" as she poked Jax in the ribs playfully.
~~~

Rick's heart clenched at seeing her being so affectionate with another man. *No! Fuck! No! She's mine. Not his!*

"I don't recall you complaining last night." Jax turned toward Fiona enough for Rick to see him wag his eyebrows suggestively at her. "And it was you moaning that woke me up this morning."

Fiona shook her head, as they started walking toward the back of the plane, where Rick could no longer hear their flirty banter.

Fucking hell! Rick thought as he took his seat. *They're fucking sleeping together. They haven't even known each other for two fucking weeks, and they're fucking sleeping together.*

Fuck! Fuck! Fuck! I have to figure out how to get any thoughts of ever being with her out of my head.

It's obvious I was right when I first met her and knew I was too old for her. Jax is closer to her age, and they clearly have more fun together than she'd ever have with me. Not to mention, he's probably a hell of a lot more gentle with her than I could ever be.

I just wish I hadn't started to believe the Heart's Destiny, love-at-first-sight bullshit was real before realizing she didn't feel it with me.

"You okay, Boss?" Cooper Stafford took the seat across from Rick. The concerned expression on the face of his oldest friend in the company brought Rick back out of his head to realize half the crew was staring at him, as he scowled because of his thoughts.

Cooper had been with the company for seventeen years, starting when both he and Rick were twenty years old, and he was the only wrestler from back then still performing in the ring. Rick wanted Cooper to sit in on more of the meetings with the bookers to easily be able to transition into that role in the company whenever he was ready to retire from in-ring action.

Because of how well they'd been able to read each other in the ring back when they were booked as the top two heavyweight competitors in the company, Rick knew Cooper could tell something was bothering him. He just hoped his old friend couldn't tell exactly what was wrong.

"Yeah, I'm fine," Rick finally said, hoping his words would appease Cooper and anyone else observing him. "Just trying to decide on a few things for some storylines. I know we were talking about you putting Tank over for the title at the next pay-per-view, but what do you think about keeping it for another couple of months?"

"But I thought the whole point was to have all the babyfaces go over to give the fans a happy Valentine's Day?" Cooper looked confused by Rick's sudden change of plans.

"Yeah, but the title of the show is ***Saint Valentine's Day Massacre***," Rick pointed out. "So, I thought having all the heels go over would better fit the name of the pay-per-view." *And my mood for Valentine's Day, since the woman I want is with someone else.*

Ethan Abrams and Stone Fields took their seats beside Rick and Cooper. Ethan and Stone were both former wrestlers, who now worked as bookers for the GWA after injuries cut their in-ring careers short.

Rick noticed that Ron Langston glared at him when he had to take a seat across the aisle instead of sitting with him and the other bookers, where Cooper had taken the seat he likely wanted. But Rick shook off the uneasy feeling he had about the only booker without in-ring experience, planning to keep his eye on Ron for the next couple of weeks to see if there was a problem he needed to deal with through his human resources department.

He can still hear our conversation from across the aisle, so he knows he's more than welcome to offer his opinions during this discussion.

"That would be a definite swerve to the fans," Stone commented on Rick's proposed plan.

"But after keeping the tag titles on the Twins last month, we really need to give them to Dark Chocolate and Red to keep their angle going," Ethan pointed out.

"Shit, you're right. I didn't think about that." Rick slammed his head back into the headrest in frustration. "I guess we'll give the fans a happy Valentine's Day then, with all the faces going over."

At least somebody should have a happy Valentine's Day. Lord knows, mine's going to be miserable knowing Fiona is spending it with Jax.

<p style="text-align:center">~~~</p>

Leah Mae Wright
Friday, January 25, 2019, Fort Myers, Florida

After an exhausting trip to Disney the day before when they were in Orlando, Fiona agreed with the other women, who suggested relaxing beside the pool at their Fort Myers hotel instead of going sightseeing once again. As much as she loved seeing new things in every city, her feet needed a rest from anything that required a lot of walking for at least a day or two.

Jax had opted to go with the other single guys, who were going on a two-hour fishing charter that afternoon, and Kay was off work for a couple more days, so Fiona was left there without the two people she'd become the closest friends with since starting her job with the GWA. Luckily, Randi had convinced some of the single female wrestlers to join the moms at the pool with the kids, so Fiona had at least one person she considered a friend there while she was getting to know the other women well enough to start considering them all friends. Well, when the moms weren't occupied with their kids in the pool, anyway.

She laid her towel out on the lounge chair beside Randi before taking a seat and starting to slather on the sunscreen. She felt a little self-conscious in a bikini, since she was curvier than the other women around her. But since she hadn't thought of packing a swimsuit, she was stuck with the only style she could find in the hotel gift shop. With showing so much more skin than she usually did, Fiona knew better than to go without sun protection with her fair complexion. She'd turn into a lobster if she spent more than five minutes sunbathing without it.

"I'll get your back if you'll get mine." Allissa Walters, one of the female performers that Fiona didn't know that well, pointed at Fiona's bottle of sunscreen with her hand holding her own. She was in the lounge chair on Fiona's other side, so she turned to face her to make it easier to swap sunscreen bottles.

"Thanks. I was regretting not getting the spray-on kind to be able to reach the spots I normally have covered while sightseeing."

"I was gonna wait to see if she got brave enough to ask Rick to put it on her back before I offered," Randi chuckled as Fiona and Allissa exchanged bottles.

"That's because you're as bad as your sister at trying to play matchmaker." Allissa shook her head at Randi while Fiona covered the tan brunette's back with sunscreen.

"They're trying to match you up with someone too?" Fiona asked Allissa, as they turned around for Allissa to put Fiona's sunscreen on her back.

"Oh, yeah. Only Randi isn't as particular about it as Kay." Allissa and Fiona traded back bottles of sunscreen before laying back on their loungers to chat while they sunbathed.

"I'm not particular about it because I'm not trying to fix you up," Randi protested while holding up her own bottle of sunscreen. "I just want to hang out with you while hanging out with my man, and my man is hanging out with his friends. So, the other guys are around, but I'm not trying to fix you up with any of them. Now put some sunscreen on my back, so I don't burn."

"Uh-huh, sure." Allissa rolled her eyes at Randi. Before she could get up to take the sunscreen bottle from Randi, one of the other women wrestlers sitting on Randi's other side took it and started applying it to their friend. "That's why you insist I sit next to Dean every chance you get."

"Just because you'd be my first choice for a potential sister-in-law, doesn't mean I'm trying to fix you up with him," Randi grumbled before taking her sunscreen bottle back from the stunning African American woman, saying a quick "thanks, Emerald," putting it in her bag, and flopping down on her lounger. "Although, you could do a lot worse than Dean, so I don't see why you don't want to go out with him."

"Why wouldn't you want to go out with Dean?" Fiona inquired. "He's a nice guy and easy on the eyes."

"Dean's a player," Allissa argued, shaking her head as she got comfortable on her lounger.

"Really?" Fiona looked at Allissa, trying to gauge in her body language why she thought that about Dean. "I've known him for as long as I can remember, and I've never seen him behave in any way that wasn't gentlemanly."

"He hit on me the night of my try-out match back in October. Not when we were backstage, but at the bar afterward. Instead of treating me like a colleague, or an equal since I'm also a wrestler, he lumped me in with the ring rats as an easy lay, which I am not. His asshole attitude trumped any thoughts I initially had about him being hot."

"That's just Dean being Dean. He flirts with everyone." Randi waved her arm around like she was waving off Dean's behavior. "He even flirted with me the first day I met them, when James was too shy to speak to me while they were at lunch."

"Yeah, exactly, he flirts with everyone because he's a player. And I have no desire to be one of the throng of women he calls Darlin' because he can't remember their names."

"And I keep telling you he only calls you Darlin'," Randi protested. "I think it's his pet name for you, like James calls me Angel."

"I've never heard him call anyone else Darlin' either." The gorgeous African American woman Randi had referred to as Emerald looked toward the other woman with them, whose name Fiona couldn't remember. "Have you?"

I should probably ask their names again, but I hate to be rude and ask in the middle of the conversation.

"No, he normally calls everyone by their gimmick name or their first name if it's part of their gimmick name," the Asian American beauty replied.

Fiona thought back to all the times she'd been around the Hunters over the years, trying to remember a time when Dean used the term of endearment the way men often did in Texas. "I have to agree with that," Fiona finally said when she couldn't recall a single time Dean had ever used the term. "Luke Walker calls everyone Darlin', but I've never heard Dean call anyone Darlin' before."

"See, and Fiona has known them since they were newborns, so she would know if it was something he called everyone." Randi turned and gave Fiona a triumphant smile as Allissa shook her head at them.

"Why don't we go back to fixing Fiona up with Rick?" Allissa suggested, obviously over the subject of Dean Hunter.

"No, let's not." Fiona held her hands up to object to her further humiliation. "I think the way he's been avoiding me for the past couple of weeks speaks volumes about what a bad idea it is to fix me up with him."

"Oh, he might be keeping his distance, but his eyeballs aren't." Randi subtly nodded in Rick's direction.

When Fiona turned to look across the pool where Rick was playing Marco Polo with his daughter and the older kids, she only caught a glimpse of his eyes on her before he turned away. She took advantage of the fact that he was no longer looking in her direction to peruse what she could see of his body through the crystal-clear, pool water.

Frick-n-frack! I just thought he looked hot in a suit and tie or the jeans and Henley he wore in Tijuana. He's got boulders for shoulders and just the right amount of chest hair. And while he's got more of a dad bod than the guys who still wrestle for the GWA, I don't think the ripples I see just a little lower are all from the water. I can't really complain that he's thicker in the middle and doesn't have a six-pack like the other guys, since I too have my abs hidden beneath a layer of fat. Though I wouldn't mind licking the water off his abs, whether they're well defined or not. Fiona licked her lips at the thought.

"You might want to stop drooling before he looks at you again and catches your lusty look for him," Randi whisper-shouted, catching Fiona's attention and causing her to turn away from the glorious sight of Rick in board shorts to look at her friend.

"I'm not drooling," was Fiona's flustered response to Randi's quip.

"No, I'd say it's more like licking your chops, wanting to take a bite out of the boss," Allissa teased with a grin.

Fiona couldn't help but giggle at Allissa's accurate assessment.

"So, why aren't you flirting a little more to show him you're interested?" Fiona was surprised that Randi asked the question, considering what she knew about her upbringing as the youngest of the Lee family.

"There are just too many reasons we'd never work," Fiona sighed, shaking her head while still holding Randi's gaze.

"Oh, like what?" Randi smirked, as if she was prepared to negate all of Fiona's reasons.

Yeah, like that's possible. It's obvious to me that it's just an unrequited crush, so why doesn't everyone around me seem to see that?

"First of all, he's my boss." Fiona started counting off the reasons on her fingers. "Second, it was made clear to me that the last English tutor was fired for flirting with every man in the company."

"And the GWA isn't like other companies," Randi refuted. "There's not a policy against dating the boss here. As for that Stacy chick, it wasn't flirting with Rick that got her fired. It was flirting with the guys in relationships and pissing off all the women that got her fired. Since you're only going to flirt with Rick, you have nothing to worry about when it comes to your job."

"There's also the fact that I'm closer to his daughter's age than his," Fiona argued. "He told my dad on Thanksgiving that he'd treat me like his own daughter to convince him it was safe for me to take the job."

"Oh, he might want to be your Daddy, but I don't think he looks at you as if you were his daughter," Emerald laughed as the other women joined in agreeing with her.

"And I don't think you're right about the age difference," Allissa added. "How old are you?"

"Twenty-seven." Fiona gave Allissa a curious look as she answered her question.

"Then you're definitely wrong about the age difference. Rick is only thirty-seven, so you're only ten years younger than him and fifteen years older than Britney."

"Wait, how do you know their ages?" Randi asked Allissa.

"Because I overheard Britney and Tia talking about their ages when your nieces joined the tour the week after I did," Allissa replied with a shrug. "And I was here for the impromptu birthday party the guys had for Rick in November."

"Wow, I really suck at guessing ages," Fiona sighed. "I thought he was at least in his mid-forties."

"Well, regardless of whether he's ten years older than you, or the almost twenty years older you thought he was, the age difference isn't a factor." Randi waved her hand around, as if she was shooing away a fly. "Large age gaps are obviously accepted in your hometown, with there being an eight-year gap between Kay and Anthony, and a seven-year gap between Bobby and Brooklyn."

"Wait, I thought Bobby's girlfriend's name is Brie?" Fiona gave Randi a quizzical expression, confused by Randi using the wrong name for the most recent woman to fall for a Burleson.

"Sugar!" Randi exclaimed, her face flushing more than it should for the amount of sun they'd gotten while covered in sunscreen. "I, uh, meant to say Brie. I just got my B names mixed up with that heiress disappearing about the same time Bobby met Brie."

"Girl, give it up," Allissa chuckled. "You are a terrible liar."

"Fine, but ya'll can't say anything to anyone about this." Randi held up her hands, extending a pinky to each of them to swear them to secrecy. Once they'd all made their pinky promise, Randi revealed the story of Brie Brooks really being Brooklyn Barns, and how Bobby was keeping her safe while trying to protect her from the fallout of everything her father was doing back in Georgia.

"Seriously? That sounds like a storyline Kay would come up with for a book." Fiona knew Hazel had pulled a matchmaking stunt to move Brie in with Bobby, but she thought the whole forced marriage and runaway bride part sounded like something added by a writer to add intrigue to a novel.

"No, Kay didn't come up with that one," Randi giggled. "But Brie is using part of her story for her next book. It should be released anytime now."

Fiona pulled her Kindle out of her bag to look up the latest Brie Brooks release, thinking she'd read it first before deciding whether or not to recommend it to the kids. Seeing her Kindle in hand, the ladies changed the subject to discuss their own recent book recommendations.

With the other women no longer focused on her crush on Rick, Fiona relaxed and enjoyed the rest of their time at the pool. Especially when she stole glances at Rick in nothing but a swimsuit from across the pool.

She also finally got up the courage to ask the other two ladies to reintroduce themselves, so she could finally call them by name. By the time they left the pool, she considered Aiken Pearson, the Asian American woman who went by the ring name Amethyst Stone, and Teagan Shields, the African American woman who went by the ring name Emerald Stone, as two of the three new friends she made that day. Though she wasn't sure she believed they were really "sisters from different misters" as they claimed for their tag-team name, the Precious Stones.

Chapter Nine

Rick was struggling to get through the last week after realizing Jax and Fiona were together. To make matters worse, he realized he'd lost his chance with her right before the tour took them through Florida and the Caribbean, where Fiona had ditched the tights and sweaters to show off more of her fair skin in her dresses and sandals. Not to mention the sexy swimsuit she'd worn at the hotel pool a couple of days before, when the weather was surprisingly warm enough to swim. It was all he could do to look away from her, where she was sunbathing, to play pool games with Britney and the other families.

Now that they were in the Bahamas, where it was even warmer than it had been in Florida the previous week, Rick feared he'd lose control of his inner beast, if he saw Fiona frolicking at the beach in that skimpy two-piece with Jax.

Fuck! Maybe a beach excursion for everyone isn't our best plan for a midday activity. I should probably try again to look up something historical in Nassau that Jax can take the kids to see. Even if Fiona goes with him, it'll be better than seeing them together on the beach.

Or maybe I can talk Britney into heading in from the beach early to bake in the bungalow before we have to go to the arena?

Just as he was unloading his and Britney's bags into their bungalow for them to change for their midday plans, his phone rang in his pocket. He dropped their bags just inside the door, pulled out his phone, and swiped the screen to answer the call from the unknown local number.

"Rick Robertson," he said in lieu of a polite greeting.

"Mr. Robertson, this is Gia at the front desk of the Seabreeze Resort." Though the woman on the phone tried to sound upbeat, Rick could tell there was a problem he didn't want to have to deal with over the phone. "We're having an issue with the reservations for a couple of your employees and need you to come back to the front desk to help us clear up the matter."

"I'm on my way," he barked gruffly into the phone before disconnecting the call.

"What's wrong, Daddy?" Britney asked as he turned to get her attention to walk back to the main hotel with him.

"There's a problem with some of the reservations, so we have to go back up to the front desk for a few minutes." Rick locked their bungalow and followed his daughter, who skipped her way back up the path from the bungalow to the main building of the resort, where the hotel was housed.

Fuck! Rick internally cursed when he saw Fiona and Jax at the front desk as soon as he walked into the lobby of the main hotel. *Why couldn't it be anyone but her with a room issue?*

"Miss Fiona!" Britney squealed as she ran up to Fiona and hugged her.

"Hey, Britney," Fiona replied as she returned Rick's daughter's embrace.

Damn, I really shouldn't be jealous of my daughter right now.

"I'm sorry for having to bother you with this." Fiona turned to look up at Rick with trepidation written all over her face as she released Britney.

"What seems to be the problem?" Rick looked at Fiona only briefly before turning to direct his question to the front desk clerk, who he assumed was Gia.

"It seems that Ms. Harrison and Mr. Nolen were last-minute additions to your company reservation," Gia stated. "And, unfortunately, the additions weren't noted until after all our other rooms were already booked. Therefore, we don't have a room available for either one of them."

Fuck! And since we had to fly over the ground crew for these island shows and get them hotel rooms, too, instead of them having the tour buses to sleep on, I'm sure it's my fault the resort is totally full.

Leah Mae Wright

Guess that's something else I need to check on for the European tour coming up, so this doesn't happen again.

"We offered to share a room, but they don't even have one available," Jax explained. "And none of the other resorts nearby had openings either."

Shit! I suppose we could ask Cage to bunk with us in the bungalow and give Jax and Fiona his room. As much as Rick hated the idea, he pulled out his phone and texted Cage in preparation for making the suggestion.

> **Rick: I need you to come back to the front desk. The hotel is overbooked and we're going to need to double up on a couple of rooms.**

> **Cage: Be right there.**

"Miss Fiona can have a slumber party with me," Britney suggested before Rick could offer his own solution. "And Mr. Jax can bunk with Uncle Cage."

"I wouldn't want to impose," Fiona said nervously before being interrupted by Jax saying, "That sounds like a perfect solution."

"If you have space in the other rooms you've booked, and doubling up works for all of you, then I can update your reservations for tomorrow in our resort in Puerto Rico." Gia looked back and forth between them. "So, you don't have to deal with this issue again when you get there."

"Let me check with Cage to see if he's okay with a roommate for a couple of days before we commit to anything." Rick knew if his friend was booked in a room with a single bed, they'd probably have to switch things up to his original thought of Cage crashing in their bungalow and giving the love birds in front of him the single room to share. "What type of room do you have Cage Dalton in?"

Gia turned to her computer and typed what Rick assumed was Cage's name to look up the booking. "Mr. Dalton is in a two-queen tonight since we didn't have enough kings available. Do you want me to make sure that's the same for tomorrow in our sister resort?"

"Yes, please." Rick smiled at Gia, knowing he was being a bastard for wanting to keep Fiona and Jax apart for as long as possible.

"What's the plan, Boss?" Cage asked as he approached the front desk.

"How do you feel about a roommate for a couple of days?"

"Fine, not the first time we've had to double up when a hotel is overbooked." Cage shrugged.

"Awesome! Tonight is going to be so much fun." Britney took Fiona's hand and started pulling her away from the front desk and toward the exit without regard to Fiona's luggage, which was still sitting by the desk.

"Don't worry, I've got it." Rick held up a hand to stop Fiona from protesting her need to grab her bags before going with Britney.

"I guess that means you get to show me to our room, Big Guy." Jax grabbed his own bags and grinned up at Cage.

Rick double-checked with Gia that everything was set up for both resorts before picking up Fiona's bags and following his girls to the bungalow.

Fuck! Fiona is not my girl! I have to quit thinking like that. Rick mentally berated himself as he watched Fiona's hips sway in her sexy sapphire dress.

Though Jax certainly wasn't acting like she's his girl either. If she were mine, there's no way I'd let her share a bungalow with another man, even under the pretense of bunking with said man's daughter.

Fuck! How am I going to sleep tonight in my king-sized bed, knowing Fiona is just a few feet away in the bunk beds in Britney's room? Or worse, if she decides she'll be more comfortable unfolding the sofa bed in the living room of the bungalow, since it's bigger than the twin beds in Britney's room?

At least if she bunks with Brit, there will be two closed doors and my daughter between us to keep me from trying anything with her tonight. With as bad as I want her, I don't think the one door between my room and the living room will be enough to stop me from hunting her down in my sleep.

"This is our room, Miss Fiona." Britney pulled Fiona along until they were both standing at the doorway to the smaller bedroom in the bungalow. "Do you want the top bunk or the bottom?"

"Oh, I'm not picky." Fiona smiled shyly. "You pick which one you want, and I'll take the other one."

"Then I'll take the top bunk and you can have the bottom one. Daddy, bring Miss Fiona's bags in here, so we can change to go to the beach."

Yes, please, Daddy, Rick imagined Fiona saying if his daughter wasn't around. *Fuck! As hot as that would be, it's kind of creepy to think of her calling me the same thing my daughter does. But maybe we could go with Padre or Papa.*

"I can take those from here," was what she actually said as she reached out to take her luggage from Rick, bringing him out of his perverted mental rabbit hole.

Rick didn't say a word as he handed Fiona her bags, not wanting to let on how his thoughts had veered to naked, naughty time with the young teacher. He walked back to the door to grab his own bags after passing Britney's through the door to the girls' room.

Out of the frying pan and into the fire, he thought as he changed into his swim trunks and water shoes to hit the beach. *If I thought seeing her in a swimsuit across the pool made me hard, my dick is going to be granite with her sharing my space for the next two days. And I'm not sure I'll be able to hide it from her in swim trunks and pajama pants.*

~~~

Monday, January 28, 2019, 10 p.m., Nassau, Bahamas

Fiona was a bundle of nerves as she boarded the shuttle bus to go back to the resort at the end of the night. She had been able to maintain her composure all day, but only because it was mostly like any other day. She'd enjoyed seeing Rick in his swim trunks again while they were at the beach, but from a distance since most everyone in the company was also there. When Britney wanted to do a little baking in the bungalow before going to the arena, Rick had left the two of them to fiddle in the little kitchenette with the rest of the girls and their moms while he went ahead to work.

Since the resort was providing shuttle services for them while they were in Nassau and San Juan, Fiona and Britney had caught a later shuttle to the arena, along with Jax, Cage, the Traversons, and a couple
~~~

of the other GWA families. Their afternoon and evening were pretty standard with Fiona working with the kids, and only seeing Rick in passing and when they all ate dinner together in catering.

Now that they were all headed back to their hotel rooms for the night, Fiona was nervous about being alone with Rick and Britney. Well, not so much Britney. But she wasn't sure what she would do when Britney went to bed, and she still needed a couple of hours to wind down at the end of the day.

Will it bother him if I stay up in the living room to watch a movie before bed? Will he stay up and watch with me? Or leave me alone to fantasize about him in his bed just a few feet away?

Obviously, I can't touch myself in bed tonight to thoughts of him the way I normally do. Even if I wasn't sharing a room with Britney and could be alone in my room to masturbate, I would die of mortification if he heard me call out his name and came to see what was wrong.

Fiona hoped her blush at the thought faded enough to not be blatantly obvious as they exited the shuttle.

"Have fun tonight, Doll." Jax grinned at her as he turned toward the hotel, and she turned toward the bungalows with Rick, Britney, and the rest of the families that had just exited their shuttle.

"See you tomorrow, Jax." Fiona shook her head, lightly chuckling at her friend's excitement about spending the night with his crush, even as she wondered why Cage was walking with the families toward the bungalows, instead of toward the hotel with Jax.

If only I could be as free-spirited and easy-going as Jax, Fiona thought as her friend called out, "See you in a few, roomie," to Cage.

Fiona smiled as the boys ran ahead of them and the girls skipped by her on the way to the bungalows. *Or as energetic as these kids.*

"You'd think the beach today would have drained some of their energy," Kay said from somewhere behind her.

"I was just wishing I had as much energy as them," Fiona giggled, turning to look for her friend.

"The beach would have worked to tire them out some, if ya'll hadn't refueled their energy stores with cookies this afternoon." Anthony waved his hand toward his wife and the other women around them.

Leah Mae Wright

"I don't recall you turning down any of those cookies when our daughters kept feeding them to you this afternoon, Cookie Monster," Kay playfully teased her husband.

"Cook-ieee!" Anthony growled out a surprisingly good impression of the *Sesame Street* character while scooping his wife up in his arms.

"Ya'll need to get a room," Archer and Addison's dad, Tanner Everett, chuckled at Anthony and Kay.

"Headed there now," Anthony replied as he took off after the kids, running toward their bungalow while still carrying his wife.

"I see why Kay fell for a younger man," Cheyenne Fields, River and Skye's mom, said with a grin.

"You'd better not be getting any ideas about trading me in for a younger man," her husband, Stone, growled.

"Oh, no, dear, I'm perfectly happy with my older man." Cheyenne batted her eyelashes dramatically at her husband. "But I can see the benefit to having a man around who is young enough to have the energy to keep up with the kids when we old folks get tired."

"Anthony's not that much younger than us," Holland Everett pointed out, shaking her head.

"No, but Kay is our age and pregnant for the third time." Cheyenne motioned between herself and the Everetts. "It was hard enough being pregnant while trying to keep up with our schedule in our twenties. Can you imagine trying to do it now, while also trying to keep up with two kids? That's why she needs a twenty-something-year-old man backing her up."

"Oh, yeah, good point," Holland giggled as they turned off the main path to head to their bungalow.

Fiona was thankful the families dispersed to head into their individual bungalows before they noticed she was with them and started asking questions. Not that she was worried about them asking why she was staying in Rick's bungalow, since they already knew about the booking mix-up earlier in the day. She was afraid they'd start asking about her age and when she was planning to have kids.

She didn't want to have to explain her P.C.O.S. to her new friends and have them feel sorry for her, or start asking questions about her options for having children because of it.

And I don't want to let it slip that I would love for Rick to father my future babies, regardless of the fact that he's ten years older than me and won't have the energy of youth to keep up with them when I'm worn out from pregnancy, if we were lucky enough to conceive, she thought as Rick unlocked their bungalow and Cage stepped inside.

Rick held up a hand to stop her from following Cage inside, confusing Fiona. She wasn't confused long, when less than two minutes later Cage emerged from the bungalow.

"All clear, Boss. Have a good night." With that, Cage walked back down the path toward the hotel, while Rick and Britney called out their "goodnight" wishes for him.

Fiona barely got her own "goodnight" out before Rick opened the door for Fiona and Britney to enter the bungalow before him.

Britney immediately started chattering as she practically ran to the bedroom to change into her pajamas. Fiona couldn't hear half of what she said, but she distinctly heard something about a "bedtime snack" that included "cookies and milk."

She went to her suitcase and dug through it for her toiletry case and pajamas while she waited for her turn in the guest bathroom to change for bed.

It's really too hot here for flannel pajamas, she thought as she tried to decide what she should wear to bed that night. *But I can't exactly wear an oversized t-shirt or short, silk nightgown when I'm not alone in the room. Flannel PJ's it is. Surely, they cover enough that I don't need to sweat to death in a robe, too.*

Fiona was second-guessing her sleepwear decision the whole time she was brushing her teeth and washing her face to get ready for bed. When she came out of the bathroom to find Rick on the sofa in the living room in pajama pants and a t-shirt, with Britney beside him in pajamas that almost matched the ones she was wearing, she decided she'd made the right choice.

On the coffee table in front of them was a plate of cookies and three glasses of milk. The sight hit Fiona straight in the heart. She felt as if her secret dreams of making a family with them were coming true before her eyes.

"Miss Fiona, come sit by me and share our snack," Britney implored, patting the sofa beside her.

"Um, yeah, give me a minute to put away my stuff." Fiona held up her armful of clothing and her toiletry bag to show Britney, as if the little girl couldn't figure out what Fiona had to put away. She took a moment to school her features as she packed up her things, not wanting to go back to the living room until she knew she wouldn't cry at feeling like they were including her while having family time.

Once she felt like she could stall no longer, Fiona walked back out to the living room and took the seat beside Britney, on the opposite end of the sofa from Rick.

"Is this your usual routine?" Fiona asked, motioning to the cookies and milk on the table in front of them.

"Yeah, we have a bedtime snack almost every night," Britney answered while dunking a cookie in her milk. "But Dad usually orders it from room service, since most of the hotels we stay in don't have kitchens for us to be able to make our own."

"Well, thank you for including me tonight." Fiona smiled at Britney before picking up her own cookie and taking a bite.

"Please eat as many of these as you want." Rick motioned at the cookies still piled high on the plate. "Otherwise, Brit will insist I finish them off."

"That's because there's not enough to share with everyone tomorrow." Britney spoke with her mouth full of cookies.

"But I already have to double up my run in the morning to work off the ones you gave me at dinner." Rick smiled as he shook his head at his daughter. "And I don't have time to triple it in the morning, if you insist I eat another half dozen cookies tonight."

"Is that the secret to getting in a workout with our schedule?" Fiona looked at Rick as she asked the question, and almost cracked up laughing at the milk mustache he was sporting after taking a drink.

"What?" He arched an eyebrow at her, and Fiona wasn't sure if he was asking her to elaborate more on her question, or what she was smiling about.

Not wanting to give away how much she was enjoying seeing this new side to her normally broody boss, Fiona opted to elaborate more on her previous question. "The only way to get a workout in our busy schedule is to go running first thing in the morning?"

"Oh, yeah, for me especially. Well, when we're in a city with an MMA gym that's affiliated with mine in New York, I'll go see if I can find a sparring partner or hit the heavy bag, instead of running or using the weight room in the hotel. Some of the performers hit the gym in the hotel while we're doing our midday excursions, but they also have time to work out in the ring, while you're teaching the kids, and I'm making sure everything is set for the show that night."

"You should go work out with Daddy in the morning, Miss Fiona," Britney mumbled between bites of milk-soaked cookies.

"I would if I could get my internal clock to reset, so I could get up early like I used to." Fiona smiled down at the precocious child between her and Rick. "But with all the time changes and the excitement of seeing so many new places, my inner morning person has been replaced with a night owl."

"Speaking of night owls." Rick pointedly looked at Britney and bopped her nose with his finger. "You need to hurry up and finish your snack and hit the rack, Pumpkin."

"I know, I know!" Britney popped the last piece of cookie in her mouth and downed the rest of her milk along with the chunks of cookies floating in it. "I just got started late because of waiting for Miss Fiona to join us."

Britney jumped up and took her cup to the sink. "And I'm gonna go brush my teeth again, too." Britney darted into the bathroom before Fiona could formulate the words to tell her goodnight.

"If I'd have realized we were having cookies, I'd have waited to brush my teeth, too."

"Don't feel obligated to eat them if you don't want them. I'll find something to put them in and hide them in my suitcase, so she doesn't know they weren't all eaten tonight." Rick shrugged. "Then I'll eat one each afternoon while she's in the classroom until they're all gone, so they won't go to waste."

He's such a wonderful dad, Fiona thought just as Britney returned carrying a washcloth from the bathroom.

"As funny as your milk mustache is, Dad, you have to wipe it off because I don't want to wear it to bed." Britney handed Rick the washcloth in her hand, which he promptly used to wipe the milk out of his facial hair.

"Better?" Rick looked up at his daughter and smiled.

"Much!" Britney leaned down to hug her dad. Rick returned the embrace, and they each kissed one another on the cheek before she said, "Goodnight, Dad."

"Goodnight, Britney Bear. Love you."

"Love you, too."

Fiona averted her eyes, not wanting to get caught spying on their father-daughter moment. Looking down at the cookie crumbs on her lap, she was surprised when Britney's arms came around her next. Fiona barely had the chance to return the hug before Britney was pulling back to kiss her cheek the same way she'd done with her father.

"Goodnight, Miss Fiona!"

Fiona rushed to return the light brushing of her lips over the child's cheek. "Goodnight, Britney. Sweet dreams."

Fiona felt awkward once the little girl left the room. *Should I try to go to bed too? Or should I brave asking him about watching a movie?*

Rick stood and took his cup and the plate of cookies to the kitchenette. Fiona was mesmerized by watching him do something so domestic as bagging up the extra cookies and cleaning up the dishes.

"Are you done with your milk?" Rick's question brought Fiona out of her lust-induced haze.

"Oh, um, almost." Fiona picked up her cup and chugged the milk, as if she was back in college chugging a beer at a frat party. Not that she'd personally chugged beer at a frat party when she was in college, but she had seen it done. *How sad is my life that this milk is the first time I've actually chugged a drink?*

As soon as the cup was empty, she stood and carried it to the sink, where Rick was just finishing washing the others. He reached out for her to hand him the cup.

"I can get this one." Fiona felt guilty for him having to wash up after her and didn't hand over the cup.

"It's no big deal, Fiona. I'm used to washing up after our bedtime snacks." Rick smiled as he took the cup from her hand and dipped it in the sink full of water to start washing it by hand. "Besides, I figured Britney has already derailed your normal nighttime routine enough. So, I can take care of this while you go do what you would normally do if you were in your own room tonight."

Yeah, I can't do that tonight, Fiona thought of her nighttime ritual of masturbating to thoughts of the hunky man in front of her. She turned her back to him and walked back over to the sofa, hoping he didn't notice the blush that marked her cheeks at the thought of what she would normally do to go to sleep at night.

"I normally watch TV for a little bit to let my mind shut down. But I don't have to if the noise will keep you or Britney awake."

"Once Britney's asleep, a bomb could go off in here and not wake her up," Rick laughed. It was a joyous sound that Fiona reveled in, since she didn't hear it often. "I often do the same, so maybe we can find something we'll both enjoy watching."

"Sure," Fiona squeaked as she picked up the remote, turned on the television, and curled her legs up under her on the end of the sofa where she had previously sat. "Do you prefer a specific show or type of movie?"

"I usually just flip channels until I find something funny." Rick rejoined her in the living room, taking his seat at the other end of the sofa.

"Well, then, by all means, find us something funny, Boss." Fiona tossed him the remote, too afraid she wouldn't be able to control herself if their hands touched by handing it to him normally.

Rick caught the remote against his broad chest and grinned at her before turning to the television to flip the channels. They settled on a Will Farrell movie Fiona hadn't seen before, quietly watching from opposite ends of the sofa.

"Um, I should have probably suggested this earlier, but we can have you share a room with one of the female performers tomorrow night, if you'd rather." Rick ran a hand through his hair, as if he was nervous to say the words.

"Oh, um, yeah, whatever." Fiona felt like she was stumbling over the words as she said them. *I guess we're both feeling pretty awkward with the situation tonight.* "I'm fine wherever there's room for me, but I understand you not wanting to share your family space with an employee."

"Oh, no, it's not that," Rick protested, running a hand through his hair once more. He mumbled something she couldn't understand before raising his eyes to hers and continuing. "I just thought you'd be more comfortable bunking with someone you're closer to, like maybe Allissa, since I saw the two of you talking more the last few days. Or maybe we can have Cage bunk with us, and you and Jax can share a room, since you seem so close to him."

"Sure, if Allissa doesn't mind, I'll be glad to bunk with her tomorrow." Fiona turned back to the television, not able to handle looking Rick in the eye as she teared up at his rejection. "But please don't move Jax from Cage's room unless Cage is uncomfortable with him being there."

She couldn't stand the thought of Jax not having the opportunity to see if Cage played for his team, just because Rick was uncomfortable with her in his space. *I mean, I don't know if Cage is gay, but I don't have Jax's gaydar to know what his preferences might be. And if they do have a mutual attraction, then they deserve the time together to explore where it might go between them.*

"Why would Cage be uncomfortable sharing a room with Jax?"

Fiona wasn't sure how to answer Rick's question. While Jax wasn't blatant with his sexuality, he certainly didn't try to hide his attraction to men. But Fiona still didn't feel like it was her place to out him to their boss if Rick didn't already know.

Surely, Rick already knows. Right? I mean, how could he not have seen it in the last three weeks? I figured it out the first time I really talked to Jax. And Kay knew enough about Jax to fix him up with her friend in Tulsa after only being around him for five days. So, yeah, Rick has to already know, so I'm not really outing my friend by telling Rick about Jax's crush on Cage.

"Well, I don't know what Cage's preferences are, but Jax has a crush on him. While I'm sure Jax would never mention it if he didn't think Cage was also interested in him, he's also not very subtle when he's talking about guys he thinks are hot. So, if Cage isn't gay, he could be uncomfortable sharing a room with Jax, whether he knows Jax is crushing on him or not."

"Huh," Rick grunted, leaning back into the corner of the sofa and extending his arm across the back.

Fiona wasn't sure how to take Rick's noncommittal response, so she kept her focus on the movie, sitting quietly while Rick seemed to think over the situation. He was lost in thought for so long that she fell asleep before anything more was said between them.

Chapter Ten

Rick knew he had to still be dreaming as he held Fiona in his arms, but he was confused about why they were both wearing pajamas when they had both been completely nude in his earlier dreams.

Too bad I can't control my dreams, he thought as he enjoyed the feel of her laying on top of him. *If I could plan them out the way I plan our wrestling shows, I'd definitely have us skin on skin, instead of being separated by my cotton and her flannel sleepwear.*

Although, she was super cute in her flannel pajamas last night. That's probably why I'm dreaming we slept cuddled on the couch in our pajamas after the movie.

The night before started invading his dream of Fiona lined up so perfectly with him that he could rock his hips and rub his cock between her thighs.

Fuck! As much as I want to relive her telling me that Jax is gay and not her lover, and especially how she sleepily admitted to having her own crush on me, I want to stay here with her knees on the couch on either side of my hips, so I could fuck up into her if we weren't wearing clothes. Wait, was that real or part of the dream? Damn, it was probably part of the dream. There's no way Fiona has a crush on me, the same way Jax has a crush on Cage.

Damn, I wonder if that's why I've never seen Cage with a woman in all the time I've known him? Of course, I've never seen him with a man either, so maybe I was right in assuming it's his injuries after the SEALs that keeps him from hooking up with anyone. Either way, if he's not interested in Jax, he'll let the guy down easy, just like he's done with the ring rats and unruly fans who've tried to sneak backstage over the years.

Not wanting to waste his dream time with Fiona by thinking of his other employees, Rick focused on what he could imagine feeling if she was really sleeping on top of him. Not only the heat of her pussy pressing into his cock, but also the feel of her breasts pressing into his chest, her head resting on his shoulder, her firm ass under his right hand, and her silky strawberry-blonde hair weaved through the fingers of his left.

Fuck! She feels amazing in my arms. Her body is the perfect fit for mine. This feels so good, so right. It's a damn shame it's only a dream.

Rick was so convinced it was only a dream that he didn't stop his body's natural instinct to dry-hump her, even as he wished he could manipulate the dream to magically make their clothing disappear, so he could fuck her instead. His dick was so hard, a combination of dreaming about Fiona and his normal morning wood, that he was afraid he'd wake up in the morning to find he'd come in his pants, like when he had wet dreams as a teenager.

Aww, fuck it! Coming with Fiona in my arms, even in my dreams, is worth having a mess to clean up in the morning.

Rick's pelvic thrusts sped up as he pressed down on her ass with his hand to increase the friction of them grinding together. Fiona moaned as her hips joined his in grinding together. Her hands gripped his biceps, giving him just a bite of pain as her fingernails dug in.

"Oh, yes, Rick," Fiona cried out, shuddering in his arms as she reached her release a few seconds before him.

"That's it, Fifi, come on my cock," Rick growled as his balls drew up and he shot his load in his undershorts. "Fuck! Fifi!"

His whole body convulsed in orgasmic bliss, just as his phone buzzed for the five o'clock alarm he had set to be able to go for a run around the resort. That was when he realized he hadn't dreamed everything that just happened.

As he opened his eyes to look for his phone to turn off the alarm, his dream woman didn't disappear from his arms. Rick lifted his hand from her ass to reach over to the coffee table, grab his phone, and turn off the alarm, hoping it wouldn't wake the sleeping beauty on top of him, whose face was turned toward the back of the couch, where he couldn't tell if she was awake or not.

Fuck! Fuck! Fuck! It might not have been a wet dream, since I grew out of them over twenty years ago, but I did just come in my pants like a teenager, while dry-humping my employee when I thought I was still asleep.

And I have no idea how to get out from under her without waking her up and making it blatantly fucking obvious that I molested her in her sleep. How the hell am I going to smooth this over without being sued for sexual harassment, or ending up in jail for sexual assault?

The only silver lining Rick could find in the situation was that he wouldn't have to hide his erection from her, since his cock had deflated in mortification at what he'd just done.

Since she hadn't stirred when he turned off the alarm, Rick decided to try to slip out from under her before the wetness in his underwear soaked through his pants. *Fuck, I don't want her to wake up with a wet spot on the outside of her pajama pants!* He gently scooted to the edge of the couch, so he could put one foot on the floor for leverage and have space on the sofa to roll her off of him.

All was going well until he realized rolling her onto her side with her head turned in the awkward way it was on his shoulder would put her face down on the couch. As he gently tried to reposition her head, so she would end up laying on her side facing out from the back of the sofa, Rick realized Fiona was awake.

And obviously mortified at what just happened, since she's trying to hide her face and won't let me turn her head.

"I'm so sorry, Fiona…" Rick's words trailed off as he tried to figure out how to apologize for his behavior without embarrassing her further.

"Don't," Fiona groaned as she pushed herself up off of him. She retreated to the far side of the couch and buried her face in her hands. The way she dipped her head hid everything her hands didn't cover behind a veil of strawberry-blonde locks. She mumbled something into her hands, but Rick couldn't understand whatever she was saying.

He sat up and backed as far away from her as he could get and still sit on the sofa. *Shit, I can't sit here and talk to her about this while my cum soaks through my clothes.*

"Listen, we need to talk about this…" Rick stood and started walking toward his bedroom door. "But I'd rather not do it when my daughter could wake up and overhear us. So, I'm going to go clean up and change into my running gear. Why don't you do the same? And then we can talk everything out while we jog around the resort."

He took Fiona's head bob as her assent to talk while they ran and rushed through his early morning routine, so they had plenty of time to talk without anyone overhearing them.

After he rinsed off in the shower, brushed his teeth, and changed clothes, he found Fiona dressed for a run in the living room. She was in shorts, a t-shirt, and sneakers with her hair up in a ponytail. Seeing her in the sporty outfit would have normally caused his cock to tent his shorts, but he was too appalled with himself to respond as he normally would just from being around her.

Fiona wouldn't look him in the eye as they quietly exited the bungalow. *God, I can't believe how colossally I fucked things up between us this morning,* Rick thought as he locked the bungalow, and they started walking toward the trail that looped around the whole resort. *Thank fuck, I wasn't as rough with her as I fantasize about actually fucking her. If I had been, she probably wouldn't have even come on this run to give me the chance to apologize.*

"I want to apologize again," Rick started, but Fiona cut him off.

"No, there's nothing to apologize for." Fiona shook her head, though she still wouldn't look in his direction. "If anyone should apologize, it's me. I'm the one who invaded your space, and apparently attacked you in my sleep."

"No, you didn't," Rick protested, wanting to reach out and take her hand or tip her chin up to look her in the eyes, but knowing he couldn't after the way he'd behaved earlier. "You were peacefully sleeping until I woke up and thought I was still dreaming. I should have realized I was awake instead of physically acting out what I thought wasn't really happening."

"We can't help what we do in our sleep." Fiona picked up speed when they reached the trail and Rick trailed along behind her, letting her set their pace. "And you weren't the only one who couldn't tell the difference between dreams and reality. So, how about we both skip the apologies, just forget it, and pretend it never happened."

"If that's what you want." Rick caught up and they jogged side by side. *But I don't want to forget it and pretend it never happened. I want to talk about it and figure out how much of what I thought happened in the last seven hours was real and not a dream. Especially if you coming apart in my arms and crying out my name when you came was real, so we can repeat it a few times, and maybe be more to each other than boss and employee.*

They jogged in silence for about half a mile before his curiosity got the better of him, and he had to ask her about the events of the night before to make sure what he remembered of them was real and not his convoluted dreams.

"So, is it true that Jax is gay and has a crush on Cage? Or was I dreaming all that, too?"

"Yes, that's true." Fiona's tone was relaxed as she answered, but then she seemed to tense up before she reached out and grabbed his arm, stopping them in their tracks. "Wait, you didn't know Jax is gay before I said something last night?"

"No." Rick shook his head in response to her question. "I honestly thought the two of you were an item."

"Frick-n-frack! I'm such a horrible friend! I didn't mean to out him, but Jax is gonna be devastated that I did."

Before Rick could reassure her that he wouldn't say a word, Fiona continued her tirade, talking with her hands as much as her mouth. "You can't fire him for being gay. That's discrimination and I'll back him in a lawsuit against you if you do. If he'll even talk to me after he finds out I mentioned his sexual orientation to you…"

"Stop!" Rick shouted, cutting her off and gripping her biceps to calm her down. "I'm not going to fire Jax or anyone else for their sexual orientation."

He stopped himself before he said what he was thinking. *Hell, if I were going to fire him for anything, it would have been when I thought he'd stolen my girl.*

"You're not?" Fiona looked up at him with a shocked expression.

Fuck! Does my displeasure at Fiona and Jax becoming fast friends come off as me being homophobic? Damn, I wouldn't think jealousy would come off as bad as that.

"No, I don't care who my employees are involved with, as long as they don't cause problems with the rest of the company by hitting on people who are already involved with someone else." Rick was getting hot under the collar at anyone thinking he was in any way homophobic and had to restart their jog to cool his temper as he ranted. "Gay, straight, bi, poly, trans, whatever makes people happy is fine by me. In fact, I extend the benefits of marriage to everyone I employ, regardless of whether their home state recognizes the legality of their form of commitment to one another. If you'd have met any of the same-sex couples in our corporate office in New York, or if the Inglemans weren't out while Tait rehabbed his knee and Kori has their second child, you'd know that."

"Who are the Inglemans?" Fiona asked as she caught up with Rick on the trail.

"Reid, Tait, their shared wife, Kori, and their son, Xander," Rick explained as they jogged along, knowing he wasn't disclosing anything to Fiona that the throuple wouldn't proudly explain to her themselves once they were back on tour with the GWA. "Reid and Tait use the ring names 'Cannon' and 'Missile' and are part of the Heavy Artillery faction with Taylor 'Tank' Olsen. When they first started with us, Tait had already changed his last name to Reid's because his parents wouldn't accept that he was gay and same-sex marriage wasn't legal yet where they're from. After a couple of years of touring with us, they met Kori and realized she was the missing piece of their hearts. Most of the company attended their commitment ceremony and now they have a three-year-old son and are expecting a daughter next month."

"So, wait, are they out for Tait's knee rehab or Kori's maternity leave?"

Rick had to chuckle at how quickly Fiona changed the direction of their conversation.

"Both, I guess." Rick half shrugged as he kept pace with Fiona. "Tait blew out his knee almost a year ago. But it wasn't like an ACL tear. It was the cartilage that was ripped from the bone. Anyway, he had to have microfracture surgery, which is where they shave off the damaged cartilage and drill into the femur to allow the bone marrow to leak out and regrow new cartilage from the stem cells. He's as good as new now, but he wasn't even allowed to walk without crutches for the first two months after the surgery and was in a knee brace for several more months. The doctor cleared him to return to the ring last month, but since Kori was seven months along it didn't make sense for them to come back for a couple of weeks just to go home again when Kori hit the point of pregnancy that her doctor said she couldn't fly to have the baby. But they'll be back sometime in April."

"So, now the whole family is home on Kori's maternity leave? How many months of maternity leave do you give your employees?"

"Technically, Reid and Tait are home on paternity leave, since Kori isn't on the GWA payroll. And before that, they were home on family medical leave for Tait's knee. As for the amount of leave, regardless of the type, it all depends on the individual situation. I leave that up to the medical professionals to decide and don't have set limits."

They continued talking about how Rick dealt with the absence of crew members when they had to be off on leave, from the restructuring of angles, when performers were injured or off having children, to the hiring of temporary employees to fill positions, like Anthony's, when the time came for his and Kay's baby to be born.

Rick wasn't sure how they got so far off from their original discussion as they finished their jog around the resort. He really wished they'd have gone back to it to figure out what was real and what was just him dreaming that morning and the night before, but he was glad their conversation had continued cordially without him worrying about her hating him for his early morning, sleep-addled behavior.

Fuck, I wish I knew if her saying she had a crush on me was real or just me dreaming, Rick thought as they went to their separate rooms to shower, change, and get ready for the rest of the day. *Unless I hear from her that she's actually interested in me, I can't pursue her. No matter how much my dick wants me to.*

Fuck! I guess I'll just have to continue keeping things professional between us, and let her make the first move if she's as attracted to me as I am to her. And hope she can handle my rougher tendencies, if anything ever happens between us.

~~~
~~~

Tuesday, January 29, 2019, 9 a.m., Flying from Nassau, Bahamas, to San Juan, Puerto Rico

As she waited in line to get through Customs to board the company plane, Fiona was torn as to whether or not she should approach Allissa to ask about sharing her room when they got to Puerto Rico. On the one hand, if she bunked with Allissa, then she wouldn't have to worry about a repeat of the awkwardness of the early morning. But on the other hand, she also wouldn't have the opportunity for more alone time with Rick.

But do I really want to risk any more alone time with him, after barely getting past the mortification of dry-humping him in his sleep this morning?

Fiona still couldn't believe her only man-made orgasm in half a decade was when they were both half asleep and didn't realize they weren't dreaming. She felt her cheeks heating, as she recalled shouting his name when she came from dry-humping him like a horny teenager.

Her only consolation in the whole situation was that Rick had also orgasmed from the experience. Although, she couldn't be sure he was dreaming about her being the woman he was with when it happened.

He called me Fifi when he came. She pondered what that meant as the line moved forward with some of her coworkers already completing the customs check. *That could be a cute nickname for Fiona. But the only other time he's called me that was when he was drunk in Vegas. And who's to say that was actually a reference to me, and not a former lover that he mistook me for while he was drunk or asleep?*

Since he only calls me Fiona when he's stone-cold sober and wide awake, I can't imagine he was referring to me with the nickname. So, no, he probably wasn't dreaming about me this morning. Which means I need to avoid alone time with Rick until we've both had enough time to forget this morning ever happened.

Fiona was momentarily brought out of her inner musings, as it was her turn to show her passport and have her luggage inspected. But as soon as she was cleared to head to the plane, her thoughts turned right back to what she should do about the room situation in Puerto Rico to keep from making things uncomfortable with her boss.

If only I could call Charlotte and ask her advice. She'd probably be hurt that I haven't confided in her sooner about everything that's happened so far. But I'm sure she'd understand my need to keep my feelings to myself for a little while, would forgive me for the delay in sharing, and would give me the best advice for how to handle my one-sided attraction to Rick going further.

Fiona looked around as she boarded the plane, contemplating whether or not she could confide in any of her new friends. *Who can I sit with that won't try to push me for details about last night with Rick? With the way they've all tried to play matchmaker here lately, probably none of them.* Her gaze skimmed over Kay and the other women on the plane before landing on Jax, who was deep in conversation with Cage.

Wow, maybe last night did work out for him to see if there's more than his crush between them. Fiona smiled at her friend as she walked by him, but she moved on to where Britney was calling for her attention a couple of rows back.

"Miss Fiona, come sit with us." Britney patted the seat beside her to indicate where she wanted Fiona. Tia was in the rear-facing seat across from Britney, leaving the two aisle seats open in their pod quad. The Staffords were across the aisle, which wasn't surprising since Connor and Cody seemed to follow Tia and Britney around like little lost puppy dogs.

Fiona stowed her bags and took the seat, buckling up before asking the girls their plans for the afternoon. She knew Jax was talking to them the day before about going to Old San Juan to see a couple of forts, but she didn't think the girls sounded too enthusiastic about that outing.

"It depends on if Mom's morning sickness stretches into the afternoon or not," Tia shrugged. "If she has to go rest in the bungalow, then Daddy might send us off with the boys to check out the forts while he stays to take care of her. But if Mom's feeling up to it, she wants to go to Casa Blanca."

"I thought Casablanca was a city in Morocco," Fiona mused, wondering if there was someplace in San Juan that had something to do with the classic film by the same name.

"Yes, it is, but that's not where we might go today," Tia explained. "Casa Blanca means white house, but the one in San Juan is actually the oldest residence in the city and was originally built for Juan Ponce de León when he was governor there, back in the fifteen-hundreds. Now it's a museum."

Fiona was once again in awe of Tia's vast array of knowledge. "Well, that sounds like fun." Fiona smiled at Tia before turning to Britney. "And what are you planning to do this afternoon?"

"Well, I'm hoping since you're still staying with us in our bungalow, maybe we can spend some more time in the kitchen." Britney looked up at Fiona hopefully. "Do you think we can talk Dad into that, since he has to go to the arena to set up for TV tonight, and I don't really want to go with Uncle Cage and the boys to the forts?"

"Oh, um, maybe," Fiona stuttered, her plan to ask Allissa about rooming with her for the night going out the window as soon as she saw how excited Britney was at possibly spending another day baking with her. "It can't hurt to ask, right?"

"Right!" Britney smiled brightly and surprised Fiona by reaching over to hold her hand as the plane took off.

While the girls mostly talked amongst themselves during the short flight, Britney surprised Fiona once more by latching onto her as they deplaned. Rick gave her a quizzical look when they walked up to him hand in hand to go through Customs in San Juan, but he didn't say a word about it.

"Dad, since you have to go straight to the arena once we're checked in at the resort, can Miss Fiona and I fix our own lunch in the bungalow? I wanna learn to make more than cookies while we have a kitchen we can cook in." Britney gave her dad puppy dog eyes that Fiona would struggle to say no to if they were directed at her.

"I thought you were going to Old San Juan with Cage and the rest of the kids?" Rick quizzically raised an eyebrow at his daughter.

"They're going to look at forts, Dad." Britney rolled her eyes and shook her head at the same time, making Fiona wonder how she could combine the movements without making herself dizzy. "We've seen like a dozen forts in the last year and the only cool one was the one that sank into the Gulf of Mexico. Since we can't snorkel around either of the forts they're going to see today, I'm good with skipping them."

Fiona struggled to stifle her laughter at Britney's reasoning. She glanced up at Rick just in time to see him suppress his urge to smile at his daughter's antics as well.

"I don't mind if you want to make lunch." Rick gave Britney another questioning look. "But you've got a couple of hours to kill before you have to be at the arena and making lunch shouldn't take up that much time. So, what else are you planning to do this afternoon, if I let you stay at the bungalow without Cage or I there with you?"

"Girl stuff!" Britney smiled mischievously. "It's not anything bad. Just stuff that I can't do with you or Uncle Cage around and need to talk to a woman about. And since I don't have a mom, I figured a female teacher was the best person to talk to about girl stuff."

Oh, dear Lord, what kind of hornet's nest have I just walked into? Fiona wasn't sure if she should be the one to have the birds and bees talk with Britney or not, but she could see Rick wasn't exactly comfortable with talking to his almost teenage daughter about it either. So, she took a deep breath to give her the courage to volunteer for the job, since Britney obviously felt more comfortable with her than with her father.

"You couldn't have had this talk with Nonna while we were home for Christmas?" Rick shifted his weight from foot to foot, obviously uncomfortable having this conversation while in the Customs line.

"I tried," Britney groaned, throwing up her hands in exasperation. "But she hasn't had a period since before I was born, so she has no clue what current brand of tampons is the most comfortable. And there's no way I'm using those pads that looked like diapers that Nonna has in her guest bathroom when I get my first period."

Fiona covered her mouth to keep from laughing at the mortified expression on Rick's face, though there were several people in line behind them that didn't. She was surprised to see him blush as his daughter continued describing the maxi pads.

"For one, they're huge. I don't think they would fit in my panties, even if I had to try to use them. And for two, if I could get them to fit in my panties, I'd be walking bowlegged from trying to straddle a balance beam between my legs."

Fiona took pity on Rick and interrupted Britney's dramatic display. "How about we save this talk until it's just you and me in the bungalow?"

"Yes, please," Rick groaned, looking at his daughter before turning to Fiona and adding, "Thank you."

After getting through Customs, it was almost two in the afternoon before they were done checking in at the resort and had their grocery delivery to fix lunch. Fiona knew she was short on time if she and Britney were going to make it to the arena by three, so she picked an easy recipe to teach Britney how to make chicken quesadillas for lunch. With the pre-cooked chicken strips and diced vegetables she'd requested, it only took them fifteen minutes to put them together and bake them until they were perfectly browned.

Fiona finally got brave enough to ask the little girl what girl stuff she wanted to talk about when they sat down at the little table in the kitchen area of the bungalow to eat their lunch.

"Okay, now that your dad's gone to the arena, what did you really want to talk to me about?"

"How do you know I want to talk about more than being prepared for my first period by knowing which tampons to use?" Britney gave Fiona a quizzical look.

"Because if you were too embarrassed to talk to your dad about your period and tampons, then you wouldn't have mentioned them while standing in the airport with such a big audience."

"Yeah, I guess that wasn't very smart, huh?" Britney giggled. "I wonder why Dad didn't figure out I already know about the right tampons and stuff from talking to Tia and Noelle?"

"Probably because he was too embarrassed to talk about that stuff in front of all his employees. Which makes me wonder how he's going to handle going to buy your supplies in the future." Fiona giggled along with Britney before confirming the brand she used was the brand Britney thought she'd want to try when the time came. Fiona gave Britney the extra box she had in her suitcase, so the preteen would be prepared without having to embarrass her father to go to the store in a rush when she got her first period, before redirecting their conversation back to why they were actually there for the afternoon. "So, what did you really want to talk to me about?"

"I want your help to find my dad a wife, so I can have a mom again." Britney's statement was so matter-of-fact that it stunned Fiona into silence for a long moment.

There was a lot to try to comprehend behind Britney's words that wasn't obvious from the simple statement. *Is Rick actually interested in getting married again? What happened in his relationship with Britney's mom? Why isn't Britney's mom in her life now? Does Britney want to find her father someone to love? Or is she just missing her mom so much that she's trying to find a way to fill that hole in her own heart?*

Frick-n-frack! How am I supposed to respond to that?

"Okay," Fiona finally replied, drawing the word out to fill the silence as she contemplated her next words. "I take it, since you didn't want to talk to your dad about this, that he doesn't know you're on the hunt for a wife for him?"

"Not exactly." Britney looked down at the table. "I've hinted that he should date and try to find a wife. But whenever I point out a woman I think he should ask out, he just says he doesn't date. It's been seven years since he divorced Colleen, and I haven't seen him go on a single date."

Colleen? Is that Britney's mom? Or her former stepmom? It has to be a former stepmother. Surely, she wouldn't call her mother by her first name.

Should I ask her to give me what she knows of her father's marital history? I'd rather hear that stuff from Rick, but I can't really help Britney deal with her feelings about her parents if I don't know the history that caused them.

I need to stop and think about this for a bit. I can't look at his past relationships as if he and I were in a relationship now or could be in the future. I have to leave my attraction to Rick out of this conversation and focus on what Britney needs. And she needs me to know the history, so I can help her deal with her feelings now.

"Okay, since I'm new around here, you've already lost me. Who's Colleen?"

"My egg donor." Fiona's jaw dropped at the unexpected statement. Britney giggled before continuing her explanation. "That's what Tia said I should call her, since she's never acted like a mother to me. She wasn't really acting like a wife to my dad, either. She had boyfriends coming to the house whenever dad wasn't home, which was pretty much all the time, since he was on the GWA schedule while she and I lived in New York."

"What? How?" Fiona sputtered, shocked at Britney's statement.

"I was five, not deaf, dumb, and blind." Britney rolled her eyes. "At least when she had her boyfriends come over during the day, I had a nanny who took me to the park. But strange voices in the house would wake me up when they came over at night, and I did not need to hear any of that."

Britney waved her hand in front of her face as if she was erasing a chalkboard, and Fiona wondered if it was her way of erasing the mental pictures of her memories.

"Okay, so they divorced seven years ago," Fiona hoped to redirect the conversation away from her mother's indiscretions. "Since you travel with your dad all the time, I'm assuming he got full custody of you. But do you ever see your mom? Like at the holidays?"

"No." Britney shook her head and slightly lifted one shoulder, as if to shrug it off. "I haven't seen her since the day Dad came home and kicked her and her boyfriend out of the house, while I was at the park with the nanny when I was five. But she was a bee with an itch, who just wanted Dad's money in the divorce, so I'm glad she didn't fight him for custody of me."

"A bee with an itch?" Fiona giggled at the twelve-year-old creatively calling her mother a bitch without saying the word.

"That's what Nonna calls her," Britney giggled and grinned at Fiona. "Well, what she's called her since I heard Dad call her the actual word and asked what it meant, anyway. She probably calls her the real word when I'm not around, like Dad does."

Fiona just shrugged, knowing she couldn't speak for the actions of others.

"So, since Dad doesn't date, I'm hoping you can help me figure out a way to find him a wife and me a mom."

"Well, it's going to be kind of hard to marry him off, if he doesn't even want to date," Fiona pointed out.

"Yeah, I know, but the only reason he hasn't dated is because I haven't found the right woman to introduce him to. I'm sure it won't be hard once we find the perfect woman for us. If we can find her, then he'll be able to see her and fall in love at first sight. Then they can get married and give me a mom again. And maybe even a brother or sister."

Britney was so confident in her declaration that she almost had Fiona convinced it was possible. If it wasn't for the fact that Rick had been so mortified that morning when they woke up and realized they'd been dry-humping, Fiona would have gladly volunteered for the position of wife and mother.

But he's clearly not interested in me, so maybe it's best if I help Britney find his perfect woman. It'll hurt to see him with someone else, but it'll be worth it to see both him and Britney happy.

"So, what attributes are you looking for in this perfect woman?"

"She has to be able to travel with us all the time." Britney started counting off her points on her fingers. "She has to be cool with spending the day with me when Dad has to be at the arena. She has to be smart and fun and ready to love me as much as she loves Dad. That's probably the most important attribute to me. I'm tired of being the only kid I know who doesn't have a mom, so she has to be willing to adopt me, and be my real mom when she marries my dad."

Fiona felt a sharp pain in her chest when she realized Britney was describing her to a T, but she couldn't step into the role because Rick wouldn't want her to.

Does he really want anyone to? Maybe I should talk to him about this? Clearly, all the qualities Britney is looking for are motherly qualities, not necessarily what Rick wants in a wife.

Does he even realize that when Britney pushes him to date it's because she wants a mom more than she wants him to have a wife? Probably not.

I can let her talk all this out, but I can't help her with her plans without talking to him about them first. Great! That means I can't go to bed at the same time as Britney tonight to avoid him. I have to stay up and talk to him tonight after Britney goes to bed, so he can figure out how best to help his daughter with her longing for a mom.

And regardless of whether or not he wants to go along with Britney's scheming for a mother, I can be there for her until the right woman steps into the role permanently.

"You're most like what I want in a mom of anyone that works for the GWA, so I figured you'd know more women like you to introduce to my dad the next time we go to Heart's Destiny. And since Miss

Leah Mae Wright

Randi said Heart's Destiny is the love-at-first-sight capital of the world, Dad will fall in love with her when you introduce them next time we go there. It'd be nice if you could come up with someone for him when we're there in February for the pay-per-view weekend. But if it takes a little longer, maybe we'll be able to convince him to go there for our next holiday break. Unless you like Dad and me enough to marry us?" Britney's impish grin stole the last of Fiona's heart.

As much as she wanted that, Fiona knew she couldn't get Britney's hopes up about anything happening between her and Rick. "I like you enough." Fiona smiled and reached over and tapped Britney's nose with her fingertip. "But I don't think your dad likes me that way. So, we'll just have to keep having girls-only days together, even if you find someone else to be your mom."

Though it'll crush my heart if you find her and she's not me.

"Deal!" Britney smiled. "And maybe you can help me figure out if River likes me, or *likes me, likes me* 'cause Tia seems to think he's too young to know yet."

Thank goodness! Preteen boy talk is much easier to deal with than adult relationships.

~ ~ ~

Tuesday, January 29, 2019, 10:30 p.m., San Juan, Puerto Rico

Rick wasn't sure what was going on with the way Britney rushed through her bedtime routine to go to bed in record time. If it wasn't for the fact that Fiona seemed to be dawdling in the bathroom since Britney gave them each a hug and kiss goodnight, Rick would have thought his daughter was trying to play matchmaker by making herself scarce, so he and Fiona could have more time alone that night.

Although, I guess Britney could be trying to push us together without realizing Fiona's trying to avoid me. Thank fuck, she didn't overhear any of the events of this morning to pick up on why that is, or tonight would have been even more awkward.

Rick finished cleaning up the dishes from where they'd microwaved the leftover quesadillas the girls had made for lunch for their bedtime snack. He smiled as he recalled how proud Britney had

140

been of successfully making them when she insisted he had to try them for their snack. Rick was surprised at how well they reheated and wished he'd have gotten a taste of them at lunch when they were fresh.

But there was no way I could have stayed at the bungalow long enough for lunch without giving in to my desire to kiss Fiona. Just the thought of her doing domestic tasks with his daughter sent strange feelings to his heart that he wasn't prepared to deal with yet, if ever. *And I absolutely can't touch Fiona in any way, especially after this morning.*

Rick wondered if he should apologize once more, as he sat there waiting for Fiona to finish her nightly routine in the bathroom, so he could be polite and say goodnight to her before going to change, knowing he'd only toss and turn in his empty bed. He knew better than to think he could stay up and try to watch another movie with her, but he couldn't make himself go to his room for the night without at least seeing her one more time.

Fuck! I'm acting like a dirty old man, sitting here just long enough to see what she's wearing to bed tonight, so I have the visual to jack off to once I'm in my room for the night. I can't be this guy!

Just as Rick stood to go to his room, the bathroom door opened, and Fiona stepped out in another pair of flannel pajamas.

How the fuck does she make the same thing Britney wears to bed look so damn sexy?

"Goodnight, Fiona." Rick started to walk to his bedroom for the night.

"Oh, um," Fiona stuttered, looking dumbfounded by his abrupt departure. "Can you, uh, give me a few minutes before going to bed? I, uh, need to talk to you about something."

Rick stopped in his tracks, not making it more than a couple of steps from the sofa, much less past her to his room. "If it's about this morning, I'll gladly apologize again. But I thought we were forgetting, and pretending it never happened."

"No, it's, um, not about that." Fiona shook her head, but her eyes darted to the doorway leading into the room she was supposed to share with Britney. "Let me put this stuff away and then maybe we can go out on the deck to talk?"

Figuring out that Fiona didn't want Britney to overhear whatever she had to say, Rick nodded in agreement and stepped over to the sliding glass doors leading out to the deck off the kitchen that had a great view of the ocean just a few yards away.

Hopefully, she can just quickly tell me what feminine hygiene products to buy for Britney, and we can both escape the night unscathed, he thought, as he took a seat in one of the lounge chairs on the deck.

Less than a minute later, Fiona was slipping through the sliding glass door to sit daintily on the second lounge chair.

"I, um, need to talk to you about my conversation with Britney this afternoon." Fiona wrung her hands together nervously as she spoke.

Yeah, their conversation obviously went deeper than the best feminine hygiene products. Rick sat there silently waiting for Fiona to gather her thoughts, or maybe her courage, to finally explain.

"Wow, this is even harder to talk to you about than I thought it would be." Fiona lifted her chin, looking up at the starry sky, as if she was looking for a higher power to come down from the heavens and say the words for her.

"I promise I won't freak out when you tell me what kind of tampons to buy my daughter." Rick smiled at Fiona, hoping to ease her anxiety.

"Oh, no, you don't have to worry about that." Fiona lowered her head to look him in the eyes as she waved a hand at him. "She'd already had that discussion with Tia. And since I use the same brand, I gave her the extra box I had in my suitcase, so she's prepared whenever it happens."

"Oh, thank fuck," Rick exclaimed, bringing a hand to his heart dramatically to lighten the mood with a little levity. "I was having a hard enough time prepping myself for taking her shopping for them later in the week, but I've been worried all day that I'd have to make an emergency run for supplies while we're on the island and wouldn't be able to get the right brand here."

"Yeah, I was kind of surprised you didn't ask me to discreetly add them to the grocery list for the concierge this afternoon," Fiona giggled. "Britney and I already have a plan in place to keep her stocked up in the future, so you don't have to worry about going shopping for them either."

"How much do I owe you for discreet tampon delivery?" Rick pulled out his wallet to cover the cost of the box Fiona had already given Britney.

Fiona held up a hand in the universal symbol for him to stop. "No, you don't owe me anything for that."

"But it's an expense I should be covering for my daughter," Rick objected, opening his wallet.

"Consider it payback for covering my admission to Mullme," Fiona argued, shaking her head and retracting her hand, so he couldn't slip a twenty into it. "Besides, I have a feeling the amount of money in that envelope from Vegas that was over and above what I actually won that night is more than enough to cover a lifetime supply of tampons."

Damn, I was hoping she hadn't figured out it was more than her winnings.

Knowing he couldn't refute her statement, Rick put the twenty back in his wallet and slipped it back into his pocket. He only gave her the slightest grin of acknowledgment that she was correct before changing the subject to keep from having to explain the extra money from Vegas. "So, since you didn't need to talk to me about tampons, what did you need to talk to me about tonight?"

The relaxed woman in front of him vanished in an instant, replaced by the nervous Fiona, who could barely speak when she first came outside.

Fuck! That wasn't my intention.

Before Rick could figure out how to lighten the mood once more, Fiona began to speak. "Britney actually wanted to talk to me today about helping her find a mom."

"She what?" If it was physically possible, Rick's jaw would have hit the floor at Fiona's statement. "Why the hell does Britney want to find her mom? She knows the shitshow Colleen made of our lives, so I can't imagine why she'd want to go through that hell again."

"Not *her* mom, *a mom*," Fiona clarified, placing special emphasis on her words to make them clear. "With what she said about her *egg donor* today, she made it clear she doesn't want your ex back in either of your lives."

"Then what exactly does she want?"

"She tried to present it as wanting to find you a wife," Fiona shrugged. "But in talking to her, it became clear that she feels like she's missing out on the motherly relationships all her friends have by not having a motherly figure in her life."

"Shit!" Rick tucked his chin to his chest and roughly pulled both hands through his hair. "My mom tries to do all that motherly stuff with Brit, but it's hard with our schedule."

"Yes," Fiona nodded in agreement. "That's why she listed traveling with you and spending the day with her when you have to work as two of the most important attributes she's looking for in the next Mrs. Robertson."

"She gave you a list of attributes for the woman she's looking for?" Rick couldn't believe what he was hearing.

Hell, maybe I should just be glad Britney hasn't already picked her out and started to plan our wedding.

"Yes, and they all pertained to being her mom," Fiona confirmed. "Well, one of them was that the woman has to love Britney as much as she loves you, so she'd be willing to adopt her. But that was the only time she mentioned you while describing this hypothetical woman."

"Well, at least she expects this woman to love me." Rick had to laugh at the absurdity of the situation. "So, how exactly does she expect you to help her find this mythical woman? And what did you tell her when she dropped all this on you?"

It was hard to see with only moonlight illuminating her face, but Rick noticed that Fiona blushed at his questions. *Shit! I bet Brit tried to recruit Fiona to be my wife and her mom.*

"I'm supposed to introduce you to any women I know in Heart's Destiny that meet her qualifications the next time we go home on a holiday break," Fiona admitted sheepishly before giggling. "Apparently, Heart's Destiny is the love-at-first-sight capital of the world, so you'll instantly fall in love if you meet the right woman there."

Fucking hell! She's not wrong about that. It's too bad I think it already happened when I first met Fiona, but she doesn't seem to feel the same.

Fiona looked down at her bare feet as her blush deepened before whispering, "She, um, also asked if I like the two of you enough to marry you."

FFFFUUUUCCCCKKKK! Rick screamed in his head, not able to even breathe as he waited to hear how Fiona responded to Britney's proposal.

"I told her that I like her enough to want to have girls-only days with her, even if she finds someone else to be her mom. But I didn't commit to playing matchmaker for you because I figured Hazel and Susan Burleson more than have that covered in Heart's Destiny."

"That they do," Rick chuckled to cover for his heart splitting in two from her not commenting on how much she liked him.

"Anyway, I just wanted to let you know that if you've been hesitant to date again because of Britney, you don't have to be. You might actually put her mind at ease by going on a date or two, so she knows you're looking for someone who might one day become her mom." Fiona was back to looking down at her feet as she softly said the words.

Fuck! If only I could ask you on a date, sweet Fifi, I'd probably consider that as an option. But I have no interest in dating anyone else.

"And I'm sure I'm not the only woman who works for you, who will be glad to spend some one-on-one time with Britney, when the other kids are off doing things with their moms. I know it's not the same as a motherly bond, but she'll still benefit from having some strong female role models."

"Thank you, Fiona." Rick reached over and patted her hand on her lap to show his appreciation for her not only telling him, but also for her doing what his daughter needed when he couldn't. "I have to think some things over and talk to Britney about all this, but I'd like to take you up on your offer to spend girl-time with her. Since I have to be at the arena all day on Tuesdays for live TV, maybe we can schedule that as your day with her?"

"Sounds like a plan, Boss." Fiona nodded, then stood abruptly to walk back into the house. "Goodnight. See you in the morning."

With that, she disappeared inside before he could wish her sweet dreams.

Rick sat there for a while, looking out over the moonlit ocean, and contemplating the events of the day. He wished Fiona had shown at least a little interest in dating him to see if Britney's marriage idea had merit. But he couldn't get a good read on her while sitting there in the mostly dark night.

Why was she as nervous as she was to talk to me about Britney's matchmaking plans? Was that because she's not interested in me as anything more than her boss? Did she think I would assume she is interested in me and is using Britney as her way in?

Surely, she realizes that I know she's not manipulative like that. I mean, we haven't spent a lot of time alone to really get to know each other. But we're around each other in groups enough for me to see how genuine and giving a person she is, so I'm sure she's noticed my personality traits as well.

And what about our early morning, dream dry-humping? She admitted to also thinking she was dreaming. Does she dream about me regularly? Or was it just last night after being stuck in our bungalow?

She called my name when she came, so I know she knew she was with me, even if she did think it was a dream at the time. People don't dream about having sex, or even dry-humping, with someone they aren't interested in. Do they?

No, not and enjoy it anyway. I mean, if I dreamed about having sex with Colleen, I'd be fighting her off in the nightmare, not enjoying it like I do when I dream about Fifi.

So, if she's dreaming about me, then she has to be at least a little attracted to me. Right? Then why doesn't she flirt a little or give me some kind of sign that it would be okay for me to flirt with her?

Fuck! What am I thinking? Her father is an overprotective small-town preacher. She's lived a mostly sheltered life. Any sexual experience she does have is minimal at best. She probably doesn't know how to flirt, much less subtly signal me that she's interested in me flirting with her.

Fuck! I've been waiting for her to make the first move, when I should have realized she needs me to be the aggressor. If I keep waiting for her to show an interest in me, then we'll never stand a chance of getting together.

All this time I've been fighting my attraction to her because of not knowing whether or not she feels it too, when I could have been working towards more with her.

Hell, I already knew I couldn't keep using Britney as an excuse not to date, since she's been pushing me to ask out every pretty woman she sees as a potential mom for the last few years. Now that she's made it clear to Fiona that she'd be okay with us dating, I really can't use her as an excuse not to ask Fifi out.

I can't risk a sexual harassment suit by being too overt in my pursuit of her, though. I'm going to have to take this slow, so I don't scare her off.

Smile at her more. Find innocent reasons to touch her, and hope she feels the same tingles I do. Maybe invite her to join me on more morning runs.

If I play my cards right, I might even be able to kiss her by Valentine's Day.

And maybe I can figure out how to take things slow and build up to my rough and rowdy fucking style, so she'll fall for me enough to want to try it.

Chapter Eleven

Rick walked into the bungalow after his morning run and was surprised at what he saw. Britney was showered and dressed for the day, sitting at the small table in the kitchen area of the open plan main room eating breakfast. Fiona was still in her pajamas from the night before, standing at the stove and plating up bacon, scrambled eggs, and toast.

The domestic scene before him made his heart skip a beat. *If this is what it'll be like if I convince Fiona to try a relationship with me, then I can't wait to make it happen.*

"Perfect timing." Fiona spun around and sat the plate on the table. "Have a seat and chow down, Boss."

"This time," Britney giggled.

"What's so funny?" Rick tousled his daughter's hair as he walked by her to fix himself a cup of coffee.

"I didn't time things right earlier." Fiona rolled her eyes at Britney and Rick had to stifle his chuckle at his daughter's annoying habit being used against her for once. "So, I had to eat the first batch before it got cold while waiting on Brit to get out of the shower. But I think I've redeemed myself by getting my second attempt at Brit's breakfast and now your breakfast timed just right, so it's warm and ready for ya'll while I go get my shower."

"Thank you, Fiona." Rick smiled warmly at her as he took his seat at the table and dug into his breakfast. The first bite exploded with flavor on his tongue, where she'd added the same peppers, onions, and cheese to the scrambled eggs that they'd used in the quesadillas the day before. "You didn't have to do this. I was planning on breakfast in the hotel restaurant before we fly out to Charleston."

Fiona shrugged as she put the pans in the sink and ran them under the faucet. "I had to use up all the raw food we ordered yesterday, so I figured this was the best way to do that."

"Well, at least leave the dishes for me while you go ahead and shower." Rick appreciated her efforts, especially as tasty as her cooking was, but he didn't want her to feel like she had to do all the domestic tasks.

"Oh, no, Brit's up on dish duty." Fiona shook her head as she turned off the faucet, dried her hands, and started walking toward the bedroom.

"Yeah, Dad, Miss Fiona cooked while I was in the shower, so now I get to clean while she's showering." Britney smiled as she scooped some of her cheesy southwestern scrambled eggs onto her fork.

"Division of labor is the only way we can get it done on time," Britney and Fiona said in unison before giggling.

"I take it that's something the two of you have discussed more than once," Rick chuckled along with them.

"Yep," Britney replied, while Fiona nodded as she went into the bedroom. A couple of minutes later, she carried a bag into the bathroom and shut the door without saying another word.

"Are we really not going to have time to go sightseeing today?" Britney asked between bites.

"Sorry, Britney Bear, but with going through customs, both here and when we get to Charleston, and having an over three-hour flight, we'll barely have time to grab lunch before we have to be at the arena." Rick hated disappointing his daughter, but he couldn't do anything about flight times interfering with their schedule.

I should probably start preparing her now for the crazy way our schedules are going to be affected by the long flight times and time zone changes when we go to Europe in a month, Rick thought as he ate.

"But don't we gain an hour by flying west?" Britney asked as she finished her breakfast.

"Yes, but that hour won't even cover the extra time for going through one customs office," Rick explained. "Remember, we got lucky with short customs times in Miami and Nassau, but when we arrived here in San Juan yesterday, it took us two hours in the customs office. So, if we get to the airport at nine, and have to spend another two hours in customs to get everyone through to board the plane, it'll be eleven before we leave. Subtracting an hour for the time change still puts us landing at one in Charleston. Even if we didn't have to go through customs again, it'd leave us with another short sightseeing window like yesterday here. And if it's another two hours in customs, it'll make us all late for the arena with no time to do more than grab lunch in a drive-thru."

"Oh." Britney's shoulders sunk as she picked up her dishes and walked them over to the sink.

Rick finished his breakfast while watching his daughter start to wash the dishes. It was the first time he'd ever seen her complete the task, and it kind of made him kick himself for not letting her assume some responsibility for cleaning up after herself sooner. *I guess, at least, I'm not still packing and unpacking her bags for her daily.*

Realizing he had other things he needed to talk to Britney about while Fiona was otherwise occupied, Rick put chores for Britney on the back burner in his mind. He carried his dishes to the sink and grabbed the hand towel to dry the dishes, so they could be put away.

"You don't have to help me, Dad," Britney objected to his assistance.

"I know, but I need something to do with my hands while I talk to you about something before Fiona comes back out of the bathroom."

"Oh, okay," Britney relented, her expression wary, as she handed him a plate as soon as it was rinsed, instead of putting it in the dish drainer with the other dishes she had already washed, and Rick had started to dry.

"It's nothing bad." Rick smiled at Britney as he finished drying the plate, and she went back to scrubbing the pan that had been soaking. "I just wanted to know if you enjoyed your day with Fiona yesterday."

"Yes, we had a lot of fun," Britney beamed.

"Good, I'm glad to hear that." Rick wasn't sure how to approach the subject without letting Britney know Fiona had told him all about their talk the day before. He wanted his daughter to feel like she could confide in him about wanting a mother figure in her life, but he was happy she'd at least felt comfortable sharing with Fiona. So, he didn't want to make it appear to Britney that she couldn't confide in Fiona without word getting back to him. "Last night after you went to bed, she asked me if it would be okay for the two of you to have more girls-only days together."

"Yeah?" Britney barely looked at him out of the corner of her eye, as she continued washing the pan while Rick dried the rest of the dishes. "And what did you tell her?"

"I told her that I'd have to check with you first to make sure you wanted more girls' days with her," Rick replied, inwardly smiling at the interest he saw in his daughter. "But if you wanted to, we could schedule time for just the two of you every Tuesday when I'm at the arena getting set up for live TV."

"Really?" Britney's eyes lit up with excitement, as she gave him a wide smile.

"Yeah." Rick returned his daughter's bright smile. "I mean, we'll have to limit it to just things you can do in the hotel if you don't want Cage tagging along, so you can have girl talks. And he'll still have to drive you to and from the arena, or if you want to go sightseeing without me. But I like the idea of you and Fiona becoming friends."

"Yeah, is that because you like her?" Britney rinsed the frying pan before handing it to him to dry.

Damn observant kid! Rick tried to hide his smile as he answered his daughter. "Yeah, of course, I like her. I wouldn't have hired her if I didn't."

Britney rolled her eyes and shook her head, as she turned back to the sink to start washing the baking sheet that had been used to make toast and keep the bacon warm. "I know you like everyone you hire. But do you *like,* like, Miss Fiona? Like as more than my teacher and your employee?"

Hell yeah! But I'm not telling my daughter that I've already started falling for her.

Although, maybe asking what Britney thinks of me dating Fiona might get her to open up to me the way she did with Fiona yesterday.

"Possibly, but I don't know her that well yet, to say for sure," he lied. "Would it be okay with you if I asked her on a date to figure out if we could *like,* like, each other?"

"That would be awesome, Dad," Britney whisper-shouted, obviously not wanting to alert Fiona to their conversation any more than he did. "But when would you ever be able to go on a real date with her, when we're always on our crazy schedule?"

"I was thinking on the nights you go have slumber parties with your friends, I could take her out after our shows." Rick almost laughed at the incredulous look Britney gave him. "What? Is that not a good idea?"

"No, that's a fine idea." Britney waved the baking sheet at him when she finished rinsing it, spattering water droplets across his t-shirt. "But with alternating who hosts and with both Noelle and Tia's parents being on alternate flight schedules, it's only once or twice a month that I stay over with them. No woman wants to wait a couple of weeks between dates like that. So, you're going to have to do afternoon dates, with me and Uncle Cage tagging along, like when we were in Tijuana."

"You think outings like Tijuana would make good dates?" Rick finished drying the baking sheet and put it away in the cabinet Brit pointed to while she drained the dishwater and wiped down the counters. "What if I want to kiss her? I can't really do that with you and Cage watching, like we're animals in the zoo or something."

"If you want to kiss her, then we'll look the other way, like we do when the other adults kiss each other while any of us kids are around." Britney shrugged. "But she's not going to want to kiss you if you don't spend time getting to know her first, so she should really go on every outing with us, even if you aren't calling them dates yet."

"Yeah, I was thinking the same thing," Rick chuckled, as he pulled his daughter in for a one-armed hug. "Figured I'd try to talk to her more when we all go somewhere as a group first, maybe flirt a little. Then once she's more comfortable with me, and if she shows she's interested in me by flirting back, then I'll ask her out. What do you think?"

"Sounds like a plan, Dad. But you might want to shower first because if you try flirting while smelling like a sweaty wildebeest, she'll probably run away before you can even ask her on a date." Britney pushed him away with one hand while holding her nose with the other. "Now I have to go change to get your stinky, boy sweat off me, so I don't reek the whole way to Charleston."

Rick laughed at his daughter's antics as he walked toward his bedroom to rush through a shower before packing up for the day.

Fiona didn't seem to mind getting sweaty with me yesterday morning. And hopefully, she won't mind getting sweaty with me in the future. Though I should probably start off by just inviting her to jog with me and work up to the sweaty, bedroom activities I'm really looking forward to doing with her.

~~~

Wednesday, January 30, 2019, 10:30 p.m., Charleston, South Carolina

Fiona was exhausted by the time she walked into the hotel in Charleston, South Carolina, after the GWA show. It wasn't that her job was exceptionally tiring. Working with the kids for a few hours a day was more fun than work. She was more worn out from the long flight, even longer time in customs offices, and gaining an extra hour to the day by flying west one time zone. Since it was already almost midnight in the city she woke up in at six o'clock that morning, she figured she'd at least not have to stay up until midnight in Charleston to be able to fall asleep as soon as her head hit the pillow.

She followed Rick, Britney, Cage, and Jax onto the elevator after riding with them from the arena to the hotel. She wasn't sure how rooming with them on the islands when they had shuttles to take them to and from the resorts had translated into her riding with them all day once they were back in the states. But she was glad that Cage would follow Rick and Britney to their suite to clear it before going to his own room, so she could have a few minutes alone with Jax when they exited the elevator on a lower floor.

"I, uh, need to apologize to you," Fiona stuttered as soon as the elevator doors closed behind them.

"For what, Doll?" Jax looked confused as they started walking down the hall to their rooms.

"I, um, accidentally informed Rick that you're gay. I thought he already knew when I said something about you having a little crush on Cage. If I'd have realized he didn't know, I wouldn't have said anything like that. I'm so sorry." Fiona knew she was rambling as she rushed out the apology and what it was for, but she felt so guilty for her actions that she couldn't slow her tongue once she got on a roll.
~~~

"Oh, Doll, there's nothing to apologize for." Jax laughed, giving her a one-armed hug, as they continued down the hall. "I'm surprised he didn't already know. I don't exactly hide it well."

Relieved that Jax wasn't mad at her, Fiona smiled at him, as she revealed what Rick had said the next morning when he informed her he hadn't known before she said something. "When he told me he hadn't known before I said something, he actually said he thought you and I were together."

"Oh, that is hilarious!" Jax roared with laughter. "Not that you aren't cute as a button and would totally be my type if I were into women." He shook his head at her confused expression. "I mean, it's hilarious how into you he is that he only sees you and not the rest of us whenever you're around. The poor man was probably too blinded by jealousy at how fast you and I became friends that he didn't notice we were ogling him and his bodyguard instead of each other."

"I doubt that's the case," Fiona objected, shaking her head as they stopped in front of her hotel room. "He was probably just too busy with running the company to notice. Besides, it was made very clear over the past couple of days of me staying in his bungalow that he doesn't look at me the way you seem to think he does, so he wouldn't have been jealous, even if his original assumption was correct."

"You mean, that scrumptious man didn't make a move the entire time you were staying with him?" Jax's eyebrows rose so high they almost met his hairline as he looked at her incredulously.

Fiona shook her head, unable to vocalize what could possibly be construed as a lie after her early morning, dream, dry-humping session with Rick less than forty-eight hours before. She hadn't completely figured out what all had happened yet. And she didn't feel comfortable talking it out with Jax when she had no idea how to explain it to herself.

It can't really mean anything if we were both half-asleep and still caught up in dreamland. Just because I was dreaming about him, doesn't mean he was dreaming about me. So, I can't consider his orgasm as a sign he's into me, when he could have been dreaming about some nameless, faceless woman. I was probably just in the right place at the right time to reap the rewards of my own orgasm.

"Wow! I'm surprised. Even Cage flirted a little, and after talking to him, I know it's going to take a long time, if ever, for him to be ready for more than friendship. I would have thought the boss would have done a lot more than that with the way he practically eats you with his eyes."

Fiona skipped over Jax's comments about Rick, choosing instead to get excited for her friend getting to flirt with his crush. "Wait, he was flirting with you, and you don't think he wants more than friendship? From what I've seen, Cage doesn't flirt, like ever. So, if he was flirting with you, then it has to mean he's into you, too. Right?"

"It was just a little banter and innuendo when we were talking." Jax waved his hand around and shook his head. "There were no accidental touches or longing looks to indicate he wants to be more than casual friends. But it was nice to talk at night while we laid in our separate beds, just to get to know him a little better. And I'm not giving up completely. I'll be his flirty friend until he's ready to explore more."

"Well, I hope he surprises you by being ready for more, sooner than you think he'll be." Fiona smiled hopefully at her friend.

"I'll cross my fingers, but I won't hold my breath," Jax joked, crossing the first two fingers on both hands. "And I'll hope for Rick to make a move on you sooner than you expect, too. Now, I must go get my beauty sleep. Goodnight, Doll."

"Goodnight, Jax." Fiona turned and opened her hotel room door. She was staggering on her feet as she rushed through her evening routine and barely flopped on the bed before she was out like a light.

Thursday, January 31, 2019, Charleston, South Carolina

After having to jog for his workout the past couple of days, Rick was glad to be back in a city with a fight school on the reciprocal use program with his gym in New York, so he could get in a more intense workout. He left his daughter asleep in her bed, knowing she wouldn't leave the room until he returned, even if she did wake up earlier than her normal seven in the morning.

As he was standing in the hallway waiting for the elevator, Cooper Stafford stepped out of his suite, also dressed for a workout. "Hey, Boss, you hitting the weight room early this morning, too?"

"MMA gym downtown," Rick replied, shaking his head. "You want to skip the weights this morning and come be my sparring partner?"

"Oh, hell, yeah," Cooper chuckled, as he pulled his phone out of his shorts pocket. "No way I'm passing up the chance to get you in the ring again."

"You inviting all the guys to come see me kick your ass in an octagon?" Rick asked when he saw Cooper texting as they got in the elevator.

"Naw, I know I wouldn't get this chance again if they were all there to see me whip your ass." Cooper shook his head, as he put his phone away. "Just letting Tiff know about the change of plans. She probably won't need to reach me while we're gone, but I don't want to take any chances on not telling her, and then her or the boys needing me and being worried when they can't find me where I'm supposed to be."

"Yeah, I get that." Rick felt a twinge of jealousy at the relationship Cooper had with his wife. If he was being completely honest with himself, he was jealous of several of the relationships of his employees. And that jealousy had nothing to do with the sexual side of those committed relationships.

Rick envied them for the way they all seemed to have deep emotional connections with their significant others, which he hadn't even really had back when he was married. It wasn't just the not having someone to worry about him if he wasn't where he was supposed to be either. He knew his daughter would worry. That was why he informed Cage the night before of where he'd be doing his early morning workouts. Should an emergency arise, Britney knew to call Cage if he didn't answer his phone. And the Traversons were her second call if Cage had to leave the hotel to find Rick.

But having his employees as part of his emergency plan with his daughter wasn't the same as having a spouse to care for, who also cared for him. He longed to have that bone-deep connection with a woman that made him want to share every minute detail about his day with her, and to have her share every minute detail of her day with him.

While he considered several of the guys he worked with good friends, he never had the connection with any of his friends that he often saw they had with their significant others. *Damn, I wish I could have that with Fifi. But as much as I want to have that connection with her, I have no idea how to develop it.*

As they got in his rental SUV to drive the few blocks over to the MMA gym, Cooper helped get Rick's mind off of Fiona. "Hey, I was thinking about ideas for TV next week, since it's our go-home show before the pay-per-view," he said as they buckled their seatbelts. "Maybe instead of doing the individual run-ins to make it look like the faces are all injured going into Sunday's title matches, maybe we could book a six-man tag match with me teaming up with the Dangerous Twins against Tank, Dark Chocolate, and Red. Then empty out the locker room for the final beatdown of all the faces as we go off the air."

"That's not a bad idea." Rick nodded in agreement as he drove the short distance to the gym. "We haven't had a good six-man tag match since two-thirds of Heavy Artillery went out on medical leave. And with not having another three-man faction in the last year, the fans would never expect a six-man tag, much less turning it into an unofficial battle royal to end the show."

"We could turn it around at the Massacre and have the babyface locker room clear out to take me out at the end of the night," Cooper suggested as Rick parked.

"No, we're ending the **Saint Valentine's Day Massacre** pay-per-view with the tag-title match." Rick was still shaking his head at James Hunter's plan to propose to his girlfriend in the middle of the ring after the Dangerous Twins lost their titles.

"Oh, you already have a finish planned to close the show?" Cooper asked as they walked into the gym.

"I didn't," Rick chuckled. "James wants to propose to Randi in the middle of the ring, since we're in San Antonio for their families to be there."

"That would probably go over better if they weren't heels. And maybe if they were going over to retain the titles." Cooper laughed as they finished signing in and made their way through the facility to where there were several rings and octagons set up for different types of fight training.

"The Twins can claim they're heels all they want, but they're really tweeners, especially since Randi joined them at ringside." Rick grabbed his sparring gloves out of his gym bag and tossed his extra pair to Cooper. "Hell, with Dark Chocolate and Red using a dirty finish to go over and James proposing center ring, the night might end in a double turn whether the boys want it or not."

"That might actually be a good thing with the women's division already being heel-heavy since signing Allissa," Cooper said as they each took off their shoes, put on the sparring gloves, and got in the closest ring to the bench, where they left their phones sitting on top of Rick's gym bag. "If Randi turns face with the Twins, it'll even things back out in the women's division. And if it's a double turn, then the tag division will stay equal, too."

"Yeah, until Heavy Artillery comes back in a few months," Rick admitted as they locked up in a collar-and-elbow tie-up to start their sparring session. "Hopefully, we'll find another heel tag team in the tryouts we have coming up in the next few months."

Cooper tried to slip his arm around Rick's neck to get him in a side headlock the way a lot of the old-school wrestlers tended to start pro wrestling matches. Knowing his friend's initial moves, Rick ducked down to evade the headlock and took Cooper to the mat with a double-leg takedown. By surprising the champ with the move, Rick was able to quickly move through a spinning toe hold to catch Cooper in a figure-four leglock.

"Geez, Boss!" Cooper tapped out quickly to get Rick to release the hold. "Aren't you supposed to be covered in ring rust after moving behind the scenes? With speed and agility like that, you should still be wrestling."

"Trust me, I'm plenty rusty," Rick laughed as he jumped back up to his feet and Cooper did the same. "Normally, when I go for these early morning sparring sessions, I can barely keep up with the young guys in the octagons. I only got the better of you this time because I knew what you were going to try first."

They went through another sequence, with Cooper getting the upper hand before the subject changed once again. This time to something Rick wasn't sure how to explain to his longtime friend and employee.

"So, what's up with you and the new English teacher?" Cooper asked as they were locking up for the third time.

Rick was so distracted by Cooper's question, he found himself locked in an armbar before he could counter it.

Unsure if he should confide in his friend just yet, Rick deflected the question with one of his own while tapping Cooper's arm with his free hand to get him to break the hold. "Why do you think there's anything going on between Fiona and I?"

"Um, let me count the reasons." Cooper held up his left hand and pointed to each finger with the pointer finger on his right hand as he counted. "One, she stayed in your bungalow both nights when we were in the Caribbean. Two, I saw the two of you jogging together in Nassau. Three, the way you look at each other whenever you don't think anyone else is paying attention. Four, Vegas. Do I need to list any other reasons after that? Even a blind man can see there's something between you two, so forget you're my boss for a few minutes and talk to me like the friends I think we are."

"I don't know." Rick threw his hands up to switch their sparring session from focusing on wrestling moves to more boxing punches and mixed martial arts strikes, so they could both remain upright while they talked. "I'm attracted to her, but I don't know if it's going to go anywhere or not."

"Why not?" Cooper swung a right hook that Rick quickly blocked. "She seems to be just as interested in you as you are in her."

"But she's ten years younger than me, and I'm her boss." Rick threw a jab that Cooper easily blocked.

"So?" Cooper tried an uppercut next.

"What if we give things a shot and then she decides she's not ready to sign up for life with an old man and a teenage girl? Or she's lived too sheltered a life to be interested in all the dirty things I want to do in the bedroom? What if we try dating and things don't work out? That would make work awkward for all of us. Do you realize how hard it is to find teachers willing to travel with us? It took me a year to find Fiona to replace Stacy. And six months to find Jax when we realized we needed a history teacher. I don't want to have to go through that again, if she decides to leave because she can't handle working with me after trying to be more than boss and employee." Rick punctuated each sentence with a punch, only half of which Cooper blocked.

"And what if she's *The One*? You know when you find *The One*, your bedroom proclivities tend to mesh together. Even if they aren't perfectly aligned at first, you make those things work for the one you love." Cooper went on the offensive, throwing rapid-fire punches in the same manner as Rick had just done. "What if she's the love of your life? Are you going to deny yourself life-long happiness to avoid the risk of having to hire another teacher? What if you're the love of her life? Do you really think she'll stick around forever if she has to pine for you from across the room every night in catering, with no chance of actually being with you?"

The thought of Fiona leaving the company because she couldn't handle working with him and not being with him scared Rick so much he dropped his guard, and caught a left hook in the jaw. Thankfully, Cooper wasn't punching at full force, so it wasn't a knock-out blow.

Rick staggered back to lean on the ropes, holding up a hand to stop Cooper from continuing their sparring session. "How am I supposed to know which of those is the most likely scenario?"

Cooper raised an inquisitive eyebrow at Rick, as if he didn't understand Rick's question.

"How do I know she's *The One*? I thought I'd flirt with her a little bit to see if she's interested. But what sign am I supposed to look for to know it will all work out between us, so I know it's safe to do so? How'd you know Tiffany was it for you?"

"There's not a specific sign to look for." Cooper shook his head before hopping down out of the ring to go get a drink of water, since Rick was taking a breather. "When you meet *The One*, you just know."

Rick turned to lean on the ropes and watch his friend as he contemplated what Cooper said.

Is it the instant attraction and constant arousal whenever she's around that I'm supposed to recognize as "knowing" she's **The One***?*

Or is it the possessive caveman inside me that "knows" she's mine and keeps wanting to come out and claim her?

Do our bedroom proclivities already align with one another because we're soulmates? If they don't already and we try to mesh them, do I give up the intense rough fucking and bedroom dominance I prefer? Or does she try to see if she can handle me?

Fuck! Could she possibly be hiding kinky tendencies behind her prim and proper veneer? Maybe I've been worried about her not being able to handle my primal needs for no reason?

"Based on that look," Cooper pointed at Rick's face as he walked back toward the ring. "I'm guessing you know she's your soulmate, but you're not sure you really believe it yet."

Fuck! Do I believe she's my one and only? I certainly feel more for her than I ever have for another woman. But, shit, I barely know her, so how can I be sure?

"I know I feel something for her," Rick admitted as Cooper got back in the ring. "But I barely know her, so I'm not sure what I really feel for her yet."

"So, get to know her," Cooper shrugged, as if that was an easy answer to all of Rick's questions. "You said you were planning to flirt with her a little, so follow that plan to get her to spend more time with you. I'm sure it won't take more than a couple of dates before you learn all you need to be convinced she's perfect for you."

Rick hesitated to respond, still thinking over his plan to pursue Fiona.

Rick's hesitation gave Cooper the perfect opening to rib him a little. "Unless you're getting too old and have forgotten how to flirt in your old age."

"We're the same age, Jackass!" Rick didn't hesitate to push off the ropes and throw a roundhouse at his friend to restart their sparring session. "And if either one of us has forgotten how to flirt, it's you after being married for fifteen years."

And I'll prove I still know how to flirt, starting this afternoon on our group outing to Discovery Place in Charlotte. I just hope Fiona is ready to start flirting back.

Chapter Twelve

Sunday, February 3, 2019, Washington, D.C.

"What part of the Smithsonian are we visiting first?" Fiona asked the question to the group as a whole, as they exited the shuttle buses that took them to the National Mall from their hotel halfway between it and the arena, where the GWA show was happening that night. She was unsure if they were sticking together as a group, or all going to separate areas based on what they were most interested in seeing.

"The kids all have a list of things to find in the American History Museum," Jax pointed out. "So, if we don't start there, we at least need to make sure they all have enough time there to find something on the list to write their reports about."

"We want to start at the Castle," six-year-olds Courtney Westbrook and Laci Kirby said in unison.

"Ugh, no castles," Laci's older brother, Dillon, complained.

"Sorry, son," Laci and Dillon's father, Donovan, who everyone referred to by his ring name, Olympus, said while shaking his head. Fiona still wasn't sure she'd ever be able to remember everyone's names, when all the wrestlers had two they used interchangeably when they weren't performing. "The visitor's center is in the Castle, so we have to go there first to find out where everything else we want to see is located."

Several of the older boys grumbled as they started walking toward the Smithsonian Castle. "Look on the bright side, boys," Stone Fields chuckled. "At least it's not a princess castle like in Disney."

A few of the girls complained about his comment, but Fiona missed what they said when Rick put his hand on the small of her back to guide her along the sidewalk as they walked through the snow. Fiona shivered from the tingles caused by his touch, even though they weren't actually touching skin on skin.

Fiona had to wonder if the small of her back was a little known erogenous zone, or if the overwhelming tingles she felt in her core whenever Rick touched her there were simply because it was him touching her.

She felt the heat of his hand even through several layers of clothing and her heaviest coat. She wasn't sure she'd ever get used to the way she felt whenever he touched her, even though he seemed to be doing it more and more since their group outing in Charlotte a few days before.

"Are you too cold? Do you want my coat to stay warm as we're walking between the buildings?" Rick immediately started unbuttoning his overcoat without giving Fiona a chance to answer his questions.

"Oh, no," Fiona replied, holding up a hand to stop him from wrapping his coat around her, since she wasn't actually cold while already bundled up in the one she bought first thing when she got to New York the day before she started working with the GWA. "Just somebody walked over my grave. I'm not really cold."

"Somebody walked over your grave?" Britney looked around as if she expected to see a headstone nearby. "I don't see any graves here. And why do you need a grave when you're still alive?"

"Not literally, silly." Fiona giggled as she playfully poked Britney with her glove-covered finger to get her attention when the little girl kept looking all around them. "That was something my grandma used to say whenever we'd shiver for no apparent reason. I'm not even sure what she meant by it. I just repeated it out of habit since she's not here to say it."

"Are you close with your grandma?" Rick buttoned his coat back up as they continued walking.

"I was." Fiona smiled at the memories of her time with her grandma. "Until she passed away a few years ago."

"I'm sorry for your loss." Rick briefly touched her lower back once more, as he opened the door and guided her through. After holding the door for everyone else to enter, Rick stepped up between Fiona and Britney, placing a hand on each of their backs. "What about your other grandparents? Are you close with any of them?"

Leah Mae Wright

"I never met my dad's parents." Fiona shook her head as they waited in line to get a map of all the Smithsonian facilities in the area. "And my grandpa moved to Houston right after my grandma died. He remarried six months later and spends all his time with his new wife's family. We hardly ever hear from him now."

"What a weird co-winky-dink." Britney grinned over at Fiona. "You only knew your mom's parents and I only know my dad's parents. We should start a club for people who only know one set of their grandparents."

"Maybe," Fiona replied, noticing a sign for tours of the Castle, and hoping to steer the conversation back to the outing of the day. She pointed to the sign, directing Britney's attention to one of their options for the day. "There's a Castle tour about to start. Do you want to do that? Or go to one of the other buildings first?"

Apparently, it wasn't just Britney whose attention was piqued at hearing her mention a Castle tour. Several of the girls started squealing in excitement at the suggestion. When the boys started grumbling, the families started to split along gender lines, with the boys going with their dads to the Air and Space Museum, while the girls and their moms stayed for the Castle tour.

Fiona felt a twinge of disappointment when she thought Rick might go with the guys to the Air and Space Museum and leave her and Britney with the other women. But as the boys led the way for their fathers out of the Castle, Fiona realized Rick was one of three men who stayed with the women and girls.

Well, duh, Fiona! She mentally chastised herself for wondering why. *Rick doesn't have a son to want him to go to the Air and Space Museum, so he's naturally going to go with his daughter. And Cage is going wherever Rick and Britney go because it's his job as their personal security.*

Fiona turned to look at Jax, who was the third man to stay behind, as the group started walking behind the tour guide. *And since the guys aren't going to the American History Museum until we all meet back up in an hour, Jax is going wherever Cage goes.*

She gave her friend a knowing smile as their eyes met. Jax darted his eyes to Cage's backside before looking back at Fiona with a huge grin. Fiona stifled her giggle at her friend, not wanting to draw any attention to herself or Jax when the kids should be paying attention to the tour guide.

They meandered through the Smithsonian Castle, as the tour guide told them all about the artifacts they were viewing and where they could see the complete collections in other Smithsonian buildings throughout the city. Instead of paying attention, Fiona found her thoughts wandering over the past few days of outings.

Rick seemed to be taking every opportunity to ask her questions about her life. It was as if he wanted to get to know her more than a normal boss and employee relationship allowed. At Discovery Place in Charlotte, he'd noticed her interest in the makerspace and disappointment when there wasn't a class available in that area for the kids at the time they were there. His observations led to a long discussion about the various things she'd made over the years after learning to sew.

The next day, when they were at Naval Station Norfolk for a bus tour before the GWA show on base for the sailors and their families, they talked about their family members and friends who had served or were currently serving in the military. Fiona's admiration of the man had grown tremendously when she found out that every show the GWA performed on a military base was free for active duty service members, veterans, and their families.

He didn't limit that to Navy bases, either. They had gone from Naval Station Norfolk to Dover Air Force Base, performing two free shows in a row. While touring the Air Mobility Command Museum and discussing their opinions on skydiving for fun, Rick had told her about the other military bases coming up on their schedule in the spring and summer. He also joked about making up the cost of the free shows by charging the politicians double the normal ticket prices at the shows in Washington, D.C., which they had every few months.

Fiona had been glad to hear they would be back in Washington in the summer, so they could tour all the outdoor monuments she wanted to see, when it wasn't so cold and snowy outside.

Wow, I guess he wasn't just asking about me the last few days. I've gotten to know more about him, too. Not just as a boss, but as an admirable person.

Too bad it's all been strictly platonic. Not that it could be anything but platonic with his daughter and the other kids around. But it would be nice to see a longing look, or have him ask for a moment alone to kiss me the way I've been dreaming of since I started this job. Or maybe have a repeat of our dream dry-humping that goes a little farther than before.

Who am I kidding? He obviously doesn't think of me in that way. All these getting to know each other talks, and his touching my back to guide me around, are just his way of treating me like another daughter, just like he told my dad he would.

I need to get over this school-girl crush and figure out how to keep my own thoughts about Rick strictly professional from now on. Otherwise, I'm setting myself up for a broken heart.

"Hey, Doll, come check out this Cooper Hewitt wallpaper." Fiona was brought out of her own head by Jax looping his arm through hers and dragging her away from the rest of the group to a display of reproduction wallpaper from the 1770s to the 1950s.

Once they were far enough away from everyone else that only she could hear, Jax whispered, "What's going on with you? Your emotions are written all over your face. And you've just gone from your normally happy, lovely self to looking downtrodden and sad."

"I'm fine, just thinking," Fiona whispered back, not really wanting to rehash everything at that moment.

"Well, quit thinking about whatever just made you sad. I don't like seeing my friends unhappy."

"I'm not unhappy," Fiona protested. "Just trying to be realistic and quit allowing myself to read more into other people's behavior than is really there."

"Is this because of the way Rick has stepped up his game with you the past few days?" Jax arched an eyebrow at Fiona.

"Rick hasn't stepped up his game with me," Fiona argued, though it didn't sound like much of an argument when her words came out so softly that Jax could barely hear her. "He treats me just like he treats everyone else. There's no game between us."

"How can you still not see it?" Jax rolled his eyes at her before vehemently whisper-shouting his observations. "That man has been a lot more talkative on our outings for the last few days, but *only* with you. And the way he's acting like the protective, possessive caveman, with his hand on your back every chance he gets to walk beside you, is so hot, he's going to melt the snow between here and the American History Museum, just as soon as we step outside."

Fiona shook her head at Jax's over-dramatic way of expressing his opinion. "While that may be hot, it doesn't mean what you think it does. He does the same thing with Britney, so it's obviously just him treating me like another daughter. The way he told my dad he would back when I first got the job."

"Oh, no, Doll, not by a long shot. With Britney, his hand is on her mid-back and all fatherly protection. With you, it's creeping toward your ass, like he's barely containing himself from grabbing a handful of your badonkadonk."

Fiona giggled, surprised to hear the term from a country song about a girl's backside coming from her big city friend, who claimed to not like country music. Before she could comment about his use of the term, Jax continued.

"Granted, he's extremely subtle with his flirting, but it's obvious to more than just me that he's trying to get you comfortable with him touching you in a friendly manner." Jax imitated the various ways Rick had touched her hand, arm, shoulder, and back the last few days to prove his point. "So, eventually, you'll be ready for him to touch you in a not-so-friendly manner." Jax backed away and waved his hand at her torso to indicate her female parts without coming close to actually touching her inappropriately. "And if your sad expression earlier was because you're trying to convince yourself that he doesn't want more, then you need to give it up and be happy to know that man wants a whole lot more with you."

"Jax," Fiona started to refute her friend's opinion.

"No, don't argue." Jax held up a hand to get her to stop speaking, probably hoping it would get her to stop arguing with him. "I know you've lived a mostly sheltered life down in Texas, but you have me now to point out when a man is giving you lusty looks. I know what desire looks like in a man's eyes, and that man wants you. *Bad.*"

Fiona really wanted to believe Jax's adamantly whispered statement. But even if she believed Jax was right about Rick's recent behavior being subtle flirting because he was attracted to her, she had no idea how to respond to it in order to get him to move past subtlety.

Jax's smile widened when she asked for his advice on how to flirt back without risking her job.

"Oh, that's simple, Doll, mimic his behavior."

It was Fiona's turn to raise an eyebrow at Jax questioningly.

"You've already done a little of that by asking him questions about himself whenever he's questioned you the last few days," Jax explained, talking with his hands. "Now you need to step it up by touching him a little more. Touch his hand or forearm whenever you're talking to him. Straighten his collar when it's flipped up or his tie when he looks frazzled backstage. And take his arm when we catch up with the tour, since you'll be walking up behind him, instead of him coming up from behind you to put a hand on your back."

"Okay, yeah, I can do that." Fiona looked around to try to figure out which way they needed to go to find the rest of the people on the tour, who had apparently left the general area she and Jax were currently standing in alone. "If we can find them without getting lost."

"Don't worry, Doll." Jax took her arm once more to lead her the way he wanted her to go. "I watched to see which way they went, so I'll help you find our men and all the ladies we're supposed to be touring with easy-peasy."

Jax turned out to be a very good guide through the Castle. They caught up with the tour group in less than five minutes.

Rick gave her a genuine smile when she looped her arm through his just before they finished the tour back at the reception desk where they'd started. Fiona returned the smile and enjoyed walking on his arm out of the Castle to stroll through the snow to the American History Museum.

Maybe Jax is right about Rick being interested in me, after all? But I'm still not going to hold my breath waiting for more than a platonic friendship with him, just in case he's wrong.

~~~

Tuesday, February 5, 2019, Pittsburg, Pennsylvania

After their short flight from Philadelphia to Pittsburgh, Rick surprised both Fiona and Britney by insisting on them spending their girls-only day at the hotel spa, since they couldn't do any cooking with only a mini-fridge and microwave in the family suites. Fiona wasn't sure
~~~

what to expect when she and Britney stepped off the elevator on the floor dedicated to the hotel spa, but it seemed like a nice relaxing place to spend the afternoon.

The reception area was decorated in soft blues and greens with a rock fountain in one corner to give the space a tranquil feel. They also had soft instrumental music playing that added to the serene ambiance.

"What all do they do in a spa?" Britney looked around in awe at the facility, as they stepped up to the glass-topped, teakwood reception desk.

"I'm not sure." Fiona smiled at the woman seated behind the counter. "But I'm sure this nice lady will be able to help us both navigate our first spa experience."

"I most certainly will," the woman said, standing to greet them. "I'm Britney."

"No, I'm Britney." The twelve-year-old Britney standing beside Fiona poked her thumb into her chest.

"Really? Darn, that means the appointment scheduled for Britney today must be for you and not me." The receptionist Britney snapped her fingers and poked out her bottom lip in a faux pout. "I was hoping my boss was being nice and pampering me, instead of making me work today."

"Sorry, but my Daddy booked the appointment for me and Miss Fiona." Britney waved her hand between herself and Fiona. "But if you point out your boss, maybe I can convince them to give you a spa day today, too."

"That's very sweet of you, but my boss isn't here today, so I'll have to try to talk her into it another day." The receptionist smiled warmly at them. "Now, I have Britney and Fiona down for our deluxe package, which starts with a massage, followed by a facial, manicure, pedicure, and your choice of hair services. If you'll follow me, I'll show you to the changing rooms to get started."

They followed the receptionist down the hall to the changing rooms, where she directed them to strip out of everything but their underwear, put on the robes and flip-flops provided by the spa, and lock up their belongings in one of the lockers. Once they had both changed and had their things locked up, they were taken to another room where two massage tables were set up side by side. They were given instructions on where to hang their robes, so they could each lay face down on a massage table and cover up with the sheets provided to prepare for their massages.

"Where are we supposed to leave the flip-flops? Or are we supposed to leave them on like our panties?" Britney asked as soon as the receptionist left the room.

"I doubt they want any dirt tracked in from outside between their clean sheets, so I don't think we're supposed to leave them on," Fiona replied after looking around and not seeing a designated space for them. "I guess we just put them under the table when we lay down, so they're close by for when we get back up, and are out of the way of the massage therapists while they're walking around the tables to do the massages."

They took off their robes to hang them up and get on the tables. "Miss Fiona, I think you were supposed to take your bra off, too," Britney pointed out as she crawled between the sheets on the closest massage table. "It's going to be in the way when the masseuse is rubbing your back."

"She said to leave our underwear on." Fiona felt herself blush at realizing Britney was probably right about her needing to remove the bra. "Do you think she just meant panties when she said underwear? Not both bra and panties?"

"How am I supposed to know?" Britney's response was slightly muffled from already having her face down in the opening of the headrest on the massage table. "I don't wear bras yet."

Fiona felt like a naïve idiot as she quickly removed her bra and stuffed it in the pocket of her robe before getting on her own massage table.

"Your bras are much prettier than Nonna's. Do you think we can convince Dad to let you take me shopping for some when we're in Heart's Destiny this weekend for the pay-per-view, since it's a safe enough town that Uncle Cage didn't have to come with us last time we were there?"

"Um, maybe," Fiona replied, wondering if Destiny Dresses carried training bras, or if they would need to go to the mall in San Antonio, where Rick would probably insist on either him or Cage accompanying them.

"Cool, it'll have to be Friday when we get there, since we have the Fan Expo on Saturday."

"That works for me, since I'm off work both Friday and Saturday and I really want to go volunteer at the shelter on Saturday like I used to before taking this job." Fiona made a mental note to call Louella later to ask about her stock before talking to Rick about the possible shopping trip.

"Oh, I almost forgot to tell you that you don't have to fix Dad up with anyone this weekend when we're in Heart's Destiny."

While Fiona was relieved to hear Britney no longer had plans to play matchmaker for her father, she had to wonder what had changed. "Oh, why not?"

"Because Dad and I talked after we made those plans last week. He wants to date you, so it would be weird for you to try to fix him up on dates with other women."

"Oh, no, you must have misunderstood him," Fiona objected, unsure why Britney would have that idea after their previous conversation. "I'm sure he just meant he didn't want to be fixed up with anyone, not that he wants to go out with me."

"No, I didn't misunderstand him. He doesn't know we were planning to find him a wife. He actually asked me if I thought it would be okay for him to ask you on a date. That's why he's been so flirty with you all week."

Fiona was floored by Britney's matter-of-fact statement. And really glad they were both lying face down on the massage tables, so the little girl couldn't see her reaction.

"He has it all planned out to flirt with you a little more each day until you start flirting back. Then he'll know it's okay to actually ask you on a date. Well, a date other than our sightseeing trips that he's trying to treat like dates with you for now. Although, it seems like you've been flirting back the last couple of days, and Dad's too clueless to realize it, since he hasn't asked you out yet. You might have to ask him out first. That is, if you want to go out with him. If you don't *like him, like him*, then I guess you can still introduce him to some of your friends this weekend."

Before Fiona could comprehend what Britney was telling her and formulate a response, there was a knock on the door and the two massage therapists walked into the room. They introduced themselves before getting started, but Fiona was too lost in thought to remember their names.

Rick has been intentionally trying to flirt with me? Because he wants to date me? And he's apparently talked over his plan to get my attention with his daughter. Jax was right all along, and I've been too blind to see it.

But now that I know he's as interested in me as I am in him, what am I supposed to do about it? Obviously, flirting back isn't working, if he hasn't recognized it since I started trying to reciprocate his subtle flirting in D.C., but I'm too inexperienced to know how to step that up.

Frick-n-frack! Aren't we a pair? Between my lack of experience and his reserved nature, neither one of us are good enough at flirting to make it obvious to the other that we're interested in one another. Maybe Britney's right and I should ask him out first to actually move us past this awkward subtle flirting, pseudo friend zone we've fallen into lately?

But when could we actually go on a date? Eating dinner together in catering doesn't seem like it would count, since the rest of the company is always there, too. And I wouldn't want to take away from his time with Britney in the middle of the day to go on a date while everyone else is sightseeing.

It'll pretty much have to be this weekend when we have Friday and Saturday nights off. But there's not really any place in Heart's Destiny to go on a date and have any privacy to see what could develop between us. Maybe I could invite him to my apartment for dinner?

I could pick up some steaks and the ingredients for a cheesecake on Friday while I'm out shopping with Britney. Then if I make the cheesecake Friday night, I'll have time to cook the steaks and baked potatoes on Saturday after volunteering at the shelter for a dinner date at home on Saturday night.

Would inviting him to my place be too forward? He won't think it's an invitation to my bed, will he?

I mean, I'm not opposed to sleeping with him early on in our relationship, if it happens naturally. But I'm not sure I want our first time to be in my apartment over my parents' garage. I'd be absolutely mortified if we were loud enough for Mom and Dad to hear us. And I have a feeling Rick has the skills to make me scream when I come.

Honestly, I'm surprised I didn't wake Britney up last week by screaming his name when I came from dry-humping him. I guess she really does sleep like the dead the way Rick said.

As the masseuse kneaded out the knots in her upper back, Fiona drifted off to sleep thinking about the possibilities for a date with Rick.

~~~

Friday, February 8, 2019, Flying from Little Rock, Arkansas, to San Antonio, Texas

Rick really wished he'd have thought to ask his employees where they wanted to stay for the pay-per-view weekend earlier in the week, instead of waiting until they boarded the plane to fly into San Antonio that morning. He already knew the people from the area would want to stay in their homes instead of in a hotel in San Antonio, but he hadn't realized his daughter wasn't the only person not from the area who wanted to stay in Heart's Destiny until their flight out on Monday.

"Hey, Dean," Rick called out as soon as they got off the ground in Little Rock and could move about the cabin. Rick motioned for Dean to come take the seat across from him when he looked up to see it was Rick calling his name.

"What's up, Boss?" Dean walked up the aisle before sitting down where Rick directed.

"I apparently screwed up by not reserving a block of rooms at the B and B for this weekend," Rick admitted, shaking his head. "I thought it wouldn't be a big deal when it was just Britney and I planning to stay there this weekend. But it seems like most of the roster wants to stay there instead of the hotel I booked in San Antonio. Do you think it'll be a problem for your mom to accommodate us on such short notice? Or should I just make the announcement that we're staying in San Antonio?"

"Naw, it won't be a problem," Dean chuckled. "After everyone had such a good time there at Thanksgiving, we thought this might come up when we realized the pay-per-view was in San Antonio. So, we made sure Mom reserved all the rooms in the Plantation House for the
~~~

GWA this weekend when we were home for Christmas. James also suggested Mom keep the same arrangement for each of our holiday breaks this year, so it won't be an issue for us to all be able to go to their wedding, no matter when Randi decides they should have it."

"Damn, that's some serious advanced planning," Rick chuckled. "And I thank you both immensely for saving my ass by booking it for me when I hadn't realized I'd needed to book it."

"No problem." Dean shrugged. "Sorry, we didn't think to tell you about it in the five-plus weeks we've been back to work since we talked to Mom."

They confirmed the plans for the tag-title match on Sunday before Dean went back to his seat to start working out the choreography with James, Liam, and Dion. Rick looked across the aisle to see his three bookers in a heated discussion and wondered what they were so riled up about.

"Stone," Rick called out to the man he considered his head booker because of his years of experience in the ring before he transitioned to booking the shows when he could no longer wrestle after an injury.

Stone Fields gave him a chin lift of acknowledgement, said something to Ethan and Ron, and finally got up out of his seat to move across the aisle to talk to Rick.

"Sup, Boss?" Even after knowing the man for years, Rick still wasn't sure if Stone's shortened word for "What's up?" was slang the way he thought he'd heard others using it, or part of his Native American dialect, as Stone had told him years ago. He'd always thought it was slang, but after fifteen years of Stone selling it, and a few other strange abbreviations, as a Muskogean term, Rick still wasn't a hundred percent sure.

"What's going on with you, Ethan, and Ron?" Rick nodded his head in the other two bookers' direction.

"Ron's trying to revert to his sitcom writer roots." Stone shook his head in disgust. "It's like he's forgotten everything he's learned in the last few years about ring psychology."

Rick was really starting to regret following the advice his father had given him that led to hiring a television writer without a wrestling background. He rubbed his temples to stave off the headache he foresaw coming when he found out what Ron was suggesting now. "What's he pushing for?"

"He's just not comprehending that angles in wrestling are supposed to last longer than one match." Stone shrugged.

"Let me guess, women's division?" Rick raised an eyebrow at Stone, knowing the issues he thought he'd quashed three weeks before were coming back up, since the only match on the pay-per-view card that was a first title match as part of a new angle was Allissa's first shot at the women's title.

"Achaffa." Stone grinned.

Rick sat and waited for his friend to elaborate on the meaning of a word that actually sounded Muskogean to Rick.

"You got it in one, Boss. Achaffa is Choctaw for one. You really should learn my language one of these days. Learning new languages helps to keep the brain sharp as we age."

"Yeah, I'm afraid I might have had too many undiagnosed concussions in my younger days for that to be an effective strategy for me now," Rick chuckled. "But I'll put Choctaw on my list of languages to learn right after I figure out Preteen and Teenager."

"Damn, you skipped over the easy languages to learn and went straight to the undecipherable. If you keep going for the hard stuff, you'll be trying to understand Women next." Stone grinned, almost getting Rick to chuckle along with him.

"I'd rather understand Ron's problem with the women's division for now." Rick's worry over the potential human resources issues of having a sexist booker working for his company kept his facial expression stoic.

"I don't think it's the whole women's division." Stone's expression turned serious to match Rick's. "I think it's just Allissa he has a problem with, but I have no idea what his problem is with her. She's one of our best workers."

Rick agreed with Stone's assessment of Allissa's high workrate. Because of holding her in such high regard, Rick had to get to the bottom of Ron's issues with her, so he didn't risk losing a main eventer from his roster. He didn't think Allissa would talk to him about any issues she'd had with Ron while the booker was sitting across the aisle, so he made a mental note to talk to her and the rest of the talent in the women's division in private meetings over the weekend.

He called Ron and Ethan over to make sure they were all on the same page for the pay-per-view card. He observed Ron closely as they discussed each match and its impact on the long-term angles. While he didn't argue his point of view with Rick, Ron's expression clearly changed whenever they discussed any match involving one of the female performers.

Surely, he's not such a sexist that he has a problem with Randi being at ringside for the men's tag-team title match? But if it's not blatant sexism, then what else could his problem be? Unless…shit! He could be pissed off at being rejected by one or more of the women on the roster. And not necessarily just the female talent.

Fuck! I'll fire him on the spot if I find out he's sexually harassed one of my staff. And losing his job will be the least of his problems if he's sexually assaulted one of them. Especially my Fifi.

Fuck! I'm going to have to talk to every woman on staff, and even the wives who aren't technically employed by the GWA, to make sure he hasn't behaved inappropriately with any of them. This is going to be an HR nightmare!

Rick spent the rest of the flight from Little Rock, Arkansas, to San Antonio, Texas, making plans to talk to every member of his staff over the next few days. He was determined to fix whatever issues he uncovered in his company.

He was so focused on looking at his calendar on his tablet to find the times to schedule the individual meetings that he stayed in his seat as the rest of the crew started to deplane. It wasn't until Fiona sat in the seat in front of him that he realized half his crew had already exited. Her shy smile instantly turned around his gloomy mood, brightening his day immensely.

"What can I do for you?" *My beautiful Fifi.* Rick barely stopped himself from vocalizing the term of endearment, as he tucked his tablet back into his messenger bag to give her his undivided attention.

"I actually have a couple of questions for you, but I haven't had a chance to ask you when you aren't too busy with other stuff to talk for a few minutes." Fiona looked nervous, as she tucked her long hair behind her ears and nibbled her bottom lip.

Rick wanted to pull that lip out from between her teeth and soothe it with his tongue. Since he knew he couldn't do that, he settled for smiling at her. "Ask away."

"First question," Fiona held up her pointer finger to start counting off the questions. "Can I take Britney shopping in Heart's Destiny this afternoon without you or Cage tagging along? And second question. Would you like to come to my place for dinner tomorrow night since we have a night off work?"

Rick was so surprised by the dinner invitation that he almost forgot about the first question. Before he could answer with an enthusiastic affirmative to the dinner invitation, Britney jumped on his lap, threw her arms around his neck, and started pleading her case to go shopping with Fiona. Rick wrapped his daughter in his arms to adjust her positioning as he listened to her.

"Please, Dad, I have girl things I need to buy that you and Uncle Cage don't need to see. And Miss Fiona wants to take me to the store where she buys her pretty, girl things, so I don't have to hurt Nonna's feelings by telling her I don't want to wear her granny version next time we're in New York."

"I thought we already had the tampon situation covered." Rick was confused about what was pretty about feminine hygiene products. And even more confused about why Fiona was starting to blush from the discussion of them when she hadn't before.

"That's *not* what I'm talking about, *Dad*." Britney rolled her eyes at him. "There are other things a girl *needs* to wear as she grows up that should *only* be seen by another girl until she gets married."

"Wait, we just bought you all new clothes when we were home at Christmas. Did we get the wrong size underwear since you didn't want me to open the package for you to try them on?"

Britney rolled her eyes again before looking over at Fiona. "Do you see why I had to ask you to take me? Dad's been single so long, he's forgotten what all girls wear under their clothes."

What the hell else does she need? The only thing I can think of would be a bra, but Britney doesn't have boobs yet to need one of those.

Fiona lifted her hand to cover her mouth, as she giggled from looking at his dumbfounded expression.

Fuck, she's cute when she giggles, even when she's giggling at my expense.

"You know what? You don't have to tell me. I don't want to know." Rick lifted Britney off his lap, standing her on her feet between him and Fiona. He reached into his back pocket and pulled out his wallet. He removed his personal Sapphire card and extended it to Fiona before putting his wallet back in his pocket. "I trust you to help Britney pick out whatever she needs and keep it age-appropriate without me having to see things I don't want to know my daughter is old enough to need."

"Absolutely." Fiona smiled at him as she took his card to pay for whatever they bought that afternoon.

"And you'll ride with us to Heart's Destiny, so you can direct us to your house before taking Britney shopping."

"Oh, my house isn't hard to find. It's right beside the church and I know you know where that's at."

Does she still live with her parents in the pastor's house beside the church? I guess that was an invitation to a family dinner and not a date.

"So, we'll be having dinner with your parents tomorrow night?"

"Oh, no." Fiona shook her head as her blush deepened. "I live in the apartment over the garage, so it'll just be us for dinner tomorrow night."

"Are you going to cook our dinner tomorrow night? Can I help you?" Britney's eyes lit with excitement at the possibility.

"Yes, I'm planning to cook," Fiona replied, smiling just as brightly as Britney. "And you're more than welcome to help me with it. In fact, I was thinking of getting the ingredients for a cherry cheesecake while we're out shopping today and making it tonight, so it's good and chilled for tomorrow. We can make it before I bring you back to the B and B after shopping, if you want."

"Yes!" Britney pumped her fist in the air before turning to look at her father. "Don't just sit there, Dad. We need to hurry and grab our bags, so we can get to Heart's Destiny with plenty of time for us to shop and bake."

"Lead the way, ladies." Rick motioned to the aisle that was now clear of the rest of his staff. As he watched Fiona's hips sway while she walked back to her seat to get her bags, Rick shook off his brief disappointment at realizing he wouldn't be alone with Fiona in her apartment.

At least it's a step in the right direction toward dating. And how can I be unhappy with spending the evening with both my girls? I can't. Especially when I want us to be a family one day.

He couldn't stop himself from grinning as he grabbed his and Britney's bags to carry them off the plane. He only came down from the high of enjoying his fantasy future family when they dropped Fiona and Britney off at Fiona's to go shopping, and he had to go start meeting with his employees and their wives.

Chapter Thirteen

Saturday, February 9, 2019, 10 a.m., San Antonio, Texas

Fiona took advantage of her extra day off at home to go to San Antonio to volunteer at the shelter. Since she was no longer responsible for any of the weekly tasks she'd previously performed there, she just dropped in at the time when she knew they would be starting the lunch prep because she knew that was when she could be the most useful.

She was surprised to see Charlotte was already there working with Antonio, thinking she usually scheduled her time working with him for after lunch. At least, that had been the plan back in December when Fiona was there to facilitate their first meeting, so their schedule wouldn't be thrown off when softball season started, and Charlotte's Saturday mornings were spent coaching.

"Good morning!" Fiona gave them a beaming smile when she walked up to the table where Charlotte was sitting with Antonio and his father, Roberto.

"Good morning." Roberto stood as she approached, showing his gentlemanly nature.

"Oh, don't get up for me." Fiona waved off his attempt to pull out a chair for her. "I'm headed to the kitchen. I just wanted to say hi and see how things are going for ya'll before I make it in there."

"Everything is going well. Thanks to everything you helped set up when we first got here." Roberto's smile widened as he sat back down next to his son.

"Antonio, can you say hi to Fiona?" Charlotte prompted, getting Fiona's hopes up for how far Antonio's speech had progressed in the six weeks since she'd seen him last.

"Hi," Antonio said shyly. "Fi. Fi." Antonio turned to look at Charlotte for assistance in pronouncing her name.

Though the little boy struggled to say her name, Fiona smiled at the way his attempt reminded her of the nickname Rick had called her.

"Fi-oh-na." Charlotte broke down her name into three distinct syllables and over-exaggerated the movement of her mouth as she spoke them to Antonio.

"Fi-oh-na," Antonio repeated slowly before smiling brightly at her and waving. "Hi, Fi-oh-na."

"Hi, Antonio." Fiona returned his huge grin and little wave.

They talked for a couple more minutes before she left them to finish Antonio's speech work, while she went to the kitchen to start the meal prep. She was warmly welcomed back by her fellow volunteers, who were glad to see her again after six weeks of being away.

Fiona easily fell back into the routine of chopping vegetables for both stew and salad to be served later in the day, as the other two volunteers in the kitchen asked her endless questions about the places she'd visited in her new job.

Halfway through the meal prep, Charlotte came into the kitchen to assist, bombarding her with even more questions about the cities she'd visited since they last talked. Once everything was in the final stages of the cooking process, the other two volunteers went out to set up the dining room, leaving Fiona and Charlotte to clean up what they could of the prep bowls, cutlery, and cutting boards.

As soon as they were alone, Charlotte's questions turned from general questions about the places Fiona had visited to more personal questions about what was going on with her feelings for Rick. Fiona filled Charlotte in on the time she shared a bungalow with him and Britney while in the Caribbean.

"Wait, so you actually shared a bungalow with him for two nights and *nothing* happened between you?" Charlotte raised an eyebrow at Fiona while standing there holding the towel she was using to dry the dishes as soon as Fiona could get them clean and rinsed. "I don't buy it. You've got that guilty look you get whenever your mom asks about what book you're reading and it's smutty."

"Well, nothing *really* happened." Fiona kept her eyes focused on the cutting board she was scrubbing as she confessed to sleeping on top of him the first night. "We sat up watching a movie after his daughter went to bed the first night. And after I told him about Jax being gay, he got really quiet. Like all conversation stopped, so I tried to focus on the movie. But the next thing I know, I'm waking up from a dream about him while laying on top of him on the couch. And while I might have O'ed in my sleep, he didn't even kiss me."

When Charlotte didn't say anything, Fiona filled the silence by rambling on about the rest of the intimate interaction she'd had with Rick. "I'm not sure if him squeezing my bottom was real or part of the dream, but we both admitted to rubbing against each other the next morning, thinking we were dreaming. He called me Fifi again, but I'm not sure if it was real or part of the dream. And after the embarrassment of his apology, while trying to get away from me as fast as possible, when his alarm went off and woke us up, I wasn't about to ask him to find out. Then we went for a run and decided to forget about it and pretend it never happened. Instead, we talked more about Jax, and his crush on Cage, and went back to our normal friendly interaction."

"And then Britney embarrassed him by talking about tampons in the middle of Customs to set it up where she and I could talk alone, so she could ask me about helping find her dad a wife and her a mom. So, the second night after she went to bed, I had to tell him about that. I had to rush off to the bunk beds in Britney's room as soon as I could, so I didn't volunteer to be the one to marry him and adopt her."

"And since then, we've only been sort of alone together in the car with Britney and Cage from San Antonio to Heart's Destiny yesterday, which isn't really alone. It was more like our outing in Tijuana that kinda felt like a date and kinda felt like family time. But all our outings since have been with other families going sightseeing, so we haven't really had the opportunity to talk, much less kiss or do any of the things I dream about doing with him alone every night."

"Not that I'm sure he'd want to do any of that with me, no matter what Jax and your matchmaking sister-in-law say about him being interested in me. Although, for the last week and a half, he has been innocently touching me as we're walking through various places and our conversations have turned a little more personal, even with everyone else around. Britney says that's his way of flirting, so I tried returning it to gauge his interest in me. But he didn't step it up even then, so I asked him over for dinner at my place tonight. I originally thought it would be a nice first date, but I'm not sure it'll really be a date, since Britney is coming, too."

Fiona sucked in a deep breath after not pausing to breathe as she rambled. When she glanced in Charlotte's direction to see her friend's reaction, she saw Char open and close her mouth several times, like a fish out of water. Not sure she was ready to hear all the thoughts obviously running through Charlotte's head right then, she decided to change the subject.

"So, what else is new with you? Anything interesting with Ian? Have you got the results of your DNA tests back yet?"

Please go with the change of subject and tell me about the long-lost relatives you're finding online after doing the DNA tests on your birthday, Fiona mentally begged her friend.

"No, not yet." Charlotte shook her head as she seemed to be going with the change of topic. "But we'll come back to what I've found on the family tree after we break down everything you just spit out at me."

"Can we not and say we did?" Fiona gave Charlotte a pleading look as she rinsed off the cutting board that she'd scrubbed so hard in one spot while rambling that she was surprised she hadn't worn a hole in it.

"No," Charlotte replied as she took the cutting board from Fiona's hand and started drying it. "I'm not going to make you tell me about every sightseeing trip or which ones felt like dates, but you are absolutely going to explain sleeping on top of him and how you ended up asking him on a date that might or might not be a date tonight."

"I thought I explained both of those things pretty well already," Fiona giggled as she washed the next bowl. "But I guess I can try again."

Charlotte grinned at her as Fiona explained once more how she fell asleep on January twenty-eighth in Nassau and woke up early the next morning in the middle of a dream about being intimate with Rick.

"So, you were really dry-humping him when ya'll were dreaming about having sex with each other? And you cried out his name when you came, and he called you Fifi when he came?"

"Yes, we were both rubbing each other while having dreams about S-E-X, but I don't know for sure that he was dreaming about me," Fiona admitted. "The only times he's called me Fifi were when he was asleep then and when he was drunk in Vegas. So, I don't know if he was referring to me, or if I just reminded him of someone in his past named Fifi when he was in an altered state of mind."

"What are the chances he'd know both a Fiona and a Fifi in his lifetime?" Charlotte shook her head as she reached for the bowl Fiona just rinsed off. "No, Fifi is definitely the pet name he calls you in his head. He's just not ready to use it all the time yet."

"You think?" While Fiona was hopeful that was the case, she still couldn't make herself believe it just yet.

"I don't think. I know." Charlotte nodded to emphasize her point. "So, did he O too? Or was that part of your dream?"

"I think he did." Fiona half-shrugged one shoulder, not totally sure one way or the other. "He had a wet spot on his pajama pants when he stood up, but he didn't really shrink much when he was still laying there under me afterwards. So, I can't say for sure that he did, since the wet spot could have been from me."

"Maybe he's a shower and not a grower?" Fiona barked out a laugh at Charlotte's crass question. Char laughed along with her before changing the subject. "So now that we know he's into you and probably O'ed from dry-humping while dreaming about you, tell me about asking him on a date for tonight and how it ended up not necessarily being a date."

"As everyone was getting off the plane yesterday, I went and sat down in the seat facing him and asked him two questions," Fiona explained as they finished up the dishes. "First, about taking Britney shopping without him or Cage tagging along. Then if he'd like to come to my place for dinner."

"And Britney wasn't sitting right beside him to think you were including her in the invitation?"

"No, she was back with the other kids." Fiona waved her hand behind her, as if she were indicating where Britney was on the plane at the time of the initial invitation. "But while he was thinking over his answers, Britney walked up and started trying to talk him into saying yes to me taking her shopping, since that was the only thing she knew I was asking him. Once he agreed to our shopping trip, he insisted on driving us to my place, so he'd know where I live. When I said it was the house by the church, he asked if dinner would be with my parents. I then explained it would just be *us* in my apartment over the garage."

"And you specifically used the word *us*?" Fiona nodded to answer Charlotte's question. "I wonder if he realized you just meant the two of you when you said *us*?"

"I don't know," Fiona shrugged. "But Britney jumped on the opportunity to spend time in the kitchen with me once dinner at my place was mentioned in her presence, and I couldn't tell her that I was inviting him on an adults-only date."

"Ah! I get it now." Charlotte bobbed her head. "And while I agree that ya'll need some one-on-one time, maybe it's better that your first few dates include his daughter."

Fiona was torn as to whether or not she agreed with Charlotte. On the one hand, yes, Britney absolutely had to be included in her time with Rick for them to have a chance at one day becoming a family. But on the other hand, Fiona didn't want her relationship with Rick to be all about his daughter, either. She felt guilty for feeling that way and she said as much to Charlotte.

"I feel selfish for wanting him all to myself during his very limited free time, when he would normally be with his daughter," Fiona admitted sheepishly.

"That's not selfish," Charlotte disagreed. "You absolutely need to have one-on-one time with each of them to develop the individual relationships and not just the overall family dynamic you feel like you're falling into when ya'll do things together. But with ya'll's crazy schedule, your one-on-one time is probably going to be limited to late at night after his daughter goes to bed. So, you might as well enjoy the family bonding time while you can and work up slowly to the overnight dates."

Considering Fiona preferred to wait until she really knew someone before sleeping with them, she found herself easily agreeing with Charlotte, even though she secretly wanted to progress things with Rick faster than she had with any other man. They dropped the subject while they served lunch alongside the other volunteers.

Afterwards, when they tackled the dishes once more and it was just the two of them in the room, Charlotte finally opened up about the last month with Ian. She rehashed the changes he wanted to make to the seventh-grade syllabus before getting into the details of their more recent interactions.

"Oh, and get this!" Charlotte exclaimed, obviously hot under the collar about whatever Ian had done. "He insisted on coaching baseball instead of softball, which was fine by me, so I don't have to coach with him. But instead of taking the normally scheduled days of Tuesday and Thursday field time for the baseball tryouts and practice days, he wants to use the field five days a week. It's frustrating enough trying to juggle our game schedules with the high school teams to make sure we don't double-book the fields on Saturdays during the season. But we've had our practice schedules coordinated for years, so there's no point in making our schedules more frustrating by changing up what already works."

"And what did he do on the first day of tryouts to try and stop me from arguing with him about it not being his day on the field? He kissed me! Right there in the middle of the field in front of all the kids coming to try out and their parents. Now everyone in school is talking about us being a couple."

"And Mom's matchmaking is getting even more out of hand. Since Ian's sister started working on the ranch and brings his son with her every day, Mom has been sending him to the barn every time I go out there. It's not that I don't enjoy spending time with Brody and teaching him about the horses. The kid is adorable and much more fun to be around than his father. But I can't go on a long ride to clear my head and destress because Ian insisted he can only ride with me in the corral where Cait can see him from whichever house she's working in at the time. Like I'm not good enough on a horse to supervise his son on a trail ride."

Fiona was glad to realize she wasn't the only one who rambled when she was stressed out and trying to deal with relationship issues.

"And Mom, bless her heart, thought she could fix the issue last weekend by inviting Ian to go on a trail ride with me, so he could see how safe Brody would be with me. That ended up being a nightmare because Ian, the idiot, would only listen to Anthony, JJ, and Justin the whole time we were out on the trail. He has absolutely no respect for women."

"And the guys let him get away with that?" Fiona had to interrupt her friend's ranting to get her to clarify what exactly happened. She knew the Burleson men would never allow anyone to disrespect their sister and cousin in the way Charlotte was describing.

"Oh, no," Char fumed, shaking her head. "He was so subtle with his selective hearing that I don't think they even noticed he was ignoring my directions just to get one of their attention later to ask how to do what I just told him."

"I'm sorry, Char. I wish I knew how to help you deal with him." Fiona felt bad for being frustrated in her slow progress with her relationship with Rick when her best friend was dealing with the aftermath of kissing another frog.

"Just listening to me rant about him is the most helpful thing you, or anyone else, can do for me at this point. But once I convince my vajayjay that there are other dicks in the sea, we'll have to schedule another girls' night out on one of your holiday breaks from traveling the world."

"Deal," Fiona agreed, laughing with her friend once more.

They finished cleaning up the kitchen at the shelter just in time for Fiona to leave to get ready for her dinner with the Robertsons, and Charlotte to put on a dress to go chaperone the Valentine's dance at the middle school.

As she drove home from San Antonio, Fiona envisioned how she wanted the night to go. She planned to put the potatoes in the oven as soon as she got home, so they had plenty of time to bake most of the way before Rick and Britney were due to arrive. Then she would teach Britney how to make the steaks that had been marinating since the night before.

Unless Rick wants to cook them on the grill instead of searing them on the stove and cooking them the rest of the way through in the oven with the last few minutes of the potatoes' baking time.

She planned to set the table on the little deck overlooking the park across Quarter Horse Drive from her parents' house. She wondered if they might want to watch a movie after they ate.

If they stay late enough for a movie, maybe Britney will fall asleep while they're there to give Rick a chance to kiss me before they go back to the B and B for the night. I might not be ready to have sex with him tonight, or even able to since I'm on my period, but a goodnight kiss sure would be nice.

~~~
~~~

"I don't understand. Why aren't you going with me to dinner with Fiona?" Rick was confused about why his daughter was packing an overnight bag, instead of changing clothes for their dinner plans at Fiona's house, and hadn't thought to tell him about her change of plans until right before they were supposed to arrive for dinner. "You're the one who accepted the invitation yesterday."

"Yes, but that was before I realized she was inviting me to invite you. And before Tia invited me to stay on the ranch tonight." Britney continued to pack, as if her statement actually cleared up her father's confusion.

"We already figured out that you can still stay with Tia when I drop you off at the ranch after dinner with Fiona. It's impolite to skip out on dinner with Fiona after accepting the invitation." Rick really thought he'd taught his daughter better manners than what she was currently exhibiting.

"Dad," Britney whined as she rolled her eyes at him and finished stuffing her clothes for the next day into her bag. "Miss Fiona wasn't really inviting me. Don't you see?"

"No, I don't see." Rick shook his head, ready to pull his hair out from trying to figure out what his daughter wasn't saying. *I really wasn't joking with Stone yesterday when I said I need to learn to speak Preteen, so I can comprehend what my daughter is hinting around at all the time.*

"All your flirting the last week and a half worked." Britney waved her hands around, as if she was presenting him as a correct answer on a game show. "Miss Fiona invited *you* over for a date. I didn't really accept the invitation because she didn't invite me. I just started talking about making dinner with her *after* she invited *you* over for a dinner date. And neither one of you corrected me about what it was supposed to be."

Huh? Rick was momentarily dumbfounded by his daughter's observation of the situation. *Was Fifi really asking me on a date? She did initially ask before Britney walked up. Did she just add Britney in because she started talking about helping to cook as if she was included in the invitation?*

Fuck! I'd love to spend the night alone with Fifi. But I don't want to make her uncomfortable by showing up alone if she didn't intend it to be a date.

"Quit thinking so hard, Dad." Britney reached up to rub the line between his eyebrows that she teased him about getting whenever he thought too hard about the angles he wanted to develop at work. "Just relax and enjoy your first date with Miss Fiona. And hurry up and get ready to go, so you have time to drop me off at the ranch without being late."

Rick wasn't sure whether following his twelve-year-old daughter's advice was his smartest move or not, but he decided to give it a try as he walked into the bathroom connecting their rooms at the bed and breakfast to freshen up for the evening.

What's the worst that can happen? If Fifi didn't intend it to be a date, we can still have a nice dinner and a cordial conversation. And maybe I can change her mind and convince her to go on a real date with me after one of our shows next week.

And if she did intend it to be a date with just the two of us, maybe I can finally get a taste of her.

After brushing his teeth and combing his hair, he called out to his daughter to ask for more dating advice. "Do you think I should change into something more casual? I could go with jeans and a Polo, so I look more relaxed in her home."

"No, Dad, you're going on a date, not hanging out with the guys after work. Stick with a suit," Britney shouted from the other room. "Change into a freshly pressed shirt from the wrinkly one you wore all day at the expo, though, so she knows you're taking the time to look good for your first date."

Rick decided to change into a fresh suit, too. *I probably should have planned my time better, so I could have taken another shower.* He shut the door between the bathroom and Britney's room, grabbed a washcloth, and made sure any place he might be exceptionally sweaty from the day at the arena was clean and dry before heading into his own room to get dressed.

Once he reapplied the deodorant he'd washed off from the morning, he got dressed and knocked on the door into Britney's room to let her know he was ready to go. They left the bed and breakfast to take

Britney to the ranch for the night, with Britney spending the whole drive giving him dating tips as if she was an expert at twelve years old.

"Remember to compliment her. And not about her looks. Women need to know you like them for more than being pretty. I wish I'd have thought to remind you earlier to get her some flowers or candy or something. But I don't think you have time to pick anything like that up now. Hopefully, she won't mind you showing up empty-handed because you can't blow this tonight, Dad. Not only is Miss Fiona a better English teacher than Miss Stacy, but I think she'll be an excellent mom for me."

Ah, so that's why Britney is so invested in this being a date tonight.

"You know Fiona wants to be friends with you regardless of whether or not we start dating, right?" While he was hopeful that he and Fiona could start a more meaningful relationship, he didn't want his daughter to worry about losing her role model if he turned out to not be what Fiona wanted in a life partner.

"Yeah, I know." Britney rolled her eyes at him as Rick rolled down the window to punch in the code Anthony had given him to get through the gate on the ranch. "And I'll be okay if she only wants to be our friend. But the universe shouted back to me that you're going to marry her, and she's going to be my mom and love us forever, so I don't want you to screw it up by bombing your date tonight."

"I'll try not to," Rick chuckled as he parked the rental car in the driveway in front of Anthony's house. He barely had the engine turned off before Britney was bounding out of the vehicle and running up to the porch, where Tia was already waiting for her.

Rick grabbed her bag out of the back and spoke briefly with Anthony to make arrangements for Britney to ride with them to the arena after the potluck at church the next day, since Rick planned to go earlier to make sure the floor was reconfigured from the Fan Expo setup to the ringside seating and hard camera setup for the live airing of the pay-per-view before the talent arrived to do a final run through of the card.

When he left the ranch, Rick drove past the church to head into town to see if the flower shop was still open. Unfortunately, Flora's Flowers was already closed for the day, so he pulled into the grocery store to see if he could find anything suitable for a first date.

Shit! I can't give her flowers or candy done up for Valentine's Day when I don't know for sure that this is supposed to be a date.

Maybe I should bring a bottle of wine to drink with dinner? Or not, because I don't think Fifi drinks alcohol. If she does, I've never seen it. Even in Vegas, she was drinking the virgin mocktails Kay was having.

Screw it! I'll just have to hope that showing up empty-handed for a first date isn't a deal breaker for her.

Rick promptly turned on his heel, rushed out of the store, and practically ran back to his car, rudely ignoring the sales associate who was trying to flag him down as if to help him.

Fuck! I need to quit freaking out like a nervous teenager going on my first date. All this rushing around is going to do is cause me to get pulled over for speeding and make me even later than I already am.

He checked the time on his phone as he pocketed it after he parked the car in Fiona's driveway. *Seven o'clock! Shit! She probably thinks she's been stood up, since I didn't make it between six and six-thirty as we planned.*

He took the stairs on the side of the garage two at a time, not wanting to be another minute late. In his haste, he rapped his knuckles on the door harder than he intended.

"Sorry, I'm late…" Rick's voice trailed off only a nanosecond after Fiona opened the door. The sight of her in a baby blue dress with a much lower neckline than anything he'd seen her in before took his breath away. He wanted to compliment her on how nice she looked, but he remembered what Britney had told him about complimenting her on things other than her looks, so he bit back the comment.

"No problem. I knew you might be late with the traffic coming from San Antonio." Fiona smiled brightly as she stepped back to allow him entry into her home. "But I'm afraid Britney's already missed the food prep. Where is Britney?"

Fiona stuck her head out the door to look for his daughter after noticing she hadn't followed him into the apartment.

"She's actually at the Burleson Ranch. That's why I'm late," Rick admitted, unsure how much of the earlier conversation with his daughter he should mention to Fiona.

"Oh." Fiona shut the door and stood there looking confused. Rick couldn't tell if she was disappointed that Britney wasn't there or not.

"I'm sorry, I should have called to make sure you still wanted me to come over when she changed her plans for tonight," Rick apologized, hoping she wasn't really upset by Britney bailing. "But she literally sprung it on me as we were walking into our rooms at the B and B to change for dinner, and I was so rushed trying to get ready while she packed her overnight bag and trying to drop her off and not be late that I didn't think to call and tell you about the change of plans."

"Oh, no, don't worry about it," Fiona waved off his apology as she stepped past him into the kitchen area of the open floor plan apartment. "Of course, she'd rather go hang out with Tia on the ranch than be the only kid here in my boring apartment."

Fiona picked up a pot holder that looked like a quilt he'd seen in the Pioneer Museum in Salt Lake City a month before, opened the oven, and bent over to remove a couple of baking dishes. As tempting as it was to stare at her curvy ass with her in the perfect position for him to take her from behind, Rick turned to look around the apartment to see her quaint country style of decorating. It was the exact opposite of the sleek modern style of his penthouse at Central Park West, but the softer, feminine furnishings felt a lot homier than anything in his condo.

The smell of fresh bread mixed with steak hit him at the same time he heard the oven door close. "Everything smells delicious." Rick turned back toward the kitchen and smiled at Fiona.

"I hope you're hungry." Fiona blushed beautifully as she looked at the feast she had spread out on top of the stove. "I may have made too much food from not thinking about the fact that we're leaving town in a couple of days, and I won't have time to finish off all the leftovers."

"I will gladly go buy a cooler to carry any leftovers on the plane Monday morning, if we don't finish it all off tonight," Rick chuckled, causing Fiona to giggle along with him.

After only a brief moment of awkwardness as they shuffled around her small kitchen to make their plates, they settled on her deck to eat the best meal Rick had eaten in a long time. He couldn't contain his moan of pleasure as his first bite of medium-well steak practically melted on his tongue. "Are you sure your degree is in English?"

Fiona gave him a quizzical look as she chewed the bite of potato she'd just taken.

"From the taste of this…" Rick held up his next bite on the end of his fork to demonstrate what he was referring to. "I think you actually went to culinary school. You've made a meal more delicious than anything I've ever had in a five-star restaurant."

Fiona lifted her napkin to her lips as she shook her head. "Please, it's good, but it's not that good."

Rick was jealous of the napkin for being able to wipe the slightest bit of sour cream from her lips when he wished he could lean over and lick it off with his tongue. "It is that good. You might have missed your calling as a chef."

"Oh, no, absolutely not," Fiona argued after returning her napkin to her lap and starting to cut into her steak. "I only learned to cook because Mom insisted on teaching me. But teaching is definitely my calling."

"Considering Britney just mentioned what a good teacher you are as we were leaving the B and B this evening, I guess I have to concede that point."

"That's high praise coming from a future Pulitzer Prize winning author." Fiona smiled between bites.

"What?" Rick was confused by Fiona's statement.

"Britney." Fiona punctuated her statement of his daughter's name with a wave of her fork. "She wants to be an author when she grows up. Her short stories are already excellent, so I can see that she'll be a contender for the Pulitzer Women's Prize for Fiction if she continues to strive toward that goal in life."

"I didn't know that." Rick leaned back in his chair, taken aback at hearing his daughter's goal in life from her teacher instead of from Britney herself. "I mean, I've always known she has a vivid imagination. But I didn't know she wanted to use it for her future career. That must be your influence in praising her writing assignments."

"Oh, no, she told Jax and me about that goal on our flight to Tijuana," Fiona disagreed, shaking her head at him. "I think Kay being able to write while maintaining the GWA schedule is what showed her it would be possible for her to be able to be an author while still taking over for you when you retire."

"Please tell me she hasn't read any of the stuff Kay's been writing." Rick felt his blood pressure shoot through the roof at the thought of his twelve-year-old daughter reading the adult content he'd heard Kay was writing about.

"No, she hasn't." Fiona reached over to pat his hand reassuringly. Rick took advantage of the situation to turn his hand over on the table to clasp hers as she continued. "In fact, after hearing that she'd been collaborating with Kay, I read Brie's latest release before adding it to the kids' reading list just to make sure it was age appropriate."

"Thank you." Rick squeezed Fiona's hand lightly in appreciation. "I think trying to play matchmaker tonight is as much as I can handle my daughter learning from Kay's foray into romance writing."

"I wondered if that was why Britney suddenly had other plans tonight." Fiona looked shyly down at their joined hands. "Especially after our conversation on Tuesday, when she told me I didn't need to introduce you to other women this weekend."

"Ah, so that's why I haven't had a harem paraded in front of me this weekend," Rick chuckled, readjusting his grip on her hand, so he could rub his thumb over her wrist. "Did she give you a reason why she changed her mind about finding me a wife?"

"She did." Fiona's blush deepened as she looked down at her plate and he felt her pulse quicken under his thumb. "But I'm not sure I believe it."

"I doubt my daughter lied to you." Rick pulled his hand back, suddenly feeling defensive of his daughter.

"No, I don't think she lied." Fiona's bright green eyes were wide when she looked up at him then, obviously realizing she'd touched a nerve with her words. "But I think she might be projecting her wishes on you without realizing you don't feel the same way she does."

"What *exactly* did she say?" Rick's question came out in a sharper tone than he intended.

"She said that you want to date me, so it would be weird for me to fix you up on dates with other women." Fiona wouldn't meet his gaze as she spoke. "But I think she's confused…"

"She's not confused," Rick interrupted Fiona. He reached across the table and lifted her chin, forcing her to look him in the eyes as he continued. "I do want to date you, and I asked Britney what she thought about the possibility on our last morning in Puerto Rico while you were in the shower."

"You, uh, okay." Fiona's eyes widened before she closed them and took a deep breath.

Rick slipped his hand from under her chin to wrap his fingers around the nape of her neck, stroked her jaw with his thumb, and gave her a moment to gather her thoughts before he broke the silence between them. "I only let Britney get away with skipping dinner tonight because I hoped she was right when she told me she thought your invitation was only intended for me. I thought this might be our first date. But if you hadn't thought of it as a date, then I hoped to use our friendly dinner to convince you to go on a date with me."

"I had originally intended it to be a date," Fiona admitted, her emerald eyes opening to meet his and sparkling with something he couldn't quite read. "But when Britney asked if she could help me cook, I realized it was probably best that it wasn't a date, since my parents are only about fifty feet away and could interrupt us at any moment."

She reached up and gripped his wrist, pulling his hand back down to the table before slipping her delicate hand in his once more. "That's why, when you showed up without Britney tonight, I decided it was best to eat out here." She waved her free arm around at the deck they were seated on and the outside space surrounding them. "So, if Mom or Dad do pop over to see who's here, there's no chance that they could interrupt a wide awake version of our dreaming the other day."

"Smart thinking," Rick chuckled before using his free hand to pick up his fork to continue eating. "I definitely wouldn't want your parents to interrupt anything like that."

"Not that I think we'd go that far on a first date," Fiona backtracked, blushing as she swapped her right hand for her left in his, so she, too, could continue eating her dinner.

"No, of course not." Rick repositioned their hands, so he could rub his thumb over her pulse point once more, enjoying the way her heartbeat seemed to speed up under his touch. "If you agree to go out with me, we'll take things as slow or as fast as you feel comfortable."

"We should probably get to know each other a little better before we decide how fast or slow we go." Fiona looked down at her plate once more, seeming like she was trying to hide from him as she said her next words. "I wouldn't want to make things awkward between us by going too far too fast and then learning something that prevents our relationship from continuing. I like Britney too much to risk my friendship with her."

"I understand and I agree." Though his dick was arguing for them to speed things up by throbbing in his pants, Rick knew it was in all their best interests to take things nice and slow with Fiona. "Britney needs you to continue being a positive female role model for her, so I don't want to do anything that might make you uncomfortable sticking around as her teacher and friend."

But, fuck, I hope you and I progress to a lot more than friends.

"So, what do you want to know about me?" Rick raised an eyebrow at her as he asked the question, thinking they'd both already started getting to know one another better in their quiet conversations while sightseeing.

Fiona tilted her head inquisitively as she observed him while she finished chewing the bite she'd just taken. Rick took another bite of his loaded baked potato to give her time to swallow before starting to question him.

Fuck! Don't think of her swallowing, dumbass! Rick mentally chastised himself when his cock overrode his self-control and started to swell in his pants.

"What's your favorite color?" Fiona finally looked up at him before taking another bite.

Before that moment, Rick would have said his favorite color was blue. But right then, looking at her in her pale blue dress was giving him blue balls, so he surprised himself when he said the only other color that popped into his head. "Emerald-green, like your eyes. They were actually the first thing I noticed about you when you came for your interview."

Fiona's flush spread from her cheeks, down her neck, to the sweetheart neckline of her dress that barely allowed him to see the top swell of her breasts. Rick fought to keep his eyes on hers. As much as he wanted to see just how far down her skin pinkened, he didn't want to make her uncomfortable by leering at her like the dirty old man he felt like whenever he was around her.

To keep the conversation flowing, and so as not to prolong her embarrassment, Rick turned the question back to her. "What's yours?"

"Pretty much any shade of pink, which is probably obvious if you look around inside and see I have at least a little pink in everything

I've bought to decorate." Fiona waved her hand toward the sliding glass doors leading inside. "I tried to make it look a little more grown-up by using it as an accent color with sage green being the primary color of everything in the kitchen and living room, but my bedroom and bathroom still give me away as never outgrowing my pink, princess stage from childhood."

Rick's smile widened at her open admittance of retaining some of her childhood favorites. *I wonder if that's why she has such an air of innocence about her?*

"What other favorites do you have?" Fiona's question brought him back to the moment. "Books? Movies? Music? Food?"

"I think you've already picked up on my favorite foods." Rick motioned to his empty plate.

"You do seem to gravitate to the meat and potatoes every night in catering," Fiona shrugged. "And I picked the cherry cheesecake for dessert because it's the only sweet I've seen you eat, other than when Britney makes cookies."

"It's not that I don't like sweets." Rick leaned back and rubbed his belly. "I just got in the habit of avoiding them years ago to stay in shape for the ring and never really added them back in when I quit wrestling every night. But yeah, cherry cheesecake is my favorite dessert and the one thing I could never resist over the years. As for meals, steak and baked potatoes are number one, followed closely by roast beef with potatoes, carrots, and gravy. What about you?"

"I actually made my favorite meal for you tonight." Fiona motioned to their plates. "But chocolate cream pie is my favorite dessert."

They spent the rest of the evening discussing their favorite things, finding they had a lot more in common than Rick expected with their ten-year age difference. The areas where their tastes differed were more likely because of where and how they were raised than the decade separating their ages.

Even though she listed several country and gospel songs among her go-to playlists, as he had expected all of her favorites to be based on being raised in a religious family in Texas, she had apparently listened to a lot of rock bands during her college years in Austin and actually classified rock as her favorite genre of music. Rick had also picked rock as his favorite, though he also listened to a mix of rock, hip hop, and rap in his younger days and their rock song favorites were from different decades.

While he didn't read as voraciously as she did, and she was more open to reading romance novels than he was, they both enjoyed novels with an element of suspense when they read. They also both picked popular mysteries as their favorite novels.

They moved inside to have their dessert when Fiona's parents popped over to find out whose car was in the driveway, since neither of them recognized his rental. Dale and Kathy Harrison ended up joining them as they ate the most delicious cherry cheesecake Rick had ever tasted.

While their conversation was pleasant, Rick still felt like a teenage boy being caught lusting after the preacher's daughter. So, he decided to make his exit without attempting a goodnight kiss as he'd originally hoped for that night.

I should probably wait until she instigates it first anyway, he thought as he made his way back to the Hunters' Bed and Breakfast for the night. Not being able to kiss her yet didn't stop him from jacking off to thoughts of her as soon as he was alone in his room, though.

Chapter Fourteen

Fiona was starting to feel frustrated by the lack of progress in her relationship with Rick as she boarded the company plane in Oklahoma City to fly to Kansas City for the day. Everything seemed to be going well on Saturday evening, when they'd both admitted to wanting the night to be a date. He'd even held her hand during the majority of their meal together. She assumed that the only reason he hadn't given her a goodnight kiss at the end of the evening was because her parents had crashed their date, just as she was serving dessert.

When she thought back over the evening, she realized that he'd pulled back from holding her hand while her parents were present as well. Not that pulling back from physically showing they were on a date deterred her parents from grilling him about his intentions, as if she was still a teenager. She still wasn't sure how he'd seamlessly redirected their conversation to telling her parents all about the places they'd visited in the last six weeks.

At the time, she thought he'd done those things to respect her wish to limit the PDA in front of her parents. But now that she was thinking back over the days since, she wondered if he had changed his mind about dating her.

He was professional but distant at church the next morning, when he apologized to her parents for not being able to stay for the potluck because of having to go to the arena to oversee everything being set up for the live airing of the pay-per-view. And nothing seemed to have changed in their normal daily outings since flying out of San Antonio on Monday morning.

Leah Mae Wright

Rick accompanied them to the Children's Museum of Houston when they arrived in the city at midday on Monday. But their interaction was no different from the week before when they were at the Smithsonian. The same could be said of their visit to the Oklahoma City National Memorial and Museum on Wednesday.

Fiona had thought about asking Britney if her father had changed his mind about dating her on their girls-only day on Tuesday, but she didn't feel comfortable discussing her feelings for Rick with his child. Not that she really had the opportunity on Tuesday anyway, since Britney wanted them to go to the Dealey Plaza National Historic Landmark District with Jax, Cage, and the rest of the older kids and their families on Tuesday while they were in Dallas.

Apparently, Tia had visited there sometime in the last year and had told the older kids about the conspiracies surrounding the assassination of John F. Kennedy, so they all wanted to explore the area together, now that they had a history teacher to teach them the true facts. The Burlesons even delayed their flight home from that morning to that night, so they could go back to the grassy knoll with everyone else.

She settled into a seat across the aisle from where the fifth- and seventh-grade girls were congregated in a quad seating area, thinking it was a good idea to keep an eye on them, since their parents were all either working during the flight or seated closer to their boys.

The three seats around her were soon filled with Allissa and the Precious Stones. Fiona was starting to get used to the interchangeable names used by professional wrestlers, after Aiken and Teagan had explained that they had to live their gimmick back when they first got started in the business to get used to answering to Amethyst and Emerald Stone when they were performing. Apparently, everyone who didn't use a variation of their real name as their ring name tended to go by their ring name more often, even after they'd been in the business for years.

"Victoria, do you know who we're swapping rooms with tonight?" Aiken Pearson, also known as Amethyst, looked pointedly at Allissa Walters, also known as Victoria Vicious, as she asked the question.

"No, I think Dean, or maybe Cage, has the list." Allissa shook her head before nodding in the direction the guys she mentioned were sitting with Jax and "Surfer" Josh Parker. "They're the ones organizing everything."

Teagan Shields, also known as Emerald, popped up in her seat to turn and look at the four men seated in a quad a few rows ahead of them and on the opposite side of the plane. Her eyes were wide as she turned back around and plopped back down in her rear-facing seat. "Wait! Dean and Josh are deciding which kids we're watching tonight?"

"No, I think it was Dean who came up with the idea, but Cage took over the planning, so they could get Rick to go along with it." Allissa half-shrugged one shoulder, as if she wasn't quite sure.

Fiona wondered what they were planning, and felt a little left out that they hadn't asked her to be a part of it, especially since they mentioned watching some of the kids for the night.

As one of their teachers, shouldn't I be involved in whatever they're doing with the kids? Or is this something they don't know me well enough to trust me with yet?

No, that can't be why they didn't include me, since they all know Rick has trusted me to take care of Britney alone on TV days.

Aiken looked over her shoulder before turning back to their quad. "Should we get with Cage to make sure the wilder guys are teamed up with someone more responsible to keep them and the kids out of trouble tonight?"

"Oh, crap, I didn't think about them teaming us up with someone." Allissa looked panicked at the realization. "I just assumed we'd swap one, single person per couple, so the kids could go to bed like normal while their parents go out for the night."

"Oh, no," Aiken giggled. "If Dean came up with this idea, it was so he could be paired up with you for the night."

Seeing Allissa's distress at the possibility of being paired up with Dean, Fiona decided to ask what was going on to see if she could help ease her friend's anxiety by volunteering to be paired up with her instead. No matter why they hadn't included her originally, she still wanted to help her new friends if she could. "What exactly are ya'll planning?"

"Those of us who aren't married or dating anyone are swapping our hotel rooms with the couples with kids for the night," Teagan explained. "We'll stay in the family suites with their kids, so they can go out for Valentine's Day after the show tonight."

"Or stay in for a romantic night without their kids in the same room to possibly interrupt them." Aiken wagged her eyebrows suggestively.

"Aw, what a sweet thing to do." Fiona turned to Allissa in the seat beside her. "Who do I need to talk to in order to volunteer to be your partner tonight, so you don't get stuck with Dean?"

"Oh, no, you're not helping watch the kids tonight." Allissa shook her head, as she held her hands up to stop Fiona from protesting further.

Undeterred by Allissa's hand gesture, Fiona couldn't stop herself from asking, "Why not?"

"Because Cage specifically said not to ask you, so you can go out with Rick tonight. If you want to turn the boss down, that's up to you. But I'm not going to be the one to upset the man who signs our paychecks by letting you commit to babysitting before he even finds out he has a sitter for the night to ask you out."

"Oh." Fiona took a moment to process everything Allissa just divulged.

Is that why Rick hasn't asked me on a date yet? Because Britney hasn't slept over with one of her friends since Saturday? And why didn't he plan something like this, so he could give me some notice about when we might be able to go out?

"Wait," Fiona whisper-shouted as she looked around at her friends. "How long has this been in the works? And why doesn't Rick know about it yet?"

"I heard Dean and Cage talking about it as we were checking out of the hotel this morning, but I don't know how long they've been planning it." Allissa lifted one shoulder in a shrug. "But they haven't told Rick yet because they want to make sure they have enough people to watch all the kids before they surprise all the parents today."

"They'd better hurry and get it all figured out if they want to tell them as we're checking in at the hotel," Teagan pointed out just as Derek York made the announcement that they were about to land in Kansas City.

And I might need to skip today's excursion to spend my time in the hotel shaving my lady bits, so I'll be prepared if we go past kissing on our second date.

~~~

Rick was discombobulated by deviating from his routine to leave the arena with Fiona at the end of the show, while his daughter went with Cage back to the hotel for the night. He still couldn't believe the single members of his roster had organized a hotel room swap to watch all their kids, so the couples with kids could all have time alone for Valentine's Day. And he was really surprised they had included him and Fiona in their plans.

After they had surprised him in the hotel lobby as they were checking in, Rick had spent most of the time touring the National World War I Museum and Memorial trying to figure out when he could ask Fiona to go out with him after the show, since she hadn't gone with them. He was so worried about why she had opted to go with the younger kids to the National Museum of Toys and Miniatures, instead of going on the same excursion as him and Britney the way she usually did, he hadn't taken the time to look up anywhere he might take her out that night.

When he finally caught up with her in catering to actually ask her out, neither one of them had any ideas for where they could go. Then he got busy with the show and had to pick up the slack from firing Ron earlier in the week, so he didn't have the chance to look up any ideas for places to go on a late-night date since. Now he wasn't sure where he was going as he pulled out of the arena parking space.

"You didn't happen to come up with any ideas for where we should go on this date, did you?" Rick glanced over at Fiona as he slowly followed the other cars toward the exit of the performers' parking lot.

"Not really." Rick barely caught the slight shake of her head in his peripheral vision while watching the car in front of him come to a stop as they waited in line at the gate. "I did a search on my phone, but the only places I saw open this late were clubs or diners."

"Yeah, I was afraid our options would be limited." Rick ran a hand through his hair, really wishing he had been able to plan their first official date better.
~~~

"Is that why you hadn't asked me earlier this week?" Rick glanced over to see Fiona looking shyly down at her hands in her lap. "Because you were waiting until we have more time off, so we'd have more options of what to do?"

"Not completely," Rick admitted, shaking his head as he pulled up to the gate and handed the attendant his parking pass. "I mean, I wanted more time to plan our date, but I'd have figured out how to make a late-night diner date work sooner than now if I hadn't had to deal with the fallout of future endeavoring Ron."

After making sure the road was clear and turning out of the parking lot to drive in the direction of their hotel, thinking he'd stop at whatever diner he saw open between there and the arena, Rick let his eyes drift off the road momentarily to glance at Fiona once more. She had the cutest look on her face as she tried to figure out what he was talking about.

Damn, she's adorable when she's confused and thinking hard to figure something out. But I don't want her to get too frustrated by not understanding me that she thinks we have too many differences to be together.

"Sorry, talking to you is so easy that I sometimes forget we haven't known each other forever, and that you're too new to the wrestling business to know our jargon. Future endeavored just means I had to fire him."

"Ron's the writer you asked me about last Friday when I dropped Britney off at the B and B, right?"

"Yes," Rick nodded, remembering back to how relieved he'd felt when Fiona had told him she'd never been formally introduced to Ron, or had any other interaction with him in her time with the company. "Though technically his job title was booker. That's what we call our show writers."

"Why did you have to fire him?" From the corner of his eye, he could see that she'd turned to examine him as he drove.

Fuck! I have to keep my temper in check, so I don't scare her by showing how fucking pissed I am at the shit Ron was trying to pull.

Rick sucked in a deep breath as he white-knuckled the steering wheel. He tried to keep his expression neutral, though he thought he might have let a little sternness or harshness show through.

"He was overstepping his role in the company, trying to act as an agent in addition to his booker duties." Rick noticed her cute, confused expression once more, and realized he had to explain the differences before he could get to the major issue he had with Ron. "Bookers plan out the angles or storylines, watch the crowd reactions, and plan out the shows to gain more interest from the fans. Agents look at what the bookers plan and help the wrestlers choreograph their matches to fit into the long-term plans. Since Ethan and Stone, the other two bookers on staff, are both former wrestlers, I don't have anyone acting in just an agent role. Ron doesn't have the in-ring experience to be able to act as an agent. My dad actually recommended hiring him a few years back, thinking his experience as a sitcom writer would be beneficial for planning long-term story arcs. But apparently, he's been getting in the ring to help choreograph the women's matches whenever the other guys weren't around."

Fiona gasped and covered her mouth with her hand as the implications of Ron's actions dawned on her.

"Unfortunately, he was so subtle with the inappropriate touching that none of the women were sure enough that it had happened to complain about it, so we have no proof to file charges for sexual misconduct." Not being able to have the man arrested was the main reason Rick was pissed off about the whole situation. "But he said some things last week that didn't sit right with me and seemed to have done a one-eighty on his opinion of one of our female performers in the last month."

"So, that's why you were asking all the women in the company about possible issues we'd had with him last weekend?"

Rick nodded. "And when I found out he was trying to turn one of our main event performers into a jobber because she refused his advances, I had enough grounds for termination, even though it's still a *he said, she said* situation and not enough for criminal charges."

"While it stinks that you can't press charges to prevent him from harassing women in the future, at least you know it won't be anyone who works for you." Fiona reached over and patted his arm reassuringly. "I hope you know how much the way you take care of everyone who works for you is appreciated."

"Yeah," Rick huffed out a self-deprecating bark of laughter as he remembered the angry reactions Tanner and Vaughn had when they found out what had been happening for months without Rick or anyone else in the company realizing it. Ron was lucky he'd been kicked out of the arena before they got their hands on him for touching their wives inappropriately. *Hell, he was lucky he hadn't even talked to Fifi, or I would have buried him in San Antonio instead of firing him.*

"So, where are we going for our date?" Fiona's voice was cheerful as she changed the subject.

"I have no idea," Rick chuckled, shaking his head, and smiling. "I've been looking for a diner, but so far the only places I've seen open were gas stations, a tattoo parlor, and what looked like a dive bar."

"Is there a bar in the hotel?" Rick nodded in answer to her question, but he didn't say anything because he didn't think a bar of any kind was the right place to take her on a date. "Then let's go there."

"Are you sure?" Rick was surprised by her vehement head bob and bright smile.

"Yeah, if it's anything like the one my friend, Charlotte, and I go to in San Antonio for our girls' nights, then we can have a drink and talk and not worry about having to drive back to the hotel afterwards."

"Okay, if you're sure." Rick made the turn off the main road through town to the side street where the hotel was located. "I was trying to find someplace other than a bar because I didn't think you drank."

"Well, I'm not a lush or anything, but I'm not a teetotaler either." Fiona giggled at his surprised expression. "Do I really come off as too much of a goody-two-shoes to drink a glass of wine on occasion?"

"No, I just haven't ever seen you drink anything but tea, juice, or water." Rick pulled into the hotel parking lot. "So, I assumed because your dad is a preacher that you didn't drink."

Fiona burst out laughing as Rick parked the car. She was still laughing, as he got out and walked around the car to open her door for her.

"You must not have heard my dad talking to Kay's dad about the champagne being served at Anthony and Kay's wedding." Rick shook his head, as he took her hand to walk into the hotel. "Yeah, my dad pointed out to Mr. Lee that Jesus turned water into wine, so it can't be a sin to drink it once in a while."

"A valid point I hadn't ever considered before," Rick chuckled along with her giggles, as they walked into the hotel bar and sat down at a table by the windows. "I guess what they say about being an ass for making assumptions is true."

"I don't think that assumption counts, since it's probably true for a lot of people raised in religious households," Fiona shrugged and gave him a shy smile.

"Thanks for letting me off the hook with that one," Rick smiled back at her. "So I don't screw up by making another assumption, I should probably ask you what you'd like to drink before I go place our order at the bar, huh?"

"I'm not nearly as much of a wine aficionado as my friend Charlotte." Fiona looked nervous, as she shook her head. "I normally just order what I remember her ordering last, if I get to the bar before her. So, you're welcome to surprise me with your choice of wine for this evening."

"You are a brave woman," Rick chuckled as he stood and stepped over to the bar. He ordered them each a glass of wine, opting for a sweet red variety, thinking it most matched Fiona's sweet personality. He also requested two bottles of water, just in case he was wrong in picking something they would both like, and they'd need something else to drink instead.

Once he returned to the table with their drinks, Rick's curiosity about her previous experience in bars got the better of him. "So, you and your friend go to hotel bars for girls' night?"

"Yeah, usually on Friday nights, when we can get a hotel room and not have to drive back to Heart's Destiny after drinking. Then the next morning, we're already in San Antonio to go volunteer at the shelter. We joke about it being penance for drinking the night before, but we actually volunteered at the shelter every Saturday, whether we drank the night before or not."

Damn. She really is an angel, and I must be Satan incarnate to want to dirty her up the way I do.

Rick watched as Fiona took her first sip of the wine he'd placed on the table in front of her. When he saw her smile at the taste, he took his own sip and was surprised to find he also liked the sweetness of the vintage the bartender had suggested. Not wanting to have to admit to his own lack of wine knowledge, Rick opted to skip asking if she liked the wine, and focused in on what she'd just said about volunteering. "So, what did you do when you volunteered at the shelter?"

"A little bit of everything," Fiona giggled. "I started out going with my parents as a child to serve meals on holidays. When I moved home after college, that morphed into going every Saturday to help with meal prep, childcare, and whatever else was needed. Over the years, I've helped the management with everything from their record keeping to fundraising."

She blushed lightly as she said the word "fundraising," making Rick wonder what was embarrassing about that.

"Since I can't volunteer every week now, I've set up automatic donations every payday to help where I can. I also sent all *our winnings* from Vegas to the shelter fund." The twinkle in her eyes and the way she said "our winnings" let Rick know she'd figured out he hadn't actually separated the money out before giving her only her share from their casino night in Vegas.

"You, ah, figured out I was too drunk to remember how much each of us won that night to be able to split it up, huh?" It was Rick's turn to feel his cheeks heat at the admission.

"Yeah, the fact that it was about three times the amount I'd won was a pretty big clue that it wasn't all my winnings," Fiona giggled.

Fuck, I love hearing her laugh.

"So, since you donated it to the shelter, can we consider my penance for that night paid in full?" Rick joked, chuckling with her.

"Yes, absolutely." Fiona grinned before taking another sip of her wine. "Since you already know pretty much everything about my family and childhood, tell me about yours."

"I grew up in New York. Mom was from a wealthy family. Dad was not. Needless to say, her family was not very impressed when she brought home a mid-card wrestler from a family of old carnies. But Dad won them over by protecting Mom from some mob rivals, and nine months later, I was born, and they got married."

"Wait, your family has mob rivals?" Fiona's eyes widened as she asked the question.

"I don't." Rick held his hands up, palms out, to stop her from thinking he was involved in any of the mob stuff his grandfather and uncles had used to gain their wealth. "But my mom's father, uncles, and brothers have been connected for decades. Dad swears his only involvement was in the early eighties when he took out one of Nonno's enemies while defending Mom and me. And I believe him, since the cops ruled it self-defense when he broke that guy's neck."

"But you were still raised in a mob family," Fiona protested, giving him an incredulous look.

"Sort of, but not really," Rick objected, shaking his head. "I mean, the seed money Dad used to start the GWA was probably mob money my nonno gave them as a wedding gift, but I've never seen any mob activity. Not when I was a kid and going to family dinners, or as an adult in reviewing the books of the company before taking over from Dad. Hell, I haven't even seen those uncles since my nonno passed away."

Fuck! I never even thought my family history might be what scares her away from being in a relationship with me. But I guess when I really look at her perceptions of what they might have done to earn their wealth, their crimes are much worse than my tendency to be rough in bed.

Shit! All I'm doing is giving her more reasons to avoid me at all costs.

Before Rick could figure out what to say to try to dig his way out of the hole he'd unintentionally dug for himself, Fiona started laughing, confusing him even further.

"Oh my goodness, I just realized how you've used your family folklore as part of your wrestling persona." Fiona reached out and placed her hand over his on the table between them, grinning up at him through her giggles. "That's why you're always in a dark suit. To look like the mobster running the show whenever you have to appear on TV."

"No, I'm always in a suit because I'm trying to show how the business has evolved from the carnie sideshow days." Rick chuckled along with her, hoping her laughter indicated she wasn't as turned off by his family history as he'd originally thought. "But that would be a good gimmick."

"What was your gimmick back when you wrestled?" Rick was thankful for Fiona's change of subject.

"I was known as 'Rowdy' Ricky Roberts," Rick admitted with a grimace at how stupid his gimmick had been. "Just a generic Jersey Guido always looking for a party."

Fiona raised an eyebrow at him, obviously not understanding the term, grinning as she asked, "Wasn't there a Guido on *The Sopranos* that exactly matches the character I'm imagining you portrayed?"

"Possibly," Rick chuckled. "But I was more of a *Jersey Shore* Guido. I was just living the gimmick ten years before *Jersey Shore* aired."

Fiona burst out laughing, covering her mouth with her free hand as she shook her head in disbelief. "No. No way."

"What? You can't picture me in graphic tees and sporting a faux-hawk?" Rick raised an eyebrow, feeling good about being the reason she was laughing, even if it was because of how cheesy his gimmick had been when he wrestled.

"The clothes, possibly, since I have seen you in jeans and a t-shirt. But I can't picture you without the beard, since you had it even in the few pictures of you I've seen in wrestling tights online."

Ah! My little Fifi searched for pictures of me in my wrestling tights. I wonder if she's touched herself while looking at them the same way I've jacked off while looking at the pictures I've taken of her with my phone?

Before Rick could question her about searching for pictures of him online, Fiona lowered her hand as her laughter died down, waving it in the general direction of his face. "Much less acting like one of those guys my college roommate and I used to laugh at on *Jersey Shore*."

"Shit, you were just in college then?" Rick shook his head. Having temporarily forgotten their ten-year age difference, her comment about being in college caught him off guard, wiping away his questions about why she'd looked for pictures of him online. "By the time it came out, I'd outgrown my party years and was only acting the part in the ring. Hell, I'd been married and a father for over three years when it first aired and was divorced by the time it went off the air."

"Oh, no, when it first came out, I was a senior in high school and halfway through my junior year of college when it went off the air." Fiona shrugged, as if the years between them didn't matter.

"Our age difference doesn't bother you?" Rick hoped he wasn't just giving her another reason to not want to be with him by asking.

"No." Fiona adamantly shook her head, as she squeezed his hand. "I mean, it might have been an issue ten years ago, when I was still in high school, but not now. Does it bother you?"

"Most of the time, no, but when it's pointed out, it makes me feel old," Rick admitted with a wary half-smile. Rick thought back to some of the things Colleen had said during their divorce, about him growing old before his time as one of the reasons she'd cheated with younger lovers, and wondered if Fiona would feel the same way when the newness of their attraction wore off. "I have to wonder if you'll eventually want to be with someone younger, like my ex."

"Wow, she did more of a number on you than Britney led me to believe." Fiona shook her head. Rick briefly thought he saw pity in her eyes, but it was quickly replaced with a fiery determination that made her emerald eyes darken.

"What exactly did Britney tell you about Colleen?" Rick couldn't believe the question had passed his lips. He wasn't sure he really wanted to know the answer.

"Just that she's a bee with an itch." Fiona grinned.

Rick couldn't stop himself from smiling at Fiona using the same term as his daughter to keep from cussing.

"And that she hasn't seen her since the day you came home and caught her with one of her boyfriends. But she made it seem like you've been a lot happier since the split. Like you weren't hurt by her betrayal. I'm guessing that's because you never let Britney see how much she hurt you."

"I have been a lot happier since the split." Rick wanted to object to Fiona's assessment that Colleen had hurt him, but he couldn't make his mouth form the words.

Was I really hurt? I was pissed. I felt like she made me look like a fool. But I don't think I loved her enough for her betrayal to hurt me. I certainly didn't feel like my heart was breaking the way I did when I thought Fifi was with Jax.

Not that I can tell Fiona that. It's way too soon for me to tell her I love her and am terrified of actually being hurt by losing her.

"I don't think I was hurt by Colleen's actions, at least not the way you think. I wasn't in love with her, so she didn't have the power to break my heart by cheating. I was more pissed off at the way she was using Britney as her meal ticket and wasn't capable of loving our daughter the way Brit deserves."

"Fair enough." Fiona raised both hands in surrender. "But regardless of whether you're protecting your heart or Britney's, you don't have to worry about me behaving anything like your ex."

"Shit! That's not what I meant…" Rick trailed off, realizing he needed to reword his statement into the apology he owed her for sticking his foot in his mouth more than once in the last few minutes. "I'm sorry. I know you're nothing like my ex. I didn't mean to…" He trailed off again, unsure how to finish his sentence.

"It's okay, I understand." Fiona reached back over and clasped his hand again, giving it a reassuring squeeze.

"I just don't see why you'd want to be with me, when you could be with someone your age with less baggage." Rick turned his hand over under hers to hold on to her as he spoke. "I'm sure your dating life was a lot more active before you started working with the GWA, and I don't want you to feel like you're settling for me because none of the guys your age who work with us are going to ask you out knowing I'm interested in you."

"Oh, Rick, that's not what's going on between us at all." Fiona looked up at him imploringly. "And my dating life has been basically non-existent since college."

Rick raised an eyebrow, unable to vocalize his questions about her statement.

"Honestly, I didn't have much of a dating life before then, either. I dated Justin Burleson my senior year of high school. We had all the typical teenage firsts, but broke up within a month of starting college because we were no longer convenient when we didn't have any classes together."

Rick had to bite his tongue to keep from growling at the realization that Anthony's cousin had taken her virginity.

"I went on a lot of first dates my freshmen and sophomore years, but not many second dates. Then my junior year, I dated Brad Kilgore for a couple of months, just long enough to realize we weren't compatible."

"Compatible?" Rick wasn't sure he wanted to know if their incompatibility was discovered in bed, hoping she'd say they split for some trivial reason.

"Like in the bedroom," Fiona whispered, blushing at the admission. "I mean, I expected him to fumble a little the first time since everyone does. But when he couldn't find the goal line after a month of trying, I realized that no matter how much I liked him, I could never fall in love with him or I'd be doomed to a very unsatisfying life, if you know what I mean."

While Rick was irrationally jealous of Brad having the opportunity to touch his Fifi over five years before, it was his grin at how cute she was in describing the unsatisfying event that he allowed to show through in his eyes, not wanting to frighten her away with his jealous rage.

"It was pretty much the same my senior year of college with Diego Gomez," Fiona shrugged. "We dated for a couple of months, but there were no sparks to push us to continue dating after college. I thought about going out with Justin again when we both moved back home after college. But then I started working with Charlotte and it would have been weird to talk to my new best friend about scratching an itch with her cousin, since I already knew we weren't a love match. And I don't do one-night stands, so I haven't even hooked up with any of the guys who hit on us when we go out for girls' night. Not that being hit on even happened all that often."

Holy fuck! She's only had three sexual partners in her life. And it sounds like none of them were completely satisfying for her.

"So, what about you? I mean, I know you were married, but I'm sure she wasn't your only partner." Fiona's blush deepened as she picked up her wine glass to finish off the last sip.

"Uh, no, she wasn't," Rick admitted, hoping his beard covered his shame at what he was about to admit. "I honestly don't know how many partners I've had because I was not opposed to one-night stands in my teens and early twenties. The wrestling business was a lot different back then, too. We didn't all travel together on the company plane, so the wives and kids stayed home while we were on tour. Our hotel rooms became party central and were overrun with ring rats willing to do whatever we wanted, just to say they'd been with a professional wrestler."

Rick shook his head in disgust at the memories of some of the things he'd done back in the day. "That's actually how I met my ex. She showed up at our hotel parties a few times, and I was too young and naïve to realize it was because one of the older guys was paying for his side piece to travel to see him whenever we were far enough away from his hometown that his wife couldn't drive to the show to surprise him. We started talking one night, and she realized that not only was I closer to her age, I was also the heir to the company, so she flirted enough to get me to take over paying for her travel and dumped him."

"I can't believe you actually started dating her after seeing her at the parties with a married guy." Fiona looked shocked.

"I never saw her there with anyone in particular. Every time I'd seen her before then, she was dancing with the other girls, putting on a show for the guys, but not looking like she was interested in anyone in particular. It wasn't until six months later, when we announced she was pregnant, and we were getting married, that the other guy pulled me aside backstage and suggested I get a paternity test before getting married."

Rick ran a hand through his hair at remembering that fight. "Our whole relationship was a disaster from the beginning. But as much as I want to block everything that happened with Colleen out of my head and forget it ever happened, I can't completely regret it because I wouldn't have Britney if I hadn't gone through it."

"I can understand that." Fiona smiled brightly at him, squeezing his hand. "I vote that from this point forward, Britney is the only aspect of our past relationships we talk about."

"I second that vote," Rick agreed as he finished off his glass of wine. He lifted his glass to her as he asked, "Do you want another?"

"No, I think I'd rather switch to water to keep a clear head for the rest of the night." Fiona lifted her bottle of water and opened it before taking a drink to demonstrate her decision.

Rick put his glass back down and did the same, agreeing that clear heads were better for him to have a chance to kiss her at the end of the night. As much as he wanted them to go further than that, he didn't want to push too fast. Not only did he need to take things slow to keep from overwhelming her because of her relative inexperience, but he also needed to talk with her about his proclivities before surprising her with them in bed. And he had no intention of having that conversation in a public bar, much less so soon in their relationship.

I have to win part of her heart first, at least. Otherwise, she won't have any reason to want to be with a beast like me.

"So, besides now being a more family-friendly traveling environment, what else has changed about the wrestling business since you first started years ago? And how did you get the GWA to change so drastically in the last twelve years?"

"I actually implemented the first of the changes seven years ago. My dad had a heart attack, and I had to go to New York to take over for him in the corporate office." Rick almost broke their pact not to talk about anything but Britney in their past relationships by admitting to that being the catalyst to his finding Colleen in flagrante delicto, but he stopped himself just in time. "In trying to schedule everything while going through my divorce, I had to find a way to travel with my daughter. So, I bought the company plane and worked with human resources to set some rules of conduct for anyone traveling with us. There were a few old-school guys who quit when I banned parties in the hotels, but for the most part, the guys all seemed to like the idea of bringing their families on the road."

Fiona listened intently as Rick continued explaining the changes he'd made when he took over for his father. As the conversation continued, he also explained the nuances of the wrestling business, both in and out of the ring, that most people didn't know about. She asked insightful questions and even came up with a few great ideas that he looked forward to implementing.

When he commented on her creativity in coming up with the tag-team name "Red Velvet" for Dark Chocolate and Red, when nobody else in the company had been able to come up with anything to tie the two of them together, she told him about her childhood dream of being a writer, which she still intended to fulfill once she retired from teaching. That took their conversation back to talking about their childhoods.

The conversation flowed easily between them, even with her teasing him a little about never breaking up with him to keep from "sleeping with the fishes" at the hands of his mobster family. When he realized she wasn't really worried about his family history tainting their future, Rick relaxed.

For the first time in his life, Rick actually felt like he'd met someone he could talk with about anything and everything, or nothing at all, and still feel at peace. Someone who could truly be his partner in life, and not just in the bedroom.

Holy Fuck! She really is **The One***. I just hope Cooper is right about our sexual proclivities meshing easily when it's true love. Because it just might kill me if my Fifi, my soulmate, doesn't think we're compatible in bed.*

Chapter Fifteen

Fiona was having such a great time getting to know Rick, she didn't want the night to end when the hotel bar closed. They had basically gone over their entire life histories with each other as they sipped their one glass of wine and bottles of water for the last few hours. She had learned everything from his favorite childhood memory to the fact that he'd only had one serious romantic relationship in his whole life.

She had laughed boisterously when staid, serious Rick Robertson had told her about his wrestling gimmick as "Rowdy" Ricky Roberts. And tried to hide her jealousy, when he'd glossed over his number of previous sexual partners by talking about how different the party scene after the shows was back when he first started in the business before he revamped the company to the family-friendly version she saw now, so his daughter could travel with him all the time.

He may have only had one serious relationship, but he definitely had more sexual experience than her three boyfriends in high school and college combined. While Fiona hated to think of how he'd gained that experience with hundreds, if not thousands, of other women, her girl parts lit up with excitement at the thought of him demonstrating it firsthand.

Her desire to learn what only he could teach her was what gave her the courage to invite him into her room to extend their night, as they rode up to her floor in the elevator. "I don't have wine, but I do have a coffee pot in my room if you want to continue our date a little longer."

"As much as I would love to continue our date, I don't think coffee in your room is the best idea for how to extend the night." Rick gave

217

her a wry smile. As the elevator doors opened, he put his hand on the small of her back to escort her down the hall to her room.

"Well, we pass the vending machines on the way, so we could get some water, or juice, if you don't want the caffeine," Fiona suggested, hoping he wasn't turning her down completely.

"It's not the caffeine I'm worried about," Rick grumbled, running his free hand through his hair, as if he was second-guessing his decision not to go into her room. "I don't want to push for more than you're ready for, Fifi. And if I go in your room where it's just the two of us, I won't be able to stop with just a chaste goodnight kiss."

Her heart fluttered when he called her Fifi for the first time since Puerto Rico. *There's no way he's drunk from one glass of wine, so he has to think of it as a pet name for me.*

"And what makes you think I'm not ready for more than a chaste goodnight kiss?" Fiona stopped walking and dug into her bag to pull out her room keycard before looking up at Rick with what she hoped was a flirty expression.

"I assumed that you needed me to back off a little, since you didn't go to the World War I Museum with us today, ur, yesterday." Rick looked at his watch to confirm the time was after midnight.

"And what did we say about assuming earlier?" Fiona grinned at him.

"That I must be a giant ass because I keep doing it?" Rick arched an eyebrow at her, as he wrapped his arms around her, settling both hands on the small of her back. Fiona giggled, but she shook her head because she could never consider him an ass for anything. "Since I'm clearly wrong in my assumption, why did you pick the other excursion today instead of going with me and Britney?"

"Well, first, because Britney needs your undivided attention once in a while." Fiona slipped her arms around Rick's neck. "And second, I didn't go on the other excursion today. I found out about the room swap on the plane and spent that time in my room on some special grooming because I knew we'd be going out tonight."

Rick visibly swallowed down a gulp at her confession, but he didn't say a word in response. Fiona pressed her body against his and felt his hard length pressed against her soft belly, even through the layers of their clothing and coats.

At least his penis is on board with my plans for the rest of our date. But I guess the rest of the man needs a little more convincing.

"I figured since we went to second base in our sleep before we even started dating, maybe we could round third on our second date. So, I mowed the playing field and hoped a night to ourselves might lead to a home run."

"You are making it really *hard* to say no to you, Fifi." Rick grinned at her, grinding his erection into her to emphasize the word hard. "But I don't want to take advantage after we've been drinking."

"We've each only had one glass of wine," Fiona pointed out. "And we both switched to water for the last couple of hours, so I doubt either one of us is even tipsy. Especially since I know from experience that it takes three glasses of wine, without anything to cut the effect over that same amount of time, for me to feel buzzed."

Fiona couldn't tell from his expression if he was starting to waiver or not, but she was starting to wonder if he was using her not being ready for more as a way to cover for his own lack of readiness to move their relationship along sexually. "But I don't want to pressure you into doing something you don't want to do either, so I will gladly accept that chaste goodnight kiss and let you go to your own bed for the night."

She pressed up on her tiptoes and lightly pecked him on the lips. She released her grip on the back of his neck, as she dropped back down and tried to turn toward her door. Rick didn't release his hold on her, however, so she didn't get very far in her retreat.

"You aren't pressuring me, Fifi. And that wasn't a kiss." Rick pulled her flush against his body, as he dipped his head to demonstrate what he classified as a kiss.

His lips were firm and demanding against hers, as he slid one hand up to cradle the back of her head. With his fingers weaving through her long hair, he angled her head the way he wanted her, just as his tongue slipped out to run along the seam of her lips.

She gasped in surprise, as his other hand squeezed her bottom, and he rocked his hips against her suggestively, allowing him to deepen the kiss. Once he had access, Rick devoured her mouth in a kiss that made her feel utterly possessed and claimed by him.

She didn't realize she had wrapped her arms back around him until the hotel keycard slipped from her grasp when it was replaced by his thick hair. *We'll pick that up later,* she thought, as she returned his passionate kiss until they both had to pull back to breathe.

Rick released her, leaving her standing there, stunned, while he bent down and picked up the keycard before he inserted it into the slot on the door.

"And that wasn't chaste," Fiona pointed out when she came back to her senses.

"No, it wasn't," Rick smirked, as he opened the door to her room and ushered her inside. "And what we're about to do isn't going to be chaste, either."

"What are we about to do?" Fiona gasped, as Rick lifted the strap for her crossbody bag off her shoulder and over her head. He pressed her back against the door, as soon as it was closed, dropping her bag and the keycard on the table right beside them, as his lips crashed down on hers once more.

Guess he prefers to show, not tell.

Rick swallowed the sounds of her giggle at her thoughts, as he kissed the rest of them right out of her head. They made out against the door for what could have been only minutes or several hours, without Fiona realizing the passage of time. She vaguely registered wrapping her arms and legs around him as he picked her up off the floor, but she had no recollection of him carrying her to the bed as she was so lost in their ardent kissing.

Their hands roamed, as they writhed against one another. They were desperate to touch each other everywhere and got frustrated quickly with so many layers of clothing in the way.

"Why did we put our coats back on just to come upstairs?" Rick lifted up off of her and stripped off his overcoat and suit jacket before pulling her up from the middle of the bed to divest her of her coat.

"I have no idea." Fiona shook her head, as she bent to unzip her boots before kicking them off. "I just put mine on because you held it up to help me with it."

"Clearly I wasn't thinking." Rick removed his tie before stepping back toward her to continue removing her clothing. He pulled her emerald-green dress up over her head and tossed it behind him before dropping to his knees to remove the leggings she wore under it due to the cold February temperature in Kansas City. He slipped her socks off with her leggings, as he lifted her feet one by one, and stood back up to stare at her standing there in only her matching green bra and panties. "You are absolutely stunning, Fifi."

She momentarily felt self-conscious about the extra weight she carried on her body, that no amount of dieting or exercise helped her shed. But when she looked into his eyes and saw the sincerity he felt behind his statement, she let her insecurities go.

Rick toed off his shoes, as he scooped her into his arms and laid her back on the bed. With his still mostly clothed body covering her almost naked one, he kissed her once more. Fiona wrapped her arms around him, as she opened her mouth for their tongues to explore.

He didn't allow her to hold him close for long, moving to trail open-mouthed kisses down the column of her neck to the valley between her breasts. He made quick work of the front clasp of her bra, freeing her mounds for him to lavish them with his oral affection.

"Oh, Rick," Fiona moaned, running her fingers through his hair as she reveled in the pleasure he was giving her. She hadn't had a guy show her breasts this much attention since high school. It had been so long she'd forgotten how much she enjoyed having her nipples sucked.

The sensation of his soft beard brushing across her skin was an entirely, all new experience to her, and one she hadn't realized she'd been missing out on with the boys of her youth. Rick was all man. A man who knew how to utilize all his assets, as evidenced by the way he alternated the pressure with his mouth, hands, and beard to bring her to the edge from breast play alone.

Just as Fiona thought she was about to come, Rick released her nipple with a pop and moved lower on the bed. "No, don't stop." Fiona tried pulling his head back to her breasts, but he wouldn't be detoured from his path.

"I'm not stopping, my sweet Fifi," Rick growled, as he kissed his way over her slightly rounded midsection. When he got to the top of her panties, he sat up on his knees between her spread thighs. "I'm just moving down to see how you specially groomed for me today."

He slipped his first finger from each hand under the side of her panties over each of her hips and slowly slid them down, lifting her legs in the air to remove them from her body completely. He tossed her panties off the side of the bed before spreading her legs and lowering his mouth to her freshly shaved mound.

Something else I haven't experienced in over eight years. All thoughts of her lackluster college boyfriends and tentative first sexual explorations in high school were wiped from Fiona's mind the first time Rick licked through her folds. It didn't just feel like her first time with Rick, but more like her first time ever. Not that she could focus to figure out why at that moment.

The feeling of his beard tickling her inner thighs, as he feasted on her as if she was the most delicious thing he'd ever tasted, was exhilarating. Combined with the visual of his dark head between her pale thighs, his oral affection made her gush with arousal.

Their gazes locked on one another's, as he lifted his head and flicked the tip of his tongue over her clit. "You taste so fucking sweet, Fifi."

Fiona was so close to the edge, his hot breath blowing over her most sensitive nub as he spoke was almost enough to push her over. Her eyelids felt heavy as her orgasm approached, but she struggled to keep her eyes open, wanting to watch the desire she saw in Rick's eyes as he took her over.

"Keep your eyes on me, Fifi. I want you to watch me lick up all your sweet cream when you come in my mouth."

"Yes, Rick, yes!" Fiona cried out, as he thrust his tongue inside her the way she soon hoped to have his manhood. She gripped the bedding under her in both hands, needing something to ground her to reality, as her world started to blur from the exquisite sensations he was giving her. He bobbed his head, his tongue moving in and out several times, but he never let her break eye contact with him.

Fiona lost the ability to form words, as Rick growled something incoherent, pulling his tongue from her channel to lap up her juices from her slit to her clit. When he reached her clit, he circled it with the tip of his tongue a couple of times before closing his lips around it and sucking. Hard.

Fiona's climax exploded through her. Her whole body seemed to spasm, with the initial tremors starting at her clitoris. Though her vision was quickly fading to black, it also tunneled in on the sight of him smiling up at her with her clit clamped between his teeth.

Fiona wasn't sure if it was watching what he was doing, or the little nip followed by him soothing it with his tongue, that sent a second wave of ecstasy flowing through her. Either way, she cried out his name repeatedly as she soared through the heights of pleasure.

She felt like she was floating on cloud nine, only vaguely aware of Rick cleaning her up, as she drifted back down to earth. He pulled back the covers on the side of the bed farthest from the door before scooping her limp body up in his arms and settling her under them.

She watched through half-closed eyes as he moved around the room, picking up their discarded clothing, draping their coats and her dress over the back of a chair, and folding her panties and bra before laying them on the table beside everything else. She reached her arms out from under the covers, beckoning him to join her, so they could finish what they started. "Come to bed. We can deal with all that in the morning."

"I'll be there in just a moment, sweet Fifi." Rick smiled at her from where he was standing and started stripping off his shirt, pants, and socks. Once his clothing joined hers on the chair and table, Rick walked over to the other side of the bed in just his royal blue boxers.

Fiona took advantage of the moonlight drifting in through the window to admire his muscular, mostly naked form, as he undressed and slipped into the bed beside her. While his muscles weren't as defined as the wrestlers who worked for him, Rick was still in excellent shape.

If it wasn't for the evidence of his arousal tenting his boxer shorts, Fiona would have been skeptical that someone as fit as him would be attracted to her. It wasn't that she was out of shape, per se, but she was definitely curvier than the female performers that he saw in their skimpy ring attire daily.

But Fiona wasn't going to let the inner voice that always made her feel bad for being thicker than her friends have a place in her head, when Rick's erection was clearly showing her there was nothing for her to feel self-conscious about. As soon as he settled in the bed and opened his arms to her, she rolled over to snuggle up next to him.

With her head resting on his shoulder, she ran her hand over his pecs before trailing down over his flat abdomen with the intention of moving his boxers out of the way, so they could continue what they'd started.

"Fifi," Rick growled, stopping her hand with his and pulling it back up to rest over his heart. "As much as I want you to touch me, holding you while we sleep is all I can handle tonight."

"I, I don't understand," Fiona stuttered, pulling back slightly from him, and feeling hurt by his rejection. "I thought you were just holding back, waiting on me to be ready. Don't you want me now that I'm ready?"

"Oh, sweet Fifi," Rick groaned, squeezing her back into his side. "Yes, I want you. Desperately. But I need us to both be sure, one-hundred percent positive, that we're all in before I can make love to you."

Fiona wasn't sure what else she could do to show him she was already all in with him. So, she rested her head back down on his shoulder and trusted he would see it when she was still there waiting for him, when he finally felt like he was ready to be all in with her.

I'll enjoy the comfort of his arms around me while I can. And, hopefully, he'll soon decide to be all in, too. I don't think I'll be able to handle it if tonight ends up being the last night I have with him.

~~~

Friday, February 15, 2019, 6 a.m., Kansas City, Missouri

Rick awoke the next morning to the glorious sensation of Fiona, naked in his arms and stroking his cock over his boxers. He kept his eyes closed and bit back a groan of pleasure, as he felt the precum oozing out of his dick from her gentle ministrations.

Her plump tits were pressed into his side, with their diamond-hard nipples poking into his ribs. Her leg was draped over his, and her wet pussy was rubbing against his thigh.

Fuck! Is she awake to know what she's doing? Or is this another dream?

Rick wasn't sure how much longer he could withstand the erotic torture of her softly stroking his cock, while soaking his thigh as she humped his leg. He certainly didn't want to come in his boxers, again, from an early morning shared dream.
~~~

He opened his eyes, expecting to see her strawberry-blonde hair spread across his chest as she slept through the sensual dream. While her hair was spread across his chest as he'd expected from feeling it before he opened his eyes, he was also met with her bright green eyes trained on him, as if she was watching to see when he'd wake up from her early morning attention.

"Fifi," he growled, his voice gravelly from sleep as much as from arousal. "What are you doing?"

"Waking you up," Fiona replied, making the blanket and top sheet fall down as she sat up and pushed his boxers down. "So I can take care of you this morning, like you took care of me last night."

He barely stopped her before she bent to take him in her mouth. "You don't have to do that, sweet Fifi."

Rick pulled his boxers back up over his cock with his left hand, while wrapping his right arm around Fiona and pulling her up to straddle his lap, as he sat up in the bed.

"But I want to," Fiona protested, wiggling in his arms until her pussy was pressed against his rock-hard cock. "I know you're not ready to go all the way, but I still want to please you in other ways until you're ready."

Yes, please! His cock was practically begging for her to wrap her pretty, pink lips around him. But Rick knew they had to talk about more than just being all in before they did anything more than him pleasing her with his mouth.

"And I want that. More than you know. But we need to talk first."

"We can talk on the plane." She wiggled against him, making his dick twitch. "But we only have another couple of hours alone…"

Rick cut her off with a kiss, hoping it would be enough to appease her for a few minutes, and would also stun her into silence, so he could say what he needed to say.

She wrapped her arms around his neck and returned the kiss with ardor, as she ground her creamy cunt against his dick. She soaked through his boxers and almost made him forget the need to warn her about what she was getting herself into in a relationship with him.

Fuck! I can't just pound into her like an animal without preparing her first, both mentally and physically.

Rick reluctantly gripped her shoulders to push her back slightly, breaking their lip lock. He found it really hard to focus while they were sitting in bed with her curvy body on full display. "Fuck, you're killing me, Fifi."

He slid his palms down her sides until he could grip her hips. He then picked her up and sat her down on the bed beside him, so he could stand from the bed and throw the blanket over her. He started to pace, as he tried to figure out how to explain the things going through his head without scaring her away.

"I'm sorry." He barely heard Fiona's softly spoken words, but they still gutted him.

"You have nothing to be sorry for, sweet Fifi." Rick turned to look at her curled up in the fetal position on the bed, as if she was soothing herself. He walked back over and sat down on the foot of the bed, reaching out to rest his hand on the lump under the covers he thought was her ankle. "If anyone should apologize, it's me. For being so selfish as to think I could sleep with you in my arms last night and not lose control before we talked things out. But I can't apologize for the best night of my life."

She looked up at him then, wide-eyed, but she didn't say anything in response. He knew he had to open up and explain why he hadn't taken things further the night before while he had her speechless.

Damn, I hope I don't screw this up.

"I want more with you, Fiona. So much more. But I can't take that step until I know you're prepared for what all that means with me. Britney already loves you and wants you to be her mom."

"And I already love her as if she was my own child." Fiona sat up, scooted down in the bed, and reached out from under the covers with one hand to place it over his on the bed between them, while using her other hand to keep the blanket in place, covering her. "I know ya'll are a package deal. And I want the whole package."

Rick turned his hand over and squeezed hers. She smiled brightly at him, and he returned her smile with a small upturn of his own lips, wary of whether her feelings would stay the same after she learned more about his proclivities.

"I know you mean that now." Rick stroked his thumb over the pulse point in her wrist to gauge her reaction. "And fuck, I hope you still mean it after you hear what I need in a relationship."

Fiona nodded her head as she opened her mouth, probably to claim that she would mean it no matter what. Rick reached out with his free hand to silence her with his pointer finger pressed against her lips.

"Hear me out before you say anything more." Fiona kissed the tip of his finger in response. Rick chuckled at the innocent way she disarmed him, even as he itched to spank her for the insolence. He took a deep breath and dropped his hand down to clasp her free hand in both of his. "I don't know if you've noticed, but I'm a very controlling person."

Fiona made a face, appearing as if she was fighting a bout of laughter at his admittance of the obvious. Rick fought his own smile, only keeping a straight face because he knew he had to, so she would understand the seriousness of the issue.

"I'm not talking about just needing to be in charge of everything with my company, but in all aspects of my life. I'm even more demanding in the bedroom than I am in the arena."

Fiona lost the fight with her smile then, breaking out in a wide one before interrupting him. "You are large and in charge, Boss. I kinda already figured that out and wouldn't want it any other way."

Rick raised an eyebrow at her, keeping his expression stern. *We'll see about that.* "That's two."

"Two?" Fiona questioned, looking confused.

"Two swats," Rick clarified. "For being insolent, disobeying, and speaking when you were supposed to be listening."

Her eyes widened and her pulse quickened, but she didn't say another word, obviously understanding that would earn her a third swat.

"Turning your ass red for being disrespectful and disobedient is only one of the dirty things I want to do to you, Fifi. I want to give you the ultimate pleasure in every way possible, but in order to earn that pleasure, you'll have to submit to me completely. I will take you whenever I want, wherever I want. I won't share you, and I'll be demanding of what I want from you. But just as I will punish you for disobedience, I'll reward you for being my good girl. Sometimes, your pleasure will come with a side of pain. I'm not a gentle man in the bedroom."

Fiona opened her mouth as if to protest. He knew she wanted to offer up his behavior the night before as evidence of the contrary, and he held up a finger to silence her.

"I can be gentle at times, like I was most of last night, but that's not how I get off. I don't intend to hurt you, but I know I'm rough, and most women can't handle how rough I can get when I'm on the brink of losing control."

Fiona gave him a look of sympathy, and he wondered if she was starting to realize what he thought was the real reason why Colleen had cheated on him—his inner caveman.

"If you wake me up with a blow job, I'm liable to pull your hair to hold your head still, while I fuck your face. Can you handle me shoving my cock down your throat?"

Her sympathetic expression changed to one of shock. But he thought he saw a hint of arousal in her eyes, as her breathing quickened.

"If I catch you off alone at one of our shows, I might find an office with a door that locks and order you to bend over the desk, so I can fuck you from behind."

Fiona's little pink lips parted long enough for her to run her tongue over them, as she wiggled under the blanket.

Ah, my sweet little Fifi has a naughty side that likes that idea.

"While I've got you there with your dress flipped up on your back, I might spank your ass. Or I might use the cream from your cunt as lube to fuck your ass. Don't worry, I'll only do that once we've got your ass trained to take me. But if you're with me, I will be fucking your ass almost as often as I'm in your pussy."

Fiona let out a little whimper and Rick hoped it was from excitement at the idea and not fear.

"Can you handle what it means to be with me, Fifi?" He held up a hand to stop her from speaking, when she opened her mouth as if to answer. "I need you to really think about that before you answer. Because I'm not going to let another woman walk out on my daughter when I'm too demanding."

"If you can't handle it, then I'll get dressed and walk out of this room and we can go back to a professional relationship, without any change to your current relationship with Britney. But if you agree to move forward with me, there's no changing your mind later. You will be mine in every way. And once I have you, I'll never let you go."

Rick searched her face, trying to read in her eyes and expression which way she might decide to go. It seemed as if a dozen thoughts crossed her mind, as she sat there staring at him for several long moments.

"I'll give you a few days to think about it." Rick stood to go get dressed and give her space to think everything over.

"No!" Fiona shouted, shattering his heart at the realization he'd just lost her.

Rick's chin fell to his chest, as he fought not to turn back to look at her, while he picked up his shirt from the day before.

"I mean, no, I don't need a few days to think about it."

Rick was hopeful when he heard her rustling in the bed behind him. But he didn't know which way she would decide, until he felt her slide her hands around his waist from behind.

"We might need to set up a safe word in case rough goes past hot discomfort to unbearably painful, but I want to be with you. However you want me." She peppered his shoulders with kisses, as she pressed her tits against his back. "And we're down to only an hour for you to have your way with me before we're supposed to meet up with Britney and Cage to go to the airport."

Thank fuck!

Rick tossed his shirt back over the back of the chair in front of him before spinning around in her arms. With a palm on each of her ass cheeks, he picked her up and stalked back over to the bed. "We'll have to talk about that safe word, and how you know about them later, because that's not nearly enough time for everything I want to do to you this morning."

"Maybe we can skip the spanking for now?" Fiona squealed, as Rick tossed her on the bed.

"That's three for trying to decide what we're doing and when." Rick shoved his boxers to the floor, stepping out of them as he crawled over her on the bed. His cock was already as hard as he'd ever been in his life, and pointing straight at Fiona's creamy pink pussy. "But I'll wait until you've earned ten before I give them to you, so I know your ass will be a bright, pretty pink when I'm done."

"I'm sorry, Sir," Fiona playfully pouted. "I was just trying to be helpful."

Rick's dick hardened even more at the word "Sir" coming from her lips, but he wasn't sure he wanted her to stick with the generic honorific. It would be much more meaningful if she came up with something only she called him.

Fuck! I don't have time to think about that now. I need to fuck her too bad to worry about what I want her to call me right now.

"If you want to be helpful, then be a good girl and spread your legs for me." Rick shifted his weight onto one forearm and his toes, as he held a plank position above her, so he could look into her eyes the whole time. He ran his free hand down her body to settle over her pussy, while she widened her legs. "You're already so wet for me. Aren't you, Fifi?"

"Yes, Sir," Fiona nodded, as she wiggled her hips to rub her pussy over his fingers.

"Lay still or I'm going to have to spank this pussy before I fuck it," Rick growled, as he parted her labia and stuck two fingers inside her.

Fiona's whole body stiffened, as her cunt gushed with cream from obeying his orders.

"Good girl." Rick fucked her with his fingers, starting slowly at first, and then ramping up the speed and intensity, as he put in a third finger to open her up to be able to take his cock with ease.

He might like to be rough and maybe pretend to force her from time to time, but he didn't want to hurt her in any way. His eight inches might not be the longest dick she could take, but he was pretty sure his thick girth would be more than she was ready for after not having sex since college.

Fiona bit down on her bottom lip, clearly fighting her need to move, as he worked her up by stroking over her G-spot.

He felt the precum dripping from his dick and knew he couldn't hold back much longer. He wanted her coming when he first slammed his cock inside her, so he could use her endorphin rush to ease any discomfort he might cause her. Rick started to circle his thumb over her clit to move them along, but first, he had to make sure she was okay with him taking her bare.

Fuck! I can't believe I forgot to stop and buy condoms last night.

"Fifi, I'm clean. Can I take you bare, or do we need to stop until I can go pick up some condoms?"

"I'm clean, too." Fiona nodded. "And I'm on the pill for my periods, so I trust you to go without the condoms."

"Thank fuck!" Rick dipped his head to kiss her then, pushing her pleasure button with his thumb and stroking her G-spot with his fingers until he felt the first flutters of her orgasm starting in her inner walls.

He broke the kiss to watch her face, as he pulled his hand from her pussy to grip his cock. He lined the tip up with her soaking wet slit and plunged balls deep in her creamy cunt.

"Rick!" Fiona screamed, throwing her arms around his neck, as her first orgasm of the morning rocked through her.

She was so tight around his thick shaft that he could barely move, even though her juices provided plenty of lubrication. So, he held still, buried to the hilt inside her, as her inner walls clamped down around him like a vise, and he enjoyed the visual of her O face from a much better angle than he'd seen it the night before while eating her pussy.

How he stopped himself from coming as the waves of her climax tried to milk his cum from his cock, he had no idea. But somehow he was able to endure the most exquisite feeling he'd ever experienced without moving inside her until her internal spasms subsided.

"Now it's my turn, Fifi," Rick growled, as he pulled almost all the way out before slamming back in until he felt the head of his cock hit her cervix. With a hand in her hair, he turned her head to kiss her, swallowing her cries as he relentlessly pounded into her. He had to know she could handle the way he fucked, so he let his inner beast loose, rutting into her like a wild animal.

Their mating was primal and rough. And the greatest experience of Rick's life. Especially when she dug her heels into the mattress and lifted her hips to meet him thrust for thrust.

When she turned her head to suck in a breath, Rick kissed his way down her neck, nipping and sucking to mark her as his. He slid his hand from her hair down to torture her tits as he continued to fuck her like an untamed brute.

"You're mine, Fifi," Rick growled against that sensitive spot on her neck just above her collarbone, where her pulse beat rapidly against his lips. "Tell me who you belong to!"

"Yes, Rick, yes!" Fiona cried out, as her nails dug into his shoulders and upper back. "I belong to you, Rick. Only you!"

The slight touch of pain she gave him was just enough to make his cock feel as if it was swelling even bigger than it already was deep inside her. His balls started to tighten, signaling that he was close to the brink.

Rick had no intention of coming without her coming with him, so he adjusted his position to make sure he rubbed her G-spot with every stroke inside her. He pushed back on his knees and hooked her legs over his forearms to change the angle of her hips, while grabbing her perky peaks with both hands. He didn't slow the pistoning of his dick in her pussy until her next orgasm had her squeezing him like a vise once more.

Rick shoved his cock as deep in her cunt as physically possible and shouted, "Fuck, Fiona!" as he filled her womb with rope after rope of his cum. He vaguely registered her screaming his name, as they simultaneously crescendoed.

Time and space lost all meaning, as he transcended to another plane of existence. For the first time in years, he didn't have a million things running through his mind. He didn't worry about his daughter or his company. There were no thoughts about maintaining his schedule or reaching out to contacts to book the tour stops for the last half of the year. All that mattered at that moment was his connection to Fiona.

Not wanting to crush her when he lost the ability to hold himself up over her, Rick rolled them without slipping out of her slick sheath. He didn't know how long they laid there with him on his back, and her wrapped in his arms and draped over his body. Just holding her as they recovered was all he needed.

Unfortunately, reality broke in when his cell phone rang from across the room with Britney's ringtone.

"Guess that means we're late, huh?" Fiona lifted her head from his chest and looked down at him with a sleepy smile.

"I don't know if we're late or not, but I'd better get it because that's Brit's ringtone." Rick pecked her lips with his, as he rolled her off of him to get up and answer the phone. When he saw the time on his phone as he went to swipe the screen, he cringed. "Hope none of the crew made special plans for Colorado Springs today, because we're probably going to miss them."

Fiona jumped up from the bed and started rushing around the room when she heard his reference to how late they were running.

Damn, I hate not being able to spend the morning going for round two. But we don't even have enough time for me to provide aftercare by cleaning Fifi up and easing any soreness she might be feeling in a hot bath.

Maybe I can sneak down to her room tonight after Britney goes to sleep to make it up to her.

"Hey, Brit, sorry I overslept," Rick said into the phone as soon as the call connected. "Tell Cage to give me thirty minutes to shower and get dressed, and I'll meet you downstairs."

Chapter Sixteen

By the time they were leaving the arena on Sunday night in Winnipeg, Manitoba, Canada, Fiona was convinced that Rick wasn't nearly as sexually rough and demanding as he'd claimed. After their morning romp on Friday, he'd only snuck in a few kisses at the arena in Colorado Springs. And while they left her breathless, they were nothing like the banging from behind he'd told her he would demand if they got a moment alone in an arena that morning.

Friday night after the GWA show, when he'd shown up at her hotel door after Britney went to sleep, Fiona thought he was there for another round. But instead, he apologized for not having time for proper aftercare that morning and gave her a bath. While she enjoyed the way he pampered her, and especially the way he fingered her to orgasm before tucking her into bed, Fiona wished he'd have let her reciprocate.

Saturday in Fargo, North Dakota, they had snuck around for a few more kisses throughout the day. But other than always seeming to have a hand on her when they were on their midday excursion and sitting together at dinner in catering, he hadn't really touched her. At least, not the way she longed for him to touch her anyway. And he hadn't come to her room again since Friday night.

So far, Sunday was more of the same, and Fiona was beyond frustrated. *It's crazy how going without sex for over four years was no big deal before. But now that I've been with Rick, I can't go four days without feeling like I'm dying with need for him.*

Fiona felt guilty for wishing she was going up to the family suite he shared with Britney, instead of to her standard room to spend another night alone in bed. She understood that Rick wanted to set a good example for his daughter, and that meant keeping their relationship in the slow lane for a while. At least, as far as anyone but the two of them knew.

Growing up with her father preaching abstinence before marriage should have prepared her for being patient and waiting until he was ready to let his daughter and the rest of the world know their relationship had gone to the next level. But she also grew up in Heart's Destiny, Texas, where everyone tended to fall in love at first sight and either got married or moved in together in record time.

So, no matter how hard she tried to be patient and set the right example for Britney, her heart wanted the instant family and quickly planned wedding that her parents and grandparents' generations had, and that her generation of friends was recently experiencing.

As she stepped into her room and started her nightly bedtime routine, Fiona thought about all the gossip from home that she'd gotten the week before. Specifically, she thought about the new couples she'd seen and heard about while in church and at the impromptu engagement party for Randi and James after the pay-per-view.

Anthony and Kay had kicked off the most recent rash of weddings in Heart's Destiny, when they met at the end of September and were married less than two months later. From spending time with Kay while traveling with the GWA, Fiona had learned that they'd practically moved in together a week after they met.

Fiona had also learned more of James and Randi's story during her time with the company. While they met on the same day as Anthony and Kay, it took them four-and-a-half months to get engaged, and they were planning their wedding for approximately eight months after the night they met. But they were basically living together on the road from the first day Randi started working with the GWA, two months after meeting James. And according to James, they would have been living together from the first night they met if he'd have been able to convince Randi to fly away with him that night.

I guess if I'm going by their timeline, Rick and I aren't too far behind, since we only met three months ago.

But then she thought about Bobby and Brooklyn, who first met at Anthony and Kay's wedding reception, and were living together less than two weeks later. Fiona knew that was a result of Hazel

Burleson's matchmaking for her son, so she didn't think they were actually sleeping together then. But there was no doubt that they were officially a couple by Christmas, approximately a month after they first met. And according to the short story Maria wrote during class time earlier that day, they were planning their wedding for April, and were expecting their first child in October.

As excited as Maria was today about having a new cousin, I can't imagine she made it up just for that writing assignment. So, they probably really are moving their relationship along at warp speed.

Fiona shook off her envious feelings as she crawled into bed, not wanting to begrudge her friends for their fast track to happily ever after. *That would be as bad as boasting about starting a relationship with Rick to my friends, who aren't quite where they want to be with their significant others yet.*

Fiona had seen quite a few longing looks the previous Sunday and knew that her hometown would see a few more weddings this year, even though the couples were still obviously fighting their attractions. She's seen several from Charlotte and Ian, when they seemed to think nobody else was watching at church.

It was the same with her high school boyfriend, Justin, and Randi's best friend, Amy, at the engagement party. For that matter, there were several possible pairings between the other Burleson girls and the single male wrestlers that were there in the diner that night, too.

And they all met the same week I met and fell for Rick. So, maybe our timeline isn't so slow after all.

I wonder if any of them were sneaking around and hooking up last weekend? Or if they're secretly dating and just don't want to let Hazel and Susan know their matchmaking worked?

Goodness, I wonder if that's what Rick and I are doing with Britney? Fiona giggled at the thought. *No, we're not exactly hiding that we're dating. I mean, pretty much everyone in the company knows we went out Thursday after the show. And with as much as we've been holding hands everywhere we go, she has to know we're dating, even if she doesn't know we're serious yet.*

Though I wonder how serious we really are, since we've only made love once? Surely, if he was really serious about me, he'd have come to my room last night or tonight for more? Unless he thinks I'm still sore from Friday?

No, surely not. I mean, yeah, I was sore on Friday because it's been so long and he's so big. But he has to know it doesn't really take this long to recover, right?

Fiona tossed and turned, contemplating how she should go about telling Rick that she didn't need that much recovery time. Giving up on going to sleep with her mind running a mile a minute, she grabbed her Kindle from her bag and read a few chapters of the latest release by Lexi Blake, a romance titled ***Evidence of Desire***. While the story was nothing like her real-life romance with Rick, it did give her an idea when Isla walked, naked, into David's shower to tell him she didn't want to go slow.

I don't want to go slow either! But how can I sneak into Rick's bedroom when we aren't sharing a suite? I can't, not without risking knocking on the door and waking Britney.

But I can text him to see if he's still up and wants company in his bed. And if he does, I can go up there in just my bathrobe to be able to get naked quickly once I'm there.

Fiona jumped out of bed and ran to the bathroom, grabbing her cell phone off the nightstand as she went. She shot off a text to Rick.

Fiona: Are you still up? Want company?

As soon as she sent the message, she stripped off her pajamas and made sure all her important parts were clean and well groomed. Just as she was finishing up, her phone beeped with an incoming message.

Rick: Does my sweet Fifi need Papa to come tuck her in?
Or do you want to come cuddle on the couch & watch a movie?

Oh, he is so scary, rough, and demanding. Not! Charlotte totally pegged him correctly as a Daddy Dom. Fiona donned her robe and sent him a message, as she walked out of the bathroom, stopped to get her room key card, and creeped through the empty hallway to the stairwell, not wanting to risk being seen in the elevator wearing only her robe by a guest coming back to the hotel after closing down a local bar.

> **Fiona: I definitely need a cuddle, Papa. What room are you in? I'm on my way to you now.**

Rick: 2101. See you soon.

Fiona was huffing and puffing after running up ten flights of stairs, making her realize just how much she'd let her fitness slip since starting her job with the GWA. She took a moment to catch her breath before she peeked out the door to make sure the hallway on the twenty-first floor was clear for her to walk to Rick's room. Luckily for her, not only was the hallway clear, but his room was also the one closest to the stairwell.

She knocked softly, and smiled brightly at him, when he opened the door before she could rap her knuckles on the door a second time.

"What are you wearing, Fifi?" Rick grabbed her hand and pulled her into the room, closing the door behind her quickly.

Fiona was too enthralled with looking him over from the top of his head to his large, bare feet to answer his question. He was wearing another t-shirt and pajama pants combo, like he'd worn in the bungalow in the Bahamas, and Fiona's mouth watered at the sight. Especially since he wasn't trying to hide the way his penis was tenting his pants like he had in Nassau.

"Fifi, I asked you a question and I expect an answer." Rick's already deep voice seemed to go down an octave, and the commanding tone would have made her wet her panties, if she'd been wearing any.

"My bathrobe and a smile." Fiona grinned at him, wondering if her cheeky response would earn her more of the swats he'd promised her on Friday morning.

Rick didn't say a word, as he bent down and picked her up, throwing her over his shoulder to walk into his bedroom. Once inside the room, he turned to shut and lock the door before placing her back on her feet at the foot of the bed.

"Now that we are someplace where we won't be disturbed," he growled, giving her a stern expression. "Explain why you are traipsing through the hotel in only your robe."

Yep, I've definitely earned a couple more swats.

"Because I've never had sex outside the United States, and I'm tired of waiting for you to take me, like you said you would." Fiona put her hands on her hips, trying to act more confident than she felt. "So, Rick, I just ran up ten flights of stairs to take you instead."

"Oh, little girl, you're going to regret that." Rick shook his head while looking at her sternly, but Fiona could see he was fighting a smile, and she knew he was enjoying her bratty behavior. "We're up to fifteen swats now, and I'm going to enjoy giving you each and every one of them tonight."

"Fifteen!" Fiona couldn't stop herself from the outburst, even though she knew it would probably add another swat or two to the total count. "How did we jump from three to fifteen?"

"Number four is from thinking you can take charge." Rick held up his hand with his four fingers extended, pointing to his first finger with his other hand. He then extended his thumb and pointed to it as he went on with his explanation. "Number five is for being practically naked in public and showing off what's mine. The other ten are for each floor you traversed while putting yourself at risk, when any number of men could have cornered you and taken advantage, or worse. I understand that the large jump in the count was a shock, so I'm not going to add one for your outburst in questioning them. But only because you haven't learned the rules yet. I will add more if you question me from this point further. I will also add more if you don't address me as Papa or Sir in the future. I only want to hear my name on your lips when you're coming for me. Do you understand?"

"Yes, Papa," Fiona answered automatically. *Hopefully, I have it right that it's Papa in private, Sir in public, and Rick when I'm coming.*

"Good girl. Now we'll go over the rest of the rules before I give you the spanking you've earned tonight. You already know that insolence and disrespect will earn swats. So will lying, talking back, or rolling your eyes at me. Putting yourself in danger will earn harsher punishments. As will letting another man see or touch what's mine. And when I say you're mine, I don't just mean the holes you will have available for me to fuck whenever, wherever, and however I want. Every part of you is mine, as is your pleasure. You don't come unless I tell you to. Understand?"

"Yes, Papa." Fiona felt her arousal running down her thigh and dropped her gaze from his in embarrassment. *So much for cleaning up before I came up here.*

When she looked down, she noticed his erection seemed to have grown larger as he was telling her the rules. Seeing the monster in his pants reminded her why it was a good thing she got so wet from just talking to him.

"You are to keep your eyes on mine unless I direct you otherwise."

Fiona's eyes snapped back up to Rick's, as soon as the words left his mouth.

"Good girl." Rick gave her a small smile before changing the direction of the conversation. "Have you ever been spanked before?"

"Only once as a child. When I realized my parents truly believed the bible verse about sparing the rod and spoiling the child, I did everything I could to keep from having the paddle used on my backside again."

Rick grimaced at her admission. "I promise I won't ever use anything but my hand."

When Rick held up his right hand to show her his palm, Fiona realized that his hand was about the same size as the two-by-four that had been carved into the paddle that still hung on the wall of her mother's kitchen. She gulped at the realization and was sure he could see her trepidation at the thought of how much this spanking was going to hurt.

"We'll use the stoplight system for a safe word tonight, so we can dial in exactly how hard I can slap your ass to be a punishment without being too much for you to handle. If at any point I go past the point you can handle, you say red, and I'll stop. If you're feeling it as an effective punishment, but it's not too much, say yellow. That's normally a signal that you need a little break but want more, so I will still treat it as such and give you a breather before administering any more swats. And I'll keep the subsequent swats at that same intensity level. If you don't say either of those because you're enjoying the spanking, I'll ask you how you are, and you'll say green to let me know we're good to keep going. Understand?"

"Yes, Papa." Fiona nodded and gave him a tentative smile.

"Do you have any questions for me before we get started with your punishment?"

"Do you have any rules about my grooming? What I wear? When I should be waiting naked in your bed for you? Or any of the diet, exercise, or language rules like I've read about?"

"Not at this time." Rick shook his head and slightly smiled. "But if there's something you've read about that turns you on to think about doing, I'm more than willing to read the books you've seen it in to consider adding more rules for you later."

"Thank you, Papa." Fiona smiled at him, already running through her list of books in her mind to come up with ideas to share with him. *I wonder what he'd think of making me talk dirty the way he does?*

"You're more than welcome, sweet Fifi." Rick stepped around her and took a seat on the end of the bed. "Now, remove your robe and lay across my lap, so we can get your punishment out of the way."

Fiona shivered with excitement, as she followed Rick's instructions, not even caring if her phone and hotel room key card fell out of the pockets of her robe, as she dropped it to the floor. She draped herself over Rick's lap with her hip bones resting on his right thigh and her ribs resting on his left thigh.

The lower portion of her breasts barely brushed against his thigh as they hung down toward the floor, with her nipples as hard as she'd ever noticed them. She felt his erection pressing into the left side of her belly and wished she was impaled on it instead of having to wait through the torture of a spanking before he made love to her.

"I don't want you to be completely quiet, but please try not to be so loud that you wake anyone else in the hotel," Rick instructed, as he placed his left hand between her shoulder blades and ran his right palm over her bottom. "I'd like for you to count them out, but I understand if you're not able to focus to do that this first time. Just know that eventually, you'll be trained to not only count your swats, but also to thank me for each one and ask for the next."

Fiona's whole body quivered at the thought of how hot that sounded. She decided to try her best to do exactly what he wanted from the very first swat, but she wasn't prepared for the way her body would respond when his first swat landed on her right cheek.

She felt the sting before she heard the smack of flesh hitting flesh. It wasn't as unbearably painful as she remembered the paddle being when she was a child, but it wasn't as soft as she'd expected him to start, either. It was just a shock to her system that stunned her into silence, as her arousal level amped up a notch or two.

She subconsciously braced for the next one, which landed on her left cheek, by pressing her palms and toes into the carpet on the floor.

Rick had given her at least five swats, with each progressively stinging a little more than the last, before she realized she'd already lost count and hadn't said a word.

"How are you feeling, sweet Fifi?" Rick rubbed the sting into her backside, as he asked the question.

"Green, Papa," Fiona answered breathlessly, surprising herself as much as Rick with how arousing she found the spanking.

Rick slid his hand down between her thighs to cup her sex. "Fuck, those first five didn't do anything but make your pussy gush. Let's see if we can get you to yellow with the next five."

He spread her juices all over his palm before lifting his hand and bringing it back down on her bottom. Fiona wasn't sure if he actually smacked her harder, or if the moisture just made it feel like it was harder. Either way, it was enough to make Fiona whimper for the first time, reminding her to count.

"Six. Thank you, Papa. May I have another?"

Rick didn't answer verbally, but she felt his erection twitch against her side, where he was obviously turned on by her responding the way he wanted to the spanking. She continued counting, thanking him, and asking for another with each swat, feeling like she was getting closer and closer to the edge with each one.

I probably shouldn't come from what is supposed to be a punishment spanking. Hopefully, if it happens, he won't notice, so he'll use this as a punishment in the future.

Not wanting him to stop and ask how she was feeling again when she was getting close to climaxing from the spanking that was way more erotic than a punishment, Fiona reported that she was still green when she counted the tenth swat. Rick didn't say anything in response, but he did pause long enough to swipe his fingers through her folds, as if he was double-checking to make sure she was being honest in her assessment.

Unfortunately, the short reprieve from the swats was enough for her to back away from the edge, and he didn't run his fingers over either of the spots he had used previously to take her over when he swiped up some of her cream. Though hearing him slurp as he sucked her juices from his fingers was hot, it wasn't enough to push her to the release she desperately needed at that moment.

Once he had licked his fingers clean, Rick continued with her spanking. Fiona counted off swats eleven and twelve, as her eyes started to water from the increased intensity. When number thirteen landed, she said, "yellow" instead of counting.

"Thank fuck!" Rick rubbed his large palm across her bottom to soothe the sting. "I was beginning to think I was going to have to come up with an alternative punishment to keep from bruising you."

Fiona was too focused on fighting her tears for any alternative punishments to come to mind. Though later, she'd realize she was glad they'd found her spanking limit, because she would vastly prefer a spanking to orgasm denial as a form of punishment.

"You have two more, sweet Fifi. Let me know when you're ready for the next one."

"I can take them both now, Papa," she said through her sniffles.

She clamped her teeth together to keep from crying out as number fourteen rained down fire on her buttocks. She didn't count it, thank him, or ask for the next one, but she also didn't say "yellow" or "red," so he quickly followed it with number fifteen on the fleshiest part of her cheeks, just below where the previous one had landed.

Fiona couldn't stop herself from crying, as Rick lifted and flipped her to cradle her in his arms. She wasn't sure why she was crying, since the sting of the spanking didn't really last that long. But she still wrapped her arms around his neck and soaked the left shoulder of his t-shirt with her tears.

Rick continued to hold her as she cried, lightly rubbing her back and rocking her, as if she was a baby who needed soothing.

"Feel better, my sweet Fifi?" Rick whispered his question in her ear, as her sobs slowly subsided.

"Yes, Papa." Fiona nodded against his shoulder. "I'm sorry. I'm crying and I don't even know why. That didn't hurt nearly bad enough for all these tears that I can't seem to stop."

"It's okay, sweet Fifi," Rick cooed soothingly. "Sometimes you just have to let out all those emotions that you haven't even realized have been building up inside you. And I'm happy to be the one to bring them out and hold you while you cry them away, so you don't have to suffer from holding them in anymore."

"Do you have a way to release your emotions like this?" Fiona lifted her head and looked into his steel-gray eyes, wanting to be there for him to release his emotions on as well.

"For the past few years, I've released my pent-up frustrations by punching a heavy bag in the gym, at least a couple of times a week," Rick chuckled. "But I have a feeling we're both going to be releasing more of them through orgasms from now on."

"Does spanking me work as well as punching a heavy bag, Papa?" Fiona smiled at him mischievously.

"Oh, no." Rick shook his head and his words, combined with the flat line of his lips, made Fiona's heart sink at the thought of not helping him as much as he helped her. Thankfully, he didn't stop with such a short answer and his continued explanation helped alleviate her insecurity of not being enough for him.

"Spanking you is much better than punching a heavy bag. I don't get out the same amount of anger because I'll never slap your ass as hard as I'll punch a bag, but I also don't feel as angry about things I can't fix when I'm looking at your sexy ass while I'm spanking you. Plus, I know I'll get to release everything else I'm bottling up in your sweet cunt once the spanking is over."

Fiona smiled up at him, happy to hear he wasn't done with her for the night and blushing at his usage of such crass words. She hoped her expression conveyed her wish for him to move on to the next part of their night, because she was pretty sure telling him she was ready for the sex to commence would earn her another spanking. While she wasn't too sore from the fifteen swats she'd just received, she was sore enough to not want any more right then.

Apparently, staying quiet and smiling at him was the right move on her part. Rick lifted her up off his lap, making sure she was steady on her feet before he released his hold on her hips to stand from the bed.

"Bend over the end of the bed, sweet Fifi," he commanded, sending a flood of arousal from her nether regions. "I want to see my handprints on your ass while I fuck you from behind."

Fiona did as she was told, reveling in the way her nipples tightened even more, as they brushed across the duvet on his bed. Rick continued giving her directions, telling her where to place her hands and feet, as well as how to arch her back and push up on her tiptoes to lift her bottom higher, while he ran his hands over her backside and between her legs.

"Fuck, that's such a hot position. Too bad your pretty pink pussy is still too low. Guess I'll just have to enjoy the visual, while I get you ready for my cock."

Rick pushed his thick finger inside her, moving it in and out like she couldn't wait for him to do with his penis. Soon a second finger joined the first, scissoring inside her to stretch her out for his large member.

It was all she could do to hold still when he spread her open with his other hand on her cheek and his thumb joined the fingers already in her channel. When his thumb slipped back out and trailed her juices up between her cheeks to press against her puckered back hole, Fiona couldn't hold back her whimper of surprise.

"Relax, sweet Fifi." Rick's voice was deep and gravelly from his heightened arousal level. "You're just getting my thumb in your ass tonight. I know you won't be able to take my cock until I buy you some plugs and get you opened up."

She tried to relax, as she felt his thumb breach her back entrance, but she wasn't sure she was completely successful. It was a strange sensation, but not unpleasant. She knew it had to be the taboo aspect of being touched back there that turned her on enough to make it feel good, as he started pumping his thumb in and out of her.

A third finger joined the other two in her vagina before Rick started alternating which hole he was pushing into while pulling out of the other one.

She felt so full. So good while being so bad. Her breathing pattern changed to a pant as Rick worked her closer and closer to the edge.

"My sweet Fifi has a naughty side," Rick growled, speeding up the movement of his digits in and out of her. "You like that, don't you, Fifi? Tell Papa how much you like being finger-fucked in your pussy and ass at the same time."

"Yes, I like it so much, Papa," Fiona panted out breathlessly.

"No, say the words, Fifi," Rick demanded. "I want to hear my naughty girl say all the dirty words."

Fiona's heart rate sped up at just the thought of saying the bad words he was directing her to say.

"Say 'I like having you finger-fuck my pussy and ass at the same time, Papa,' or I'm going to stop and not let you come," Rick ordered her.

That would be a worse punishment than the spanking earlier, Fiona thought as she was saying the dirty words he wanted to hear. "I like having you finger-fuck my pussy and ass at the same time, Papa."

"Fuck, yeah, you do. But you'd better be a good girl and wait until it's my cock in your cunt before you come."

"Please, Papa," Fiona begged, not sure how long she could hold back, while he was relentlessly fingering her.

"Please what, Fifi? Please let you come on my fingers? Or please fuck you, so you can come on my cock? Say the words, naughty girl."

"Please fuck me, so I can come on your cock, Papa," Fiona begged, as she felt the flutters starting in her inner walls.

"My sweet Fifi, such a good girl for Papa," Rick growled, as he pulled his fingers and thumb from both her holes just in time to keep her from coming.

Fiona groaned in frustration just as he gripped her hips and lifted her off her feet.

"Knees on the bed and stick that ass in the air for me, Fifi," Rick commanded, releasing his hold on her hips, as she did as he instructed.

Rick shoved his pants and boxers down to his mid-thighs as he stepped up to the edge of the bed between her splayed legs. He spread her cheeks with his hands, slipping his thumb back in her back hole, as he impaled her on his manhood.

Fiona cried out at the shock of suddenly being filled in both holes at once.

"Not so loud, sweet Fifi," Rick chuckled, as he reached around with his free hand to lightly slap her mound, just as he pulled out with his monster erection.

The sensation of having her clit spanked sent Fiona flying over the edge in a surprise orgasm.

"Holy! Wow! Rick!" Fiona gripped the duvet in both hands before pressing her face into the bed to muffle her cries of pleasure, as her whole body spasmed in ecstasy. She closed her eyes and saw fireworks going off on the backs of her eyelids, as wave after wave of pleasure crashed over her.

"Fuck, yeah, my naughty Fifi likes having her pussy spanked, as much as she likes having her ass finger-fucked." Rick's dirty commentary didn't slow the frantic pace with which he pounded into her. It also didn't stop the way he pumped his thumb in and out of her back hole.

Fiona barely registered that he was still talking, saying something about loving the visual of her red backside with him filling both holes, as one climax rolled into the next and she floated away in nirvana. Time lost all meaning, as euphoria overwhelmed her. It could have been minutes, or hours later, when she felt him still inside her, as he cried out her name and filled her with jet after jet of his cum.

She felt him resting against her back, as they both recovered from their carnal mating. He apparently recovered much faster than she did because he didn't rest on her long.

"Don't move, Fifi. I'll be right back."

Fiona replied with a thumbs-up gesture, still unable to form words, as she heard him chuckle and walk away.

"Fuck," he groaned, as he walked back up behind her from wherever he'd been. "You're so hot right now. I'd love to take a picture of my cum dripping out of your pussy, with your ass all red and your asshole opening up for me."

Yes, do it! Fiona thought, thinking it would be hot to see later.

"But I'd never want to risk being hacked and someone else seeing you like this," Rick continued his thought, as he ran a warm washcloth between her legs to clean her up.

After he wiped through her folds, over her thighs and butt cheeks, and swiped through her crack to clean up her back hole, Fiona started to move, thinking he was done.

"Don't move yet, Fifi," Rick directed. "I have some arnica cream I want to rub on your ass to keep you from bruising from the spanking."

The cream was cold as he rubbed it in, but it eased the remaining sting from the swats.

Once he was done, Rick disappeared once more to put away the supplies he'd used to clean her up and care for her after the spanking and sex. When he returned to the bedroom, he scooped her up into his arms and carried her around the bed, pulling down the covers before laying her in his bed and crawling in beside her.

Fiona knew she needed to go back to her room, so Britney wouldn't know she'd been there in the middle of the night, but she couldn't make herself move from the cradle of his arms.

"Rest, sweet Fifi," Rick whispered, cuddling her the way she hadn't realized she loved until the first time she slept in his arms. "I'll wake you up at five when I get up for my workout to sneak you back to your room."

Fiona smiled, as she moaned her agreement and snuggled into his side. She fell asleep almost instantly, not registering the end of his statement.

"And I'll be covering you up in one of my t-shirts and a pair of sweats under your robe before taking you back down there."

~~~

Monday, February 18, 2019, Calgary, Alberta, Canada

Rick was having a hard time focusing on everything he had to do at the arena in Calgary, Alberta, Canada, after the mind-blowing night he'd had with Fiona. He just kept reliving every moment, from the time she arrived at his hotel door in nothing but her bathrobe, to the time when he carried her down to her hotel room bundled up in his sweats and t-shirt, and her robe.

Fuck! Fifi in my clothes was almost as hot as her naked.

He had diligently tried to give her a few days to recover from their rough first fuck Friday morning, but it had taken every ounce of willpower he had to stay away from her on Saturday night. And there was no way he could resist her when she came to his room Sunday night.

He'd been worried that she'd be too sore for the way he liked to fuck to be able to do it again within a week, especially knowing it had been years since she'd even had mediocre sex. He was happily surprised by the way she'd shown him she could handle him, without the need for as much recovery time as he'd thought.

All day long, every time he looked at her, he imagined her as he'd seen her the night before. He couldn't remember anything they'd seen at the Glenbow Museum because he kept picturing Fiona as he'd seen
~~~

her draped over his lap while he spanked her. Her perfect, round ass on display for him with her bare, pink pussy dripping wet from every swat he delivered.

His palm had itched to do it again, until he saw her shifting uncomfortably in the hard chairs in catering that evening. *I'm going to have to reapply the arnica cream tonight after the show, so hopefully, her ass won't be too sore to sit tomorrow.*

With the way the backstage area was set up in the Calgary arena, there were no walls, or even curtains, separating the various areas backstage other than the locker rooms. So, while catering separated his makeshift office from the classroom, he was still able to see Fiona from across the vast backstage area, while he was supposed to be working and she was teaching. While Rick loved the unobstructed view, he struggled to keep from being distracted by watching her to be able to do his job.

Earlier, when he thought he was focused on interviewing the tag team, who were there for a try-out match that night, Rick immediately flashed back to being inside her bare when they explained their wrestling gimmick, Protection Detail, because it was a spoof on condom usage.

Cameron Wentworth used the ring name Trojan. His tag-team partner, Harrison Thorne, used the ring name Magnum, which was oddly appropriate since he was six-foot-seven and towered over his six-foot-two tag-team partner. Their ring attire consisted of head-to-toe, flesh-toned bodysuits. They'd also put together a sponsorship deal to toss condoms to the fans when they entered the arena to wrestle on the local Calgary cards.

Rick was glad Stone and Ethan had been sitting in on the initial interview earlier in the day to be able to bring him out of his Fiona-fog long enough to call his legal department in New York before the office closed. He not only had to get them looking into what was needed to add the GWA to the contract for the sponsorship to expand outside of Calgary, but he also had to get them started on the paperwork for work visas for the Canadian wrestlers, if he offered them a contract after their try-out match.

Damn! I need to get my mind off Fiona and go watch their try-out match!

Rick shook off his guilt for not doing his part to get the show started, as he joined his talent gathered around the monitors backstage in the open area between catering and the classroom. But no matter how hard he tried to focus on the screen to see the match between Protection Detail and the Dangerous Twins, Rick's eyes kept wandering over to where Fiona was seated at a table with Jason Moore and Baylee Grady, administering a second-grade spelling test.

"Oh, shit!" Bama Boy Mason shouted, drawing Rick's attention back to the screen they were all watching. "Didn't anybody teach that boy three-hundred pounders don't fly? There's no way I'm gonna be able to catch him, if he tries that in a match with us."

"Hell, I'm surprised Dean didn't need to take a breather after that splash," Bama Boy Dixon replied to his partner.

"If that's his finisher, we should rename it the sperminator," Stone chuckled, eliciting a round of laughter among the performers around them.

Rick somehow managed to drown out the comments of the men and women already on his roster, as he focused in on watching the performance in the ring. He knew only half the high workrate he saw could be attributed to the guys trying out, with the other half credited to the Dangerous Twins. But Protection Detail brought a new layer of ring psychology that made him want to hire them, without even waiting to hear James and Dean's opinions of how they worked during the match.

With the way they're over as faces, though, we're going to have to turn another team heel to keep from having a face-heavy tag-team division.

He looked around at the crowd around the monitors and pointed to the two teams he currently had working as babyfaces. "Bama Boys and Red Velvet, you guys need to decide which of your teams is turning heel when we get Protection Detail's visa paperwork done for them to join the roster."

"I thought you already turned us heel by naming us after a cake." "Dark Chocolate" Dion Davis motioned back and forth between himself and his tag-team partner, Red, whose real name was Liam Connery.

Rick heard Fiona giggle from where she was sitting across the room and wondered if she was laughing at something one of the kids said, or if she heard their conversation to realize he'd gone with her suggestion for the Red Velvet tag-team name. *I can't wait to get her alone in my bedroom later to ask her what she's finding so funny right now.*

Unfortunately, he still had to get through the rest of the card, and contract negotiations with the new team he wanted to sign to the roster, before they could even head back to the hotel. Then he still had to wait an hour for Britney to fall asleep before Fiona could sneak up to his room for the rest of the night.

And she'd better stay in that sexy sapphire dress, even if she takes off the leggings and cardigan before she walks through the hotel. Surely, she knows better than to earn another punishment while her ass is still sore from last night. If not, it's going to be more of a punishment for me when I have to deny her orgasms, since I can't spank her again yet.

Chapter Seventeen

Fiona was having a whirlwind of a day with her schedule thrown off by not having a GWA show due to their travel changes to leave for the European tour that night. Everything was business as usual when she woke up at five a.m. in Cincinnati to sneak out of Rick's room before Britney woke up.

They had easily fallen into a routine of her going (fully clothed) to his room an hour after they arrived back at the hotel every night after the GWA shows, making love for a couple of hours, and sleeping in each other's arms until his early morning alarm. While Rick still called it fucking, and had gotten her to call it that when they were locked behind closed doors alone, Fiona could only classify their intense copulation as making love.

Yes, Rick was rougher than anyone she'd ever been with before. But he never actually hurt her, and he always made sure she was enjoying it as much as he was by making her come multiple times every night. Besides that, she didn't think the carnality of the act determined whether it was classified as making love or not. It was the connection between partners that elevated any sexual act up to the status of making love, no matter where it fell on the intensity spectrum between gentle, vanilla sex and primal, kinky fucking.

Even the way he snuck in a quickie in the women's locker room at the gym this morning was making love. Though, I still can't believe he called the grappling moves he tried to teach me "foreplay" in front of all those guys there for MMA training.

Going to the MMA gyms he trained at in some cities was also new to their routine. Fiona wasn't sure how the workouts compared to the days they went jogging together because she didn't feel like her heart rate stayed consistently in the cardio zone as he was teaching her the wrestling moves, but she liked being close to him and spending their mornings together.

After their early morning workouts, they went back to their separate rooms at the hotel to get packed up for their day. *Or cleaned up when we don't have the luxury of a private locker room at one of his MMA gyms, like this morning.*

They normally met back up in the lobby to have breakfast and head to the airport to go about the rest of their day, just the same as they had before they started dating. But this morning, when they boarded the plane in Cincinnati, they didn't fly to the next city where the GWA had a show. They flew to New York City, and left the majority of their bags on the plane as they went sightseeing.

As it was still February, and too cold for Fiona to be comfortable with being out in the elements to see things like the Statue of Liberty, they rode around in a limo with Rick pointing out significant buildings in the city before going to the Metropolitan Museum of Art. They ate a quick lunch from a hot dog vendor in the limo before starting the tour of the iconic museum, where Fiona was most impressed by the rare drawings of Leonardo da Vinci that were on display for a limited time.

After the museum, Rick pointed out the main features of Central Park they could see from the car on the drive between the museum and his home at 15 Central Park West, where he was dropping off Fiona and Britney to spend the afternoon playing in the kitchen, while he ran some errands.

She wasn't sure what all he had to do while in New York, but assumed at least some of his tasks included stopping by the GWA headquarters to sign off on the final immigration paperwork for the new tag team he'd signed in Calgary to finally be able to join them on tour when they returned to the states after the next two weeks in Europe.

As soon as Rick escorted them up in the private elevator to his penthouse, Britney practically shoved him back into the elevator before he could even show Fiona around. "I've got this, Dad. You need to hurry with your errands, so you can be home in time for dinner at five to give us plenty of time to get back to the airport for our flight."

"We don't have to be at the airport until eight," Rick objected, not letting Britney push him back into the elevator. "So we can still eat at six and have our normal hour for dinner with an hour to get to the airport."

"No, Dad!" Britney groaned, as she shook her head and rolled her eyes at her father. "We're having a special surprise tonight, so we need two hours for dinner."

"Are you in on this surprise?" Rick looked at Fiona, as if he expected her to fill him in on whatever Britney was going on about.

"Nope," Fiona replied, popping the P as she grinned at him standing in the way of the elevator door closing with his daughter still pressing on his chest with both hands. "But you might want to hurry, so we can both be surprised by whatever Britney has planned."

"Fine, but if I'm going to be shoved out the door by the two of you ganging up on me, I should at least get a kiss goodbye before I go," Rick huffed in feigned outrage.

Britney popped up on her toes and kissed his cheek before stepping back out of the elevator opening.

"You too, Fifi." Rick pointed to his other cheek, while grinning at Fiona.

Fiona giggled with giddiness at him using the nickname, as she stepped up to kiss his other cheek. Rick surprised her by wrapping his arm around her to hold her in place when she started to step back after kissing his whiskers. He turned his head and pecked their lips together before releasing her and stepping back into the elevator to actually leave.

"Let's go check the pantry to see what all we have to order to make dinner. Then I'll give you a tour of our house while we're waiting on the grocery delivery." Britney motioned for Fiona to follow her around the corner from the entryway, past an elegantly decorated dining room with a table for twelve, and down a short hallway to a gorgeous eat-in kitchen in the northwest corner of the building, with a view of what Fiona thought was the Hudson River.

"Do you have something specific you want to make for dinner to go along with your surprise?" Fiona ran her palm across the gorgeous light marble countertop on the island, as she followed Britney to the stainless steel refrigerator.

"I'm thinking something Tex-Mex, since we can't get that here in New York." Britney rummaged through the packages in the freezer. "Can we make enchiladas with chicken breasts or steak? I think Dad used the last of the ground beef making burgers when we were home at Christmas."

"We can make chicken enchiladas," Fiona suggested, prompting Britney to remove a package of wrapped chicken breasts from the freezer and drop them into the sink in the island.

"Good, because I know who to call for the grocery store to deliver the cheese and sauce and stuff, but I don't know which butcher shop delivers here to order more ground beef." Britney walked back around the island to open a door to the pantry before asking, "What else do we need to make enchiladas?"

"Corn tortillas, enchilada sauce, and cheese for just basic enchiladas, but we can add beans, rice, tomatoes, and peppers if you want to dress them up." Fiona recited the ingredients from memory, as Britney pulled a container of rice from the pantry and checked the fridge for cheese.

"We'll have to see what the grocery store has premade for dessert, since we don't have time to make anything but the enchiladas." Britney pulled a notepad from a drawer and started making a list of what they needed.

"Or we could make sopapillas on the stove while the enchiladas are in the oven," Fiona suggested, stepping into the pantry to see if she could find the ingredients, since most of them were pantry staples.

"What are sopapillas?" Britney looked at Fiona with a confused expression.

"They're a Mexican fried dough that's drizzled with honey and a fruit sauce for dessert. I like them best with a strawberry syrup," Fiona explained, as she placed the flour, shortening, baking powder, and vegetable oil on the island. "It looks like you already have all the ingredients for them, except maybe the strawberry syrup."

"I'll add it to the list." Britney grinned, as she pulled out her cell phone and dialed to place the grocery order.

Once that was done, Britney gave Fiona a tour of the over five-thousand square foot, four bedroom, five-and-a-half bath penthouse.

Every room in the place was elegantly decorated with white walls and furniture. The draperies, rugs, and accent pillows were all shades of cream. The only pops of color in the common areas were the medium brown wood tables, cabinets, and doors throughout the beautiful home. Oh, and the wood-paneled walls in the room Britney called the library in the northeast corner of the building.

Fiona was starting to feel self-conscious about what Rick must have thought of the chaos of color in her apartment, until Britney showed her the bedrooms. First, they went through a guest bedroom right beside the kitchen that was decorated in masculine shades of green. Then they went to the room next door to it that was decorated in sunny yellows.

On the other side of the second guest room was Britney's room. It was decorated similarly to Fiona's back home, with lots of pink and purple and a princess canopy over the bed. Her room was in the southwest corner of the building, with windows that overlooked both the Hudson River and the Manhattan skyline.

As they left Britney's room, Fiona expected to go back around the center of the penthouse where the elevators and stairs were housed, past the two spare bedrooms, kitchen, laundry room, dining room, library, living room, and gallery entryway to look into Rick's bedroom on the southeast corner of the building. But Britney surprised her by opening a door Fiona thought was a linen closet to a hallway that actually led past the second master bathroom, and several closets before opening up into the master bedroom and first master bathroom. Rick's bedroom was decorated in shades of blue, with pale blue walls and navy bedding.

The room was gorgeous and masculine, but it made her question his truthfulness about his favorite color, since it was all blues and not green, as he'd told her was his favorite color.

Fiona didn't have a chance to ask Britney about Rick's color choices because there was a buzz coming from the gallery entryway that the little girl ran off to answer. Fiona caught up with her as she was pushing a button on the wall and talking with the doorman about the delivery of the groceries.

By the time the woman with the groceries had been allowed to come up in the public elevator beside the private elevator they'd used, all thoughts about Rick's room colors evaporated from Fiona's mind.

She and Britney spent the next couple of hours preparing the enchiladas and making the sopapillas once the enchiladas were in the oven, while talking about the things they were looking forward to seeing on the European tour.

Fiona was afraid they'd made way more than they could eat that evening, as they moved the two full baking dishes of enchiladas and a platter containing a dozen sopapillas to the warmer to wait for Rick to get back for dinner. But she assumed he would find some way to keep the leftovers from going to waste, just as he had with everything else she and Britney had cooked in the last month. *Or maybe Cage will stay and eat with us to help finish off some of this extra food.*

Just as Fiona was opening her mouth to ask Britney if she knew what Cage's plans were for dinner, she heard voices coming from the entryway. For a moment, she was frightened, thinking someone had bypassed the security of the doorman downstairs to enter the penthouse without permission.

Then Britney got the biggest grin and shouted, "We're in the kitchen!"

"Britney," Fiona whisper-shouted, shaking her head at the little girl, while grabbing her arm and pulling her into the pantry and pulling her phone out of her pocket to call for help. "We should hide and call nine-one-one, not announce to the intruders where to find us."

"They're not intruders, Miss Fiona," Britney objected, pulling out of Fiona's grasp, and stepping back into the kitchen. "They're my surprise dinner guests."

Fiona followed Britney back out of the pantry, just in time to see an older couple walking into the kitchen. Seeing Rick's older doppelganger with a full head of silver hair and Rick's steel-gray eyes, Fiona knew the man must be Rick's father. Which meant the tall, raven-haired, brown-eyed woman with him must be Rick's mother.

Frick-n-frack! I'm so not prepared to meet his parents! Especially with him not here to make introductions.

Do I introduce myself as his girlfriend? No, that's too juvenile for Rick to be comfortable with classifying me.

Should I just introduce myself as his employee and Britney's teacher? While those are both accurate, they don't really encompass every aspect of our relationship, especially for the last couple of weeks.

Leah Mae Wright

We really should have talked about how we're defining our relationship before I met his parents.

Frick-n-frack! Does he even want me to meet his parents yet? Them coming over now is Britney's surprise, so Rick doesn't know they're here. Is he gonna be upset that I'm meeting them now, when he's not ready to introduce us yet?

Fiona vaguely registered that Britney was making introductions, but she was too busy having a mini-panic attack in her head. Their conversation sounded like when adults were talking in the old *Charlie Brown* cartoons she remembered watching as a child. When the room started to spin and fade to black, Fiona plopped down on the floor of the kitchen and leaned back against the refrigerator to keep from hitting her head, if she passed completely out.

That was apparently a good call on her part because the next thing she knew, she was being lifted in Rick's strong arms, while someone else was pressing a cool washcloth to her forehead. Her eyes fluttered open long enough to verify it was Rick carrying her, before she closed them once more to prevent getting too dizzy while being moved over to a loveseat in a sitting area on the other side of the room.

Once Rick laid her down and took over wiping her face and neck with the washcloth, Fiona opened her eyes and asked, "What happened?"

"I'm sorry, Miss Fiona." Fiona turned her head to look at Britney, who was standing beside her dad, who was kneeling on the floor beside the loveseat he'd lain her on. "I didn't realize you'd think my grandparents were burglars and be scared by my surprise, or I would have told you about them coming to dinner before they arrived."

Fiona felt herself flush, embarrassed that it wasn't the thought of intruders that scared her into passing out. She knew it was the panic at not knowing how to introduce herself to Rick's parents because they hadn't had the relationship talk yet, but she didn't want to admit that when said parents were still hovering nearby to overhear her.

"It's okay, Britney." Fiona reached out and took the girl's hand, hoping to reassure her. "I'm sorry if I scared you by passing out like a big ol' fraidy cat. I feel really silly for fainting when I'd already realized we weren't in danger."

"Feeling better now?" Rick smiled tentatively, as he stroked his hand down the side of her face.

"Yes," Fiona replied, starting to sit up slowly. *Just embarrassed about the horrible first impression I just made on your parents.*

"Take it slow and easy, Fifi." Rick stood, as he helped her move into a seated position. "It was probably just a sudden drop in your blood pressure after a moment of fear, and we don't want you to pass out again because of changing positions dropping it again."

Fiona wasn't sure if that was the case or not, but she was glad Rick was there offering a plausible explanation that didn't make her look quite as incompetent for taking care of his daughter as she felt for fainting from a panic attack.

"Her color looks much better now," Rick's mother said, nodding as she examined Fiona's face. "More like she looked when she first walked out of the pantry."

"Why were you in the pantry?" Rick looked confused.

"Miss Fiona pulled me in there to hide from the intruders when she heard Nonna and Nonno talking," Britney giggled. "I barely had time to tell her they weren't intruders to stop her from calling nine-one-one."

"Glad to know you had a plan, even if it wasn't necessary." Rick grinned before assisting her to stand. Once he was reassured she wasn't wobbly on her feet, he continued making the introductions she'd missed Britney making earlier. "Mom, Dad, this is my girlfriend, Fiona Harrison. Fifi, these are my parents, Richard and Katarina Robertson."

I guess girlfriend isn't too juvenile after all.

Fiona smiled at the Robertsons as pleasantries were exchanged before trying to get everyone to focus on the meal Britney had helped prepare, instead of on her by turning to Britney and asking, "How would you like to serve this dinner you've worked so hard on all afternoon?"

Britney looked at her with a confused expression, so Fiona opted to clarify her question.

"Buffett style like we eat every night in catering? Or family style in the dining room?"

"Family style." Britney's face lit with excitement, as she grabbed Fiona's hand and pulled her back toward the kitchen, while calling over her shoulder at her family. "Give us a few minutes to set the table and we'll call you into the dining room for dinner."

Britney directed Fiona where to find the silverware as she pulled down plates and glasses from one of the cabinets. She showed her the secret pocket door between the butler's pantry and the dining room to make carrying everything quicker and easier.

Britney took charge of deciding to have the five of them sit at one end of the long table with Britney at the end, her grandparents on the side of the table to her left, and Rick and Fiona across from them on Britney's right. They quickly set the table with plates, silverware, and glasses.

Fiona went back and added the napkins while Britney carried in a pitcher of water. As Britney carried in the pitcher of sweet tea they'd made, Fiona carried in the two trivets to place the baking dishes of enchiladas on and put them in the middle of the table at the end they were sitting at. Finally, they each carried a baking dish.

Once the food was in place with spatulas in each dish for serving, Britney called her family to dinner. "Oh, I forgot the sour cream." Britney ran back through the butler's pantry, as everyone else took their seats.

"It certainly smells delicious," Richard said, as he pulled out the chair for his wife. "Though if it's as spicy as it smells, I'm probably going to need to take an extra heartburn pill when we get home."

Oh goodness! I didn't even think about needing to lower the spice level for people who aren't used to Tex-Mex, Fiona thought, as she took the seat Rick held out for her.

"We can cut some of the spice with the sour cream Britney's getting now," Fiona suggested, hoping it would help keep Rick's dad from having heartburn before the end of dinner.

"We can also cut it with a chilled sweet wine," Katarina pointed out before turning to look directly at Rick. "Do you have any sparkling wines in your wine cooler?"

"I only have whatever you stocked it with at Christmas," Rick shrugged, as he took his seat.

Fiona didn't know enough about wine to properly pair it with their meal, but if chilled and sweet were the key components that would cut the spice level, she thought the tea they were serving would also do the trick. Unfortunately, Rick's mother looked at her like she'd lost her mind when she suggested as much.

Britney picked that moment to come back in the room carrying the sour cream in a china serving dish and immediately picked up on her grandmother's disdain for sweet tea. "What's wrong with sweet tea? I like it. Especially after Tia told me about how the sugar and tannins stop our tongues from burning when we eat spicy food. That's why I had Miss Fiona teach me how to make it today, so we could make the enchiladas extra spicy."

"There's nothing wrong with sweet tea, Britney Bear." Rick smiled at his daughter. "Nonna's just not used to it, so she was suggesting getting her sweetness and tannins to cut the spice from a glass of wine with dinner."

"But not everyone at the table can drink wine, Nonna." Britney rolled her eyes at her grandmother.

"No, but we should all have the option to drink something we know we'll enjoy," Katarina retorted.

"How about we go look for that wine, Sweetheart?" Richard stood and reached for his wife's hand to assist her out of her chair.

Fiona wasn't sure what Richard said to Katarina while they were off in the other room, but when they returned, she seemed to be in a much better mood. Though she did give Fiona a few pointed looks throughout the rest of the meal.

All things considered, the evening wasn't too unpleasant. Rick and his father raved over the meal, showering both Britney and Fiona with compliments for their accomplishments in the kitchen. With Rick's continuous praise, Fiona was able to overlook his mother's subtle digs about their age and upbringing differences.

By the time dessert was over, and they left to head to the airport for their overnight flight, Fiona decided Katarina Robertson's poor opinion of her didn't matter all that much. *I'm dating Rick, not his parents. So, his and Britney's opinions about me are all that matter.*

Thursday, February 28, 2019, Dublin, Ireland

Rick was exhausted as he made his way to his hotel suite in Dublin, Ireland, for the night. After touring EPIC - The Irish Emigration

Museum and Dublin Castle, he'd barely stayed awake, as he went about his evening, making sure everything ran smoothly on the first GWA show in Europe. He'd planned the travel schedule to allow them to sleep on the plane, hoping it would prevent jetlag from the seven-hour flight and five-hour time difference between Dublin and New York. But with everything on his mind, and not being able to hold Fiona in his arms with everyone sleeping on the plane, Rick actually tossed and turned more than he slept.

It wasn't all the stress of the first time he'd taken the company halfway around the world to visit thirteen cities in seven countries in the next two weeks that kept him up, though it was stressful to coordinate everything with that many government entities for his whole crew. He was more focused on the way he felt like he was on an emotional roller coaster the day before.

The first part of the day had been the highest of highs, with him enjoying his time with Fiona and Britney. His errands hadn't been stressful so much as exhilarating.

First, he had Cage drop him at his office to sign off on the final paperwork to add Protection Detail to the roster. Now they were just waiting for their work visas to be approved by the U.S. government, which would hopefully happen while the company was on the two-week-long European tour, so the guys could join them when the GWA flew back to New York in the middle of March.

After he was done in the office, he took a cab to make a couple of stops before going home since he'd given Cage the afternoon off. First, he stopped in at an adult toy store to buy a set of training plugs for Fifi's ass to get her ready to take him in every hole. He couldn't wait to surprise her with them when she got to his hotel room for the night. Just the thought of what he had planned for their first night in Europe kept him hard half the time since he'd bought the toys, whether he could see her when he thought about them or not.

His final errand had been a stop at Tiffany's to pick out a four-carat square-cut diamond set on a platinum band, so he could propose to Fiona sometime in the next two weeks. He wasn't sure if he wanted to pop the question in a traditionally romantic setting, like at the base of the Eiffel Tower in Paris, or in a gondola under the Bridge of Sighs in Venice. Or if he wanted to be more true to their everyday lives and get down on one knee in catering, so everyone in the company could witness the proposal.

If he was totally honest with himself, he wasn't just vacillating between places to propose. After the disastrous dinner with his parents the previous evening, he was wondering if he was moving too fast. His mother's subtle digs at Fiona made it obvious she didn't approve of their relationship. Not that he needed her approval, but some of the things she said made him question his own thoughts and feelings about the relationship.

Rick was thankful Fiona had been unconscious for the worst of what his mother had to say, but he couldn't say her words hadn't struck a nerve with him.

I still can't believe Mom asked if Fiona is pregnant in front of Britney. Or that she insinuated it was a ploy to trap me the same way Colleen did.

Yeah, Brit knows her mother and I didn't have a good relationship, but she didn't need to know she was the only reason I married that woman.

I need to make sure I talk with her soon, to make sure she doesn't have any feelings of guilt over what Mom said. My daughter needs to know she's not responsible for Colleen's actions. And that I'd gladly go through it all over again to have her because she's the most important person in the world to me.

With that thought most prominent on his mind, he pushed aside his trepidation about Fiona being honest with him when she told him she was on the pill, as he placed his order with room service for his and Britney's bedtime snack. As soon as their cookies and milk were delivered, he sat down on the sofa to talk with his daughter.

"Hey, um, Britney Bear, I need to talk to you while we snack." Rick fidgeted in his seat, more nervous about talking to his daughter than he had been about talking to Fiona about starting to date.

"Yeah, Dad, what's up?" Britney dunked her first cookie in her milk and took a big, soggy bite.

"What Nonna said yesterday when Fiona fainted…" He trailed off, unsure how to ask if she'd been hurt by the comments about her mother.

"Don't worry, Dad." Britney reached over with the hand not holding a soggy cookie and patted his arm reassuringly. "Like I told

Nonna yesterday, I know you haven't been dating long enough to give me a little brother or sister yet."

Rick hoped his daughter couldn't see his embarrassment at not being the one to refute his mother's assumption the day before. He blatantly ignored the optimistic look Britney gave him when she said the word "yet," which seemed to indicate she wanted siblings from his relationship with Fiona.

"No, that's not the part I'm talking about." Rick shook his head, still not sure how to ask. "What she said about your mother trapping me by getting pregnant with you. You know that's all on her, right? You're not responsible for the decisions we've made in our lives."

"So, you didn't marry her just because I was on the way?" Britney gave him a look of disbelief.

Fuck! I can't lie to her.

"That's not what I'm saying." Rick ran a hand through his hair in frustration, knowing he wasn't wording things in the right way, but unable to figure out the correct way to say them. "I just don't want you to feel guilty for being the reason I married her. It was my decision to marry her, so I could have you in my life. I love you more than anyone or anything else on earth. And because I got you as my little girl, I wouldn't go back and change a thing about everything that happened back then. I'd go through it all over again, if I had to, in order to have you as my daughter and see your smiling face every day."

"I know that, Dad." Britney sat her cookie back down on the plate on the coffee table beside her cup of milk and leaned over to give him a hug. "Babies have no control over who gives birth to them. I'm just glad you're my dad, and you were smart enough to divorce my egg donor and fix it, so we don't have to see her anymore."

Rick hugged his daughter, grateful she seemed to understand what he meant and didn't seem to be bothered by his mother's words.

Once they released the hug, they went back to eating their cookies with a peaceful silence between them. At least Rick thought it was a peaceful silence, until Britney looked at him with worry etched on her young features. Not wanting to upset her by asking what was bothering her, Rick opted to word his question the way he'd been taught by the child psychologist he'd visited during the divorce to make it seem like the game they'd played when she was younger. "Hey, Britney Bear, what are you thinking?"

Britney grinned, obviously remembering some of the off-the-wall answers they'd come up with over the years, when they gave a silly answer before delving into serious discussions. "That these cookies would taste better if they were pink with purple polka dots."

Rick sat patiently, waiting for his daughter to continue with her serious answer.

"And that I hope you and Miss Fiona aren't dating just because I want her to be my mom."

Fuck! I probably put that thought in her head by bringing up Mom's comments from yesterday.

"No need to hope for that, Britney Bear." Rick smiled at his daughter and ruffled her hair. "While I'm glad you like her that much, I'm dating her because I like her."

"Dad!" Britney squealed, shaking his hand off her head. She straightened in her seat and looked at him seriously before continuing. "I don't just like her, Dad. I love her. And I don't want you to date her if you just like her. You have to at least *like her, like her,* and think you could fall in love with her to date her."

"Fine, I *like her, like her,*" Rick admitted, making a goofy face at his daughter to lighten the mood of the conversation because he wasn't ready to admit to his daughter that he thought he might already be in love. If and when he made the decision to declare his feelings, he wanted Fiona to be the first to hear the words.

"Good, 'cause she *like, likes you,* too. And no matter what Nonna thinks, she's nothing like my egg donor. She's not dating you because of your money, or even how much she likes me." Britney punctuated her statement by popping the last bite of her cookie into her mouth.

Rick nodded his agreement, as he stuffed his mouth with a whole cookie. He wasn't sure how his daughter came to her conclusion about Fiona, but he didn't want to question it and have any of his cynicism rub off on her.

I don't think Fifi's after my money either, but I can't help but wonder if her naïveté has allowed her to confuse our sexual attraction for something more meaningful. Especially if her feelings are influenced by her empathy for Britney needing a motherly figure in her life.

Hell, maybe that's all I'm doing. Thinking I'm falling in love, when I'm really just sexually attracted to the same woman my daughter wants as a motherly figure in her life. I mean, it would be easy to convince myself to marry someone I want to fuck, when I know marrying her will make Britney happy.

That's basically what I did when I married Colleen. But do I really want to repeat that mistake with Fiona? What's it going to do to Britney when Fiona and I don't want to fuck each other anymore?

Shit, maybe it is too soon for me to have bought a ring. Thank fuck, I didn't give in to the urge to ask her to marry me in catering earlier tonight! Now I just have to make sure the thing is well hidden, so she doesn't see it in the next two weeks before I can return it.

Rick was momentarily brought out of his downward mental spiral by his daughter kissing him goodnight. But as soon as Britney was in her room for the night, he started contemplating all the potential issues he might have come up if he continued to have a sexual relationship with Fiona.

Should I even continue fucking her when I'm not sure if we're really falling in love or not? Hell, if I don't, then I'm not giving us a chance to figure out if our feelings are real. Breaking it off now would just be accepting it's not love.

Fuck! I can't stop fucking her when I'm not sure how I really feel yet. But if I keep fucking her, I'm risking getting her pregnant and complicating our lives even further if we're not really falling in love.

Hell! If she lied about being on the pill, I might have already gotten her pregnant. I can't believe I lost control so bad that I couldn't hold off until I picked up a box of condoms before fucking her the first time.

And I can't start using them every time we fuck now because it would tip her off that I'm questioning things between us. And that would sabotage any chance we have of really falling in love.

Fuck! Fuck! Fuck!

I'm screwed, no matter what I do!

I might as well enjoy screwing her until I figure out what I'm really feeling. I'll just have to start pulling out and coming on her tits, unless I'm fucking her mouth or ass, so I don't take any more chances with getting her pregnant.

Rick was once again brought out of his mental spiral, this time by Fiona's light knock on the door to his suite. He took a deep breath and prepared himself as best he could before opening the door, hoping to mask his doubts from her for the time being.

That seemed to be easier than he was afraid it would be when she smiled up at him like he hung the moon. Her expression of adoration was almost enough to convince him his worries were for naught.

But lust fades and then what do we have? Rick heard his doubts in his mother's voice in his head and had to come up with some way of covering them quickly, so Fiona wouldn't notice.

She can't read my inner thoughts with her eyes closed, he thought, as he pulled her into the room and covered her lips with his. *So, maybe I'll blindfold her tonight instead of plugging her. Or, hell, maybe I'll do both. For that matter, I have enough ties in my suitcase to tie her down and blindfold her before plugging her.*

He shut and locked the door without breaking their kiss. Then picked her up and carried her straight to his bed. Fiona giggled, as he dropped her on the bed, finally breaking their lip lock, so he could turn around and lock his bedroom door to keep Britney from being able to come in and see them.

"Goodness, you seem impatient tonight, Papa." Fiona pushed up on her elbows and watched him stalk back over to the bed.

Rick loosened his tie, as he gazed at the gorgeous woman spread out on his bed. She had already discarded the leggings and boots she'd worn while sightseeing and at the arena earlier in the day, only wearing her coral dress and some slip-on sandals to come up to his room.

Yeah, I'm definitely going to enjoy fucking her for as long as this attraction lasts.

"You look sexy as fuck spread out on my bed," Rick growled, changing direction to walk toward the closet to remove his suit and grab the two ties he'd need to tie her down and blindfold her for the night before returning to the bed. "I can't wait to see how fucking hot you'll look naked and tied to it."

Fiona's emerald eyes dilated to the point he could barely make out the rings of green around her pupils. She whimpered as she kicked off her sandals, but she didn't object to his plan for the night.

"Stand up and strip," he ordered, resisting the urge to call her by the pet name he'd given her, as he struggled with himself for questioning his feelings for her. He instantly regretted the distance he was putting between them by not addressing her as his sweet Fifi.

"Yes, Papa." Fiona's breathlessly whispered words made his dick twitch in his boxers, as she stood from the bed and pulled her dress up over her head.

"Fifi, where are your panties?" Rick raised an eyebrow at her, as he ran his eyes down from her tits, barely contained by her lacy, peach bra, to her bare pussy already glistening with her arousal.

"I left them in my room, Papa." Fiona batted her eyelashes, as she reached behind her back to unclasp her bra. Rick felt the precum leaking from his cock, as she dropped her bra to the floor, revealing her perky peaks.

"Why would you leave them in your room and walk through the hotel with nothing covering my pussy?"

"Because it's been too long since you've spanked me, Papa." Fiona turned her back to him, as she crawled back on the bed, wiggling her tempting ass at him. "So, I thought I'd be just a little naughty to give you a reason to spank me again."

Fuck! Did she actually enjoy that as much as I did? Or is she just doing what she thinks I want to make us fit together, when we really don't?

Hell, no matter whether she liked it or not, I don't want her topping from the bottom to manipulate me into spanking her when I have other plans.

"No, I think you liked being spanked too much." Rick shook his head, as he crawled up behind her on the bed. "So, I'm going to have to come up with a better way to punish you tonight."

Rick grabbed Fiona's ample hips and flipped her over onto her back before covering her body with his. With her pinned beneath him, he pushed her hands over her head, tied one end of his tie around her right wrist, looped the tie through the slats on the headboard, and tied the other end around her left wrist.

He made sure there was enough give in the tie to keep from cutting off her circulation. The bonds were tight enough to keep her from being able to get out of the bed, but with only the one attachment point, he was able to flip her from her back to her front to have access to every part of her curvy body.

He covered her eyes with the other tie, carefully tying it at the back of her head without catching her hair in the knot, while explaining his plan for the night. "I'm going to torture you in every way I can think of tonight. I'm going to touch you, taste you, fuck you, plug you, and anything else I want to do to you to keep you on the edge all night. And you're not allowed to come until I tell you to. If I tell you to come, it will only be after you've proven you've learned your lesson. That might or might not happen tonight. Though I hope you will be a good girl for me and earn your orgasm soon, so your punishment doesn't have to stretch on for a few days. Do you understand your punishment, Fifi?"

"Yes, Papa," Fiona moaned breathily.

"Do you understand why you're being punished?" Rick didn't think she did, and suddenly, he desperately wanted her to know the real reason he felt he had to punish her that night.

"Because I didn't wear panties when I walked through the hotel, Papa." Fiona smiled, obviously pleased with herself for thinking she'd answered correctly.

"No, Fifi." Rick sat back on his heels between her spread thighs, admiring the sight of her without touching her. "I know your dress was long enough to keep your bare pussy hidden from anyone who shouldn't see it, so I don't actually have a problem with you not wearing panties to give me easy access."

Fiona's lips turned down, showing how confused she was by Rick not having a problem with her going commando.

"You're being punished tonight because you tried to manipulate me. I told you when we first started that I'm always in charge. Just as I want you to use your safe words if you need me to give you a break, or if I do something you can't handle, if there's something you particularly enjoy and want me to do more of, I want you to ask me for it. But unlike a safe word, which will be honored immediately, I'm still only going to give you more of what you want when it's also what I want." Rick backed off of the bed and walked over to his suitcase to dig out the anal plugs he'd bought the day before.

"Trying to manipulate me into giving you another spanking isn't going to work. In fact, feeling manipulated makes me want to do the opposite of what you want. So, there will be no spanking tonight, or any other night you're still being punished."

"I'm sorry, Papa," Fiona whimpered, as Rick walked toward the bathroom to clean the new plugs. "I didn't do it to manipulate you. I just thought it was a playful way to tease you. But I promise I'll be respectful and ask you for what I want from now on."

He could hear her continued sobbing, as she rambled out more of her apology and promises to never do anything manipulative again, while he washed the two smallest plugs in the set of six that he planned to use to open her up enough to take his cock. *Fuck! She sounds completely sincere.*

But can I really believe her when she says she didn't mean to be manipulative? Can I trust her not to try to manipulate me in the future?

Fuck! I should probably decide if I believe her about being on the pill before I try to decide if I'm able to trust her completely for anything else.

Rick took a couple of deep breaths, as he dried off the plugs and carried them and the lube back into the bedroom.

"Please, Papa," Fiona cried, her tears soaking through the tie covering her eyes. "At least tell me you're still here. I can handle the punishment you laid out, but being ignored is a hard limit."

"Shit! Fifi, I'm sorry." Rick clumsily dropped the plugs and lube on the floor beside the bed, as he rushed to release her from the bondage. He felt like a total ass for getting distracted by his own thoughts and not properly taking care of her. "I should have told you I had to go in the other room for a minute."

As soon as Rick had her wrists freed from the tie, Fiona wrapped her arms around his neck and clung to him as she continued to cry. He removed the tie he was using as a blindfold and pulled her into his arms on his lap, twisting in the bed to lean back against the headboard, as he held her.

"I wasn't ignoring you, sweet Fifi," Rick whispered in her ear, as he rubbed her back, trying to soothe her. "Not intentionally, anyway. I guess I just got too distracted by what I was doing and thinking about doing to you. I didn't even register that you were distressed by my silence. I even left the door open between here and the bathroom, so I could hear everything you were saying, while I was cleaning the plugs

I bought you yesterday. But I guess I couldn't hear as well as I thought with the water running."

Rick knew he was grasping at straws and making up excuses, but he didn't want to hurt her by letting her know he'd spiraled down into a pit of doubt, since their dinner with his parents. His logical mind knew Fiona was nothing like Colleen, and he didn't want to punish Fiona for Colleen's misdeeds. But he was still his mother's son, which meant he was susceptible to the seeds of fear his mother planted in his brain the day before.

"It's okay," Fiona sobbed, lifting her head from his shoulder, so they could look into each other's eyes. "I don't even know why I freaked out. I could hear the water running, so I knew you hadn't completely left me alone."

She released her grip around his neck to wipe at her eyes, and Rick instantly missed the feel of her clinging to him. He gently gripped her wrists to put her hands back on his shoulders and used his thumbs to wipe the tears from her cheeks.

"Actually, that's not completely true." Fiona shook her head, as she massaged his shoulders. "Being alone doesn't bother me enough to cause a freak-out like that. I mean, I've spent most of my life alone in my room every night, so I'm pretty much used to it."

"Yeah, but you're normally not tied up and blindfolded when you're alone," Rick pointed out, feeling guilty for not specifically mentioning her safe words before tying her up. If he had, then she might have remembered to say "yellow" to get him to give her a breather before continuing the night. Since he hadn't reminded her of their usage, he had to consider her tears, as if they were her saying "red" and stopping the scene for the night.

"That's true," Fiona giggled. "But that was exciting."

Rick chuckled at the cute way she wiggled her eyebrows. "I still should have waited until I had everything ready to go before I tied you up and blindfolded you. And I should have reviewed your safe words, so you could have used them before getting to the point of panicking. I'm sorry, I just wasn't thinking."

"You've seemed distracted all day. Wanna talk about it? I'm a really good listener. Though we might need to put our clothes back on first, so we can both focus." Fiona smiled sincerely, making Rick feel like an even bigger ass for having his doubts about her.

"Just jet lag," Rick lied. "I couldn't sleep on the plane, like I'd planned."

"And I'm probably making it worse by freaking out for no reason, instead of letting you go to bed early tonight." Fiona shook her head, as she tried to push up off of Rick's lap. "Is there anything I can do to help you sleep before I go back to my room for the night?"

"Don't go back to your room." Rick surprised himself with his answer, as he pulled Fiona back into his arms. "I actually sleep better with you in my bed than I ever have in my life."

Shit! I probably shouldn't admit that to her. No matter how true it is, it's still giving her something else she can use against me if this relationship goes south.

"Of course, that could be because of all the energy we normally expend by this time of the night," Rick chuckled, trying to keep their relationship focused on the physical side until he understood his own feelings well enough to be able to share the emotional side with her. *If we can ever share those emotions.*

"Well, please don't let me stop you from expending that energy, so you can get some sleep." Fiona grinned, as she wiggled in his lap, grinding her wet pussy over his cock. "I'm all yours to do with as you please, Papa."

Fuck! I can't resist her.

"Yeah, you are," Rick growled, just before slamming his lips over hers. He kissed her long and hard, as he rolled her onto her back and covered her body with his. He held his weight off of her by planking on his elbows and knees, as he continued the passionate fusing of their mouths.

All his plans for their evening were wiped from his mind by the brush of her tongue against his. The way Fiona ardently returned his kiss, combined with the way she delicately caressed his back and shoulders, as they made out like teenagers, made him feel as if nothing in the world mattered, but the two of them joining as one at that moment.

Even the brief realization, that he wasn't behaving like himself, was fleeting when he registered the feel of her pebbled nipples brushing against his chest. It was such a tantalizing feeling that he didn't want to move far enough away from her to remove his boxers, even though it would only take a moment to eradicate the last barrier between them.

Instead, he kissed his way across her jaw and over to her ear to whisper to her. "Push my boxers out of the way, sweet Fifi."

"Yes, Papa," Fiona answered breathily, as she slid her palms down from around his neck, over his shoulders, and caressed his pecs and abs, before finally following his orders.

"Line me up," he commanded before nibbling her earlobe.

Fiona stroked his cock with both hands, rubbing all along his length and teasing him mercilessly.

"I need inside you now, Fifi," Rick growled, rocking his hips, and brushing the head of his dick against her clit.

"Yes, please, Papa," Fiona moaned, as she pushed him down between her folds to line him up with her opening.

Instead of thrusting hard the way he normally would, Rick slowly slid through her slick slit, one agonizing inch at a time, until he was fully sheathed inside her. It was the sweetest torture for both of them, as he settled into a slow, sensual rhythm to make love to her.

There was no dirty talk. Their mouths were otherwise occupied with kissing, licking, and sucking each other wherever they could bend their heads to reach.

Though their mating lacked the rough, primal element Rick usually needed to reach his release, he found himself fighting to keep from coming too soon during the most erotic, titillating experience of his life.

Fuck! I wish I could make this last forever, Rick thought, as he lightly suckled the pulse point at the base of Fiona's throat.

"Oh, Rick," Fiona moaned, as he felt her inner walls start to flutter around his dick.

"Oh, no, sweet Fifi," Rick groaned, his need for control taking over as he pulled out, so only the head of his cock was still in her quivering pussy. "You wait for me to tell you when to come."

"I'm trying to hold it, but I'm so close, I don't know if I can stop it for much longer." Fiona swiveled her hips, unable to control her body movements from the intensity of her need for release.

"Then milk my cock as you come, sweet Fifi," Rick growled, as he pushed balls-deep into her creamy cunt, lifting his head to watch her face as she came. "Now!"

With their eyes locked on one another, Rick saw her love for him shining through, as the first waves of her orgasm washed over her. He might not be one-hundred percent sure how he felt for her, but her feelings were written, plain as day, all across her face.

Fuck! I hope I'm worthy of her love. And, damn, I want to be able to return it.

"Yes, Rick, yes!" Fiona shouted, as her pussy contracted and her whole body convulsed.

Her epic orgasm triggered his own, rendering him unable to think about the future, while he was in heaven with her right then.

"Fuck! Fifi!" Rick couldn't move in her vise-like grip, shooting rope after rope of his seed straight into her womb. He was so lost in the ecstasy of his orgasm that he forgot to worry about whether they conceived or not.

As the peak passed, Rick rolled them, so he was on his back with Fiona draped over him. They maintained the connection of their bodies, as they recovered from their mutual high, but lost eye contact when Fiona rested her head on his chest.

With her head resting over his rapidly beating heart, Rick held Fiona for several long moments before finally getting up to grab a washcloth to clean them both up.

"That was…" Fiona's words drifted off, as Rick crawled back into the bed after wiping between her thighs and putting the dirty washcloth back in the bathroom. He pulled her into his arms, unable to come up with the words to finish her sentence either. "Wow!"

Rick chuckled at her apt description, kissing the top of her head, as she rested back on his chest. "You're always wow."

"Only with you." Fiona yawned, as she snuggled in close, drifting off to sleep shortly after.

Though he was exhausted, Rick lay there holding her long into the night, unable to go to sleep, as he tried to make sense of his thoughts and feelings.

Fuck! I hope this really is love. If it's not, it's got to be the closest I've ever felt to true love. That has to mean it can last forever. Right?

Chapter Eighteen

While Fiona had enjoyed every place she'd visited since she started working with the GWA, she was exceptionally excited about their day in Edinburgh, Scotland. Her parents had proudly extolled their Scottish heritage all her life, going so far as to search baby name books for names of Scottish origin before deciding on her name. They had settled on Fiona Greer for her first and middle name because they liked the meanings together—fair, watchful, guardian.

When she looked them up when she was in school, she discovered that Fiona meant fair in the terms of complexion, rather than equitable, as her parents believed. But she didn't have the heart to tell them they'd given her a name that basically meant white, when they'd also taught her to be color-blind when it came to race.

Fiona took as many pictures as she could while touring the Palace of Holyroodhouse. She couldn't wait to send them to her parents to tell them she'd actually gotten to tour the former home of Mary, Queen of Scots.

Apparently, the Burlesons had also discovered quite a bit of Scottish in the DNA tests they'd recently done through an online ancestry site. Tia and Maria were inundating Anthony with questions about which of his ancestors had lived there centuries ago. Fiona couldn't help but grin when Maria asked if Anthony's fourth great-grandmother, Mary Burleson, was named after Mary, Queen of Scots, and Tia explained that Mary Burleson's African mother had probably never heard of Mary, Queen of Scots, since they came from completely different parts of the world.

Leah Mae Wright

After a brief discussion about the lack of shared knowledge around the world before the twentieth century, the group as a whole decided to walk the Royal Mile to Edinburgh Castle, instead of getting back on the tour buses Rick had scheduled to keep everyone from having to drive in countries with different traffic laws than they were used to obeying. They grabbed lunch at a café to break up the walk between the two historic sites they were visiting that day.

After lunch, as they walked the rest of the way to Edinburgh Castle, Fiona noticed that Rick seemed to be deep in thought, much like he was the night before.

When she truly thought about it, he'd seemed to be distracted, or not acting like himself, several times since they'd flown out of New York on Wednesday night. She wasn't sure what was going on, but she was afraid to ask him, since his mood swings seemed to have started after dinner with his parents.

I really hope his mother's obvious dislike of me isn't the problem. Although, I don't think he could have made love to me the way he did last night, if her comments about our age difference actually caused him to have doubts about us.

But then again, he hasn't been nearly as affectionate today as he normally is when we're sightseeing, so maybe he's regretting changing things up last night from his normal rough and wild to soft and sensual. I'm still not sure what made him change things up so drastically last night.

Surely, it wasn't me breaking down crying, was it? No, it couldn't be. I mean, I cried like a baby when he spanked me, too, but he still fucked me like a wild animal after I stopped crying.

And what was up with me crying like that? I know it wasn't a fear of him leaving me tied up alone. I could hear him in the bathroom, so I knew he wasn't leaving me. Shoot, if I was afraid of anything, it was what his silence meant, since he's normally Mr. Dirty Talk the whole time.

Although, he did say something about me not using my safe word. Maybe he took my saying "being ignored is a hard limit" as if I'd said "red" to get him to stop everything for the night?

Frick-n-frack, I should have said "yellow" to get his attention, instead of freaking out and rambling the way I did. I bet that's why he didn't end up punishing me last night. He didn't think I could handle the kinky things he needs in bed, so he made love to me the way he thought I needed instead.

That's probably why he's backed away from me today, too. He's questioning whether or not I can handle the things he needs in a relationship. And I have no idea how to show him I can not only handle his rough, kinky side, but it's also what I crave in the bedroom with him.

Although, I guess he doesn't really want me to show him what I want. That's what almost got me punished last night. He said he wants me to ask for what I want. But can I really do that without dying of embarrassment?

I mean, I can't even think the dirty words he wants me to say without blushing. But he does seem to enjoy it when I blush from head to toe when he commands me to say them in bed. So, maybe watching me turn pink all over is part of the appeal for him to have me ask for what I want in the bedroom?

Even knowing that's what he wants, it's still scary to think about saying those things aloud. Even though I'd only ask him for the really dirty, kinky things in the privacy of the bedroom, with the thin walls in some of the hotels we've stayed in, I can't guarantee nobody else will hear me.

And there's no way I could face my friends the next day, if one of them was in the suite next door, and overheard the things I fantasize about. I mean, yeah, my girlfriends know the things I read about, since we talk about the books we've read recently. But we aren't reading the dirty passages aloud, or even discussing some of the more risqué book scenes, other than commenting that the love scene in a specific chapter was interesting.

Well, except for back at the end of December when we had our last book club meeting in Heart's Destiny, when Kay asked if that one position was even possible, and Randi said something about getting James to try it to find out. But there were enough women there that night that I was able to avoid that part of the conversation by talking to someone else about a different scene in the book.

Fiona shook off the memory of her last book club meeting to focus on her surroundings, as they started the tour of Edinburgh Castle. They arrived just in time to hear the One O'clock Salute from Half Moon Battery before entering the massive stone building.

Britney stuck by her side, as they toured the various rooms and marveled at the artifacts. While she enjoyed the time spent with Britney, Fiona missed Rick's normal presence, with a hand on one or both of them, as they listened to the tour guide telling them about the history of the various objects they were seeing. It just didn't feel right to not have his hand on the small of her back or holding her hand.

I guess that needs to be one of the things I tell him I want more of when I finally work up the courage to ask him for what I want.

"Where are the rest of the Crown Jewels?" Courtney Westbrook asked, drawing Fiona's attention back to the display in front of them in the Royal Palace, where the crown, scepter, and sword used in Mary, Queen of Scots coronation were exhibited.

"Yeah, where are the rings, necklaces, and tiaras?" Laci Kirby asked, looking disappointed by the lack of daily jewelry in the display.

"Probably in Queen Elizabeth's jewelry box," Britney said with a shrug. "She needs to keep those with her, so she can wear them whenever she wants. But the stuff that would be used by a King can be put on display because her husband is only a Prince."

"I don't understand how she's a Queen and married to a Prince. Shouldn't he get to be a King by marrying a Queen?" Carter Westbrook asked.

The tour guide went into a lengthy explanation about royal bloodlines to clear up the kids' confusion before pointing out that crowns represent the monarch and can be worn by either gender.

Feeling bad for the callous way the tour guide corrected Britney, Fiona pulled the girl in for a one-armed hug and whispered, "I've only ever seen Queen Elizabeth wearing tiaras, so I think you're right about her letting the stuff she doesn't wear be exhibited. I mean, what woman in her right mind would want to wear something that big and gaudy, when it would probably cause a massive headache within a few minutes of putting it on?"

Britney giggled, as she returned Fiona's embrace, leaning in to whisper her agreement. "Exactly. The bling is nice, but that's all totally impractical for a woman to tote around when she has a country to run."

Seeing Britney's smile return made Fiona glad they'd had that moment alone, even though she still missed Rick's presence in their little huddle. Though she knew she needed to get brave enough to ask him for more of the affection she missed, along with a return to the kinkier copulations he'd told her to expect from him all the time, she decided that she'd take a few days to bond more with Britney before taking that leap of faith.

And maybe he'll go back to normal in the next couple of days, and I won't have to stress about asking him for what I want.

~~~

Sunday, March 3, 2019, London, England

Rick was glad he'd had the foresight to charter tour buses to take everyone to and from the airports, hotels, and arenas in every city on the European tour, as well as for their sightseeing trips to make sure they didn't miss any of the major historical attractions without having to coordinate so many families driving separate vehicles. He'd thought it was the safest way for everyone to get around in the countries that drove on the left side of the road. But after seeing how many headaches the buses saved from finding parking at popular tourist attractions the past three days, he'd emailed his executive assistant, Patrice, in New York to have her start scheduling them in every city they visited, even if they were only available for the midday excursions.

If it hadn't been for the buses taking them from the airport to the hotel, and then immediately to Buckingham Palace without having to struggle to find parking, they would have missed the Changing of the Guard. Though Rick wasn't paying much attention to the daily ceremony, as he stood back and watched Britney and Fiona huddled together at the front of the crowd to have the best view of the pomp and circumstance.

In the days since they'd left New York, he'd actually found himself stepping back and observing them more than participating with them, like he usually did on these outings. Prior to his mother stirring up his doubts about his relationship with Fiona, he'd shown her just as much affection as he'd shown his daughter, with a hand on one of them at all times while out sightseeing.
~~~

He hated the realization that in pulling back from Fiona, he'd also pulled back from Britney, since the two of them seemed to be joined at the hip on every excursion. While he hated the distance he was putting between the three of them, he couldn't think of another way to figure out if his feelings for Fiona were real, or just him trying to make his daughter happy, without separating the relationships for a little while. So, he was spending time with Britney when Fiona wasn't around, spending time with Fiona while Britney was asleep, and stepping back from both of them whenever they were doing anything together.

But, fuck, it doesn't feel right to watch them having fun together without me.

"Hey, you alright?" Cooper waved a hand in Rick's face, as he walked up to where Rick was standing off by himself.

"Yeah, fine." Rick nodded at his friend, hoping his expression covered his melancholy mood.

"Then why are you standing back here by yourself, instead of being up there between your girls?" Cooper motioned with his head in the direction Britney and Fiona were standing.

"Just giving them time together." Rick shrugged, as if it was no big deal, but he knew his friend saw through his flimsy excuse.

"Don't lie to me," Cooper huffed, shaking his head. "They have one-on-one time together every week when you have to be at the arena early for TV. And since that's started, you've been in the middle of them whenever we're all together until we crossed the pond. So, what's different about being in the U.K. that has you stepping back from your family."

"It's not the U.K.," Rick grumbled, shaking his head, and looking around to make sure none of his other employees were within hearing distance. "It was having dinner with my family while we were in New York."

Cooper raised an eyebrow, but he didn't say anything. He just gave Rick a pointed look and waited for him to elaborate.

Keeping his voice low, Rick explained the events of Wednesday evening. "Britney surprised us by inviting my parents to the dinner she and Fiona made while I was taking care of a few things in the city. There was an issue with Fiona being scared by hearing strange voices and almost calling the police for a break-in before Britney cleared up that it was my parents' voices. And then Fiona fainted from the sudden drop in blood pressure when she realized they weren't in danger. I happened to walk in just as my mom was asking if Fiona is pregnant and using the baby to trap me the same way Colleen did with Britney."

"Oh, shit!" Cooper whisper-shouted, covering his mouth with his hand to keep anyone else from noticing the expletive. "What did you say to that?"

"Nothing. Britney handled it by telling Mom that we haven't been dating long enough to give her a baby brother or sister yet. I picked Fiona up off the kitchen floor and carried her to a sofa to lay down while Britney wet a hand towel to put on her head to help revive her. Once she recovered, Fiona and Britney finished putting dinner on the table, while I made sure Mom knew not to mention the possibility of pregnancy again. Thankfully, she honored my request to drop that subject, but Mom still made it clear she thinks Fiona's too young for me, and has the same motivations for dating me as *other women in their twenties*."

"What does her age have to do with her motivation for dating you?" Cooper's expression made it clear he didn't think their age difference mattered one bit.

"She was referencing Colleen being in her mid-twenties when we first got together," Rick clarified, shaking his head, as he realized how stupid it sounded when he said it out loud. "And implying that Fiona could be after me for my money or status or whatever."

"And that's why you're backing off on your relationship with Fiona? Because you think she's like that bitch, Colleen?" Cooper scowled. "Dude, I thought you were smarter than that."

"No, I know Fiona is nothing like Colleen." Rick held his hands up, palms out, as he tried to defend himself and his recent actions. "But everything Mom said led me to talk to Britney about why I married Colleen."

Cooper's eyes narrowed as he leaned in to whisper, "You told Britney about Colleen threatening to have an abortion if you didn't marry her?"

"No," Rick adamantly denied. "I never want Britney to know about that. But I couldn't deny that I only married Colleen because she was pregnant with Britney after Mom brought it up. And when I told Brit that I'd do it all again if I had to in order to have her as my daughter and make her happy, I started wondering if part of my attraction to Fiona is because Britney wants her to be her mom. I don't want to fool myself into thinking I'm in love, when it's just lust combined with wanting to give my daughter the mother she wants. So, I'm trying to keep Britney out of my relationship with Fiona for a few days to see if I still feel like it's more than lust or not."

"And how's that going for you?" Cooper grinned, giving Rick the impression he didn't think it was working at all.

"I don't know," Rick admitted with a half-hearted shrug. "I think it's working to show me that I want more than just sex when we're together after Britney goes to bed at night. But I don't know how much of that is being influenced by watching them acting like mother and daughter, even when I'm not right there with them as part of a family."

"Having never been in your shoes as a single parent, I can't tell you how much that could be influencing your feelings. But based on the way I've seen Fiona looking at you when you're off brooding instead of walking with her and Britney, I'm concerned you might be hurting your chances with her." Cooper sighed. "Maybe you should talk to Anthony and Kay. Anthony's known Fiona forever, so he can help interpret what she might be feeling that I think I'm seeing. And Kay's been in your shoes as a single parent to know how to help you navigate a new relationship."

Rick thought about Cooper's suggestion for a moment, but he didn't get the chance to fully think it through because the crowd was breaking up with the end of the Changing of the Guard. He followed the rest of his crew to the bus that would take them around to see Kensington Palace, Big Ben, Parliament, and a few other historic sites while eating lunch on the bus before visiting the SEA LIFE London Aquarium.

With trying to see everything they could in the two hours before their reservation for a private capsule on the London Eye, Rick wasn't sure he'd have time to talk to Anthony and Kay privately before they went to the arena for the evening. But he did decide to take Cooper's advice and talk to them as soon as he could when he noticed the sad smile Fiona gave him from across the crowded bus.

Fuck! I haven't hidden my doubts about us as well as I'd hoped. She's obviously noticed I've pulled back and seems confused by the mixed signals I've been sending her.

He hadn't meant to confuse her with his change in attitude. But looking back on their most recent times together, he could see how he'd screwed up. Not only had he backed off on what felt like family time during their daily midday sightseeing. But he'd also backed off on the intensity and kink when he fucked her every night.

After two weeks of rough fucking in a variety of positions, and anal play to get her ready to take a plug and eventually my cock, I bet she's confused as hell about why I've stuck to basic missionary position and gentle, vanilla sex the past few days.

He had only intended to take it easy on her the first night in Dublin because of thinking he'd pushed past her boundaries by tying her up and blindfolding her. But after realizing the potency of their connection during slow and sensual lovemaking, he had to see if being able to come that way was a one-time thing, or if the intensity of his orgasms would decrease over time from boredom.

That was what had happened with Colleen that led him to wanting to experiment with various kinks and positions after their divorce. When she decided she no longer wanted him to be rough, he got bored with gentle vanilla sex.

Looking back, he realized it was ironic that she apparently just didn't want it rough and kinky with him, since that's how the gardener was giving it to her when he walked in on them.

He'd thought taking sex out of their relationship was working well for them at the time, but looking back now, he realized it was never going to work long term because Colleen had never been honest with him about her real desires and goals in life. Thankfully, when she'd tried to use his rough sexual tendencies against him and tried to accuse him of abuse for being dominant during their divorce, she'd been on the witness stand in the courtroom of a judge who'd been in the lifestyle for almost three decades.

Rick had to smile at the memory of how Colleen had been shocked at how her plan to get the female judge to take her side had failed miserably. Apparently, the Domme took exception with Colleen referring to primal sex with a slap or two on the ass as abuse, and told her to be glad she hadn't submitted to a sadist who preferred whips or canes for impact play.

Oh, the judge hadn't said anything like that during the court proceedings, but had asked them both to stay for a moment in her chambers after their attorneys left once the final documents were signed. She actually suggested they both look into training as Dominants in one of the more reputable BDSM clubs in the city, but to avoid going to the same club as each other. Rick didn't know if Colleen had taken the judge's advice or not, but he'd looked into it.

During the first year after his divorce, Rick had a few liaisons with ring rats, but found he only enjoyed them when the woman in question was also into rougher sex. After studying up on BDSM as the judge had suggested, even those encounters weren't completely satisfying, since they never lasted long enough for him to build the trust needed in a true Dominant and submissive relationship. That was why he'd stopped hooking up on the nights Britney spent with her grandparents or friends, and had taken care of his own need for release with his hand in the shower for the last six years.

Meeting Fiona had changed that, though. For the first time he could remember, he had a fully satisfying sex life. And it didn't seem to matter what they did in the bedroom to achieve it.

I still can't figure out how I came just as hard the last three nights from vanilla, missionary sex, as I did when I spanked her and fingered her asshole while fucking her hard, doggie style. It has to be because I was with her. With all the other factors being different, there's no other explanation for how sex is so much better with Fiona than it's ever been in my life with anyone else, no matter how we do it.

But just because it's the best sex of my life, does that mean it'll always be that way between us? Does our undeniable sexual chemistry mean we're in love? Or is it just lust?

As he exited the bus at the aquarium, Rick thought back to some of the conversations he'd had with his friends and staff members about their relationships with their soulmates. They had all said they just knew they'd met *The One*, but none of them had really been able to objectively tell him how or why they knew it was true love.

Hell, maybe I'm being too rigid in my thinking by trying to quantify love with a checklist of reasons why it's real? I should just relax and enjoy my time with Fiona while I can, regardless of whether it's true love or not.

With that thought in mind, Rick made his way to the front of the pack to speak with the group coordinator at the aquarium in order to expedite their entry. Once they were all inside and starting the tour of the facility, Rick managed to get Anthony's attention for a private chat while the women and children were all focused on one of the exhibits.

"Whatcha need, Boss?" Anthony asked once they were off in a corner by themselves where it was unlikely they'd be overheard.

"I probably need to speak with your better half more than I need to speak with you," Rick chuckled, surprised he was about to ask for relationship advice from a man who was the same age he was back when he married Colleen.

"Better third," Anthony corrected with a chuckle of his own. "Remember, Tia corrected my math in the middle of our wedding."

"Sorry, I just assumed her added pregnancy weight would increase her percentage of the equation," Rick joked.

"Shit! Don't say that loud enough she can hear you," Anthony whisper-shouted, looking to make sure Kay was still focused on the fish in the tank on the opposite side of the room. "She's self-conscious enough about the fifteen pounds she's gained so far. If she hears you think she'll gain a hundred pounds, her pregnancy hormones will have her in tears until she gives birth."

"Sorry," Rick grimaced, as he apologized for his poorly thought-out joke. "I'm clearly not thinking straight right now, but I'll make sure to refrain from any mention of weight from now on. Especially since I think Kay might be the only person I know, who can answer my questions about falling in love as a single parent."

"Well, as the man she fell in love with, maybe I can help you out." Anthony grinned. "Since I've probably asked her some of the same questions to make sure I'm not screwing up being a dad."

Rick didn't believe Anthony had questioned Kay's love for him for even a second, so he doubted Anthony had asked the same question he was about to ask, but he still found himself asking it, anyway.

"How did Kay know she was really in love with you, and didn't just confuse lust, and a desire to give her daughters a dad, for love?"

Anthony opened his mouth as if to answer, but he quickly closed it again. He repeated the process a few times, making it look as if he was mimicking what the fish on the other side of the room would do if they jumped out of the tank and landed on the floor, where there was no water.

"I actually had to convince her that she wasn't asexual when we first met," Anthony finally said, after thinking for a few, long moments. "So, I don't think lust played any part in her realizing she loves me. But I hadn't ever considered my wanting to step up and be the girls' dad as a possible factor for why she fell for me."

Fuck! Now I'm sharing my skepticism and making him doubt Kay's love for him. How the fuck do I fix this?

"No, it's obvious she loves you, just as much as you love her." Rick held his hands up, hoping to stop his friend from going down the negative spiral of thinking he'd been on for the past few days. "I know you fell for her instantly. I just wondered if she fell for you the same way before the girls factored in at all. Or if she had some tips to offer me, so I can make sure I'm not letting my daughter's wish for a mom muddle my feelings."

"Yeah, I'm not sure Kay can help with that, since she was more worried about me being like her ex and unable to love the girls than whether or not my relationships with the girls influenced her love for me." Anthony shook his head.

"I've already figured out that my mom is wrong in thinking Fiona is anything like my ex." Rick shook his head, frustrated at the memory of the things his mother had said. "So, I don't need help with that. Just how to know for sure that what I think I might be feeling is real."

"You're in luck then." Anthony slapped a hand on Rick's shoulder and smiled. "Because I know exactly how to clear things up for you."

"Yeah?" Rick raised an eyebrow, curious about what Anthony seemed to think he knew better than his wife, who had been in Rick's shoes as a single parent.

"Yeah, it's simple." Anthony nodded. "Picture your life in fifteen years. Britney is an adult, no longer living with you. Maybe she's off at college or working in a career other than wrestling, but whatever she's doing, she's not living with you or traveling with the GWA. You got the image in your head?"

Rick nodded, as he tried to imagine life the way Anthony described it, closing his eyes to envision himself still traveling and doing his current job without his daughter there every day. "Yeah, I've got it.

It'll be strange when she goes off to college or picks a career outside the GWA, but I can see it happening."

"Great. Where does Fiona fit in that picture?"

"She's my wife and in bed beside me every night." Rick opened his eyes, shocked that he'd clearly pictured the future so well that he'd spoken without even thinking about it.

"Of course she is," Anthony smirked. "Because you love her. Britney getting a mom out of the deal is just a bonus. Just like the girls, and the boys we're gonna have in the future, are Kay and I's bonuses."

"Huh?" Rick didn't realize he'd mumbled the word aloud, as he stood there trying to picture more of what he wanted in his life than just his time in bed with Fiona. But once he imagined her naked in his bed, he got stuck there in his mind and worried he was still only lusting after her. "You don't think it's just lust, since I instantly pictured us in bed together?"

Anthony scratched his head. "Yeah, I suppose that could be a factor. Okay, how 'bout this? Picture yourself in fifty years. You're old enough that you have to pop a couple of little blue pills to get it up, but the doctor won't prescribe them because of the increased risk of a heart attack, so sex is totally off the table. Do you still see yourself with Fiona?"

Just as Rick started to picture himself sitting in a rocking chair on a porch in his late eighties, Stone walked up and pointed out that the rest of the group had moved on to the next exhibit.

"What's got you guys so distracted you missed everyone walking over to see the sharks?" Stone circled his hand in the general direction of Rick's face. "And put such a weird look on the boss's face?"

"He's trying to figure out if he's really in love with Fiona," Anthony explained.

"And you didn't just tell him that his love for her has been obvious to all of us for months?" Stone smirked and raised an eyebrow at Anthony.

"Naw," Anthony chuckled. "He didn't believe it when I tried to tell him that a couple of months ago, so I was going with a different tactic to let him see it for himself."

Tired of his employees standing there talking about him as if he wasn't there, Rick looked at Stone and asked him a similar question to the one he'd asked Cooper almost a month before. "How did you know you had fallen in love with Cheyenne?"

"Simple, I got a hard-on the instant I met her and couldn't get it up for anyone but her after that." Stone shrugged.

"My dad told me only getting it up for one woman was one of the signs of being a man who'd met *The One*." Anthony pointed at Stone and nodded. "But I didn't figure asking Rick if he only got it up for Fiona would be a good way to prove it's love, since he's worried about lust muddling his brain."

"Ah, so that was what the face was all about," Stone sighed and nodded along with Anthony. "Trying to make sure he's thinking with the right head. And what did you figure out, Boss?"

"Nothing. You interrupted me when I was trying to imagine my life in fifty years." Rick pointed at Stone, trying to look irritated, when he really wanted to laugh at the goofy expressions on his friends' faces.

"Well, let's see if you can walk and picture the scene at the same time, so we can catch up with the group while describing it for you." Stone threw an arm around Rick's shoulders and swiped his other arm through the air, as if setting the scene while getting him to start walking in the direction the rest of their group had gone. "Ninety-year-old Rick is sitting in his wheelchair on the porch while looking out over the yard at all his kids, grandkids, and great-grandkids."

"I only have one kid, so that's probably not going to be a very big crowd," Rick pointed out, as he shook his head at his friend's antics.

"Naw," Anthony disagreed, getting in on the silly scenario with Stone. "With all our kids basically adopting you as Uncle Rick, you're gonna need a few acres to hold everyone coming for a weekend barbeque, whether you have more kids in the future or not."

"Exactly," Stone agreed, as the three of them kept walking past the next exhibit, where their families had already moved on. "Who all is in the yard doesn't matter. You just have to figure out who's pushing your wheelchair, so you can come hang out with the rest of us. Is it Fiona? Or some home health nurse slipping you little blue pills in the hope of you leaving your fortune to her offspring?"

Rick stopped walking, as the vision hit him square in the heart, not even registering the end of Stone's questions. His ninety-year-old self wasn't in a wheelchair. He was on an electric scooter with an eighty-year-old Fiona beside him on a pink electric scooter of her own, and they were racing a few of their older great-grandkids, who were on their bicycles, down a long driveway.

He could picture Britney in her mid-sixties with two brothers and a sister, all in their early fifties. His and Fiona's grandchildren would be in their twenties and thirties and their great-grandchildren would range in age from newborns to ten or twelve years old.

With their four kids and their spouses, their sixteen grandkids and their spouses, and at least thirty-two great grandkids, Rick could easily see over seventy people filling up their future yard, with a majority of them having a mix of his and Fiona's traits.

Holy Fuck! I'm in love with Fiona! I don't just want to fuck her. Or give Britney the mom she wants. I want more with her. More kids, more long talks, more quiet nights cuddling on the couch, more…everything with her.

And lusting after her is just part of that everything that makes up my love for her. I'm not going to stop wanting her the way I did with Colleen. No matter how old we get, I'm still going to want to fuck her every time we're alone, even if I have to pop a couple of little blue pills to do it.

Rick was in awe at the feelings flowing through him. Before Fiona, sex had been no more than a primal need for him. Yeah, he'd always made sure his partners got theirs before he took his moment of pleasure, but he'd never felt like his partner's pleasure was more important than his. But with Fiona it was different.

He still had the primal urge to rut into her like a wild animal. But that need was less urgent with Fiona. Making her come was his top priority. That was why he'd been able to enjoy gentle lovemaking the last few days, when he'd never really enjoyed it that way before. Because he got off on watching her come more than he enjoyed his own orgasms.

Hell, even if I end up with health issues that prevent me from being able to take those little blue pills to get it up, I'll still want to get her off every night with my fingers and tongue. Not because sex is our only way of connecting, but because it's one of the many ways I want to show her I love her.

"I think he figured it out." Stone slipped him into a side headlock and tried to pull him further through the aquarium, bringing Rick out of his mental revelation.

Rick instinctually wrapped his arms around Stone's midsection to pick him up in a bear hug to get out of the hold. Had they been in a wrestling ring, or on a thick practice mat, Rick would have turned it into a suplex to take him down to the mat. But knowing Stone's history of back injuries, he wasn't about to do that without a soft mat to land on. So, Rick just started walking instead, carrying his friend a few feet before Anthony reprimanded them for roughhousing in the aquarium.

"Hey, guys, come on. Ya'll are gonna get us kicked out of here, if you keep horsing around."

Rick put Stone back down on his feet before they each released their holds. They separated with raised palms to call a truce.

"While I'm glad to have Rowdy Ricky back, I hope it's because you've realized you're in love with Fiona, and not because you're planning to go back to the party boy phase of your life." Stone grinned as they started walking once more.

"Yeah," Rick nodded, grinning at his friend as they caught up with their group at the seahorse exhibit. "Now, if you'll excuse me, I'm going to go hang out with my girls."

Rick walked up to where Fiona and Britney were standing close to the glass and seemed to be interacting with a particularly large purple and orange striped seahorse.

"Isn't she pretty, Dad?" Britney smiled up at him, when she realized he was pushing his way in between her and Fiona and wrapping an arm around each of their shoulders.

"I think that's a boy, Pumpkin." Rick grinned at his daughter.

"How can you tell?" Fiona asked, tilting her head to examine the seahorse from a different angle.

"Because he's flirting with my girls," Rick smirked.

Fiona giggled while Britney rolled her eyes at him. Rick felt so much better after his realization of his feelings that he couldn't even find it in him to be annoyed by the behavior his daughter was using more and more often the closer she got to being a teenager.

"Since male seahorses are the ones to give birth, do their kids call them mom or dad?" Skye Fields asked, looking up at her dad, Stone, for the answer.

"Neither," her brother, River, answered. "Because seahorses don't talk. So, they can't call their parents anything."

"I know that," Skye groaned, rolling her eyes at her brother. "But if they could talk, would he be Mom because of giving birth or Dad because of being male?"

Guess I'm not alone in dealing with that behavior, since Britney isn't the only one who's mastered rolling her eyes.

"He'd still be Dad because of being male," Britney answered her friend without taking her eyes from the seahorse in front of her. "Giving birth doesn't make someone a mom. If it did, there'd be a lot of adopted kids with no idea what to call their female parents, since they didn't give birth to them."

Rick was surprised and proud of his daughter's simple explanation. Though it did make him wonder if she already had plans to call Fiona her mom in the near future.

Is Fiona ready for that? She said she knows Britney and I are a package deal, so maybe?

Fuck! I hope my backing off to take some time to think hasn't caused her to change her mind.

I'll just have to take things slow and get us back on an even keel before I push for more by popping the question.

Thank fuck, I figured out how I feel before going back to New York, so I didn't mess up even more by returning the ring.

Rick stuck close to his girls for the rest of the time they were touring London. Even going so far as to sneak a kiss to the top of Fiona's head while they were at the top of the London Eye. But, not wanting to seem like his mood had swung by a hundred and eighty degrees, he didn't push for too much PDA.

When she came to his suite that night, Rick thought about being more commanding and giving in to his urge to rut into her like a wild beast once more. But Fiona still hadn't asked him for what she wanted in bed, so he wasn't sure how she felt about the way he'd changed to making love in a more gentle manner for the last few days.

Fuck! If she's not asking for me to be rougher, then she must prefer the slow and sensual way things have been the last few days. Right?

As he kissed his way back up her body after undressing her, he caught a look in her eye that made him wonder. He couldn't quite figure out what he was seeing as he hovered over her, looking down into her emerald eyes. It wasn't fear, though there was possibly a hint of trepidation. It also wasn't excitement, even though there was definitely a haze of arousal.

Fuck! It's the same thing I saw in that sad smile on the bus earlier today. I thought I wiped that away by being more affectionate and attentive the rest of the day.

No matter how bad his dick was fighting to get out of his boxers and into Fiona's sweet pussy, Rick knew he had to back off and find out what was going on in her head first. With his weight resting on his elbows, he brushed her hair off her forehead with the lightest touch of his fingers, in what he hoped was a comforting manner to put her at ease. "What's the matter, sweet Fifi?"

"Nothing." Fiona barely shook her head, moving just enough to be recognizable as a negative response without breaking eye contact. She smiled, but it wasn't nearly as big or bright as normal, and it didn't reach her eyes. "Nothing's the matter, Papa."

I guess it's time to teach my sweet Fifi that she can't get out of talking to me by using the honorific she only uses when we're playing. They might not have talked about how she'd quit using it the other night, when they paused their playtime to talk for a few minutes, but Rick recognized the disconnect when it happened.

He might have only skimmed over the information on the Daddy-babygirl dynamic when he first studied Dominance and submission, while trying to figure out his kinks and how to incorporate them into his sex life years ago, because he didn't think it pertained to him at the time, but he remembered the part about bratty behavior and deflection. And he didn't want to set a precedent with Fiona, where she thought she could appease him with sex when she didn't want to talk about something that was bothering her.

"Did you forget the rules about lying to me, Fifi?" Rick raised an eyebrow, as he asked the question. "I can clearly see in your eyes that something is wrong. So, you'd better tell me what it is before I have to add to the punishment I already owe you from the other night."

An expression of surprise and excitement crossed her features at his mention of their previously abandoned night of punishment. *Ah! She's sad that I've been too vanilla for the past few days. So, why hasn't she just told me that?*

Fiona bit her bottom lip, as she thought for a moment before speaking. "It's just…" She trailed off and closed her eyes for a moment, visibly taking a deep breath, as if to calm herself, as her pretty, pink blush spread from her cheeks down her neck and across her chest.

"It's just what, Fifi?" Rick stroked his fingers through her hair, hoping to soothe her obvious embarrassment, so she could finally talk to him. When she didn't respond other than to continue her deep inhales and exhales for a moment, he brushed his lips over her forehead and whispered, "You know you can tell me anything, right? There's no shame between us, sweet Fifi. Nothing you say will change how I feel about you. So, don't be embarrassed. Just tell me."

"I know." Fiona nodded before opening her eyes to look up at Rick. She released her hands from around his neck to motion between the two of them with her right, while resting her left on his shoulder. "I just wasn't raised to be comfortable talking about this stuff."

Rick gave her what he hoped was a reassuring smile, trying to be understanding of how her religious upbringing clashed with his need for her to be open to talking about their sexual desires. "I know, sweet Fifi. That's part of why I've tried to back off on some of my more primal instincts to be the man you need. But I can't read your mind, so I need you to tell me if I'm doing something to put that sad look in your eyes. I only ever want to make you happy."

"You do make me happy." Fiona smiled, as she ran her hands over his shoulders, before lightly massaging away the tension he carried in his upper back and neck. "I love…"

Fiona paused to swallow, as if she had a lump in her throat and Rick wondered if she was about to tell him she loved him for the first time. *Fuck! I wanted to be the first one to say the words.*

"I love everything we do together," she said before he could blurt out his feelings for her. "I'm not really sad about anything you've

293

done. I just kinda wish you'd mix some of those rougher things you did before in with the gentle way we've been making love recently."

Rick grinned, glad to know he was correct in his realization a few minutes before. "Does my freaky Fifi need a good, rough fuck?"

"Yes, Papa." Fiona returned his grin with a wide, bright smile, excitement lighting up her whole face.

"Then you're in luck, because I also need to fuck you hard tonight." Rick had more to say, but he had to kiss her long and hard first. Fiona opened for him, allowing him to plunder her mouth with his tongue, as she squeezed him in her arms.

When he finally broke the kiss to breathe, Rick couldn't hold back his words any longer. "I want you to know, no matter how I'm fucking you, whether I'm being gentle or rough, if I'm in your pussy, your mouth, or your ass, with my cock, my fingers, or my tongue, I'm always making love to you, Fifi. Because I love you, Fiona."

"Oh, Rick, I love you, too." She peppered his face with kisses, as she made her declaration.

Feeling as if his heart was going to burst along with his cock from hearing those words from her sweet lips for the first time, Rick couldn't wait a moment longer to be inside her. He shifted his weight to his left side, so he could reach down with his right hand and shove his boxers out of the way while returning her kisses.

He hitched her leg up over his hip and lined up with her soaking wet slit, plunging balls deep in her cunt with one stroke. Fiona cried out at the sudden invasion, but Rick swallowed her screams by covering her mouth with his.

She wrapped her legs around his waist and returned his ardent kiss, as he pounded into her mercilessly. The scrape of her nails on his back drove him wild. Both of them needing just that slight touch of pain with their pleasure.

Rick knew she'd be sore the next day from the way he was taking her, but he felt no remorse, since she'd made it clear she missed his rougher tendencies the last few days. She wasn't the only one who missed their darker desires, even as they enjoyed the slow and sensual.

Fuck! I should have grabbed the plugs out of my suitcase before we got started.

Deciding he'd have to wait until the next night to plug her the first time, Rick pushed up on his knees, pulling completely out of her, so he could manhandle her onto her hands and knees.

"Did my naughty Fifi miss my fingers in her ass, too?" Rick spread her ass cheeks with both hands, as he shoved his cock back into her dripping wet pussy.

"Yes, Papa." The words came out breathy, as Fiona arched her back, pressing her ass into his hands and her cunt farther onto his thick dick.

"Tell me what you missed, Fifi. I want to hear my dirty girl say the words. Especially the filthy, dirty words you only say with me." Rick used his thumbs to spread her cream from her drenched pussy up to her puckered little asshole to lubricate the digits' entry.

"I missed you finger-fucking my ass while you pound your dick into my pussy, Papa."

"Fuck, yes, you did," Rick growled, alternating the strokes of his thumbs in her ass with his cock in her cunt. "Your tight little cunt is making it obvious how much you love having me play with your ass while I fuck you. You keep clamping down and not letting me pull out when I shove my thumbs deeper in your ass."

"I can't help it. It feels so good." Fiona was panting as she shifted her weight back and forth, trying to match his rhythm.

Rick couldn't tell if she was trying to push back more when he pushed his dick in her pussy, or when he pushed his thumbs in her ass. But it was very clear, she wanted more of both. He was happy to oblige her, pounding harder when her inner walls started to flutter, as she got closer to her peak.

"Fuck, you feel amazing, Fifi. So wet. So tight." His dirty talk pushed her over the edge.

"Oh, yes, Rick!" Fiona bit down on the duvet, as the waves of her release squeezed his cock like a vise.

Every time the pressure lessened for a moment to make him think her orgasm was passing, another wave would hit and clamp down on him once more, even tighter than the previous one. It took everything he had to hold back his orgasm, and not let her milk the cum from his cock, as he continued to rut into her like a wild animal. But he was determined to get her off at least once more before he shot his load.

Now that he'd envisioned what their future children would look like, he no longer worried about whether she was really on the pill or not. He wanted to make babies with her. The sooner the better.

As soon as she agrees to marry me, I'll ask her not to refill her prescription. So we can get started trying right away.

The thought of Fiona round with his child made his balls draw up, ready to fill her womb with his seed. Though she was just coming back down from her first high, Rick needed to get her ramped back up quickly, or she wouldn't get the second before he reached his release. So, he amped up the dirty talk, instead of just continuing to grunt like a pig, as he pumped in and out of her.

"Fuck, I can't wait to fuck you with a plug in your ass, so I can play with your tits at the same time."

Fiona moaned around the wad of duvet in her mouth, as her flutters started once more. She pushed back harder, never losing their synced-up rhythm.

Rick's balls bounced against her clit, as he fucked her with a ferocity even he hadn't realized he possessed. It was the most intense, carnal mating he'd ever experienced. It was such a mind-blowing coupling that he could barely grunt out her name, as they exploded in ecstasy as one.

"Fiona!" Rick shoved in as deep as he could go, holding still deep inside her tight, wet heat, as the spasms of her creamy cunt around his cock pulled every drop of cum from his body.

With the head of his dick pressed into her cervix, each wave of her release triggered a jet of his semen to shoot straight into her womb. He was barely able to hold himself upright, as the aftershocks rumbled through him.

When Fiona collapsed down into the bed, Rick pulled out of her and slumped down beside her. He pulled her into his arms, holding her close, as they caught their breath.

Once he recovered, Rick scooped Fiona up into his arms and carried her into the ensuite bathroom to clean them both up in the shower. As he washed their combined cum from her body, he continued getting her to open up about her sexual likes and dislikes, and even explained a little more about his past, so she could understand his sexual proclivities a little better.

After washing and drying each other from head to toe, they crawled back into bed and whispered, "I love you" once again before falling asleep in each other's arms.

The way we were meant to be.

Chapter Nineteen

Monday, March 4, 2019, Paris, France

Fiona was having the time of her life on the European tour. It wasn't just the variety of things they'd seen so far, though she'd loved how they'd changed things up from the castles and historical sites in Dublin and Edinburgh on Thursday and Friday, to some fun things like the Beatles Magical Mystery Tour in Liverpool on Saturday, and the SEA LIFE London Aquarium and London Eye mixed in with the historical sites of London on Sunday. She also felt closer to Rick, since they'd started talking more about their feelings the night before.

After declaring their love for the first time, they'd ended up saying the words multiple times throughout the night. Their conversation in the shower had started out with him asking her more about what she liked sexually and hadn't been brave enough to ask him for yet. But it quickly morphed into more of a discussion about the things she'd read about in books and was curious about, since she hadn't actually tried anything kinky before being with him.

That led to his explanation of how he'd discovered his kinks, which actually gave her a better understanding of his issues with his ex-wife and how that relationship affected his psyche than he probably realized. He'd made it clear that he'd never felt like he was in love before, but even though he hadn't loved his ex-wife, she had still broken his trust.

Though Fiona also hadn't been in love before, she hadn't had a bad break-up to know firsthand how he felt, so she was relying on her ability to empathize to be understanding of his feelings. She was in love with a man with trust issues, so she had to figure out how to show him that he was safe entrusting his heart to her.

Fiona knew it would probably take years for him to get past those issues to be able to completely trust in her. But she was a patient woman, and now that she understood where he was coming from, she was more than willing to spend the time waiting for him to be ready to move their relationship to the next level.

Earlier that day, as they were touring the Louvre Museum in Paris, Fiona realized that his distance during the first few days in Europe was because of his mother's distrust of Fiona feeding his trust issues. Thankfully, it only took a few days without her influence to get him back to acting normal again. But Fiona still wasn't sure how to win his mother over, when she probably wouldn't see her except the few times a year when the GWA traveled through New York City.

I just have to hope that being myself with Rick and Britney will be enough for them to tell Katarina who I really am as a person when they communicate with her from the road. Maybe if she hears enough about me over the next couple of years, she'll eventually start to trust me with her son and granddaughter.

After they left the Louvre, she continued enjoying what felt more and more like family time with Rick and Britney, while having lunch at a café near the Eiffel Tower. They took a ton of pictures together at the base of the tower, several of which she emailed to her parents when they got to the arena that afternoon.

After seeing Rick and Britney in several of the shots she'd sent them over the last month, her parents had started asking questions about her relationship with Rick, when they responded to her messages. Fiona was glad her busy schedule kept them from talking on the phone often, since it was much easier to admit to dating her boss via email than when she was actually talking to her mom and dad.

She'd been a little worried when she first told them, thinking they might object to the relationship because of him being her boss. She thought for sure there would be comments about him being older than her, having a child from a previous marriage, and possibly influencing her to have sex before marriage, as well, in order to try to dissuade her from continuing to see him. But she'd been pleasantly surprised to find out her parents actually approved of her relationship with Rick.

Though they probably wouldn't be as happy about it if they knew about me sneaking in and out of his bed on a daily basis, Fiona thought as she finally made her way to Rick's room in their Paris hotel that night. *Not that I'd ever tell them about our bedroom activities.*

Fiona shook off the grossed-out feeling of thinking about talking to her parents about sex, as she lightly knocked on the door to Rick's suite. All thoughts of anyone but her and Rick quickly fled her mind, as he opened the door. He had already removed his jacket and tie, and was standing there looking good enough to eat in his navy-blue slacks and pale blue button-down.

Rick pulled her into his arms before shutting and locking the door, silently leading her to his bedroom before taking her lips in a passionate kiss, once they were locked away in their private oasis for the night. He had made it clear he preferred her to follow her instincts and return his kisses however felt right to her, whether he'd explicitly instructed her to or not, so she did just that. She wrapped her arms around his neck and explored his mouth with her tongue, the same way he was exploring hers.

She reveled in the feel of his hands, as they traversed her body. Rick squeezed her bottom in one hand, while running the other up her back to cup her nape and guide her head the way he wanted her to move. Fiona melted into him, loving the feel of his erection pressing into her belly.

"Fuck, Fifi, I can't get enough of tasting you," Rick growled when he broke their kiss to take a breath. He proved his point by trailing his lips and tongue down her neck before starting to take little nips with his teeth, which drove her nuts.

Fiona could only moan in response, too caught up in the pleasure to think of how she should reply. Not that she had much time to think because a moment later Rick was pulling back and moving to sit on the end of the bed, leaving her standing there dazed.

"I believe I still owe you a punishment that got interrupted in Dublin." Rick rubbed his jaw, as if he was thinking hard about what he wanted to do to punish her.

"Yes, Papa." Fiona remembered being excited about the things he'd told her he planned for that night, but she couldn't remember why she was being punished.

To be totally honest, she thought the things he'd described sounded more like funishment than punishment, so she wasn't going to argue that feeling disconnected from him that night was actually more of a punishment. She didn't want him to think she'd already been punished and decide to do something else instead, so she made a mental note to talk to him the next morning about the differences. She thought she understood the differences from the romance novels she'd read recently, but she wanted to verify that Rick's proclivities in the bedroom aligned with her understanding, and didn't just feel like they were straight out of the pages of some of her favorite books.

"I've already prepped everything, so we won't have any reason to pause our play unless you feel uncomfortable." His lips lifted in the slightest smile, and Fiona could see the regret in his eyes from the night he left her bound to the bed while he went to clean the plugs he planned to use on her.

Fiona returned his smile as she stood there, enjoying the feel of his eyes on her.

"Remember to use your safe words if you need them. Yellow to take a breather and red to stop everything. Though I don't think anything I have planned tonight will be more than you can handle." He winked.

"Yes, Papa."

"Then we'll begin as soon as you strip for me." Rick's grin widened, as he pulled his phone from his pocket and started playing some music.

Fiona didn't recognize the songs, or know the names of the artists on whatever Pandora station he'd picked, but the grinding beat of the music seemed to be designed to match their sexual pace. She started dancing more than stripping, teasing him some by lifting the hem of her purple dress almost high enough for him to see her panties before dropping it back down to shimmy some more.

Rick groaned as he watched her, obviously appreciating watching her dance, even as he was getting impatient for her to undress. He rubbed his hand over his erection, which was prominently tenting his trousers, making it evident he was enjoying the show she was giving him.

"You do know that the longer you tease Papa, the longer you'll be waiting for an orgasm tonight. Right, Fifi?" Rick arched an eyebrow at her, as he toed off his dress shoes.

"No, Papa, I didn't, or I wouldn't have taken so long."

Eager for the pleasure awaiting her, Fiona quickly pulled her purple dress over her head and stepped out of her black pumps. She released the front clasp of her lavender bra and dropped it to the ground, barely waiting for the straps to clear her hands before looping her fingers in the sides of her matching lavender panties to shimmy them down her legs.

Rick chuckled at her hasty switch from sultry to speedy stripping, unable to hide his amusement under his normal stoic expression. Fiona grinned at him, as she popped back up to standing, presenting her naked self to him.

Rick shook his head, as he schooled his expression and stood. He walked around the bed, placed his phone on the bedside table without stopping the music, and picked up the pink silicone plug and bottle of lube he had waiting there.

"Bend over the end of the bed, Fifi," Rick directed, turning, and walking back toward her just as the song changed.

Fiona stepped up to the end of the bed and bent over just as Rick's phone blared the words "face down, ass up," causing her to burst out laughing at the timing of the song change. She couldn't be sure if she actually heard Rick chuckle over her laughter or not, but she liked that they could find humor in their intimate moments.

"Reach back with both hands and pull your cheeks apart for me, Fifi," Rick commanded, sobering her instantly.

Fiona turned her face into the mattress, trying to hide her blush of embarrassment, as she followed his instructions.

"Good girl."

Those two words did something to Fiona that she didn't quite understand. They would have sounded condescending coming from anyone else. But from Rick's lips, when she was obeying him in the bedroom, they infused her with a sense of pride in herself for pleasing him.

She felt her arousal dripping down her legs at the same time she felt Rick drizzle the lubricant between her cheeks. She slightly jumped and her whole body stiffened, as she was shocked by the cool fluid dripping on her puckered back hole.

"Relax, Fifi," Rick chuckled, as he rubbed the lube around with the tip of the small pink plug. "This isn't much bigger than my fingers, so it won't hurt a bit if you just relax and let me put it in."

"Yes, Papa," Fiona sighed, as she willed her whole body to relax. She focused on her breathing, as he worked the tip in and out of her bottom in a similar manner to how he'd used his fingers and thumbs on her before.

Rick continued to work the pink plug in and out, going a little deeper each time until he finally worked the widest part of the plug past her tight ring of muscles to seat it completely inside her.

Being plugged felt different than when he used his fingers back there during sex. It wasn't unpleasant, just unusual. She felt full, almost like she needed to go to the bathroom, but without the rest of the normal feelings of a bowel movement.

"Fuck, that's so much hotter in real life than it was in the videos," Rick growled, his voice deeper and more gravelly than usual from arousal.

"Have you done this before, Papa?" Fiona felt a twinge of jealousy at the thought of him doing these things with other women in the past, but she hoped his statement meant he'd only watched videos in the past.

"No, Fifi. Like I told you the other night, I started exploring BDSM after the judge suggested I check out a club after my divorce. I managed to visit a couple of times, but with my schedule, going to a club for master's training just didn't work. So, the majority of my research has been online and video conferencing with a mentor a few years ago. I haven't had any opportunities for practical application, since I decided not to join a club I couldn't use ninety percent of the year."

At hearing his answer, Fiona released a breath she hadn't realized she'd been holding. She knew from their talks that he had always been rougher in the bedroom. And as irrational as it was to be jealous of his past lovers, she'd hated that he hadn't reserved that intensity for her. But knowing the other things they were exploring were just between the two of them, that they were still having firsts together, eased some of the jealousy.

"Crawl up on the bed, lay on your stomach, and reach your hands over your head," Rick instructed, bringing her back to the moment with him.

"Yes, Papa." Fiona felt the plug with every movement, as she gingerly climbed onto the bed. It filled her in a way she'd never experienced before, and she wasn't sure how to crawl without risking it coming out. "Um, Papa?"

"Yes, Fifi?" Rick sounded amused at how she'd stilled and used his play title as a question, but Fiona knew better than to turn her head to look at him, choosing to imagine his smirk instead of actually seeing it.

"How do I keep the plug in my bottom? It feels like it's trying to slip out when I move my legs."

"You might want to squeeze your ass tight around it," Rick chuckled. "If it comes out, I'll have to go get the next size up."

Fiona swallowed down her trepidation, as she contracted her glutes. *Hopefully, this works. 'Cause I don't think bearing down like I'm trying to poop will hold it in, and that's the only other way I know how to squeeze back there.*

She cautiously started to crawl toward the head of the bed, moving much slower than she knew Rick wanted her to move, but unable to go any faster. She was afraid if she tried, the plug would shoot out of her lubricated backside like a little pink rocket.

As she pictured passing gas and shooting the plug back at Rick, Fiona started giggling. With each tentative movement of her hands and knees forward, her giggles increased. She feared she'd lose the plug for sure, if she ended up in a full-on belly laugh.

"Is that little plug tickling you, Fifi?" Rick's words were infused with his own light laughter.

"No, Papa," Fiona giggled, trying to concentrate on crawling a couple more feet before laying down on her stomach as she'd been instructed.

"Then why are you laughing, sweet Fifi?"

"Just imagining you trying to catch the little pink rocket, if I can't hold it in, Papa," Fiona choked out through her laughter, as she crawled the last few inches.

When she got to the middle of the bed and collapsed forward onto her stomach, the little plug slipped out. She pushed back up onto all fours to dip her head and look between her legs to see how far it had flown.

"Well, that's not how I pictured it coming out at all." Her disappointment killed her laughter.

Rick shook his head and tried to hide his smile, as he reached down and picked up the plug. "Guess it's a good thing I already have the others cleaned and ready for you. You can lower your shoulders and head, but keep that juicy ass up, while I take this to the sink and grab the next one."

He stepped into the ensuite bathroom, as Fiona lowered her top half into the mattress. She maintained her position, eagerly anticipating him coming back to insert the next plug. She turned her head to watch him coming back into the room with the next size of plug, and her heart rate sped up when she noticed how much more it flared out in the middle than the last one.

"Relax, sweet Fifi." Rick gave her a reassuring smile as he walked on his knees from the side of the bed to come to her side. "You can take this, I promise."

"Yes, Papa." Fiona returned his smile, as he moved behind her.

Rick rubbed his hand that wasn't holding the plug over her bottom for a moment before pulling the bottle of lube from his pocket. "Reach back and hold your ass open for me, Fifi."

Fiona followed his instructions without saying a word and was rewarded with another "good girl" coming from his lips. She focused on her breathing and tried to relax, as he repeated the process from earlier.

First, he drizzled more lube on her opening. Then he worked it in with the tip of the pink plug. He took his time and mimicked making love to her with the plug for several moments.

Fiona relaxed even more, enjoying the sensations that were bringing her closer to the edge than she thought possible without him actually touching her with anything but the plug. *Wow! Who knew that's an erogenous zone for straight people?*

Finally, Rick pushed the widest part of the plug inside her, seating it fully and making her feel even more full than before. "So, fucking, hot. Now let's see if you can keep this one in while laying down to get into position for your punishment."

Fiona tightened up as much as she could, and gingerly moved into the original position Rick had directed her to take on the bed, as he backed off the bed and placed the bottle of lube on the bedside table. He picked up his ties that were laying there before moving back on the bed.

He was so gentle, as he secured her wrists, one at each end of his tie, with the middle of the tie woven through the slats of the headboard. He double-checked that they were tight enough she couldn't easily escape, but not so tight that they cut off her circulation. Then he took the second tie and tied it around her head, covering her eyes.

He explained once again that he was punishing her for trying to coerce him into spanking her, instead of submitting to his control, and that her punishment was not being able to come until he said she could, no matter how much he worked her up to it. He reiterated her safe words and their proper usage, making sure she could repeat them back to him to know she was prepared to use them if necessary.

"And remember not to lose the plug, sweet Fifi. No matter how I touch you, move you, fuck you, you have to hold that plug in, or I'll have to go to the next size and start your punishment all over again."

"Yes, Papa. I'll hold it in." Fiona was already panting and barely able to get the words out. She was so aroused by the preparations that she was afraid she'd explode in orgasm as soon as he touched her.

"Fuck, you look so hot. I might just have to stand here and look at you for a little while."

Fiona bit back a moan of frustration, needing him to touch her more than anything.

"Spread your legs wider, Fifi. And arch your back, so I can see how wet you are for me." Rick's voice was deep and commanding, as he moved around the room to look at her from various angles.

Fiona heard the rustle of fabric and assumed he was undressing, as she spread her legs as wide as she could and arched her back to lift her bottom and expose her womanhood to him.

"Fuck, that creamy cunt has already made a wet spot on the bed," Rick groaned, as she felt the bed dip at the end between her feet.

She wasn't sure what the strange popping sound she heard was until she smelled menthol and felt Rick's strong hands start to massage her calves. He worked his way up her body, massaging in the sports cream she knew he used for muscle soreness after a hard workout.

Fiona hadn't ever thought a massage could be arousing. But when Rick moved from her calves to her hamstrings and then her glutei, she quickly changed her mind. He didn't touch her anywhere the menthol cream couldn't safely go on her body, but that didn't stop her girl parts from tingling in anticipation.

She thought he might be spending extra time on her gluteal muscles, trying to get her to lose the plug, but she knew better than to say anything about his underhanded tactics for trying to get her to move up to the bigger plugs faster. She just had to hope that squeezing her sphincter wouldn't push the plug out, since she couldn't tighten her glutes when he kept massaging them to make the muscles relax.

Finally, he moved from her buttocks to her back, squeezing more of the sports cream from the tube to really work all the knots out of her tense muscles.

"You should have been a masseuse, Papa. That feels better than the lady at the hotel spa a few weeks ago." Fiona heard the breathiness in her voice and knew her arousal was evident to Rick in more ways than one.

"No, sweet Fifi, these hands are only meant to massage you." Rick brushed her hair out of the way to massage her neck for a few minutes before lifting his hands from her body and backing away.

Fiona felt herself stiffen, wondering what he was going to do next. Apparently, Rick noticed, pausing to reassure her before leaving the room. "I'll be right back, sweet Fifi. I just have to go wash my hands, so I don't get this cream anywhere it shouldn't go."

She heard more rustling, just after his weight was lifted from the bed, then his surprisingly soft footfalls, as he walked to the ensuite bathroom once more. She was surprised at how loud the water running in the bathroom sounded, even over the music that was still playing.

I guess losing the sense of sight really does heighten our other senses.

He was only gone a few moments before she felt him reenter the room. It was strange how she sensed where he was, as he quietly moved around the room. She knew he was standing at the foot of the bed, so she made sure she arched her back to hold the position she knew he wanted her in for him to see her most intimate areas.

The anticipation of what he was going to do next was killing her, especially when he wasn't talking to give her any kind of clues. With her adrenaline running on high, she squealed when he gripped her ankles, lifted her completely off the mattress, and flipped her over onto her back before dropping her back down.

She wasn't sure if she was more surprised at being flipped over, or from the plug staying in place when he flipped her.

"Remember to be quiet, Fifi," Rick admonished, though she could hear the laughter in his voice. "No matter what I do to you, you have to stay quiet, so we don't disturb the neighbors."

"Sorry, Papa. I just wasn't expecting you to move me like that," Fiona whispered, circling her wrists to make sure the pressure on them from the flip didn't tighten the ties too much.

"Of course, you didn't expect it, that's why I did it," Rick chuckled, as she felt the bed dip under his weight once more. "Surprising you with everything I'm doing to you is what makes this punishment so fun for me."

He teasingly ran his hands up the front of her legs, massaging some when he got to her thighs, even though he didn't use the sports cream to really dig into the muscles. He changed tactics, lightly running his fingers over her lower torso, but avoiding the area between her legs where she really wanted him to touch her. His fingers almost tickled, as he moved up over her belly and ribs. Only to change the pressure once more when he reached her breasts.

He kneaded her mounds and pinched her nipples, making them tighten even harder than they already were from everything else he was doing. He quickly replaced his fingers with his mouth, continuing to squeeze the bulk of her breasts with his hands, as he suckled and lightly bit her nipples.

Rick worked Fiona up to the edge quickly with breast play alone, and almost pushed her over the edge when he lowered his body onto hers. She couldn't stop her moans of pleasure, as he teased her mercilessly with the weight of his torso pressing into her mound.

Just as she thought she was about to come, he released her breasts and pushed up off of her, breaking all contact. Fiona let out a frustrated groan, which was only met with a chuckle from Rick.

Next, he trailed something soft over her skin, starting at her feet, teasing up the inside of her legs until he tickled the apex of her thighs. She writhed and wiggled, needing more pressure on the sensitive nub he was barely touching with the unknown soft object.

When she was right at the point of not being able to take much more, he replaced the soft item with something that felt sharp against her skin. She wondered if it was a razor, with the way he scraped it over her mound in a manner similar to the way she shaved.

But, no, it can't be. Unless it's a straight razor, since it feels like a single thin blade.

Her breathing quickened with the fear that he might slip and cut her most sensitive areas. As he trailed it over her abdomen and then across her breasts, she no longer felt aroused by what he was doing. She didn't think Rick would do anything to cause her harm, but she couldn't stop the fear from overwhelming her at the thought that he could accidentally cut her with whatever he was running over her body.

"Yel-yellow," she stuttered out.

Rick lifted the object from her left breast immediately. "What's too much, sweet Fifi? What do you need for us to be able to keep going?"

"I just need to know what you're using, Papa. I like the feel of it scraping my skin, but I can't stop the fear of being cut by whatever you're using."

"Oh, sweet Fifi, I would never use anything that could cut you." Rick ran a hand over her head, pushing up the tie he was using as a blindfold.

When she opened her eyes, she saw him holding up the key card for the hotel room. "Wow, I feel foolish now."

"Nothing to feel foolish about, Fifi. Without being able to see what I was using, you had no way of knowing it wasn't a knife. And now we know you like the sensation, but not the danger. So, from now on, whenever I want to tease you by alternating between soft and sharp, while I have you tied down and blindfolded in the future, we both know it's perfectly safe, so you can enjoy the experience without fear."

Rick gave her a small smile before placing the hotel key card and the tie from one of the hotel bathrobes on the bedside table. "But since you're not supposed to be enjoying your punishment, we're done with that for tonight."

"But I said yellow, not red, Papa," Fiona protested. "So, you're supposed to just give me a breather and then go back to it."

"Oh, I'm going to go back to your punishment, my naughty girl." Rick moved from her side to kneel between her legs, stroking his hard, thick penis, as he grinned down at her. "I'm just not going to use those tools any longer. Now I'm going to tease you with my fingers, mouth, and cock, until you beg me to let you come."

"Oh." Fiona tried to hide her excitement, as she realized he was finally going to touch her where she wanted him to most of all. But she wasn't sure how successful she was when he shook his head and grinned before running his hands up her thighs.

He didn't replace the blindfold, allowing her to watch as he started a new onslaught of teasing by fingering her to the brink of orgasm before pulling out at the last second. He sucked her cream from his fingers before bending down to drink straight from the source.

His tongue was magical and had her writhing in mere moments. He maintained eye contact with her the whole time, repeatedly working her up and backing away at the last second to keep her on edge for what seemed like hours.

Finally, he pushed back up to a kneeling position and lifted her lower body by her ankles. He shoved a pillow under her low back to hold her up off the mattress and propped her feet on his shoulders before lining up his erection with her slit.

"Are you ready to be Papa's good girl?" Rick rubbed the head of his penis against her clit, teasing her even more before taking her.

"Yes, Papa."

"Remember, good girls don't come without permission. They lay there and let Papa do whatever he wants, and ask permission to come if it feels good." Rick gripped her by the hips and rammed his erection into her, shoving all the way in until his balls bounced against the base of the plug in her backside.

The feeling of both holes being filled to capacity elicited a squeal that Fiona tried her best to bite back, knowing she needed to be quieter. She clamped her mouth shut, so only whimpered sounds could escape.

Rick didn't see the need to be quiet, however, grunting loudly, as he pounded into her over and over. "Fuck, you're even tighter with the plug in your ass. I'm not sure I'll be able to fit when we move up to the big one."

"That's not the big one?" Fiona screeched, forgetting he'd mentioned going bigger if this one slipped out the way the first one had.

"Oh, no, sweet Fifi," Rick growled, not stopping the way he was roughly fucking her, as they discussed the plugs. "There are four more we have to work you up to taking before you'll be able to take my cock in your ass."

Fiona wasn't sure if she was excited, or frightened, at the realization that he was planning to fill her up with a plug as big as his erection in her back hole, while he was in her front hole. Not that she could focus enough to think about how that would feel when he rocked his hips and hit that secret spot inside her that only he had ever found.

"Oh, Papa," Fiona whisper-shouted, needing to cry out in pleasure, but trying to stay quiet enough not to disturb the neighbors.

"Yeah, you like that, don't you, Fifi? My cock's the only one that makes you come. Isn't it, Fifi?"

"Yes, Papa," Fiona moaned, as her climax built inside her.

"That's right. You're mine, Fifi. Mine to tease. Mine to punish. Mine to fuck. You're all mine, Fifi. Every. Part. Of. You. Is. Mine!" Rick punctuated every word with a powerful thrust so deep inside her, she knew he had to be pushing into her cervix.

"Yes, Papa!" It felt so good. Fiona wasn't sure she'd be able to hold back the massive orgasm that was building in her core. So, she did the only thing she knew Rick wanted. She begged. "Please, Papa. Please let me come. I… I… Please, Papa."

"Fuck, yes, come, Fifi!" Rick commanded, pounding into her ferociously and driving her completely over the edge. "Come. On. My. Cock. Now!"

"Yes, Rick!" Fiona cried out his name, as the waves of ecstasy took her under. She felt like she was floating and drowning all at once, as her body convulsed in the ultimate pleasure.

It was the most intense orgasm of her life. It was so intense that she wasn't sure if she passed out, or had an out-of-body experience. She barely registered Rick joining her in orgasmic nirvana, repeatedly grunting her name with each jet of cum he shot into her womb.

She wasn't sure how long she laid there, watching the colorful light show behind her closed eyelids, and feeling like she was floating in a pool of endorphins before Rick untied her wrists and carried her to the bathroom. But he'd apparently removed the plug from her backside and ran them a bubble bath before he lifted her limp body into his strong arms.

"I love you, Rick." Fiona curled up against his chest in the warm water, trusting him to take care of her as she drifted off to sleep, barely hearing his reply.

"I love you, too, Fifi."

~~~

Tuesday, March 5, 2019, Paris, France

Rick wasn't surprised when he slept through his early morning alarm, after his late-night activities with Fiona the night before. But now, as he slipped on a pair of pajama pants and a t-shirt, sans underwear, he found himself trying to figure out how to sneak her out of his suite without his daughter realizing she'd been there all night.

"Let me make sure the coast is clear before you leave." Rick brushed his lips over Fiona's forehead as he passed her at the foot of the bed. He made sure she was out of the line of sight of the bedroom door before he opened it and looked around the main living area of the suite. He saw the light on under Britney's door and assumed she was already up and probably in the shower. He closed the door once more before turning to Fiona, who was slipping last night's dress over her sexy lavender underwear. "She's not out of her room yet, so you should be able to head out now, if you hurry."

"See you on the plane, Papa." Fiona pushed up on her tip-toes and pecked her lips on his cheek, as she walked past him to the bedroom door.

Rick couldn't contain his grin at her being playful in the morning, as he returned her quick peck. "See you soon, sweet Fifi."

With her shoes in her hand, she tip-toed out of the bedroom, trying to exit quietly to keep Britney from hearing her leave.

Rick watched from the doorway, not wanting to make too much noise in the communal space of the suite to draw Britney's attention before Fiona left the room. He planned to rush over to relock the main door, as soon as it closed behind her.
~~~

Unfortunately, they hadn't timed things as well as he'd hoped. Britney's bedroom door opened when Fiona was only halfway across the main living area of the suite. Britney stopped in her tracks, with one hand on the door and the other on the handle of her rolling suitcase.

"Miss Fiona?" Britney looked back and forth between Rick in the master bedroom doorway and Fiona, who had frozen in place halfway between him and the main door to the suite.

If it wasn't for the fact that they'd just gotten caught by his twelve-year-old daughter, Rick would have laughed at how cute his Fifi was acting like a statue, still on her tip-toes, as if that would stop Britney from noticing she was still there.

"Why are you sneaking out?"

Fiona dropped down to stand flat on her feet before turning to look at Rick. The look on her face was clearly a cry for help in how to answer his daughter's question.

Rick wasn't sure what to say to Britney. They had both been extremely uncomfortable when the sex education module had come up in her online learning portal the year before, so he'd tried to avoid any mention of sex with his daughter after they got through that embarrassing semester. Now he was stuck with no idea what other excuse he could use for why Fiona was in his room overnight, and extremely uncomfortable with the prospect of having to discuss his sex life with his preteen daughter.

Maybe this is one of those girl talks Fiona can have with her without me around? Rick shrugged, hoping Fiona would get his unspoken message and take the lead on this conversation.

"Well, I have to go back to my room to get ready for the day, and didn't want to wake you up on my way out."

"Oh, okay." Britney nodded, as if that was all the answer she needed.

Rick was thankful they seemed to have skipped over the reason Fiona was in their suite altogether.

"But maybe you should just bring your stuff to our suite when we check in at the hotel, instead of getting your own room, so you don't have to sneak in every night and back out every morning." Britney grinned at Fiona, as she rolled her suitcase to the living area, where they would start stacking their things to have them ready to take downstairs when they checked out of the hotel, before turning to look at Rick. "Oh, and Dad, now that we all know that I know Miss Fiona is spending the night every night, I'm not going to wait until my birthday or Christmas to ask for noise-canceling headphones, like Tia suggested. If you order them now, they should be waiting for us when we get to New York next week."

"I'll place that order today." Rick nodded at his daughter, as she walked back into her bedroom.

"That's it?" Fiona looked at him with a shocked expression on her face. "No embarrassing questions or awkward conversations? She's just okay with…" Fiona's voice trailed off for a moment, as she waved her hand in the air between her and Rick. "Everything? Like it's no big deal?"

"I guess," Rick shrugged, a little surprised that Britney hadn't made a bigger deal of things. "Though with how uncomfortable we both were when she had a sex ed module we had to discuss for school, I wouldn't be surprised if she saves the embarrassing questions for your girl time later today, so she doesn't have to talk to me about it again."

Fiona's eyes widened, and her jaw dropped momentarily. "And how do you want me to answer those questions, if she does ask me later?"

Rick walked over to pull Fiona into his arms, sensing she needed his reassurance and comfort, as much as she needed his advice for having that talk with Britney later. Fiona wrapped her arms around his waist and rested her face against his chest, relaxing some in his embrace.

"However you feel comfortable answering them, Fifi. I trust your judgment in knowing what's appropriate to discuss with Britney." Rick rubbed his hands up and down her back and bent his head to kiss her on the top of her head. "And from now on, I'll take the lead when it comes to discussing sex with our sons, and let you take the lead with our daughters."

"You'd better not be saying that just because Britney is your only kid," Fiona giggled. "Because I'm gonna hold you to it. Even if we don't work out and I end up having sons with someone else, I'm gonna bring them to you for the sex talk."

"Then I guess it's a good thing I already know we're going to work out." Rick shook his head, as he lightly tickled Fiona to keep her giggling. "And we're going to have two sons and another daughter, so the responsibility for sex talks will be even."

"Oh, is that so?" Fiona laughed, pulling back to look up into his eyes. "You've already got them planned, huh?"

Rick barely had time to grin and nod before she was shaking her head.

"You know it doesn't work like that, right? You can't just place your order for what you want and expect me to pop out three kids to your exact specifications. I mean, I could have issues and end up not being able to even have one baby, much less three."

"Then we'll adopt," Rick shrugged. "It doesn't matter how we end up adding to our family, Fifi. I know we're going to have a big one. In fifty years, all four of our kids will be happily married, as will all sixteen of our grandkids. And you and I will be souping up our motorized scooters to be competitive in driveway races with our three dozen great-grandkids."

"You're crazy." Fiona shook her head, as she laughed at him.

"Crazy about you," Rick agreed, catching her face in his hands, so he could hold her still long enough to kiss her once more. "And it was that vision I had of our future that proved it to me."

Rick captured her rebuttal by covering her mouth with his. He knew he didn't have time to do more than kiss her, or they'd be late for their flight to Lisbon, Portugal, and risk delays and other issues with the first time the GWA's weekly television show was broadcast from Europe. So, he kept the kiss mostly chaste, instead of giving into his desire to claim her one more time in Paris.

"Now hurry up and get your stuff packed up in your room, so we can check in together at the hotel in Lisbon."

"Yes, Sir." Fiona saluted him playfully, as she pulled away, slipped her shoes on her feet, and headed for the door.

Damn, that girl is going to be the death of me. But what a way to go!

Chapter Twenty

In the past few days, Rick had enjoyed just how perfect his life was now that he had Fiona by his side. Life hadn't changed that much with her sharing his and Britney's suite each night. She had been sneaking into his bed every night for over two weeks before they'd taken the step to make their relationship seem more permanent by having her openly checking in with him when they first arrived at the hotel each day. So, he knew it wasn't just having her in his bed every night that made the last few days seem more perfect than before.

They also hadn't changed anything about the rest of their daily schedule. Rick and Fiona still worked out together most mornings before grabbing a bite of breakfast with Britney on the way to the plane. They did their own thing on the plane, so the girls could have fun with their friends while he worked. When they landed, they checked in at their hotel and sent their things to be laundered as needed. They would then go on their daily sightseeing tours and grab lunch before going to the arena to work for a few hours, have dinner together as a family, and then go back to the hotel, where he spent his nights making love to Fiona in all the dirtiest ways he could think of to pleasure them both.

On Tuesday in Lisbon, Portugal, Rick had gone to the arena to set up for the GWA's weekly TV show, while Fiona and Britney went with the rest of the crew on a bus tour through the city. Then, on Wednesday in Madrid, Spain, Rick had rejoined the group on the daily excursions, enjoying touring the Prado Museum with his girls. Thursday in Barcelona, Spain, Friday in Marseille, France, and

Saturday in Milan, Italy, had been similar, with more bus tours to view some beautiful churches and a couple of museum visits.

His favorites had to be the Leonardo da Vinci National Museum of Science and Technology and seeing Leonardo da Vinci's painting of the Last Supper, both in Milan. The former was because of how much fun Britney had in the interactive laboratory, and the latter because of how much it seemed to fascinate Fiona.

The fact that nothing had really changed, except the feeling of permanence surrounding his relationship with Fiona, solidified Rick's decision to ask her to marry him. He was done metaphorically kicking his own ass for the doubts his mother had planted in his head that had made him question the speed at which their relationship was progressing.

He was madly in love with her and had come to realize that love didn't happen on a specific timeline. It didn't matter if love took years to develop, or if it was instant, the feelings wouldn't go away when they were real. So, he no longer saw any reason to delay in legally making them a family, since they were already living as one.

Rick had decided on their flight from Milan to Venice that he would pop the question under the Bridge of Sighs. Unfortunately, when they got to the location to board the boats for their scheduled tour of the Grand Canal, he found out the Bridge of Sighs was over one of the smaller waterways, and wouldn't be included in the tour on the larger boats he'd reserved, so everyone in the GWA could tour in groups of twelve.

Fuck! Should I just propose under one of the other bridges, so our closest friends can be there to witness it? Or should I leave Britney with Cage on the Grand Canal tour, and take Fiona on a gondola ride under the Bridge of Sighs?

I'm sure there are other bridges that will be just as romantic to propose under. But what if she thinks I'm moving too fast with a proposal? Do I want to make her feel pressured to say yes because of having a large audience when I propose?

Rick glanced over at Fiona, who was standing beside Britney with their friends. She was gorgeous in the green dress he loved seeing her wear most of all the rainbow of colors she had in her suitcase.

No. I want her to say yes because she's ready to be my wife. While I hope her wearing my favorite dress is a sign that I'm supposed to propose today, I don't want to embarrass her by doing so with an audience, just in case she's not ready yet. So, I have to figure out how to get her alone on a gondola ride under the Bridge of Sighs.

Knowing his daughter would want to be in on the plan to propose, Rick waved Britney over to talk a few feet away from everyone else. Luckily, Fiona seemed preoccupied with something Kay was saying, so she didn't notice Britney slipping away to where he was standing. Or if she did, she realized she was going to him and didn't feel the need to follow.

"What's up, Dad?"

"I need your help," Rick whispered, putting an arm over Britney's shoulders, and turning them away from Fiona, so she couldn't even figure out what they were saying by reading their lips. "I want to propose to Fiona today under the Bridge of Sighs, but I just found out this boat tour doesn't go under that bridge."

"That's the one you're supposed to kiss under to have true love last forever, right?"

"Yeah, how'd you know that?" Rick couldn't believe his twelve-year-old daughter had heard the folklore surrounding the bridge.

"The girls were talking about it on the plane this morning." Britney waved her hand in the direction of her friends. "I guess Mr. Anthony doesn't have to worry about making sure they go on a different boat than Mr. Cooper's family to keep Connor from kissing Tia today, after all."

"No, I guess not," Rick chuckled. "But I still need your help in figuring out how to get Fiona to come with me on a gondola ride, instead of going on one of these boats with everyone else, so I can propose under the right bridge."

"Can you get a gondola from here to go to the Bridge of Sighs?" Rick nodded in answer to his daughter's question. "Then it's simple. You book it to leave at the same time we do, and when we start to board the boats, I'll go with Uncle Cage, so you can pull Miss Fiona aside to tell her you have a date planned for the two of you instead."

"You're okay with doing this tour without us? You don't want to come with me to be a part of the proposal?" Considering how much Britney wanted him to get married and have Fiona adopt her, Rick was surprised his daughter didn't want to be there to witness the proposal.

"I thought you'd want to come with us and ask her to be your mom, too."

"Well, yeah, I want her to be my mom, but I don't want to watch you guys kiss under a bridge when I ask her." Britney rolled her eyes at him. "You need to make your proposal romantic, but when I ask her to be my mom, it needs to be when we're doing something together like mother and daughter. I'll wait until I know she loves you enough to marry you, and ask her when we have another girls-only day."

"Clearly, you've already thought this out." Rick had to stifle a chuckle at the way his daughter was mimicking his normal stoic expression as she spoke.

"Since I first saw you two making goo-goo eyes at each other on her first day working with us." Britney grinned mischievously. "Now, do you have the ring?"

Rick nodded, not wanting to risk anyone else seeing it to pull it out and show it to his daughter.

"Then go schedule your gondola before they tell us to board the boats for our tour." Britney pushed him in the direction of the desk, where he'd gone to check them in for their boat tour.

Rick took care of the logistics and got back over to the area where Fiona was standing, just in time to clasp her hand to prevent her from following the group to board the tour boats.

"We have other plans for the afternoon, Fifi," he whispered in her ear, as he held her in place.

"Oh, and what might those plans be, Sir?" Fiona grinned cheekily.

"A date on a gondola." Rick returned her grin before directing her away from the larger boat dock to the smaller dock where their gondola was waiting.

Rick watched, as the first of the boats with the GWA crew took off toward the Grand Canal from Giardini Ex Reali, as they walked over to the gondolas.

Thank Fuck, I picked a boat tour that's located between the two canals, so we can all meet back up here after for lunch and the walking tour I have scheduled.

"This is so perfect," Fiona said once they were seated side by side in the small boat and on their way toward the smaller canals in the opposite direction of the way everyone else went on the tour boats. "Exactly how I always pictured seeing Venice."

"I hope you don't mind that we're going through the smaller canals instead of the Grand Canal, like everyone else." Rick knew Fiona wanted to see as many sights as possible, so he hoped she wouldn't mind missing the bigger attractions they wouldn't get to see on the walking tour later.

"No, not at all." Fiona shook her head as she squeezed his hand. She had her phone in her other hand and was already taking pictures of the scenery they were passing.

Rick couldn't take his eyes off Fiona to look at what she was photographing, thinking she was more beautiful than any of the sights of Venice.

"I'm sure the kids will have lots of pictures to share when we get to the arena, so I won't miss a thing. Besides, we're in Venice. We have to ride in a gondola. Though I do kinda feel bad that everyone else had to ride in motorboats instead."

My sweet Fifi is always worried about everyone else. One of these days, I'll convince her it's okay to put herself first once in a while.

"They didn't have enough gondolas for everyone," Rick explained. "We were lucky they had six motorboats available at one time to do our midday tour. The ground crew has to go at two different times this evening, so they can all go on the tour."

"I didn't realize you'd booked these tours for everyone in the company, and not just those of us available to go sightseeing in the middle of the day." Fiona turned to look at him, admiration shining in her emerald eyes.

"Yeah, I couldn't bring the company to Europe without making sure everyone had the opportunity to see all the sights," Rick shrugged, thinking it wasn't that big a deal, since he'd actually had his administrative assistant work with their scheduling department to book all the excursions. All he'd done was authorize the payments for everything. It was the staff in the corporate office that had done all the work.

The gondolier started pointing out the sights, as they turned into one of the smaller canals, so they sat there quietly cuddling together, listening to him, and looking at the beautiful architecture of the area.

"Up ahead, you'll see the Bridge of Sighs. It connects the Palazzo delle Prigioni Nuove to the Doge's Palace." The gondolier continued with detailing the history of the bridge along with the folklore about kissing under it, but Rick didn't hear anything he was saying over the sound of the blood rushing in his ears.

Fuck! I hope I can get the words out over all these nerves!

Rick slipped off the seat to go down on one knee in front of Fiona. Her eyes widened, as the boat rocked slightly from his movement. He released her hand long enough to reach into his pocket to pull out the ring box. He opened the box to present her with the ring, at the same time he reached for Fiona's left hand once more. "Fiona, my sweet Fifi, I love you so much."

When she realized what he was doing, Fiona covered her mouth with her right hand, still holding her phone in the same hand.

"I know we've only been dating a month, and some people will probably think we're moving too fast, but I disagree. I think we're running behind, since I fell in love with you the first moment you walked into the room for your interview back in November. Waiting almost six weeks to see you again, and then another six weeks to start dating you, was a torturous waste of time when we should have been together. And I don't want to waste another moment before I can call you my fiancée and, hopefully, really soon, my wife. Will you marry me?"

"Oh, Rick, I love you, too. So, so much. And I really want to say yes to this wonderfully romantic proposal, but I can't."

Rick felt as if his whole body was deflating at her rejection. He knew he should get up off his knee on the floor of the boat, but he was frozen in place.

"Please don't be upset. I want to marry you." Fiona dropped her phone in her lap and cupped his jaw with her hand. "I do. I really do. But I can't let you put that ring on my finger until you ask my dad for my hand. I know that's old-fashioned, but so am I. So, I need you to respect that about me, and get my dad's blessing before I can say yes."

Rick took a deep breath, closing the ring box and putting it back in his pocket, as he resigned himself to waiting to ask her until after he had a chance to talk to her father.

Should we call him right now? Fuck, what's the time difference between here and Texas? Six or seven hours? Seven, because it's a six-hour difference between here and New York. So, it's four-something in the morning. Fuck, way too early to make that phone call. Waking him up from a sound sleep is probably not going to get him to give us his blessing.

"Okay, I can do that. Now kiss me, while we're under this bridge, so we can still take advantage of the true love legend, even if it is too early in Texas for me to call your dad right now to ask for your hand."

"Oh, no, mister! You have to ask that question in person. No phone calls…"

Rick cut off her objection to him calling her father by wrapping her in his arms and covering her mouth with his, just as the shadow of the Bridge of Sighs fell over them. As always, their kiss was impassioned in a way he'd never experienced with anyone else. It was as if the rest of the world ceased to exist beyond the two of them.

The only thing that registered in his brain, besides the two of them connecting through the kiss, was the ringing of church bells. At first, he thought he was imagining the chiming, thinking he was so caught up in Fiona that he was imagining the bells that would ring throughout the church when they kissed for the first time as husband and wife.

But as they broke the kiss to take a breath, the gondolier extolled what a blessing it was to have the bells of Campanile di San Marco toll, as lovers kiss under the Bridge of Sighs. Rick had always heard the legend to be about kissing under the bridge at sunset. But since their schedule wouldn't allow him or Fiona to be there at sunset, he was glad to know their timing didn't negate the folklore of having a long and lasting, true love relationship.

"Wait!" Rick held up a hand, deciding to clarify what the gondolier was saying, as a way to joke around with his sweet Fifi. "Kissing under the Bridge of Sighs, just as the bells of Campanile di San Marco toll, is like God blessing the union of the couple?"

"Sì," the gondolier nodded, as he affirmed Rick's understanding in Italian.

"Surely, your dad would agree that God's blessing bests his, so you can say yes now." Rick hoped his grin was enough to show her he was joking and didn't actually expect her to agree to marry him until after he'd manned up and talked to her father. But when she looked at him with a shocked expression, he wasn't sure his tone had been light enough to relay the way he meant to tease her a little.

Before he could make the words "I'm joking" come out of his mouth, Fiona grinned back at him and shook her head. "That might work on my dad, but it would never work on your mom. So, I still can't say yes until I know she's not going to have me offed by your mob relatives for daring to marry her son."

Rick's grin widened, as he was amused by her turning the teasing back on him. "You don't have to worry, sweet Fifi. That would never happen. My uncles have a code they live by that doesn't allow them to harm women. So, if she wanted to fit you with cement shoes, she'd have to do it herself. And since they aren't made by Jimmy Choo or Louboutin, she wouldn't have a clue where to get them."

They both laughed at his carrying on her joke, as he retook his seat beside her. They enjoyed the rest of the gondola ride through the city, as Rick mentally made plans to talk to both their parents, just as soon as they traveled close enough to them to have face-to-face discussions.

~~~

Sunday, March 10, 2019, 11 p.m., Venice, Italy

Fiona couldn't believe how many of her friends had commented on her not accepting Rick's proposal until he spoke to her father first. Apparently, Britney had filled everyone in on his plan to propose, while they were on the boat tour. Though Fiona wasn't sure how, since they'd been on six different boats at the time. But she supposed that once one person asked to see the ring, as soon as they met back up for the walking tour, word spread quickly to anyone who hadn't been on the boat with Britney.

She had felt guilty for not immediately agreeing to wear his ring when a few of the women told her she was crazy for letting their parents' opinions matter in their relationship. But then Kay had stood up for her and said she wished she'd stuck to her principles and made Anthony speak to her dad face to face instead of over the phone when he asked for her hand.

Then Randi made a comment about how James had been smart enough to fly her parents in for the proposal, so she knew he had a face-to-face discussion with her dad. That solidified Fiona's resolve to wait until Rick had her father's blessing to agree to marry him. Even though the conversation also revealed that James had been telling
~~~

Charles Lee that he was marrying his daughter via text for a couple of months before he actually got his blessing in person.

Maybe I should ask for tips on how James wore Charles down, Fiona thought as she brushed her teeth after having pizza for a bedtime snack with Britney. *So, I can start a text campaign to convince Rick's mom that I'm the perfect woman for her son.*

Not wanting to dwell on the negative thoughts about Rick's mom not liking her, Fiona shifted her thinking to build the anticipation for what was about to happen with Rick. They were moving up to the next to the largest plug for the next two days, and she was both excited and anxious about it.

She was anxious because it was bigger than anything she'd had inserted back there before, and she wasn't sure two nights each of using the second, third, and fourth sizes was a sufficient amount of training to open her up enough to take it. But she was also excited because the fifth plug was shaped to look like three balls, just like the third one had been.

Rick had shown her just how good it could feel when he moved the third one in and out during their play. She just hoped the increased size for number five wouldn't negate the extra tingles she got from those three areas where it widened out the same way number three had. *But I'm sure Rick will be gentle and use lots of lube to keep it from hurting.*

Fiona stripped off her clothes, knowing Rick preferred her to sleep naked to allow easy access for any middle-of-the-night mating that might come up. *And he always seems to be Up for that.* Fiona giggled at her thoughts, as she put her clothes in the laundry bag before exiting the ensuite bathroom to find Rick already lying in bed waiting for her.

He, too, was already naked, lazily stroking his erection, as he watched her walk toward the bed where he was stretched out. The sight was mesmerizing, making her ache to be the one stroking him. *Or better yet, sucking him.*

Fiona's mouth watered at the thought, giving her the courage to playfully ask permission to do the one thing he hadn't allowed to happen between them yet. "Papa, may I suck on your special lollipop?"

"My special lollipop?" Rick chuckled, shaking his head. "No, not if that's what you're going to call my dick. But if you're a good girl, and ask if you can suck my cock, I'll consider letting you suck me off, while I plug you."

Fiona felt herself blush from head to toe, as she crawled into the bed and begged, "Please, Papa, may I suck your cock?"

"Fuck, Fifi, I love the way you turn pink all over when you say dirty words." Rick scooted up, so he was reclining on the bed with his torso propped up on a couple of pillows at the headboard. "Such a good girl deserves a reward, so I'll let you suck me, while I'm plugging you. Come over here and straddle my chest, facing the foot of the bed."

Fiona crawled over the king-sized bed and got into the position he directed her to, as Rick reached over to the bedside table for the lube and plug.

"Now bend over and lick me, while I fuck your ass with this plug," Rick commanded, his voice deep and gravelly, making her tingle with anticipation for what was about to happen.

Fiona bent over as directed, pushing her backside toward his face in a way that she would have been way too self-conscious to do a month before. But somehow, in their short time together, Rick had made her feel more comfortable doing things she'd never thought she'd be brazen enough to do.

She stuck her tongue out and licked the head of his penis, tasting the salty precum that was already oozing out of the tip. She didn't have much experience with performing oral sex on a man, and none in this position, so she was tentative in her initial attempt at pleasuring him with her mouth.

She licked him from tip to base, glad he manscaped daily, so she didn't worry about swallowing any long, loose hairs.

"Use your hands, too, Fifi," Rick directed, just as Fiona felt the first cool drops of lube drip on her back hole. "And show me how much of my cock will fit in your mouth."

It was a struggle to balance, to stay bent over the way she was without her hands on the mattress, but Fiona somehow managed to lift them both and wrap them around the base of his dick. He was so thick, it took both of her hands to encircle his girth, as she started to stroke him.

Thank goodness he tapers down some toward the head or I'd never be able to get my lips around him, she thought as she sucked the bulbous head into her mouth. *Though I guess the coronal ridge is just as large as the root, so maybe I could still get him in my mouth, if he was the same thickness all along the shaft.*

Fiona desperately tried to distract herself by thinking about his penis in her mouth, as Rick started pushing the plug into her anus. But when her lips passed the coronal ridge and brushed his frenulum, Rick moaned in pleasure and pushed the first ball of the plug past her sphincter, shocking her into moving her whole body forward away from the intense pressure. She swallowed another couple of inches of his length, as her hands squeezed him at the root.

"Fuck, Fifi," Rick groaned, bucking his hips to push his shaft even deeper into her mouth. "Stop. Don't move or I'm never going to be able to focus to get this plug in your ass."

Fiona smiled around the erection in her mouth, at the giddy feeling she got from being able to distract him from his task. Rick didn't acknowledge her smile as movement, other than to slap her left butt cheek with his free hand, while starting to move the plug in and out of her anus once again.

She held as still as she possibly could, while trying to relax enough for him to finish inserting the plug. Her task of holding still became quite difficult when Rick teased his fingers through her feminine folds.

He rubbed over her clit several times, pushing her close to the edge without letting her go over before sliding back to her slit to insert two fingers into her vagina.

My pussy, Fiona thought, trying to make herself at least think the dirty words Rick wanted to hear her say when they were alone. *He's finger-fucking my pussy while fucking my ass with the plug and my mouth with his cock.*

Just thinking the words turned her on even more than she already was, causing her to gush with cream to ease the way of his fingers in and out of her.

"Fuck, Fifi, you're so fucking perfect," Rick growled, as he started rocking his hips in time with his fingers and the plug. "Taking me in every hole like a good little slut."

Fiona cringed at the term, not sure if she liked him using it to describe her or not.

"Relax, sweet Fifi. I know you only let your inner slut out for me. I'm not calling you a slut in a derogatory way. Think of it as a term of endearment to show how much I love being the only man you trust enough to be slutty with in bed."

Not just in bed, Fiona thought as she relaxed, allowing him to push the second ball of the plug into her ass. *I trust you with every part of me, no matter where we are, Rick. So, I guess I have to believe you mean it as a term of endearment.*

Rick must have felt her capitulation to him, as he intensified his movements to bring her to the brink. He twisted his fingers in her pussy, finding that secret spot only he could locate to take her over the edge, just as he pushed the plug the rest of the way into her ass.

"Fuck, yes, Fifi," Rick whisper-shouted to be commanding without being too loud. "Come from taking me in every hole at once. Be my good little slut and come for me now!"

Fiona didn't register the rest of his words, as her whole body convulsed in orgasmic bliss. She literally saw stars from the intensity of the climax, and she knew they were only getting started on their night.

She wasn't sure how she kept from biting down on Rick's dick, as every muscle in her body contracted with wave after wave of pure pleasure.

As she was recovering, Rick slipped his arms between her thighs and slid down the bed. He replaced his fingers with his mouth on her pussy, lapping up the evidence of her arousal, as if he was starving and she was the meal that would save his life.

Rick wrapped his arms around her, pressing her pussy into his face by pushing down on her hips with one hand, while the other gripped her hair to control the movement of her head. He bucked his hips up, as he pushed her face down, fucking her mouth with his cock, while fucking her pussy with his tongue.

Fiona took the briefest moment to mentally acknowledge her first sixty-nine, as she swirled her tongue around his shaft, praying he didn't trigger her gag reflex when he hit the back of her throat. She didn't have time to think, much less worry, past that one brief moment, as Rick expertly plied her body up to another euphoric crescendo.

He was truly a master at the art of orgasm, working her up repeatedly with his mouth and tongue all over her pussy, while pressing his thumb on the base of the plug to heighten the experience with gentle movements in her rectum.

Fiona tried diligently to maintain suction on his dick in her mouth, while using her hands to stroke the part that was too big to fit without choking her. But it was really hard to focus when he kept making her come over and over and over again.

She wasn't sure if she was really giving him a blow job, or if he was fucking her face. But either way, she assumed they were both enjoying it, when he pulled his mouth away from her core long enough to warn her that he was about to come.

"Fuck, Fifi, you feel so good. I can't hold back any longer," Rick panted, punctuating his words with thrusts into her mouth. "I'm about to come. So fucking good. You'd better sit up now, if you don't want to swallow every drop."

Fiona didn't heed his warning, gripping his shaft tighter, as she sucked harder. She was eager to taste him on her tongue, as he filled her belly with his cum.

"Oh! Fuck! Fifi!" Rick cried out, punctuating each word with a thrust of his hips, plunging his cock into the back of her throat before diving in once more to devour her pussy.

Fiona felt his cock swell, as he pushed in and held himself deep, but she barely tasted his salty flavor, as he shot his load down her throat. Knowing he was so far back in her mouth that his cum bypassed the majority of her tastebuds was enough to make it easy for him to bring her to climax right along with him.

Her body melted into his, as she collapsed from the intensity of their mutual release. She wasn't sure which one of them realized she needed to roll off of him to release his cock from her mouth to be able to breathe. But she was grateful one of them had when she came back into her body from the orgasmic realm only Rick could take her to.

Fiona twisted around to cuddle up beside Rick, while they both caught their breath.

And maybe a little cat nap before round two.

Chapter Twenty-One

Fiona was in a strange mood, as she finally exited Customs to go board the plane to head back to the United States. She had so many wonderful experiences, which she'd never forget, in the last thirteen days in the thirteen European cities they'd visited, that she hated for the tour of Europe to end. She had especially enjoyed their time in Rome on Monday, when they'd seen the Colosseum, Trevi Fountain, the Vatican Museum, and the Sistine Chapel. But she was also excited to be back on American soil to see the sights of the northeast for the next couple of weeks before venturing back into Canada for the first few days of April.

In addition to the melancholy of not wanting to leave Europe, and excitement for the new places she'd soon be seeing in the US and Canada, Fiona was also feeling nervous about going back to New York City. It wasn't the city she was nervous about seeing. It was Rick's parents, whom he insisted on meeting for an early dinner after their ten-hour flight.

Since they would gain six hours with the changing time zones between Naples, Italy, and New York City, if they took off within the next hour, they'd land in New York City between two and three in the afternoon local time. Fiona had a feeling she'd really feel jet-lagged after that flight, and would appreciate the fact that the GWA was taking the night off to rest before their flight to Allentown, Pennsylvania, on Thursday morning.

Maybe I should try to sleep on the flight again, so I'm not too irritable to deal with Rick's mom at dinner, Fiona thought, as she followed Britney on the plane. *And maybe I can convince Brit to sleep some, too. Although, she's used to these long days with our normal schedule, so she'll probably still be wide awake, even after dinner with her grandparents.*

On second thought, maybe I should keep Britney up for the whole flight, so she'll want to go to bed early tonight. If she stays up to her normal bedtime, there's no way I'll be able to stay awake for any alone time with Rick tonight.

And after spending an evening with his mother, he and I are going to need all the alone time we can get, to keep her negativity from causing him to have second thoughts about me again.

As she settled into the pod beside Britney and facing Rick, Fiona felt horrible for having thoughts of how to manipulate the two of them. Yes, her intentions were good, for the three of them to remain a family regardless of what his mother thought about her, but she wasn't a manipulative person, and hated that she even thought about trying such behavior.

She was quiet, as the rest of the crew boarded the plane, still nervous about how the rest of the day was going to go. But as Rick and Britney dominated the conversation, she started to settle in, deciding to just relax and enjoy the rare flight when Rick didn't have to work, so they could spend the time as a family.

And whatever happens when we land, we'll deal with it together, as the family I hope we'll truly be one day soon.

~~~

Wednesday, March 13, 2019, 4 p.m., New York City, New York

Rick wasn't sure what he'd been thinking when he decided to meet his parents for an early dinner at Carmine's Italian Restaurant on Broadway. While the food was excellent, and the time of day made it easy to get a reservation, since it wasn't too crowded like it would be for a normal dinner time, trying to talk to his parents while jet-lagged wasn't his brightest plan.

And I didn't even think about the fact that Britney, Fiona, and I have just spent the last four days in Italy, so my girls are probably ready for something other than Italian food.
~~~

Fuck! I hope Britney remembers to mind her manners and doesn't comment on how the food compares to authentic Italian food in Italy.

As his parents greeted them just inside the entrance of the restaurant, Rick realized it wasn't his daughter's manners he needed to be worried about.

"Oh, I didn't realize your…" Rick's mother's words trailed off, as she cleared her throat before continuing. "*Girlfriend* would be joining us. I thought this was just a family dinner. Shouldn't she be at the hotel sleeping off the jet lag, so she can do her job tomorrow?"

Seeing the hurt look on Fiona's face was heartbreaking for Rick. He knew his sweet Fifi would never stand up for herself with his mother, so he stepped up to do it for her.

"Fiona is family, Mother," he growled. "It might not be official yet, but it will be, just as soon as I can speak to her father face to face to ask for his blessing and get her mother started on planning the wedding. And if you keep being snippy and rude to my future wife, you won't be invited to the wedding."

"Richard Giovanni Robertson, how dare you speak to me like that," his mother howled.

Rick cringed at his mother's use of his full name, looking over at Fiona to see if she registered the name, or if she was still in shock at the audacity of his mother. Thankfully, she still seemed to be stunned at his mother's first words, so she didn't seem to register his mother's revelation of his middle name. Rick was relieved she didn't hear the name he disliked, though he knew he'd have to share his middle name with her eventually.

Oh, how he wished he'd been named Richard Aaron Robertson, Junior at birth. But no, his mother had to give him her father's name as a middle name to avoid the Junior title she thought sounded gauche.

"Katarina, enough," Rick's father barked, putting a temporary end to the rude exchange, just as the hostess walked up to seat them for dinner.

Rick gave the hostess his name for the reservation and stepped between Fiona and Britney to guide them to the table they were being directed to for their meal. He pulled out the chair at the end of the table for Britney before seating Fiona in the first chair to Britney's right on the side of the rectangular table. He then took the seat to Fiona's right, leaving the two seats on the other side of the table for his parents. Thankfully, his father understood the need to put his mother across from Rick before taking his seat beside Britney and across from Fiona.

While he'd rather take his girls home and not deal with any more of his mother's antics, Rick knew he had to clear the air with her before Fiona would accept his proposal. And he wasn't going to let his mother continue to take her hostility toward Colleen out on Fiona. It was not only misplaced, but it was also highly unwarranted. Rick knew Fiona was nothing like his ex, and he wasn't leaving the restaurant until his mother knew it, too.

They sat in uncomfortable silence, as the hostess passed out menus and told them their waitress would be with them shortly. But as soon as she stepped away, Britney broke the silence.

"Can we please have plain garlic bread for the appetizer? I don't like that sauce and stuff they put on the bread we got last time we ate here."

"Of course we can, Pumpkin," Rick smiled at his daughter, grateful for the subject change. "What kind of pasta do you want?"

"I liked the penne we got last time, so we can get that again. And the eggplant. You'll like that, Miss Fiona. It's almost exactly like the eggplant we got for lunch in Naples yesterday."

Rick hated that he'd missed lunch with his girls in Naples, while at the arena to set up for the live television broadcast. But he was glad Britney had noticed something Fiona enjoyed eating then, and was bringing her into the conversation about lunch by mentioning it.

"You should really get the broccoli or spinach instead of the eggplant," Rick's mother interjected. "And I'd prefer the calamari to the penne."

"Oh, no!" Fiona held her hands up in the universal sign for "stop," just as Britney turned slightly green. "No calamari unless you're trading seats with me, so I'm not in the splash zone."

"Sorry, Mom," Rick chuckled, glad to see Fiona animatedly joining the conversation, instead of being intimidated by his mother. "We learned in Barcelona that Britney can't even handle being at the same table with calamari. So, if that's what you want to eat, you're going to have to request to be moved to the other side of the restaurant."

"Please stop saying the C word," Britney groaned, covering her mouth, as if she was already close to puking just from the mention of the squid dish. "And don't laugh at me, or I'll aim at you when I vomit."

"Oh, sweet girl, we're definitely not laughing," Fiona consoled Britney, reaching over to clasp her hand and give it a reassuring squeeze.

"You can switch seats with Dad, 'cause he laughed." Britney pointed at him.

"Not at you, Britney Bear." Rick shook his head and felt guilty for chuckling a moment earlier. "I was laughing at the mortified expression on Nonna's face. It was the same look she gets when she doesn't think farts are funny."

"Well, I agree with you this time, Nonna. Puking isn't funny." Britney almost kept a straight face, but she couldn't stop the slight lift of her lips as she added. "At least, when I'm the one puking, it's not funny. Cody puking from being puked on was kinda funny, even though I couldn't really laugh about it at the time."

"Serves him right for flirting with my daughter by teasing her," Rick grumbled, barely containing his chuckle at the memory of karma hitting Cody instantly.

"He wasn't flirting, Dad," Britney groaned, shaking her head, and rolling her eyes. "We're friends, but we don't like each other that way. So, you don't have to act like Mr. Anthony to keep us from kissing because it's not happening."

"Hey, I'll admit I'm a protective dad, but I'm not a neanderthal. I haven't threatened any of the boys to keep them away from you the way Anthony has for his girls." Rick raised his hands in surrender. "But I make no promises about sitting back and enjoying the show when karma does it for me. Or stepping in if the boys' antics ever go past a little harmless flirting."

"Like you have to say anything to threaten them when you give them the look." Britney rolled her eyes again.

"If it's any consolation, I think he gives Anthony that look more than he gives it to the boys," Fiona interjected, giggling. "And his look is way less scary than the one my dad gave all the boys when I was growing up."

"No way," Britney objected. "Pastor Dale is way too nice to have a scary look like Dad's."

"You can ask Anthony, or the Hunters, if you don't believe me." Fiona lifted one shoulder in a nonchalant half-shrug. "Being a couple of years younger than me, they weren't ever on the receiving end of it, but they sat through the smiting sermons when Anthony's older brothers and cousins were."

"Damn, I thought that was just in my head when we were there in February." Rick shuddered at the memory of how Pastor Harrison's sermon felt as if it was directed at him.

"What happened in February?" Rick's dad looked back and forth between Rick and Fiona.

"We had the **Saint Valentine's Day Massacre** pay-per-view in San Antonio," Rick replied. "And stayed in Heart's Destiny for the weekend."

"That's when Dad and Fiona had their first date," Britney explained.

"Which was interrupted by my parents joining us for dessert," Fiona said with a smile. "And my dad started interrogating us about dating."

"And the next morning at church, Fiona's father gave a sermon about Sodom and Gomorrah, that felt as if it was directed at me. But I thought I was imagining the way it felt like a warning because he didn't seem to have any issues with us dating in any of our conversations." Rick shook his head, suddenly worried he might not get Fiona's father's blessing to marry her as easily as he thought he would.

"Oh, no, you weren't imagining it," Fiona giggled. "Daddy never had to clean his hunting rifle when I went on dates like my friends' dads did, when he knew the subtle threat of having God smite sinful boys worked just as well."

"Having been the recipient of threats from a dad with a gun, I'd have to disagree," Rick's dad chuckled before turning to his wife. "But you'll find that the right man won't be discouraged from going after his lady love by any threat from an overprotective parent."

Rick had a feeling his dad's words had more to do with his mother than with overprotective fathers. He reached over and picked up Fiona's hand, bringing it to his lips to brush the briefest kiss on the back. "You're right about that, Dad."

His mother opened her mouth as if to disagree, but shut it quickly when the waitress arrived to take their order.

"We might need a few more minutes," his mother started to wave the young woman away.

"Actually, I know what we want." Rick waved his hand between himself, Fiona, and Britney. "So, we can go ahead and order, while my parents are looking at the menu to see if they want to add anything."

The waitress nodded for him to give their order.

"Three Little Louie's Lemonades, garlic bread, Caesar salad, penne alla vodka, eggplant parmigiana, and broiled porterhouse with tartufi and Italian cheesecake for dessert."

Britney and Fiona passed their menus to Rick for him to hand all three of theirs to the waitress. The waitress then turned to look at his parents to see if they wanted to order anything more, or if the large family-sized portions he'd ordered would be enough for the whole table.

"That all sounds good to me." Rick's dad nodded and handed over his menu.

"I'd like to add the veal marsala and a bottle of the Cristom Pinot Noir," Rick's mother added before handing over her menu.

If it wasn't for the fact that they'd dropped Cage off at the hotel for the night, Rick would have been tempted to join his mother in drinking to get through the rest of the meal. But he wouldn't, knowing he still had to safely drive his girls home afterward.

"So, tell me about all the places you visited on the European tour," Rick's dad directed Britney, obviously trying to steer the conversation away from their family issues.

Britney dominated the next hour of conversation with detailed descriptions of every major sight they saw over the last two weeks. Rick thought it was the perfect topic of conversation to make dinner go down easier, until she got to their day in Venice.

"I went with Uncle Cage and my friends on a motorboat through the Grand Canal, while Dad took Miss Fiona on a gondola ride to propose…"

"You proposed?" Rick's mother interrupted Britney, her fork clanking to her plate, as she dropped it in shock.

Leah Mae Wright

"Yes, Mother. As I told you when we first arrived, I will be marrying Fiona." Rick reached over to take Fiona's hand, wanting to comfort her when he noticed her shifting in her seat anxiously.

"I suppose this means I was right the last time we saw you and she is pregnant." His mother's tone was accusatory, as she glared at Fiona.

Fiona covered her mouth with her free hand, as her eyes widened, clearly surprised at the accusation.

"Not that I'm aware of at this time." Rick shook his head and squeezed Fiona's hand. "But I wouldn't be upset if she is. In fact, just as soon as I can get my ring on her finger, I intend to start trying to get her pregnant."

Fiona turned her stunned eyes from his mother to him. "While I appreciate you defending me, I can assure you I'm not pregnant."

Rick turned to look into Fiona's eyes as he spoke, wanting to make sure she knew there was no accusation in his words, as he mentioned his most intimate observation of their last month together. "Are you sure, Fifi? We've been together almost every night for about a month, and you haven't had a period."

"Yes, I'm sure." Fiona rolled her eyes at him. "And while I'd rather have this discussion in private, I'll gladly air my business to the world to quash your family's suspicions of me. My last period was the week before the pay-per-view in San Antonio, which was perfectly timed for me to pick up my prescription for birth control while we were home that weekend to be able to start my new supply of pills on the eleventh of February. And the pills I take keep me from having a period for three months, so I'm not due to have my next period until May sixth, when I'll skip a week of taking my pills."

Rick made a mental note of the date, knowing they would need to discuss their options for birth control between then and the end of May when they would be back in Heart's Destiny. *Though maybe I'll convince her not to restart it before then to try to have our babies soon.*

Fiona paused to take a deep breath and turned to glare at Rick's mother. "And for the record, I'm on the pill to regulate my periods because of medical issues that are going to make it difficult for me to have children, if it's even possible for me to get pregnant in the first place. So, you don't have to worry about me using an accidental pregnancy to trap your son, since it's probably going to require medical intervention for me to conceive whenever we decide we're ready to try."

"Fuck," Rick groaned under his breath, hating that he'd stepped into such an emotional minefield with his parents and daughter at the table. Not that anyone else at the table heard him, or acknowledged him if they did hear him, as Fiona calmly continued to defend herself against his mother.

"I get that you don't like me and don't want me to be with Rick. I even understand why you feel that way when you know absolutely nothing about me. His witch of an ex did a number on your whole family, so you're naturally going to want to defend him and Britney from going through that painful situation again. If I was in your shoes, I'd probably have similar concerns. Though I hope I won't ever make anyone my loved ones date as uncomfortable as you've tried to make me."

Wow, I knew Fifi is highly empathetic to the feelings of the people she cares about, but I didn't realize that extended to my mom, Rick thought, as Fiona was speaking. Then he chuckled at her subtle reprimand of his mother's behavior.

"But he's a grown man, and one of the smartest men I've ever met. So, you have to step back, and trust that he's perfectly capable of defending his own heart from the wicked women of the world. Just like I have to trust that he's truly over everything she put him through, and isn't going to punish me for his ex's sins that I would never commit."

Rick had gone into the meal expecting to be the one standing up for Fiona and their relationship to his mother, but he was pleasantly surprised to see his previously shy, sweet Fifi showing her backbone, while calmly defending herself. So, he plastered on a smile, and let her continue. He would silently support her by holding her hand and would only step in if necessary.

"I hope in time, you and I will get to know one another well enough that you will no longer have any doubts about my love for Rick and Britney, or my character as a human being. But in order for that to happen, you're gonna have to tone down the hostility toward me. Not because I can't handle it, but because I don't think any of us want Britney exposed to that kind of behavior."

"I think you're about twelve years too late to keep me from being exposed to hostile behavior," Britney interjected, grinning, as she reached over and patted Fiona's arm. "And since our family business is to broadcast fake fights to the world, I think it might be a losing battle to try now. But we can try booking you and Nonna in a match at the next pay-per-view to settle this feud."

"No, Fiona's right." Rick understood his daughter was trying to lighten the mood with her reference to settling things in the ring, but he needed to know she understood the difference between the acting on the GWA shows and the passive-aggressive way his mother was treating Fiona. "You're old enough to know that professional wrestling is acting, and not how you should handle disagreements in real life. But you don't need to grow up thinking it's okay to mistreat people because you're afraid of what they might do in the future, especially when you don't know them."

"I know that, Dad." Britney nodded somberly, clearly feeling more chastised than he intended. "I guess I didn't think it through enough to set up the joke properly."

"Son, you can't very well reprimand the girl for trying to defuse the situation with humor," Rick's dad laughed. "I mean, she learned that tactic from you, after all. So, you can't punish the apple for falling at the base of the tree."

"I'm not reprimanding her." Rick held his hands up in surrender. "I just wanted to make sure she understood the difference between wrestling and reality."

"If anyone should be reprimanded, it's Nonna for acting like a bee with an itch toward Miss Fiona," Britney pointed out. She shrugged when her grandmother looked at her with a shocked expression. "I mean, really, Nonna. I'm twelve, and even I know better than to act like that, whether the person deserves it or not. And Miss Fiona doesn't deserve it. Not like my egg donor does, and you just ignore her if she happens to show up somewhere we're at. So, if you can't be nice to Miss Fiona, why can't you just ignore her, like you do my egg donor?"

Rick wanted to hear his mother's answer to Britney's question, but he wanted to know when they'd seen Colleen recently enough for Britney to know about it, and why he hadn't been informed of her reappearance in their lives at the time, more. His eyes darted to his mother. "When did you see Colleen?"

His mother floundered, apparently flustered by both his and Britney's questions.

"She apparently moved into our building last summer," his father started to explain. "So, we've run into her a few times in the lobby, but no words have been spoken when it happens."

Rick wanted to ask questions about why she was back in the city, and how she'd afforded a condo in their building on Park Avenue, since he didn't think the generous settlement she'd gotten in their divorce was enough to buy in their exclusive building. But he didn't get the chance because his mother finally spoke.

"You're right, Britney. I should definitely be the one being reprimanded. I have been taking out my irritation at Colleen on Fiona, and it was completely uncalled for and inappropriate." His mother turned to look directly at Fiona as she continued. "I'm sorry, Fiona. I'm not normally like that, but I didn't even realize what I was doing until you pointed it out just a few minutes ago. Now that I recognize my recent behavior for what it is, I promise, I will try my best, not to let it happen again."

She lifted her napkin to dab just under her eye to stop her tears from falling. "And I hope we can start over getting to know one another, so you can one day forgive me for my atrocious behavior toward you."

Fiona released his hand to reach through the platters on the table to extend her hand to his mother. "Like I said earlier, I completely understand where you're coming from, so there's nothing to forgive. And I'd love to start over getting to know you."

His mother clasped Fiona's hand and gave her a tentative smile. "Hello, I'm Katarina Robertson. It's so nice to meet you, Fiona. My son and granddaughter have told me so many wonderful things about you."

"Yeah, that would never work on pay-per-view," Britney joked, waving her hand between Fiona and her grandmother, and getting a laugh from everyone around the table.

The rest of their meal was much more jovial. Though it didn't last long because he and his girls were all tired after their long trip back to the states.

They hadn't gone back to the discussion about Rick's proposal to get into the specifics about why it would be another month or two before Rick could talk to her father to get his blessing before they officially became engaged. But his mother still surprised him, as they were leaving, by asking Fiona to give her phone number to her mother, so they could start making plans for the wedding, as soon as their engagement was official.

Her statement got Britney to start talking out all her ideas for the wedding, as soon as they were in the car and on the way home. Rick mostly listened, as his daughter rambled about wedding colors and going dress shopping, but finally spoke up when they started talking about possible wedding dates.

"I don't want to wait until the fall." Rick shook his head at the suggestion of planning their wedding over either their Labor Day or Thanksgiving break. "I know I'm probably not going to have a chance to talk to your dad until we're there for James and Randi's wedding on our Memorial Day break. But I've seen how fast the ladies of Heart's Destiny can put together a wedding, so I think we can plan it for the week we're on break for Independence Day."

"That's because the Burlesons were paying for everything." Fiona shook her head. "Yeah, I can schedule everything for that week with no problem. But my family isn't as wealthy as the Burlesons, so it'll take us a little longer to save up the money to pay for it."

"There's no need to save, sweet Fifi." Rick reassuringly kissed the back of her hand, as they pulled into the parking garage for his condo. "I'll pay for everything."

"After paying for a hundred people to tour Europe for the last two weeks, surely, even you need to save a little to be able to pay for something as expensive as a wedding," Fiona objected.

"I don't think Miss Fiona realizes just how rich you are, Dad," Britney giggled.

"Well, no, I guess I don't," Fiona shrugged. "But money doesn't really factor into why I love you, so it hasn't mattered enough for me to even be curious about. Besides, my parents are just old-fashioned enough that they're probably going to insist on paying for the wedding, which means we'll need to give them at least six months, maybe even a year, before they can afford it."

"Then I'll just do like Anthony and James, and let my mother have free rein to plan everything. I'm sure she won't mind going to Heart's Destiny to insist all the vendors charge everything to me." Rick grinned over at Fiona. "Should I send her now to start working on softening up your parents? Or have her meet us there over our Memorial Day break?"

Fiona's jaw dropped in shock at his suggestion.

Oh, sweet Fifi, I'm going to have so much fun teasing you for the next sixty or seventy years.

~~~

Wednesday, March 13, 2019, 8 p.m., New York City, New York

Fiona was dead on her feet after such a long day, but she knew she needed to stay up to talk to Rick about the events of the day. In the course of healing the rift with his mother earlier, they'd only briefly touched on her reproductive issues. And she knew he needed to know everything about her condition to be able to decide if he really wanted to be with her, when she might not be able to give him more children.

She also needed to talk to him about what he wanted to do in May when she would have to skip three weeks of her pills, instead of the normal one, because of not being able to be in Heart's Destiny to go to the doctor to renew her prescription. While she wouldn't mind spending that time continuing as they were sans condoms, she also had to make sure he knew she understood if he wanted to suit up to protect against the very slim chance she could get pregnant.

"I thought she'd never get tired enough to go to sleep this early." Rick dropped down on the sofa in the library next to Fiona, where she'd been staring out at what she could see of Central Park an hour after sunset, while Rick was helping Britney with her math module. "We could solve the world's energy crisis if we could figure out a way to siphon ten-percent of her energy off and share it in some usable form."

"I think you're just feeling your age ¡and having trouble keeping up with her," Fiona giggled, as she leaned over and rested her head against Rick's shoulder.
~~~

"Oh, that's definitely part of it," Rick chuckled. "But I swear she has more energy than I ever have, even when I was her age." Rick wrapped his arm around Fiona's shoulders, effectively moving her head to his pec.

Fiona listened to the steady thud of his heart beating under her ear for a moment before bringing up the subject she dreaded talking to him about. "Does her never-ending well of energy causing you to feel your age affect your thoughts on having more kids?"

"No, not really." Rick bent his head and kissed the top of Fiona's. "Other than maybe thinking I should probably have them before I turn forty, if I'm going to have more. And maybe find ways to increase my cardio to be able to keep up with them later."

"So, you definitely want more kids?" *Will you still love me if I can't give them to you?*

"Before I met you, my answer to that question would have been no. I couldn't imagine I'd ever find someone I'd want more kids with, and I didn't want to risk more *baby momma drama,* like I had with Colleen. But now, yeah, I can definitely picture us having more kids. In fact, it was imagining my life in fifty years, with you by my side as we were having a family barbeque with a massive yard full of our four kids, sixteen grandkids, all their spouses, and almost three dozen great-grandkids, that convinced me what I feel for you is true love."

Fiona vaguely remembered him mentioning something about that in Paris.

"And how do you see yourself in fifty years if I'm not able to have kids?" Fiona held her breath without realizing it, as she waited for Rick's answer.

"I still see the same scene playing out."

Fiona's heart sank, as she thought he meant he'd still have more kids with someone else by his side.

"Only instead of looking like a mix of us that I pictured before, we'd have a more diverse group of kids and grandkids because I have no idea what our adopted kids will look like. Remember, I told you we'd adopt when you asked me this same question in Paris."

Fiona released her breath, relaxing some at hearing his willingness to adopt when they were having a serious discussion. She hadn't let herself take his words to heart in Paris because they'd been joking around at the time. At least, she thought they were just joking around, and not seriously discussing their future.

Prior to meeting Rick, she had mostly resigned herself to probably having to adopt to have children after her P.C.O.S. diagnosis during her second year of college. But she'd also held onto a sliver of hope of one day being able to have children of her own because she knew most men seemed to struggle with raising kids they'd played no part in producing.

While she would still love to have at least one child with Rick that would be a mix of the two of them, she was also relieved that he was one of the few men she'd met that didn't seem to care about the DNA link to his future children.

"How many children do you want?" Rick shifted in his seat, as if he was uncomfortable asking the question. "I mean, I pictured us having four, but I'm willing to adjust that number to whatever you want."

"Four sounds perfect to me," Fiona sighed. "I hated growing up an only child and was always so jealous of Justin and his siblings. They had the perfect size family, with two boys and two girls, so they had built in best friends."

"Yeah, I guess that's what I pictured, too," Rick huffed. "I was lucky to have the other wrestlers' kids to hang out with on weekends when I was a kid, but I always wanted a brother to have someone closer when I wasn't in school, or there weren't other kids around. I still don't understand why Mom and Dad didn't have more than me."

"I figured out why my parents didn't have more when I got my diagnosis, and I realized that Mom had all the same symptoms. I decided then to apologize for all the years I'd begged for a baby sister." Fiona felt a little silly for having still wanted a sibling at twenty-one.

"What exactly is your diagnosis? I know you said it could require medical intervention to get pregnant, but is that just because it would be difficult, or would it be dangerous for you to carry a baby?"

"I have polycystic ovary syndrome, commonly referred to as P.C.O.S. It's caused by a hormone imbalance that affects ovulation. Before I got on the pill, my periods were irregular and unpredictable. And horribly painful when the cysts would develop on my ovaries.

But with the problem being ovulation, it just makes it hard to get pregnant, not unsafe."

"But being on the pill helps?" Rick rubbed his hand up and down on her back, comforting her as they talked.

"Yeah, a lot. Now I have one normal period every three months instead of two, three, or four painful cycles of cysts in the same time frame." Fiona snuggled into Rick's side, wrapping her arms around his waist.

"So, if you have to be on the pill to keep from having those painful cysts, we'll just look into adopting whenever you're ready to expand our family," Rick said matter-of-factly.

"There are other medications I can take to try to get pregnant that should improve ovulation and decrease the risk of cysts, too. I haven't done a lot of research on them, but they seem to be used for multiple egg retrieval before in vitro fertilization, and that wasn't on my radar as a single woman. But we can look into that too, if you want to try to have kids before we decide to adopt exclusively."

"We can definitely do that if you want," Rick agreed, squeezing her closer to him. "You just let me know when you're ready and I'll make it happen, however you want to add to our family. But only if it's not going to bring back your painful symptoms. As much as I'd love to have a kiddo or two who looks just like you, I'd rather adopt than have you suffer through painful cysts."

"Well, the good news about the possibility of pregnancy is that I wouldn't have to worry about those symptoms for nine months," Fiona chuckled. "And since Britney pointed out how rich you are today, I guess I don't have to worry about IVF being too expensive to be an option for me anymore either. So, I'd like to try at least once before we start adopting."

"Then we'll try as soon as you tell me you're ready." Fiona could hear the smile in Rick's voice, even though she couldn't see his face in their current position. "Maybe I can go to your doctor with you in May and start asking questions about the process."

"You're welcome to come to the doctor with me, but Doc Hayes will probably just refer me to a fertility specialist, since he's a general practitioner." Fiona inwardly cringed at the thought of talking to the man old enough to be her father about her female issues again. It was hard enough to tell him about her diagnosis when she moved back to

Heart's Destiny after college to get him to take over prescribing her birth control to regulate her periods.

Maybe I'll just ask Kay about the doctor she sees in San Antonio to find an OB-GYN.

"Speaking of my appointment in May, you realize I'm going to be off the pill for three weeks instead of my usual one because of not being there in time to renew my prescription? Right?"

"I wondered about that when you said something about skipping the week of May sixth earlier." Rick rested his cheek on the top of her head. "I was going to tell you about the pharmacy we use, to have medications mailed to us, so you don't have to pick things up in Heart's Destiny all the time."

"Oh, that'll come in handy in the future," Fiona nodded. "But I'm out of refills, so I have to go for an appointment to get a new prescription. I've already scheduled it for Wednesday, the twenty-ninth."

"Then I'll plan on going with you on Wednesday, the twenty-ninth." Rick kissed her head once more.

"Um, we, uh, should also probably talk about what we're going to do for those three weeks," Fiona stuttered, unsure why she was still nervous about broaching this subject with Rick.

"What do you mean?" Rick sounded confused by her statement.

"Well, I know we'll have to stop having sex while I'm on my period, but that'll only last four or five days, of like twenty-two, that there's a slight chance I could get pregnant." Fiona felt herself blush as she mentioned sex and wondered if she'd ever stop being embarrassed when talking about it.

"Oh, my sweet Fifi, we don't have to stop having sex just because you're on your period," Rick chuckled. "Even if you're having cramps and can't handle vaginal penetration, there are so many other things we can do then. And you might need the orgasms for the endorphin release to ease your pain."

"I'm not worried about the pain," Fiona objected. "I'm worried about the mess and just the overall ick factor."

"Then you'll leave your tampon in and I'll play with your clit while fucking you in the ass," Rick growled in her ear. "No mess, no ick factor. Well, other than the mess of my cum dripping out of your ass afterward, but I'll happily clean that up."

Rick picked her up and shifted her around onto his lap, so he could bring their lips together in a passionate kiss as she straddled him. Fiona forgot what they were talking about as he drugged her with his kisses for several long moments and was confused when he broke their lip lock to speak once more.

"As for the risk of getting you pregnant in those three weeks, I know it's very slim, but I'd be happy if we had a miracle and started adding to our family now. However, I'll also gladly wear a condom, if you're not ready to try for babies yet. You just let me know what you want, and I'll make it happen. But in the meantime, I'd like to take you to my bed and get started practicing on your ass."

Fiona wasn't sure if she was excited or anxious, knowing it was her last night with the training plugs. She wasn't sure if he was going to wait until the next day to attempt anal sex for the first time, or if he was planning on trying it when he removed the plug in an hour or two.

She knew it would be a first for both of them, but she trusted Rick had researched everything to make sure he wasn't going to hurt her when they tried it for the first time. But even after enjoying the plugs for the past nine days, she was slightly apprehensive about whether or not Rick would fit.

"Relax, sweet Fifi," Rick ordered, as he stood from the sofa with her in his arms. "I may not have done this before, but I know I'm going to have to be gentle back there."

Fiona wrapped her arms around his neck and her legs around his waist, as he carried her through the library, living room, and gallery to get to his bedroom. She was surprised he could see where he was going with the way he was kissing her neck as he walked. But he made it with no problems, kicking the door shut behind them and turning to lock it without lifting his lips from her skin.

"Get undressed and bend over the end of the bed while I get your plug out of my suitcase and wash it again," Rick instructed, as he lowered her feet to the floor and released his hold on her.

"Yes, Papa." Fiona smiled at him, already starting to strip off her peach dress. Since she'd removed her boots as soon as they arrived at the penthouse, she didn't have to sit down to take them off before she removed her leggings and undergarments. Though she did take the time to put her clothes in the laundry bag in her suitcase before walking naked back to the bed to get into position.

Knowing he would be putting in the plug before doing anything else, Fiona reached back and pulled her buttocks apart, as soon as her face hit the mattress.

"My sweet Fifi. Always such a good girl." Rick praised her, as he walked up behind her. He drizzled the lube over her puckered entrance before starting to spread it around with the tip of the plug.

Unlike previous nights when he'd plugged her, Rick didn't spend much time teasing her with the plug before seating it fully in her rectum. She heard the pop of the lube cap closing before the thud of the plastic bottle landing on the hardwood floor. Then she felt Rick's hands gently pushing hers off her butt cheeks.

"Hands above your head," Rick directed, as he stroked his palms over her buttocks.

Fiona followed his instructions, eagerly anticipating what he would do to her next. She didn't have to wait long to find out.

Rick stroked his hands over her backside, down between her thighs to tease his fingers through her soaking wet folds. He pushed two digits inside her, as his other hand lifted from her body, and she heard the distinct sound of his zipper. "Fuck, Fifi, you're always so wet for me."

"Only for you," Fiona moaned, loving the way he touched her.

Since they were both exhausted from their long day of traveling, it was a good thing Fiona was ready for Rick. He took no time for foreplay, lining up the head of his cock with her entrance and sliding into her all the way to the root.

"Fuck, Fifi, you're so tight. Even tighter than normal with that plug in your ass." Rick gripped her hips to control their movements, squeezing tight enough that Fiona knew she'd see his marks on her the next day.

Fiona felt so full, taking more than she'd ever felt before. The sensations Rick was creating in her body left her speechless. She was thankful his constant stream of dirty talk didn't include any questions she had to answer because she couldn't think, much less form words, as he gradually increased the speed and intensity of their lovemaking.

"Fuck, Fifi, you have a greedy little pussy. It keeps squeezing my cock, trying to keep me inside you. Like you can't get enough. Feels. So. Good." Rick punctuated each word with a thrust into her.

Fiona's breathing rate increased, as she rocked her hips, matching his rhythm stroke for stroke. Her breasts rubbed on the soft, navy-blue duvet on his bed. She loved the feel on her hard nipples, but worried they were so hard they might tear the material.

"Your greedy, little pussy needs to come. Doesn't it?" Rick reached around with one hand to rub her clit, working her up even more than he already was from hitting her G-spot with each stroke.

"Yes. Papa." Fiona forced herself to form the words, almost too caught up in the sensations he was creating in her body to make more than a trilling sound come from her throat.

"Then be my good, little, cum slut, and come for me," Rick commanded, sending her over the edge.

Her whole body convulsed, as wave after wave of pleasure spread from her core outward. She bit down on the duvet to muffle her screams of ecstasy, unsure how soundproof his bedroom was, and not wanting to wake Britney.

As she floated down from her orgasmic high, she felt Rick pulling the plug from her anus. He didn't bother taking it to the bathroom to clean, dropping it with a thud to the floor. Then he pulled out of her vagina, and she felt the blunt head of his cock taking the place of the plug.

"Oh," she moaned, tensing slightly when she realized what was happening.

"Relax, my sweet Fifi. Let me have all of you." Rick slowly pushed past her ring of muscle, opening her up more than even the largest of the six plugs he'd used to prepare her with just the head of his cock entering her.

He took his time, being more gentle than she could ever remember him being, even more so than he'd been in Dublin, when he took things easy on her after her crying jag. He rocked back and forth, rubbing his coronal ridge in and out to relax her before pushing further inside her.

The whole time he was working his length into her tightest opening, Rick talked her through what he was feeling and seeing, as they both experienced anal sex for the first time. The situation was so surreal that Fiona zoned out, focusing on the unusual taction, and the strange sense of belonging to Rick that it evoked, more than his words.

She had never felt more connected to another person in her life, and knew it had to be that sense of connection that had her on the edge again already.

"Fucking amazing," Rick growled, as he bottomed out in her rectum.

"Hmmm," Fiona moaned. She agreed with Rick's sentiment, but she couldn't form the words to say so. She was too caught up in the pure pleasure he was giving her, as he slowly pulled out and then pushed back in.

"Can you handle more, my sweet Fifi? Can I go faster? Harder?"

"Yes, Papa," Fiona nodded, unsure how she'd managed to get the words past her lips.

Rick gradually increased his speed and intensity, testing her limits, while pulling her cream up with his hand from her lower lips to coat his shaft to ease the way for his dick in her ass. Using her arousal as additional lubricant, he eventually worked up to fucking her ass so hard his balls bounced against her clit. He praised her the whole time for being his "good girl" and his "anal slut" to the point that Fiona started to think the terms were interchangeable, identical in their meaning of being perfect for him.

Fiona found herself coming once more, her sex clamping down on nothing but air, as her inner walls contracted in climax. "Oh, yes, Rick," she uttered, as she peaked, barely loud enough for him to hear her.

"Yes, come, sweet Fifi. Come from me fucking you in the ass." Rick didn't slow his rhythm, continuing to pound into her, prolonging her orgasm, until he joined her in simultaneous erotic ecstasy.

She felt him stretch her further, as he seemed to swell with each spurt of his ejaculation. While Fiona reveled in the emotion she felt at being the reason he experienced such pleasure, she wasn't prepared for the difference in the physical feelings of him coming in her rectum, as opposed to her vagina.

Theoretically, she realized that what went in had to come out no matter where he came, but the practical application of that theory definitely changed in urgency depending on which orifice he filled. When he came in her vagina, she could lay there and recover, knowing only a little would ooze out before he grabbed a washcloth to clean her up. But she had no time to recover when he came in her rectum.

As Rick started to collapse forward over her back for his own recovery, Fiona pushed up on her hands, squealing, "Frick-n-frack!" She wasn't sure how she managed to twist out from under Rick to disconnect them before running to the closest of his ensuite bathrooms.

"Are you okay, Fifi?" Rick appeared in the doorway, just as she plopped down on the toilet with what felt like explosive diarrhea.

It was such a close call, she didn't think her backside even made contact with the seat before she passed gas along with the contents of her colon.

"No!" Fiona covered her face with both hands, mortified that Rick was standing in the doorway watching her poop. She knew she was being ridiculous, since he'd just had his penis in her bottom, but she couldn't stop the embarrassment from pinkening her from head to toe. "Please go back to the bedroom, or clean up in the other bathroom. I'll be fine. I just need you to give me a few minutes of privacy."

Fiona punctuated her statement with some of the most awful sounds she'd ever heard coming from her backside, which only strengthened her resolve to hide her face to keep from seeing Rick's reaction to her most disgusting bodily function.

"Oh, um, take your time," Rick chuckled, as he backed out of the room and shut the door.

"It's not funny," Fiona groaned, as her bowels protested their earlier activity, but she was pretty sure Rick didn't hear her.

She wasn't sure how long she sat there, turning the inside of his toilet into the most grotesque version of a Jackson Pollock painting she could imagine. Once she thought she was emptied back out, she went straight to the shower. Toilet paper alone wasn't enough to make her feel clean after that experience.

"Romance novels with anal sex scenes should at least warn a girl about the mess afterwards," she grumbled, as she scrubbed her buttocks under the warm water. "Or give us more info on how to prep to avoid the explosive consequences of trying it at home. Maybe I should have used an enema beforehand? I'll make Rick ask Jax about how to better prepare for this before I consider letting his penis near my rectum again."

Once the evidence of her anal annihilation was cleaned up, Fiona wrapped herself in one of Rick's fluffy blue towels before she braved walking back into the bedroom.

Rick was laying in the bed, already under the covers with her side pulled down for her to be able to slip right into bed. "Feel any better?"

Fiona shrugged, praying she got it all out and wouldn't have to rush back to the bathroom in the middle of the night. She didn't bother removing the towel, as she climbed into bed.

"Do you at least think you're finished sharting?" Rick raised an eyebrow at her, smiling, like he thought the situation was funny.

"I hope," Fiona groaned, covering her eyes with her arm.

"I'm sorry, sweet Fifi," Rick cooed, wrapping his arms around her, and pulling her to the middle of his king-sized bed. "I didn't think of the consequences of giving you a cum enema. From now on, I'll pull out and cover your back with my cum instead."

Fiona nodded into his chest, still too embarrassed to look him in the eye, as she agreed with his plan for their future anal experiences.

"But if I accidentally lose control and forget to pull out sometime in the future, I hope you'll realize you have nothing to be embarrassed about, and let me take care of cleaning you up."

Fiona couldn't even fathom a time she wouldn't be embarrassed by this situation, so she didn't dignify his statement with a response. She just cuddled in close to him, and let the topic die, as she drifted off to sleep.

Chapter Twenty-Two

Fiona found herself reflecting on everything that had happened in the three weeks since they'd returned to North America after the European tour, as she rode on the bus the GWA chartered for their midday excursion from the hotel where they were staying to the actual falls in Niagara Falls, Ontario, Canada. So much had happened, both on the GWA tour of the northeastern United States and southeastern Canada and at home with her friends in Texas, that she was glad for the relative normalcy of her relationship with Rick.

The first thing she'd recognized as a major event in the company had been when the tag team of Harrison Thorne, who used the ring name Magnum, and Cameron Wentworth, who used the ring name Trojan, and were collectively known as Protection Detail, joined them on tour when they flew out of New York for their first show back in the States in Allentown, Pennsylvania.

Then, just a couple of days later, Rick signed a new female performer to join them at their show in Atlantic City, New Jersey. Rylie Long used the ring name Chastity, so Rick decided to have her act as Protection Detail's manager, as well as wrestle, thinking the name went too perfectly with their gimmick to pass up the tongue-in-cheek sexual innuendo. It set them up, so they could start a feud with the Dangerous Twins and Leigh during their first appearance on the GWA's weekly television show.

Speaking of Rylie, I wonder what she and Liam are doing on the bus with the families today? Are they really just friends like they've both claimed after we all saw them hanging out together the past couple of weeks? Or are they the next couple to get together on tour?

In addition to the new members of the roster, the Inglemans had rejoined the tour while they were in Maine on the last Saturday in March. They hadn't been back a week yet, and Fiona already knew she liked the throuple and their two kids. Since Kay had gone home on Wednesday for her five days off while the other flight crew worked, Fiona was the first to volunteer to help Kori with baby Talia and three-year-old Xander while her husbands met with Rick and the writers.

Being around four kids under four years old every day was feeding her baby fever as much as, if not more than, the Burleson baby boom that seemed to be starting in Heart's Destiny. After her talk with Rick on their night off in New York, Fiona actually felt hopeful she would be able to have babies of her own for the first time since her polycystic ovary syndrome diagnosis in college.

Though Kay and Brooklyn both being pregnant probably doesn't constitute a baby boom in the Burleson family. But with Charlotte telling me about Justin finally making a move on Amy, and her hooking up with Ian a few more times in the last six weeks, I'm sure there'll be more Burleson babies coming in the next couple of years.

Thinking of her talks with Charlotte momentarily brought her down at the memory of hearing that Roberto Reyes had quit bringing Antonio into the shelter for Charlotte to work with him on his speech. Nobody knew what happened to them since the last time they'd been seen the first week of March, and Fiona was afraid they might have run into some kind of immigration issues.

I really hope they weren't sent back to the same area of Mexico they fled from, and are back stuck in the middle of cartel crossfire. I wish Charlotte could have told me more, but at least I know she's got her brothers and new cousins looking into their disappearance. So, even if they can't tell me anything during their investigation, at least I know someone is looking for them, and will make sure they are safe.

In addition to knowing the Burlesons were looking into things, Fiona also had Rick to talk with about her fears for the little boy and his father. He couldn't do much more than reassure her that the Burlesons would make sure the Reyes family was safe. But for some reason, being held in his arms when he said the words made them feel more true than when she'd heard the same sentiment from Charlotte.

Fiona pushed everything else from her mind, as the buses pulled up at the falls. She pulled her black cardigan closed over her red dress, as she stepped off the bus, wishing she'd remembered to grab her coat to wear in the fifty-degree weather.

"You cold, Fifi?" Rick wrapped an arm around her shoulders to help warm her up.

"A little cool, but I'll be fine," Fiona admitted, snuggling into Rick's side, and wrapping her arms around his waist. She was in awe at how he wasn't cold in his black slacks and button-down with no jacket. "I keep forgetting I'm not in Texas, where the overnight low is warmer than the daytime high temperatures here in Canada. And I should probably go back to looking at the local weather online before going out, instead of going by how many layers you and Britney wear, since ya'll are much more accustomed to the cold than I am."

"Well, stick close and I'll share my extra body heat." Rick grinned and wagged his eyebrows suggestively. "And I'll remind you to grab a jacket before we leave the hotel from now on."

Fiona agreed, as the group started separating into smaller groups to go through the various attractions. While Dan Traverson led the smaller group with the elementary-age children toward the Niagara Parks Power Station for a scientific view of the importance of the falls, Jax led the middle school group toward the entrance for the Journey Behind the Falls for a historical perspective. Halfway through their excursion, they'd swap groups, so all the children would experience both lessons.

Fiona knew she should probably be helping Jax corral the kids the way Ivy was helping Dan, but she decided to stay with Rick when it looked like Cage was doing a pretty good job helping Jax. "Do you think those two are ever going to hook up? Or are they just going to keep fighting their attraction to one another?"

"You're asking the wrong person that question," Rick chuckled. "I'm not a matchmaker like everyone else in the GWA."

"I didn't think I was either," Fiona shrugged, as they entered the tunnel behind the falls. "Until I realized how happy I am with you, and started wanting all my friends to be just as happy."

They quit talking so much when the kids started reading every plaque on the walls, as they weaved through the tunnels. Then, as they got to the area of the tunnels with the cut-out sections of rock to the backside of the waterfalls, it was almost too loud to hear each other talking. The same seemed to be true when they got to the observation deck, so they quietly stood with an arm around each other to appreciate the majesty around them.

Until Rick bent his head to speak close to her ear for her to be able to hear him over the roar of the waterfall. "You sure we can't do a video call with your dad, so I can propose again, while we're here in this place that's almost as beautiful as you?"

Fiona blushed at the compliment, but she still shook her head no at the video call suggestion. She felt a little guilty for not accepting his proposal until he spoke with her father face to face. But after the face-to-face interaction she'd had with his mother three weeks before, Fiona felt it was only fair that he showed her family the same respect she'd shown his.

She realized at that moment why she felt so strongly about him asking for her hand in marriage. It wasn't that she was old-fashioned enough to believe she was property to be handed over from her father to her husband, as the tradition had originated. If her father didn't like Rick and refused to give them his blessing, she knew she'd still marry Rick.

It was simply a matter of him showing his respect for her and her family by honoring their tradition. She didn't need a grand gesture or fancy proposal, but she did need to feel like he thought she was worth stepping out of his comfort zone for, to show his love for every part of her.

Not that I can explain any of that to him right now, Fiona thought with a sigh as she leaned into Rick's side once more. *But maybe I can talk to him more tonight once we get back to the hotel.*

~~~

Thursday, April 4, 2019, 11 p.m., Niagara Falls, Ontario, Canada

Rick was determined to convince Fiona to say yes to his marriage proposal without making him wait until their Memorial Day break to talk to her father in person. It wasn't that he had a problem with following the tradition of asking for his blessing. Though he did think
~~~

it was an antiquated tradition when he was the one having to ask, he hoped his daughter's future spouse would one day ask for his blessing before marrying Britney.

The problem was that Rick was impatient. At least, he was impatient when it came to seeing his ring on Fiona's finger. He knew he would have to go back to his normal, high level of patience when it came to waiting for the actual wedding. But he couldn't stand the fact that she wasn't wearing the engagement ring as a symbol to show the world she was taken until then.

So, as they were going through their normal nightly routine with a bedtime snack for Britney, and then brushing their teeth and undressing for bed, Rick was planning how he was going to convince Fiona to wear his ring now, even if he still had to ask for her father's blessing at the end of May.

I'll tie her up again and tease her to the point she'll do anything I ask to be able to come. She won't be able to refuse to wear my ring then.

It sounded like the perfect plan in Rick's head. He could enjoy touching and tasting every inch of her, while torturing her in all the ways he knew she loved most.

We'll probably both explode in a massive, mutual orgasm when I slide the ring on her finger.

As he finished undressing, and sorting his clothing into the laundry and dry cleaning bags he would deliver to the front desk at the hotel in Buffalo, New York, the next day, Rick grabbed a couple of his ties to use to bind Fiona to the bed.

If we keep doing this regularly, I should probably pack a few more ties when we're in New York City for the GWA show in mid-May, so we don't accidentally tear one of the ones I wear regularly. Or maybe I can find a specialty store somewhere between now and then, where I can pick up proper bondage equipment, so we don't have to wait a month before playing like this again.

When he turned away from the closet, Fiona was walking out of the ensuite bathroom, already undressed, and carrying her clothes toward the closet. He pecked her lips with his, as they passed each other between the bed and the closet.

"Hurry to bed, Fifi. I have plans for you tonight." Rick held up the ties in his hands to give her a hint of what was to come.

"Yes, Papa." Fiona grinned at him, as she practically skipped to the closet to put her things away.

Rick wasn't sure she'd bothered sorting her clothing, much less folding it, as she stuffed everything in the laundry bag.

I hope she didn't shove her boots in there with her clothes. Rick cringed at the thought, knowing she didn't share his penchant for folding his dirty clothes before putting them in the bag to be laundered. He didn't get the chance to ask where her boots were, however, because he was too busy trying not to laugh at how she rushed past him to jump on the bed. *Damn, and I thought I was eager to get things started tonight.*

Fiona positioned herself in the middle of the bed, with her arms extended toward the headboard and her legs spread, without him even having to direct her into the position. *Fuck, she's perfect!*

Rick made quick work of wrapping the first tie around her wrists and through the slats on the headboard to secure her to the bed. After double-checking that he didn't have the bindings too tight around her wrists, he reminded her of her safe words, eager to get started playing with her. He then secured the second tie around her head, covering her eyes, so she didn't see him get the ring out of the bedside table to place it on the pillow beside them before covering her body with his.

"Am I being punished for something, Papa? Or are we just playing like this for fun tonight?" Fiona licked her lips, as Rick trailed a hand down her body to start teasing her.

"It's mostly just because I like playing like this with you, sweet Fifi," Rick whispered against her skin, as he kissed his way down her neck. "But if you don't follow my every instruction, and answer my every question correctly, I can turn our playtime into a punishment by teasing you without letting you come."

"I promise I'll be a good girl, Papa, and do everything you want, so you don't have to punish me." Fiona practically purred the words, as her whole body quivered with excitement at what was to come.

"Hmmm, let's hope that's the case." Rick stuck his tongue out to trail it down from the base of her throat to swirl designs between her tits. "Since you can't really do much while blindfolded and bound, we'll start with my questions. Where do you like me to use my mouth on your body the most, sweet Fifi?"

"Oh, these are hard questions, Papa," Fiona moaned, writhing beneath him. "I love the feel of your mouth on me everywhere."

"Ah, but you have to pick one spot, so I know where to start teasing you. So, tell me where it's going to be. Your dripping, wet pussy? Or your diamond-hard nipples?"

"While I love your mouth on my pussy and my nipples, Papa, I think I love your mouth on my mouth most of all." Fiona puckered her lips, anticipating his kiss.

Rick chuckled, as he moved back up to grant her wish. *Only my sweet Fifi would pick kissing over having her pussy eaten.*

Neither of them spoke for several long minutes, as they kissed passionately. When he finally broke the kiss, Rick moved back down her body to lavish more open-mouthed kisses over her bountiful breasts. He suckled her nipples, easing her toward the edge before backing off and moving down her body.

"And when I eat your pussy, do you prefer I fuck you with my tongue? Or suck your clit while I fuck you with my fingers?" Rick lightly ran his fingers over her mound to find the wetness between her thighs without actually doing either of the things he asked about.

"Yes, Papa," Fiona cooed, causing Rick to chuckle at her non-answer.

"Yes to which, sweet Fifi? Fucking you with my tongue? Or sucking your clit while fucking you with my fingers?"

"I like it best when you alternate both with licking me everywhere, Papa. Just doing one or the other can quickly feel like too much and be more annoying than arousing."

Good to know. It wasn't exactly the answer Rick expected, but he was glad to hear she liked all his favorite ways to eat her, and not just one.

"As you wish, my sweet Fifi." Rick rewarded her honesty with a thorough tongue lashing of her pretty, pink pussy. Once again, he brought her to the brink before backing off and not letting her climax too soon.

He repositioned himself, sliding a little farther down on the bed before pushing her knees up on either side of her chest, exposing her puckered asshole for him to play with next. "What do you think about me wanting to fuck your ass with my tongue?"

"I, um, don't know about that, Papa. That seems rather unsanitary."

Rick looked up just in time to see Fiona make a face at the thought. Since her cunt didn't seem to get any creamier at the thought either, Rick opted to just use his fingers back there for the time being. He still hadn't convinced her to give anal another go, so he knew anal oral was a long shot before he even asked.

He teased her anus with the tip of his finger for a moment before he lowered her legs and crawled back up over her, kissing his way up until the tip of his cock brushed through her lower lips to press against her clit.

Fiona sucked in a breath, as her pussy flooded at the prospect of him entering her.

"You want my cock in your tight, little pussy, Fifi?"

"Yes, Papa," Fiona agreed breathlessly.

"What are you willing to do to get me to fuck you, Fifi?"

"Anything you want, Papa." Fiona rocked her hips, coating the underside of his hard-as-a-rock cock in her juices.

"Anything? Are you sure about that, Fifi?"

"Yes, Papa." Fiona nodded her head adamantly.

"You'll let me fuck you hard until I come, even if I don't let you come with me?" Not that he ever wanted to come without her, but he wondered if she was willing to deny herself for him.

"Yes, Papa." Fiona's breathing rate picked up, as her arousal increased.

"You'll let me make love to you, slow and gentle, until we both come together?"

"Yes, Papa." Fiona's hips rocked faster, letting Rick know she'd reached the point where she'd agree to anything he wanted.

"You'll agree to marry me and let me put my engagement ring on your finger right now?"

"Ye…no!" Fiona broke off her affirmative answer in the middle of the word to shake her head with her adamant refusal.

Rick pushed up off of Fiona, sitting back on his heels to stare down at her in confusion. He couldn't believe she'd said "no" so vehemently, just as he was about to slide his ring on her finger. He floundered for a moment, trying to figure out what to say in response to her shocking refusal.

Apparently, his quiet withdrawal from her lasted too long for Fiona, who softly whispered the safe word to get him to pause their play. "Yellow."

"Fuck," Rick cursed under his breath, as he moved to remove the blindfold and untie her wrists.

Fiona sat up as soon as she was freed, reaching for his hands with both of hers and clearly seeing the ring he had slipped on the tip of his pinky to keep from losing it while untying her. "I'm sorry I'm frustrating you so much by not being able to accept your proposal yet."

"You don't need to apologize, Fifi." Rick moved up to lean against the headboard and pulled Fiona onto his lap while they talked. Even if he couldn't get her to wear his ring yet, he needed to feel physically connected to her while they discussed their feelings. "I'm sorry I'm so damn impatient that I can't wait to see my ring on your finger."

"You know it doesn't matter if I say yes now, or at the end of May, we'll still be able to plan our wedding for our Independence Day break." Fiona wrapped her arms around his waist, as she nuzzled her face against his shoulder.

"Will we?" Rick wasn't so sure. He knew they loved each other, and both wanted to get married, but he couldn't stop worrying that if her father didn't give his blessing, then Fiona would refuse to marry him. Losing her was his greatest fear, and he didn't know how to deal with it other than to have that symbol on her finger showing she was his forever. "Or will I lose you completely if your dad doesn't give his blessing?"

"Oh, Rick." Fiona lifted her head and pressed a way too brief kiss to his lips. "I don't care whether Daddy gives us his blessing or not."

"Then why won't you wear my ring now? Is this just an excuse for you to have a few more weeks to decide if you love me enough to marry me?" Rick was even more confused than before.

"No, I know we're getting married, whether my parents agree or not." Fiona shifted on his lap to straddle him, cupping his jaw in both of her tiny hands. "Not just that we're getting married, but we're getting married in July, and I'm adopting Britney, just as soon as you can push the paperwork through the courts. And I'm more than willing to get started with planning everything and doing the paperwork now to make sure it happens when we want it to. I just can't say yes to a proposal and wear your ring until you do this one thing."

"If you know all that and your parents' opinion doesn't matter, then why does it matter if I ask for their blessing before you'll wear the ring to show the world we're together?" Rick still didn't understand what she was thinking. He wanted to provide for her every want and need, but sometimes he needed to understand the logic behind them before he could.

"Do you know what I like most about romance novels?" Fiona blindsided him by changing the subject so abruptly.

"The graphic sex scenes?" Rick joked, thinking he was being as random as she was in switching the subject.

"Well, those are definitely a high point, but no," Fiona giggled, shaking her head. "It's how the couples are so in love they'll do anything for each other. That no matter what else is going on in their lives, they always put each other first. It's completely unreal and impossible to do a hundred percent of the time in real life."

"No, it's not. You're always first in my life," Rick disagreed, knowing his perspective of the priorities in his life had changed since he and Fiona got together.

"No, I'm not," Fiona argued. "Britney's number one, always. For both of us. And when we have more kids, they'll be tied for number one with her. And all your responsibilities to the GWA are number two. But that's fine because I don't expect to be number one in your life all the time until after we retire, and our kids are grown."

Rick tried to focus on what she was saying, but it was becoming increasingly hard to comprehend when she was wiggling on his lap. The feel of her wet pussy rubbing against his cock was exceptionally distracting, so he gripped her hips and held her still, hoping he could concentrate enough to understand her convoluted explanation.

"I'd like to say I'm a rational woman, who doesn't need the grand gestures and elaborate, romantic proposals like in romance novels. But there are certain times in life, when even a rational woman needs to be shown she's the top priority for her man. I don't need you to ask for my hand in marriage to get permission to marry you. I need you to do it to show me that you see everything about me, including the traditional values of my family. To prove that you respect and love every aspect of me enough to step outside your comfort zone to follow my family traditions. To put me first in your life for that small window of time by doing something just because I want you to, even though it makes absolutely no sense to you."

She was right about her choice of tasks making absolutely no sense to him, but he thought he understood where she was coming from in her reasoning. She needed to feel special to him. *Fuck! I thought I was showing her daily how special she is to me. I'm obviously going to have to step up my spoiling of my sweet Fifi.*

"I'm not asking you to leave Britney and the GWA to go speak to my parents immediately. I'm not even asking you to fly them in to see us to keep from impacting our schedule. Just to ask them next time we're in town and see them. Is that really too much to ask?"

"No, sweet Fifi, it's not." Rick leaned forward and brushed his lips over her forehead. "And now that I understand the why behind it, I'll settle for starting to plan everything now to appease my inner caveman that keeps demanding I show the world you're mine."

And I'll work on ideas to go above and beyond your expectations for showing you that you're number one in my life, Fifi.

"You know your inner caveman is more than welcome to mark me as yours in other ways," Fiona teased, rocking her hips once again.

The squelching sound as she soaked his dick in her arousal made it evident to Rick that his Fifi was open to all kinds of options for how he might mark her that night. "Oh, really? Like a few little bite marks?"

"Yes, Papa," Fiona agreed breathlessly.

Completely forgetting about his earlier plans to have her tied down and blindfolded for the night, Rick lifted Fiona by her hips and lowered his mouth to her perfect rack. He nibbled and nipped for a few agonizing moments, as he rocked his hips to line up his cock with her soaking wet slit. He thrust up as he pulled her down, impaling her on his dick at the same moment he bit down a little harder on the inside of her right breast.

"Oh, yes, Rick!" Fiona cried out, grabbing his head with both hands and slightly pulling his hair, as she took pleasure in the pain.

He quickly released the bite, only wanting to leave a faint mark, not draw blood. He turned his head slightly to leave a matching bite mark on her left breast, as he lifted her halfway off his cock.

He controlled the intensity of their fucking by syncing his upward pelvic thrusts with each time he pulled her hips down. Fiona relaxed and let him move her however he wanted, only grounding herself with her hands in his hair.

"Oh, Rick, I love it when you take me like this."

"That's because you're mine to take whenever and however I want," Rick growled before latching onto her nipple to torture her with the edge of his teeth, as he continued to pound his dick into her pussy.

"Yes, yours. All yours. Forever." Fiona panted each word, as the walls of her cunt clamped down with her first orgasm of the evening.

"Fuck," Rick groaned, desperately trying to hold back his own climax because of how good it felt when she squeezed him like a vise. "Yes, Fifi, come on my cock! Show me how much you love it."

"Yes! Rick! Yes!" Fiona continued chanting his name, as the waves of her release washed over her and flooded out on him.

"Fuck, yeah. Squirt on me, Fifi," Rick commanded, even though his direction came after she'd already done just that. He moved his head to her other breast, lightly nibbling her other nipple to prolong the pleasure pain combo that made her come like a freight train. "Fuck, you like that, don't you, Fifi."

Fiona moaned in response, but she was too far gone to respond coherently. She went lax in his arms, allowing him to keep fucking her, as she recovered from her intense orgasm. Rick cradled her to his chest, slowing things down, so he didn't blow his load too soon.

He basked in the sensual slide of their bodies connecting, until she recovered enough to lift her head from his shoulder once more. Their eyes locked and words became unnecessary, as Rick picked up the pace of their lovemaking.

She understood his unspoken command to ride him, as he released the bruising grip on her hips to reach around and tease her asshole with his fingers. Fiona rode him like a rodeo queen, while he finger-fucked her ass and ate at her nipples until they turned cherry red.

They frantically fucked for hours, murmuring dirty words to one another about how full she felt with him filling her both in front and in back, how tight and wet she felt on his cock, and how much he loved seeing his marks on her tits while he fucked her.

Rick wasn't sure how he held out until she'd come three more times before he finally let go and filled her with his cum, as she came for the fourth time. Every time her inner walls squeezed his cock, it felt as if she was trying to milk him of every drop in his balls.

He gladly gave her everything he had, until they both collapsed into one another, completely sated.

"I don't know how you keep making it better and better every time." Fiona shook her head against his shoulder, as she breathlessly panted the words.

Rick barely got out the lightest chuckle, still trying to catch his breath.

"It has to be how you overwhelm me by being everywhere at once."

Rick appreciated how the position they were in allowed him to fill her pussy and ass, at the same time he was able to get his mouth on her tits, but he could only nod in agreement with her assessment, as he was still catching his breath after the most intense orgasm of his life.

"With as much as you liked me biting your nipples, maybe we should get them pierced, so I can adorn them with jewelry that will make it easier to stimulate them in other positions," Rick suggested when he could finally form words once more.

"I think you just want to come up with a different way to get me to wear your diamonds before we go back to Texas," Fiona giggled, her breath tickling against his neck. "But I think I can live with that, if you can figure out how we can sneak off to get them pierced without having to explain it to Britney."

"I'll get right on that," Rick chuckled with her. *Piercing places are open overnight, right? Maybe we can schedule it the next time Britney has a sleepover with Tia or Noelle.*

They sat there cuddled together, still connected, for several long moments before he finally felt strong enough to move. He scooted to the edge of the bed before standing with her in his arms to carry her to the shower to clean them both up.

Rick took his time, making sure she knew how precious she was to him, as he took care of her before bed. His mind was whirling the whole time, with ideas for how he was going to show Fiona that she was number one in his life, multiple times a day for the rest of their lives. Starting with telling her how much he loves her first thing every morning, just before falling asleep every night, and every chance he got in between.

Chapter Twenty-Three

Monday, April 22, 2019, 11 a.m., Flying back and forth between Austin, Texas, and Heart's Destiny, Texas

Rick was as nervous as he could ever remember being, as he sat in the co-pilot's seat of Anthony's Cessna Citation Ultra Encore Plus, as they flew from Austin, Texas, to the small airfield between Heart's Destiny and San Antonio, where they were picking up Fiona's parents to come to the GWA show that night in Austin. It wasn't that he was nervous about flying in the small jet that only held ten people at maximum capacity, with eight in the passenger cabin and two in the cockpit. Though it did feel strange to be in the cockpit when he had no idea what any of the controls in front of him would do if he accidentally bumped them.

No, Rick was nervous because he knew he'd be riding in the passenger cabin on the way back to Austin with Fiona's parents. He planned to use the forty-minute flight to have a private talk with Dale Harrison to ask for his blessing in marrying Fiona.

"Hey, Boss, are you turnin' green because of the size of the plane, being able to see out the front window, or the talk you're gonna have with Pastor Harrison on the way back?" Anthony grinned, as he glanced over at Rick and spoke with him through the headsets they were wearing.

"Definitely the talk," Rick self-deprecatingly chuckled. "Thank you again for doing this."

When Rick heard Anthony talking about having a friend move his plane from the private hangar, where he kept it, over to the airport in Austin, so he could fly his family home Tuesday morning to kick off his paternity leave, Rick had asked if it would be possible to use his plane to surprise Fiona with her parents at a show. As soon as Anthony heard Rick's idea for how to see Fiona's father sooner than their Memorial Day break to ask for her hand in marriage, he'd jumped at the chance to spend more time in the air, while helping Rick with his plan.

Rick had originally planned on Anthony going to get them and bringing them to the arena, where he'd talk with them while Fiona was occupied with the kids in the classroom area. But then Anthony had pointed out that they needed some way to cover for where he was going without his family, so they'd concocted a cover story of Anthony wanting to take Rick flying to show him his plane.

They'd then explained their plan to Britney and Anthony's family, so they could keep Fiona distracted for the afternoon. The girls were having one last afternoon cooking lesson together before the Burlesons went home to Heart's Destiny for the next four months or so to have their baby boy.

"No problem. You know I'm trying to sneak in all the extra flying while I can before the baby's born, 'cause I'm gonna be grounded for at least a month once he arrives. So, I was happy to do it."

"And here I thought you only agreed because your wife wanted to see the results of her matchmaking before your time off," Rick joked.

"Well, there is that, too," Anthony laughed. "But seriously, you know you don't have to be nervous about asking for her dad's blessing, right?"

"No," Rick disagreed. "With the way Fiona limits my contact with her parents when they call to keep me from asking for his blessing over the phone, I have no idea what they think about me to have even the slightest clue how they're going to react to me asking to marry their daughter. That's why I had to have you call them to set this up."

"Well, trust me, whenever I see them on our time off, they're asking about you and Britney, as much as they're asking about Fiona, so I'm sure they'll be thrilled when you tell them you want to marry her."

Fuck! I hope he's right about that.

"Well, I guess we'll see in a little while," he sighed. "But in the meantime, tell me about your plane to keep me distracted from worrying that they're just coming to the show tonight to try to talk Fiona into quitting and coming home."

"They definitely aren't doing that," Anthony chuckled, shaking his head. "As for the plane, it's the upgraded business version of one of the planes I learned to fly in the Navy. Although, it's typically used for Marine transport and not what I ended up flying for most of my Naval career."

Anthony spent the rest of the flight going over all the specifications of the plane. While it all went completely over Rick's head, hearing the details he didn't understand kept him distracted until they landed.

His nerves came back, full force, as soon as the wheels of the plane hit the ground, and they only seemed to amplify as Anthony taxied over to refuel before going to his hangar, where the Harrisons were waiting.

After polite greetings, Anthony led them all onto the plane and directed them where to stow their carry-on bag before heading back to the cockpit. The Harrisons chose the first row of front-facing seats, so Rick took the rear-facing seat directly in front of Dale Harrison.

"It's so nice of you to personally come pick us up to surprise Fiona," Kathy Harrison said, as soon as they were all buckled in and ready for take-off. "I didn't realize you had more than one plane available to fly families in like this for your shows."

"Actually, this is Anthony's plane." Rick waved a hand around at the jet Anthony bought back in November. "Though I think he told Kay he bought it for her as a wedding present."

"Oh, yes, Kay has mentioned how he bought a small plane to be able to take her to see her family, or bring them down to Texas for visits." Kathy nodded.

"I assume your company plane is much bigger than this to make your travel schedule easier for everyone who works for you?" Dale's words came out sounding like a question, even though Rick thought he meant for them to be a statement.

"Yes, it's the biggest airliner I could find at the time I purchased it seven years ago. It currently seats a hundred-and-twenty people on the main deck, plus the flight crew, but we only have about two-thirds of the seats filled with people, which is why I haven't added pods in the center yet. There's room for another thirty passengers on the upper deck if I want to have it filled with the same pods we use on the main deck, but it's set up as a bedroom right now, though we don't use it. I'll probably have it reconfigured to hold our oversized luggage if we ever need all of the seats on the main deck. I would have brought it to pick you up, but my ground crew had to unload the backstage furniture from the hold, and I'm not sure this runway is big enough for it to land here. But if you'd like to see it when we land in Austin, I'll be glad to show it to you." Rick shut his mouth abruptly, afraid he was letting his anxiety show in his rambling.

"I'd like that. It'll be nice to see how our daughter is traveling all around the world." Pastor Harrison nodded, but he didn't crack a smile.

They sat quietly, as Anthony announced he was prepared for take-off to make sure they were all fastened into their seats. Kathy focused on looking out the window as they left the ground, but her husband kept his gaze directed at Rick.

Rick felt the need to loosen his tie, but he fought it off, knowing that would just be another way of showing his trepidation at what he was about to discuss with the Harrisons. As a man who was always in control of every aspect of his life, he wasn't comfortable showing any weakness to anyone he was in discussions with, personally or professionally. He especially didn't want to show his vulnerability during one of the most important conversations of his life.

Damn, I think Dad was wrong. I'd much rather face down a man with a gun than suffer under Pastor Dale Harrison's scrutiny. At least then, I'd know what to do to disarm him, so we could talk. How on earth am I supposed to convince a man of the cloth that I should be allowed to marry his daughter, when I'm pretty sure he can see through my stoic façade to know all the sinful things I've been doing with her and plan to keep doing with her for the rest of our lives?

"I'm assuming there's a reason you invited us to a random wrestling show on a Monday night," Pastor Dale said, breaking the silence. "And I doubt it's just because Anthony is using his plane to fly his family home tomorrow and has the extra space for us. Nor do I believe it's because of a surprise baby shower for Kay, since I know Hazel is planning that at the church next month."

"No," Rick admitted, steeling his spine to prepare for what he was about to say. "I just got lucky in hearing Anthony talk about using his plane to be able to invite you to the show tonight. If he hadn't mentioned his plans for having his plane in Austin, I would have had to wait another month to have this conversation with you."

"Is something wrong with Fiona?" Kathy's eyes widened, as she directed her question to Rick. "Is that why you couldn't wait a month to tell us about it?"

"No, there's nothing wrong with Fiona," Rick stated adamantly, wanting to alleviate Kathy's fear for her daughter. "Fiona is perfect."

"So, you're just impatient?" Dale arched an eyebrow at Rick.

"Normally, I'd say I'm a very patient man," Rick chuckled, surprised he was relaxing enough to admit to a potential flaw in his armor. "But when it comes to your daughter, I'm finding it hard to maintain my patience."

Dale frowned, and Rick realized his statement came out sounding much worse than it was intended.

"Not with her." Rick raised his hands in surrender. "I would never lose my patience with her, or harm her in any way. But for the first time since taking over running the GWA, I'm irritated by the travel schedule that has kept us so busy we haven't been able to be back in Heart's Destiny since our first date ten weeks ago."

Kathy leaned back in her seat and smiled, but Dale still glared at Rick. *Maybe Kathy can help soften him up, since he still seems to be likely to deliver a hard no to what I'm about to ask.*

"I realize Fiona and I have only been dating a short time," Rick continued, hoping his plea would have some effect on Dale. "But I'm in love with your daughter. I love her so much that I actually proposed six weeks ago on a gondola in Venice."

"Oh, dear, why didn't she tell us you're engaged?" Kathy covered her mouth with her hand as she gasped.

"Because she refuses to say yes to my proposal until I speak to you face to face, to ask for your blessing." Rick smiled at Kathy before turning his gaze back to Dale. "As I said, I got lucky when Anthony mentioned his plane and gave me the idea to invite you to tonight's show. Otherwise, I'd have had to wait until our Memorial Day break to speak with you. And while I understand impatience might be a flaw in my character I hadn't realized before, I can't wait another month to put my ring on her finger."

Rick wasn't certain, but he thought he saw Dale's lips turn up slightly before he schooled his features once more.

"So, I'm humbly asking for your blessing to marry Fiona." Rick hoped he was pulling off the right expression to convince Dale to agree with him.

"And when you're not traveling, where will you live? We're barely getting to see our daughter now when she just works for you. Are you going to move her to New York after the wedding and go there for your holiday breaks? Will she be expected to live there when she has to stop traveling to have babies? Why should I agree to let you marry my daughter when that's just going to make it harder for us to see her regularly?" Dale rattled off his questions rapid-fire, not allowing Rick to answer the first one before asking the next.

Rick held his hand up to stop Dale from continuing, so he had a chance to answer.

"My parents and corporate headquarters are in New York, so I'll always have to maintain a residence there. But I fully intend to buy a place in Heart's Destiny as well, so we can split our time off between our families. I have no intention of taking your daughter and future grandchildren away from you."

Dale nodded, as Rick paused to take a breath before tackling the harder topic Dale had raised.

"As far as where we'll be when we're ready to start having babies, Fiona and I have already discussed her medical issues, and will be doing more research on treatments for P.C.O.S. and the procedures for IVF to find the best doctor in the country when the time comes. Until then, we won't know if we'll be in New York, here in Texas, or anywhere else the best of the best might reside. But I'm more than willing to provide all accommodations to have both our families with us, wherever we have to go, to try having babies together."

Dale nodded once more, as his wife quietly asked another question. "Have you thought about what you'll do if IVF doesn't work?"

"Then we'll adopt," Rick replied nonchalantly. "We're already planning for Fiona to adopt Britney, so I'll just have my attorneys look into what we need to do to adopt three more children when we go to sign the paperwork."

"It won't matter to you that they don't share your DNA?" Dale looked at Rick suspiciously, as if he wasn't sure what to think of his previous answers.

"Not a bit." Rick shook his head, as he answered Dale's question, deciding to elaborate on one of the things he most loved about Fiona to show her dad why he was willing to do whatever he had to do to give Fiona children. "Do you know why your daughter decided to become a teacher?"

Dale shook his head as Kathy answered, "She's always loved to read and wanted a job sharing her favorite books."

"You're partially right," Rick grinned at Kathy. "She also loves kids. All kids. And teaching allowed her to combine her love of books with her love of children in the best possible way. Over the last few months, I've been able to see her with my daughter and all my employees' children, both while she's teaching them and while we're all together when she's not officially working. She absolutely lights up whenever she's with the kids, and her smile is blinding whenever one of them gets what she's teaching them. And while I love the way she glows when I see her holding a baby or toddler on her lap and reading them a story on the plane when she's technically not working, and the kid isn't old enough to be her student yet, I see the sadness and longing in her eyes when she has to pass them back to their parents afterward."

Rick looked back and forth between Fiona's parents before continuing. "Fiona was born to be a mom. And while I've been blessed with a daughter I can share with her, she deserves to have all the milestones that she's already missed in Britney's life with the kids she longs for, as well as the trials and tribulations raising a teenager will bring us in the next few years."

Rick looked Dale directly in the eyes, as he finished explaining. "I love your daughter and want to be the man to give her everything she could ever want or need in life. And I especially want to be the man who takes that sadness and longing out of her eyes, and makes her the happiest woman on the face of the earth for the rest of our days. So, no, our children's DNA won't matter to me because I know it won't matter to Fiona. We'll love all our kids equally, regardless of their race, ethnicity, gender, sexuality, and most especially regardless of how they come to be a part of our family. Fiona has already proven that to me by loving and accepting Britney, who is a product of my ex-wife's manipulations and condom tampering. I mean, if you need proof that DNA doesn't matter, Britney is a prime example because she's nothing like her egg donor, regardless of sharing fifty percent of her DNA."

Rick didn't mention that he'd already imagined their future children looking like a mix of the two of them. He knew his mental imagery when contemplating his feelings for Fiona had occurred before he knew they might not be able to conceive children together and would possibly end up adopting children that looked nothing like them. So, he didn't consider the specifics about what their kids and grandkids looked like in his vision of the future as set in stone, much less worth mentioning to his future in-laws.

Dale nodded once again, but this time he also started to smile. "Then I guess it's time to give you my blessing, so we can welcome our first granddaughter to the family this afternoon."

Rick reached out to shake his future father-in-law's hand. "Thank you, Pastor Harrison."

"Please, call me Dale. Pastor Harrison is reserved for my parishioners and, now that you're marrying my daughter, any teenage boys who show too much interest in my granddaughter."

Rick chuckled at how he'd been instructed to address Dale as Pastor Harrison from the day they'd first met until just a couple of seconds before, while Britney had been instructed to call him Pastor Dale from day one.

"So, when are you going to propose again? And have you thought any about when we can start planning the wedding?" Kathy's face lit up the same way her daughter's did when she was excited about something, giving Rick a glimpse of what Fiona might look like in another twenty-five years or so.

"After being denied at multiple romantic landmarks, I thought I might ask her tonight when everyone is gathered for dinner in catering. I thought maybe with the two of you there, plus the huge audience of everyone in the GWA, she wouldn't be able to say no again." Rick looked to Kathy to see what she thought of his plan.

"Excellent! I'm glad you aren't planning to wait until the next romantic landmark ya'll visit, so we can be there to witness the proposal." Kathy clapped excitedly, looking decades younger than she did when she first got on the plane.

If she's that excited, maybe she'll like my suggestion for planning the wedding over our Independence Day break, and won't balk at me paying for everything the way Fiona thinks.

"I'm thinking the week we're on our Independence Day break." Rick smiled at Kathy's excited expression before turning to look directly at Dale once more. "I also wanted to ask if you could perform the ceremony. Or, if that's not allowed, do you have another pastor whom you want to fill in for you? And if it is allowed, would you still need someone to fill in for you, so you can walk Fiona down the aisle?"

"Yes, I'm allowed to officiate my daughter's wedding." Dale grinned for the first time that Rick had ever seen.

"And if anyone's filling in for him, it'll be me," Kathy giggled. "To walk our daughter down the aisle. As for the date, that's perfect. We can go dress and tux shopping, and make any final decisions on all the arrangements while you're in town for the week of James and Randi's wedding festivities."

"That's exactly what I was thinking." Rick smiled once more, as Anthony announced they were almost in Austin, so they all needed to fasten their seatbelts and secure their belongings for landing.

Now I just have to hope Fiona says yes tonight.

~~~

Monday, April 22, 2019, 6 p.m., Austin, Texas

Fiona couldn't believe Rick had made arrangements for her parents to come to the show in Austin, since the GWA was so close to her hometown. She'd been confused when Cage had shown up at the hotel to bring her and Britney to the arena without Rick. Especially since Anthony was there to pick up his family. Then she'd started to worry when she couldn't find Rick when they got to the arena. Thankfully, he didn't make her worry through the whole time she was teaching before their dinner break. He ended her parents' tour of all things GWA with the classroom area about halfway through the three hours she spent teaching before dinner.
~~~

After briefly filling her in on their afternoon adventure to get there, her parents stayed in the classroom watching her work while Rick went back to his normal duties.

She assumed he'd had the talk with her father at some point in the time he spent with them on the flight into Austin, showing them the GWA plane at the airport, getting them checked in at the hotel for the night, and showing them around the arena. But a part of her hoped that he hadn't braved asking for her hand yet, so she could be there to witness the talk over dinner in catering.

She couldn't bring herself to ask what all they'd discussed with Rick, as she walked her parents to the catering area. Instead, she explained how her schedule worked with the dinner break before going back to the classroom with the kids whose parents were working on the show.

"So, they're still getting six hours of education a day, but it's in the afternoon and evening instead of first thing in the morning, like most schools?" Fiona's mother looked at her inquisitively. "I'd think it would be harder to keep them focused to learn late at night like that."

"They don't all stay in the classroom until the end of the show," Fiona explained. "The time we spend sightseeing counts as part of their educational time, which can be three or four hours a day depending on how long our morning flight is each day. Then we focus on teaching everything else from three to six in the afternoon. When we go back to the classroom at seven, any of the kids who are already caught up or ahead on their lessons can either go hang out with their parents or, if their parents are working the show, they can socialize in the classroom while we work with anyone who needs additional help with their lessons. As the parents finish working, they come get their kids to head back to the hotel, or go do something as a family. So, the kids start thinning out by eight, with only three or four still socializing by the time the GWA show ends. And it's usually the older kids who're used to the schedule."

"It still boggles my mind," her mother said, shaking her head as they got in line with the rest of the families to fix their plates for dinner.

As they were going through the line, Fiona introduced her parents to the members of the GWA crew, whom they hadn't met previously at Kay and Anthony's wedding or the weekend of the pay-per-view in

San Antonio. Her father couldn't quite hide his confusion when she introduced him to the Inglemans, but he didn't say a word to make her new friends uncomfortable.

That was one of the things she was grateful to have recognized in her father. He might not completely comprehend lifestyles that didn't mirror his own, but he tried to be accepting of everyone and truly believed in following the Bible verse that instructed him not to judge.

Rick had proven himself to be similar to her father in accepting everyone, though he didn't seem to link his behavior to religious teachings. The only exception she had seen from Rick in his ability to live and let live was when he had to deal with people preying on his crew, whom he thought of as his GWA family.

Who'd have thought a mobster's grandson and a southern preacher could have similarities? Fiona giggled at her silly train of thought, as she watched Rick walking up to her, while she finished filling her plate and turned toward the tables.

As soon as he reached her, Rick took her plate and bottle of water from her hands. He sat them down on the closest table as she asked, "What are you doing?"

"Something I've been waiting way too long to do again." Rick brushed his lips over hers briefly, as he took her hands in his. "But I had to prove I could be patient and do everything else that needed to be done today while waiting for everyone to be gathered in one place to witness it this time." With that, Rick dropped to one knee and released her right hand to reach into the pocket of his suit coat. He pulled out a familiar box, opening it one-handed without taking his eyes from hers.

"Fiona Greer Harrison, I love you. Every part of you. The fun-loving, compassionate, soft-spoken, kindhearted, beautiful woman the rest of the world gets to see, and the private parts of you that only I will ever know. I want to spend the rest of my life loving you, sharing everything I am with you, and doing everything I possibly can to make you the happiest woman in the world. Will you, please, make me the happiest man alive by marrying me?"

Fiona was overwhelmed with emotions. She couldn't hold back the happy tears, as she nodded her head in agreement. "Yes, Rick. It will be my greatest honor to marry you."

Rick shot to his feet, picking her up in his arms, as he crashed his lips over hers. Fiona wrapped her arms around his neck and her legs around his waist, as he deepened the kiss. There were catcalls and whistles, as their kiss bordered on inappropriate for their audience, but Fiona and Rick blocked them all out. They enjoyed their moment of connection among the sea of well-wishers.

Until a shrill New York accent broke through their bubble. "Ricky, I know I taught you better than to risk losing the ring by dropping it!"

His parents are here too?

"Don't worry, Mom," Rick laughed, as he released Fiona's lips and placed her back on her feet. "I didn't lose the ring. I just dropped the box."

He pulled back just enough to bring her hands back down in between them, so he could slide the beautiful, square-cut diamond on her left ring finger. Fiona couldn't take her eyes off the man in front of her to look at the ring, but she remembered thinking it was perfect when she'd seen it in Venice.

"I can't believe you surprised me by bringing both our parents to the show tonight," Fiona said breathlessly, as she rested her palms on the lapels of his jacket.

Rick shook his head and grinned at her, holding her hands to his chest. "I was as surprised to see my parents here as you are."

"We hopped on the first flight we could get, as soon as Britney filled us in on the plan," Katarina explained. "We figured it would be the perfect time to meet your parents and get started on the wedding plans."

"Absolutely!" Fiona's mother exclaimed. "We really should get started if we want to have everything set up by the Fourth of July."

"You don't really want to get married on the Fourth of July, do you?" Fiona looked up at Rick, thinking how hard it would be to get the various wedding vendors to work on a major holiday. She didn't want her wedding to be the reason they didn't spend time with their families for the holiday.

"I was actually thinking about the weekend after the fourth, so we'd have time for all the other wedding stuff, while we're there the weekend before." Rick grinned. "I can't wait to see our parents go head-to-head in the newlywed game, like at Anthony and Kay's wedding. I was thinking my uncles and their wives can even come into town for the wedding and maybe one of them will be brave enough to be the fourth couple in the game."

Fiona giggled at how she imagined that would go with his colorful family history.

"So, we're looking at the sixth or seventh for the wedding," Katarina interjected while looking at her phone's calendar app.

"Oh, yes, the seventh day of the seventh month!" Fiona's mom bounced with excitement, as she looked at Katarina's phone with her. "What a perfect day for the wedding! And we'll have it at seven p.m., instead of our evening church service."

"Guess they're planning it without us," Fiona shrugged.

"We should probably grab our plates and sit down to get in on planning the other details," Rick suggested, finally releasing his hold on her.

By the time Fiona found her plate and got settled at the table, their mothers had moved on to discussing wedding colors and how big the wedding party would be. Rick pulled Britney away from her table of friends, where she'd gone with most everyone else to eat dinner after the roaring round of congratulations died down. They walked over to the buffet, so Rick could fix his own plate, while talking to his daughter. Fiona couldn't tell what they were discussing from where she was sitting, but she hoped they would hurry up and join the rest of their families, so she could ask Britney to be her maid of honor.

She knew she'd also want Charlotte to stand up with her as a bridesmaid, but she didn't want to have to choose between her childhood friends and her new GWA friends to fill the front of the church for her wedding party.

"Britney just agreed to be my best girl." Rick grinned at their mothers, as he took the seat beside Fiona. "And Cage will be my best man."

"Who are you going to have as your bridesmaids?" Katarina tapped away on her phone, taking notes of the plans electronically.

"Charlotte Burleson and…I don't know." Fiona shook her head, thinking she needed to call and check on her friend to see how she was doing after her ordeal earlier that month. *But now's not the time to think about her being kidnapped.* "I was planning to ask Britney to be my maid of honor, but Rick had to sneak in and steal her for his side of the aisle before I could."

Leah Mae Wright

"I'll be your man of honor, Doll." Jax surprised Fiona by coming over and sitting down beside her. He gave her a one-armed side hug before introducing himself to Rick's parents. "I'm Jax Nolen, Fiona's bestie. And if you pair me up with Cage to walk down the aisle, then we won't have to worry about any jealous boyfriends causing a scene at the wedding."

"Oh, I'm sure Charlotte won't have a jealous boyfriend causing a scene at the wedding, no matter whom she walks down the aisle with," Fiona's mother explained.

"Oh, no, Doll, I was talking about me." Jax waved his hand around before placing his fingertips on his own chest. "We might not be completely there yet, but I hope to have that hunk of man meat all to myself by July."

"Oh, well, then we'll definitely push the two of you together at all the wedding festivities," Fiona's mom grinned, nodding at Jax.

Fiona had to giggle at the surprised expression on Katarina Robertson's face, as her mom and Jax started to conspire to plan all the ways he could win over his man, if he hadn't already sealed the deal by the time she and Rick's wedding rolled around.

This will be an interesting couple of months of planning. And when all is said and done, I'll have my family. The man of my dreams, an almost-teenaged daughter, and the hope of more children to come.

Epilogue

The last couple of months had been a whirlwind for not only Fiona with all her wedding preparations, but also for several of her friends. Both in the GWA and back home in Heart's Destiny.

Jax and Cage had finally given in to their attraction to one another and were openly living as a couple. As glad as Fiona was for them, she hated that it had taken the danger of Allissa's stalker to bring them together. *Though if there ever was a silver lining to a stalker situation, bringing couples together would have to be it*, she supposed.

Dean also seemed to be trying to take advantage of the situation to spend more time with Allissa by insisting on being her bodyguard. But Fiona wasn't sure her friend, Allissa, was quite as open to a relationship with him as he hoped.

It wasn't just her coworkers who were progressing in their relationships recently, either. So was her best friend back in Heart's Destiny. Fiona had spoken with Charlotte several times to get updates on how she was doing after her harrowing experience with Roberto Reyes, who turned out to not be who he said he was, and had also gotten updates on Charlotte's relationship with Ian when they talked. They were now dating exclusively, even though Charlotte refused to move off the family ranch to live with him.

In those updates, she'd also heard about Justin and Amy planning a December wedding after the birth of the twins they're expecting, all about the process the Burlesons had gone through to locate Antonio in the system before he could be deported, and how he was progressing now that Anthony and Kay had adopted him.

Now that she was finally in Heart's Destiny for the festivities surrounding her and Rick's wedding and the Fourth of July celebrations, Fiona was happy to share her wedding week with the excitement of the first of several Burleson births that would be happening in the next few months. She couldn't contain her smile, as she rode with Rick and Britney to visit Anthony, Kay, and their newborn son at the Heart's Destiny Birthing Center, which had opened in conjunction with the Heart's Destiny Clinic in April.

She'd actually seen the facility for the first time in May, when she went for her appointment with Doc Hayes to renew her birth control prescription. She ended up transferring to Dr. Magnum for her female health issues, instead of seeing Doc Hayes for that appointment.

After she and Rick talked to the OB-GYN, they decided to try ditching the birth control for a while to see if the time she'd been on it was enough to reset her system to allow her to get pregnant naturally, or if she would need to try one of the P.C.O.S. medications to help her ovulate.

So far, just being off of her birth control hadn't worked, even though they practiced making babies every morning and again every night. But it had only been five weeks that they'd actively been trying, so it could still work. And if it didn't, Fiona was hopeful that the new female doctor in town knew more about reproduction than Doc Hayes to be able to help them navigate their other options, if they became necessary.

"Do we just go in the main clinic entrance?" Rick parked the car, as they looked around to see if there was a separate visitor's entrance for the birthing center.

"I don't see a separate entrance for non-patients," Fiona shrugged, as they got out of the car. "So, I guess we just go in where we'd go for an appointment, and let them direct us to the patient rooms, since it's not like a traditional hospital."

Once they were inside, the receptionist directed them to a set of stairs off to the side of the room that Fiona hadn't noticed before. The second floor of the building was set up more like a hospital ward, with a central nurse's station at the top of the stairs and hallways leading to the patient rooms. The nurse manning the desk directed them to Kay's room, which they found easily.

"Happy Birthday!" Britney squealed, as soon as they walked into the room, waving the giant teddy bear she was carrying over her head. "We brought the baby his own Britney Bear."

"Oh, Boy!" Anthony exclaimed, grinning at her with as much excitement on his face as Britney brought to the room. "That bear is big enough to need its own seat on the plane."

"Yeah, that Britney Bear will have to watch over Sam at home, so I can keep our kids and their toys corralled in one quad on the plane," Kay chuckled, as the baby in her arms yawned. From just looking at her, Fiona never would have guessed her friend had given birth that morning via C-section, since she didn't look like the incision site was causing her any discomfort as she cradled her son.

"Aww, he's so cute," Fiona cooed, as she stepped closer to the bed to get a better view of the baby. "So, you decided to stick with Sam for his name?"

"Yes, Samuel Hendrix Burleson," Kay replied. "You want to hold him?"

"Yes, please!" Fiona was so eager to hold the baby, she couldn't get to the chair beside the bed fast enough.

"Let me guess, after Sammy Hagar and Jimi Hendrix?" Rick lifted his chin in Anthony's direction, as he asked the question. "I'm surprised you went with two guitarists, instead of having a pilot or plane name in there."

"Oh, you sneaky, sneaky man!" Kay squealed, pointing at Anthony, as soon as she'd handed baby Sam to Fiona.

"What? I didn't sneak anything in," Anthony denied the allegations, holding up both hands. "You picked Samuel, not me."

"But you agreed with it, and let me believe it was to be patriotic, and not after another guitarist." Kay threw up her hands in exasperation before bringing one back down to place on her stomach, as she shifted in the bed.

"What other guitarist?" Tia asked, as she walked into the room with Hazel, Maria, and Antonio.

"Sammy Hagar," Rick answered Tia before turning to look at Anthony and shrugging. "Sorry for tossing you under the bus on that one."

"If you don't like that Sam namesake, we could say he's named after Sammy Davis, Junior," Anthony suggested.

Leah Mae Wright

"Or Samuel L. Jackson," Hazel added.

"Or Sam Cooke," Rick recommended.

"Or Sam Houston," Maria mentioned. "The first President of the Republic of Texas."

"Or if you want to stay patriotic, since he was born on July second, which was the day the section of the Lee Resolution dealing with independence was adopted, you could pick one of the Samuels who signed the Declaration of Independence, even though they didn't sign it until a month later on August second," Tia proposed. "There were three Samuels. Adams, Chase, and Huntington. But if you really wanted to be patriotic, you should have named him George, John, Thomas, or William. There were six of each of them that signed it. But please don't change his name to Button just because Button Gwinnett signed it."

"No, we're not changing his name to Button, or anything else," Kay giggled, still pressing a hand to her belly. "But it's good to know there are other options for people named Sam that he could be named after."

Fiona was too focused on cuddling little Sam in her arms to catch everything that was said about the famous people named Sam that they could consider as the little one's namesake, as the discussion went on around her when more people filed into the room. Until Antonio offered his suggestion, and she was surprised at how much his speech had progressed in the few short weeks he'd been living with the Burlesons.

"*Sam Sorts* from my book," Antonio said clearly.

"I vote with Antonio," Fiona piped up, grinning at the now five-year-old boy, who had crawled up on Anthony's lap.

"Agreed," Jen Burleson added from over Fiona's shoulder, where she was cooing at baby Sam in her arms. "*Sam Sorts* is much better than Julie's suggestion of Sam from *NCIS: Los Angeles*."

Jen's twin sister, Julie, just shrugged in response to her sister's teasing.

"Oh, wow, we've got a packed house in here tonight," Dr. Magnum said, as she walked into the room. "Now I see why Eric insisted on making the patient rooms so big."

"Yeah, you probably should have gone bigger, Doc," Bobby Burleson suggested. "We only have half the Burlesons in here right now."

"Seriously?" Dr. Magnum's eyes widened in shock.

"Yeah, we're still waiting on our dad," Anthony started pointing between him and Bobby. "Four siblings, two cousins, Uncle Jon and Aunt Susan."

"And that's just the family with the last name Burleson," Bobby chuckled. "There's also five Harpers and four Whitmans just on our side of the family that could pop up here any minute."

"How many members of your side of the family are coming to visit?" Hazel asked Kay.

"Well, Randi and James are already in town. My mom and dad are coming tomorrow because they thought he'd wait to come closer to my due date. David, Diana, and their two kids are supposed to be here tomorrow, too. Deanna is coming for the weekend. And do I get to claim Amy for my side of the family, since she's not a Burleson yet?"

"Wow, ya'll have a big family," Britney said, sounding like a strange mix of her normal New York accent and the South Texas drawl of almost everyone else in the room.

"Yes, they do," Dr. Magnum agreed. "And I need most of them to clear the room for a few minutes while I examine Kay."

It took a few minutes for everyone to play pass-the-baby before the room actually cleared of everyone, but Dr. Magnum, Kay, Anthony, and baby Samuel. They didn't go far, most of them waiting in the hallway for the doctor to do her thing before they piled back into the room, along with the rest of the Burlesons, who had shown up while Kay was being examined.

Fiona wasn't surprised to see Charlotte and Ian walk in together, since they seemed to be inseparable after their ordeal in April. She had a feeling they would be the next couple she knew planning their nuptials and making a baby announcement.

It's just a matter of time before one of them finally gives in and agrees to move where the other wants to live. And based on the way Ian is looking at Charlotte holding Sam, I'd put my money on him moving to the Burleson Ranch in the near future. Maybe we can push them a little on Sunday by tossing the bouquet and garter at them?

~~~
~~~

As she sat at Rick and Fiona's wedding reception, Allissa Walters was feeling discouraged that her stalker hadn't come out of the woodwork for the security team her boss had hired to be able to catch him, while they were all in Heart's Destiny, Texas, for the GWA's Independence Day break from traveling. *Though it has been nice to have a reprieve from the creepy notes and gifts being delivered every other day.*

Those had started shortly after the European tour, with her only other reprieve being when she was in Heart's Destiny over the Memorial Day break to be a bridesmaid in James and Randi's wedding. But that wasn't really a reprieve, since her stalker had just sent them to her mother's place an hour outside of Las Vegas that week, since he didn't know where she was to send them to her hotel.

When her mother called her, hysterical, and interrupted the wedding shower to tell her about them, Allissa had finally told her boss what was going on. With them being in Heart's Destiny at the time, Rick's head of security wasn't there to handle it, so he asked the Burlesons to call in their cousins to investigate.

Avington Security had done more than investigate. They'd also sent two, full-time bodyguards to watch over her mother and tried to send two more to travel with Allissa. She thought it was overkill to hire bodyguards for her when the company already had security at every show, so she'd turned down the extra travel companions, but gladly accepted the protection for her mother. Though she did insist they be discreet in discussing her mother's situation with Rick, so her homelife wouldn't be common knowledge among her coworkers.

With the way Dean Hunter was acting like being her bodyguard was his job, though, she was starting to question her decision to not accept the two from Avington Security.

If they were here, maybe I could avoid him a little more. But since they were obviously wrong in thinking Rick and Fiona announcing to the world that we'd be here all week for their wedding would draw the stalker to the small town, where it should be easier to find him, maybe they wouldn't be any better at protecting me than Dean has while we're on tour.

Truth be told, her complaint about Dean didn't have anything to do with keeping her safe from her stalker. It was all about protecting her heart and keeping her from falling for Dean.

She was afraid that was a battle she'd been losing, since first meeting him back on October fifth, when she had her try-out match with the GWA and signed her contract to start working with the promotion. Not that she would admit that to any of her matchmaking girlfriends and coworkers.

Dean and his twin brother, James, had caught her eye from across the arena when they were sparring in the ring, while she was talking to Holland Everett to plan out the choreography for her try-out match. But after being raised by a single mother, who earned her living in a brothel, Allissa had no plans to do more than look at the eye candy she started working with that night.

As she'd gotten to know the other women who worked with the GWA, Allissa hadn't confided in any of them about what her childhood was like, much less her lack of experience with men because of her upbringing. She'd always been embarrassed whenever anyone found out what her mother did for a living, even after she transitioned to managing the bar in the brothel when she aged out of the job she'd performed for most of Allissa's childhood.

People always made assumptions about her based on her mother's chosen profession. Assumptions about her promiscuity that Allissa had spent her whole life trying to prove inaccurate.

She may have used her looks to earn a living as a model, and probably still did a little in picking her wrestling attire to keep the interest of the fans, but she'd avoided men as much as possible all her life. She never had a boyfriend in school, never went on a date, or even attended a school dance. At twenty-three years old, she'd never even been kissed.

From the time she'd first started developing boobs, her mother, and the other women in the trailer park where she'd been raised, had all taught her that boys were only after one thing. None of them ever had a successful relationship, and some had actually had a few disastrous ones, so Allissa hadn't seen the point in even trying to date. Once she got old enough to hear the horror stories of how painful sex could be, she decided orgasms weren't worth the risk.

Leah Mae Wright

That was why it had been easy to ignore her body's irrational attraction to Dean for the last nine months. Well, at first, anyway.

He came on too strong at the club the GWA crew went to after her first show with them in October, so she slotted him into the player role with ease. His constant flirting and calling her Darlin' all the time were really annoying for the first few months, reinforcing her negative opinion of him. But then, in February, right around the same time everyone found out about the way their former booker, Ron Langston, had been treating her and some of the other female performers, Dean flipped the script on her.

Oh, he still flirted and called her Darlin', but he also started treating her like one of the guys and showing her the respect she deserved as a wrestler. While his behavior was almost exactly what she thought she wanted from him and the rest of the men on the roster, it was also disconcerting because she couldn't just lump him into the flirty, player role anymore.

So, she spent the next three months trying to distance herself from him as much as possible. But then she found herself unable to tell Randi no when she asked her to be a bridesmaid. Which meant she was paired up with Dean at every wedding event, and got to see the charming, fun-loving, small-town boy who grew up in Heart's Destiny, Texas, and put his family above everything else. That Dean Hunter was really hard to resist.

Seeing the part of him that is the exact opposite of every guy I knew of in Nevada is probably why I started having sex dreams about him then. Allissa sighed, shaking her head as she watched Dean dancing with his Meemaw. *I mean, how's a girl supposed to resist a man who dances with his mom and grandma, instead of the bevy of single women he could be hitting on? That's as irresistible as seeing him in "Uncle Dean" mode with the GWA kids.*

Even I can't fight the biological drive to want to procreate when the hottest man I've ever seen shows signs of being the perfect family man. I just hope my ovaries don't explode from trying.

"For someone who says they're not interested, you sure stare at Dean a lot." Emerald brought Allissa back to the moment with her way too loud statement.

"Just because I'm not interested, doesn't mean I can't enjoy the eye candy." Allissa shrugged, unable to really argue with her friend and fellow wrestler.

"Uh-huh, sure." Amethyst rolled her eyes before staring down Allissa. "I think you've got a classic case of protesting too much."

"I agree. And I think you should go for it with Dean. Take advantage of the way he's stepped up to be your bodyguard to see what he looks like in the buff before he gives up on you and picks up one of the local girls who've been drooling over him all week." Emerald motioned toward a table of Fiona's hometown friends, several of whom seemed to be focused on watching Dean on the dancefloor as much as Allissa had been.

Allissa remembered back to Randi's bachelorette party, when she was warned that one of Anthony's sisters had been crushing on the Hunter twins since high school, and would probably make a move on Dean, since James was off the market. She had refused to acknowledge her twinge of jealousy back then, still trying to keep him classified as a player, no matter how hard it was quickly becoming.

Shit! Maybe they're right. Even if it doesn't turn out to be a fairytale romance, can I really pass on the only man who has ever piqued my interest? If sex with Dean is as wonderful as Randi talks about it being with his twin, can I really keep fighting this attraction? Or will I always regret not knowing, if I keep resisting him long enough for him to move on to someone else?

And how am I supposed to "go for it" with Dean when I've never even kissed a boy, much less tried to flirt back with a man? Can I trust the women around me to not judge me for my past, and actually give me some helpful advice for how to go about "taking advantage" of Dean's interest in me?

Allissa was still pondering whether or not to confide in her friends about her inexperience to enlist their assistance in figuring out how to make a move on Dean, when all the single ladies were called to the dance floor.

"Come on, girl!" Emerald shouted, grabbing Allissa's hand and pulling her up from her seat. "If we've gotta try to catch the bouquet, so do you."

"Yeah," Amethyst added, grinning, grabbing her other hand, and pulling her to the middle of the crowd of local women vying for the honor of catching Fiona's bouquet. "Let's show everyone how the heel women of the GWA fight dirty for what we want, even if it's just a bouquet."

"Yeah, I'm moving away from the two of you," Allissa laughed, stepping away from her friends to the side of the crowd. "I don't need an accidental elbow giving me a black eye before TV in two days!"

"Oh, I'm sticking with you," one of Anthony's sisters chuckled, moving closer to Allissa and away from the fray. Allissa couldn't remember her first name, but she remembered the bridesmaid was the GWA pilot's sister, as well as Fiona's best friend. "Black eyes don't work for teaching middle school either."

Allissa nodded her agreement, while making faces at her friends a few feet away, and didn't see the bouquet until it almost hit her in the face. She didn't really mean to catch it. But she couldn't stop herself from grabbing it out of the air to keep the bundle of rose stems from poking her eye out.

"Guess you really are trying to avoid a black eye," the bridesmaid laughed.

"Yeah, I just didn't think it would be Fiona trying to give it to me," Allissa chuckled with her, as the ladies dispersed, so the single men could take their place on the dance floor.

With all the guys standing between her seat and the newlyweds, she didn't see Fiona whispering to Rick to change their plans for whom he should aim at when tossing the garter. Though she probably should have realized that her boss's new bride, whom she thought of as a friend, would conspire to play matchmaker at her wedding by instructing him to toss the garter straight at Dean.

"Hey, Darlin', you need to come back up for pictures," Dean hollered across the room, twirling the pink garter on his finger, and grinning at her, as the crowd of men shuffled off the dance floor.

"You think that was planned?" Amethyst giggled.

Emerald laughed along with her "sister from another mister," nodding in agreement, as Allissa begrudgingly walked back to the dance floor, where there was a chair set up that she was apparently supposed to sit in for the pictures.

There were numerous catcalls from their coworkers and Dean's local friends, as Dean got down on one knee in front of her at the direction of the photographer. Not that Allissa could hear exactly what they were saying over the blood rushing in her ears, when Dean's large hand encircled her ankle.

She vaguely registered that the photographer wanted him to lift her leg and place the garter around her calf for the photos before her vision tunneled down to just her and Dean. They locked eyes, as she had the most sensual experience of her life. Which, in her opinion, was really sad to say about her inexperience, since he only lightly brushed his hands over her leg from her ankle to her calf to put the garter in place.

Holy shit! What are those tingles? And how in the hell is having him touching my leg, making my pussy wet and my nipples hard? I thought those things only happened from me being aroused by the sex dreams I've started having.

Apparently, Dean wasn't as affected as Allissa by their moment of connection, as he was evidently able to comprehend what his buddies were shouting. He turned his head and grinned at the audience before responding. "Yeah, well, if this means we're the next to get married, then ya'll can all plan to come back here for our wedding on our Labor Day break in September."

Turning his head to break their eye contact, also broke the spell Allissa felt like she'd just been under, causing his words to actually register in her brain. Not that she got the chance to argue against a September wedding for her and Dean, when the bridesmaid she'd spoken with earlier put him in his place.

"Sorry, Dean. That week is already spoken for, so Fiona can be here as my matron of honor!"

"Guess that means we'll have to plan a Thanksgiving wedding, Darlin'." Dean wagged his eyebrows suggestively, as he turned his dark gray gaze back to Allissa.

Surely, he's only joking around. Right?

Coming Next in Heart's Destiny

<u>*Charlotte's Wedding*</u>

Heart's Destiny Series Book 5

Former DEA agent Michael Ian Campbell struggled with civilian life after leaving the agency when his wife, Mari, was killed after blowing his cover with the Rodriguez Cartel. He'd gone in with the alias of Michael Smith, trying to get the intel needed to bring down the infamous drug ring. He'd worked his way up to only a couple of levels down from the ringleader, Roberto "Rojo" Rodriguez, when Mari posted a picture of him with their son, Brody, on social media, identifying him as her husband. He barely made it out alive the day he and his family were ambushed in a drive-by ordered by Rojo to take him out.

With his cover blown and Brody now motherless, he retired from the DEA and scrubbed all records of Michael Campbell from existence, so he could safely raise his son with the help of his sister, Cait. As a parting gift, the agency created a new identity for him, using only his middle and last name. In exchange for the anonymity, Ian used his new job as a high school English teacher to funnel information back to his former partner on the lower-level drug dealers in and around the San Diego schools. Until the day he got word that Rojo Rodriguez had escaped, when the rest of the major players in his cartel were captured in a raid in South Texas, that is. With limited resources keeping the DEA and local law enforcement from having someone in Heart's Destiny, Texas, actively looking for the cartel kingpin, Ian moved there with his family to capture the man responsible for his wife's death.

Charlotte Burleson didn't know the new English teacher she had to work with was actually a friend of her brother, Jake, and a former undercover DEA agent. She only knew him as a one-night stand she thought she'd never see again, and the most infuriating man she'd ever met.

After the most intense sexual experience of her life, Charlotte woke up to an empty bed with no information on how to contact the mysterious Ian for another round. Two weeks later, he showed up at her family's late Christmas celebration and acted as if they'd never met. He continued the charade of not knowing her when he started working in the classroom next door to hers at the beginning of January.

Ian wasn't sure how to deal with finding out the hot-as-hell one-night stand he had on the night he interviewed for his new job was with the sister of a man he'd worked with on a joint task force a few years back and considered a friend. He had to keep his cover and not let on to anyone in town that he knew Jake Burleson before moving there. Not to mention the fact that he couldn't tell his friend Jake that he'd slept with his sister. So, when the owner of the bed and breakfast, where he and his family were staying until their rental was available for them to move, insisted on taking them to a late Christmas celebration, Ian pretended he'd never met Jake or Charlotte.

When he started work and realized he was supposed to coordinate the seventh-grade lesson plans with her, Ian couldn't resist pushing her buttons to get a glimpse of the fiery passion he'd seen on their one night together. But even as hot as his time with Charlotte was, he couldn't risk getting burned if Rojo Rodriguez caught wind of his presence in town and went after her, the way he had Mari.

As danger loomed, the couple fought their instant attraction and growing connection, not realizing that standing together was the only way they could win in the end.

Leah Mae Wright
DISCLAIMER: This single dad, teacher, brother's friend, instalove, alpha male, romantic suspense book contains references to past gun violence and child abuse, as well as the kidnapping and rescue of a main character, profanity, and graphic sex scenes. It is intended for adult readers (18+) who are not easily offended.

Coming Next in the GWA

Dean's Darlin'

Galactic Wrestling Association Book 2

Dean Hunter enjoyed his life, living like a rock star while traveling the world, as one of the top stars of the Galactic Wrestling Association, after growing up with wealth and privilege in Heart's Destiny, Texas. He didn't have relationships with women because he was literally in a different city at least three-hundred days a year. But after his best friend lifted the ban on dating his sister, Dean was starting to wonder if he should act on the crush he'd had on her in high school.

He contemplated how to make a long-distance relationship with his best friend's sister work, until a week after the ban had been lifted. Then, when he saw the newest addition to the women's division of the GWA roster for the first time, Dean felt like he'd been struck by lightning. For the first time in his life, he understood what everyone in his hometown was talking about when they discussed instalove, and knew he didn't feel it for his high school crush because he fell instantly for the newest woman to join the GWA roster.

Allissa Walters grew up in a trailer park about an hour outside of Las Vegas. Raised by a single mom and surrounded by the other women who worked in the brothel across the road, she learned young not to trust men. With limited resources, she had to use her physical attributes to earn a living. But instead of stripping, or becoming a prostitute, like many of the women she knew growing up, Allissa took

"

every modeling or acting gig she could find. She got lucky when one of her first gigs turned out to be as a ring girl for a mixed martial arts fight, and she caught the eye of a local fight promoter, who was looking for women to work in his independent wrestling promotion.

It took almost a year to save up the money from her modeling gigs to pay him to train her to become a professional wrestler. But from the first moment she stepped inside a squared circle, Allissa was hooked on the adrenaline of performing. She soaked up every lesson in the ring like a sponge, dreaming of the day she'd be good enough to work on bigger shows with a worldwide promotion.

She finally achieved her dream when she got a try-out match with the Galactic Wrestling Association. She signed a contract with them that night and took off traveling with the GWA the next day.

Unfortunately, dreams sometimes come true with a side dish of nightmares. She could handle the flirty, male wrestlers hitting on her. If she ignored them, they eventually backed off. She could even handle the booker who tried to get a little handsy. She was a trained fighter, after all, so spraining his wrist, as she got away from his hands, was simple. And more than enough to teach him to keep his hands to himself. But she wasn't sure what to do when she found herself the target of a stalker.

Dean was confused by what he'd done wrong to cause the woman of his dreams to hate him. But months after Allissa had come to work with the GWA, she was still doing everything she could to avoid him. None of his typical flirting techniques had worked. Neither had enlisting the help of the matchmaking women, who had recently paired off with his twin brother and best friend and now worked with Allissa closely enough to become her best friends. Even contriving situations to spend time with her had backfired.

But when Dean found out Allissa was in danger from a stalker, he was determined to protect her, whether she liked it or not. He just hoped there really was a fine line between love and hate, so maybe he could convince Allissa to cross it with him.

DISCLAIMER: This opposites attract, instalove, suspenseful, sports romance book contains threats from a stalker, gun violence during a kidnapping attempt, profanity, and graphic sex scenes. It is intended for adult readers (18+) who are not easily offended.

Books by Leah Mae Wright

Heart's Destiny Series

Galactic Wrestling Association Series

<u>Glossary of Professional Wrestling Terms</u> – Free on Book Funnel
<u>Fighting for Fiona</u> – Rick Robertson and Fiona Harrison
<u>Dean's Darlin'</u> – Dean Hunter and Allissa Walters
<u>Mistakenly Married?</u> – Liam Connery and Rylie Long, Brent Crockett and Aiken Pearson, & Josh Parker and Teagan Shields
<u>Winning Rylie</u> – Liam Connery and Rylie Long
<u>Blade's Botched Bump</u> – Brandon "Blade" Braddock and Caitlyn Sullivan (Coming Soon)

About The Author

Leah Mae Wright lives in Florida with her husband and fur babies. Her head has been filled with romantic stories for as long as she can remember, beginning with fairy tales as a small child growing up in Oklahoma and carrying through to countless ideas of her own throughout the years, as she has moved around to live in several different states. Now that her children are grown and life has slowed down, she's letting them out of her head, so they can join the libraries of her fellow fans of romance. Leah's literary world is a wonderful place that has no Covid, no real politicians, and a few unreal towns. Her favorite part about her characters living in her literary world is knowing that they are guaranteed a happily ever after.

You can keep up to date with Leah's future book plans at: www.leahmaewright.com – Be sure to sign up for the Newsletter to receive emails about new releases, sales, and freebies.
www.facebook.com/LeahWrightAuthor
www.amazon.com/author/leah_wright

https://www.instagram.com/leahmaewrightauthor/
https://www.pinterest.com/LeahMaeWrightAuthor/

Provide your feedback to the author at:
Leah's Literary World Facebook Group
LeahWrightAuthor@gmail.com
Leah@LeahMaeWright.com

You can also review Leah's books on Amazon, Goodreads, Bookbub, and Fictiondb.